INTO THE BARN

JO BOVÉ

Jo Bové/Into The Barn
Printed in the United States of America

This is a work of fiction. Names, characters, places, and incidents are a product of the author's imagination. Locales and public names are sometimes used for atmospheric purposes. Any resemblance to actual people, living or dead, or to businesses, companies, events, institutions, or locales is completely coincidental.

Into The Barn/ Jo Bové. -- 1st ed.

ISBN 9798839767027 Print Edition

ACKNOWLEDGEMENTS

I praise and thank you Jesus, my Lord and Savior, for choosing me to be the vessel to write this story. Using me and guiding me in this endeavor has been quite an experience and blessing. Praise to you Jesus for keeping me going and helping me to complete this book. Thank you for leading me in this journey, you are an awesome God!

Thank you, my sisters and friends, for your encouraging words and prayer support. Listed in no particular order are; Kathy T., Patsy B. and Linda Bjork.

To my sisters and brothers in the Sunday night prayer group, and my sisters in the woman's Bible study group, thank you for your prayers. I also thank the Graham Publishing Group for their help with editing, cover design and interior layout. Their skill and professionalism along with their patience with a first-timer is greatly appreciated.

ONE

AS THE TRAIN CAME INTO THE station Belle gathered her things anxiously. She had had a sense of someone watching her as she moved about on the cars during the trip. Ready to get off and shake off this feeling, she walked toward the midsection of the train. Finally, the train stopped and she quickly exited, looking over her shoulder to see if anyone was following her.

As she was rushing to find her friend, she turned her head a second time to check if she was being followed. Suddenly Belle crashed right into Starlit who responded, “Easy, girl—happy to see you too.” She grabbed Belle’s shoulders to steady her.

With a gasp Belle cried, “Star, I’m sorry, didn’t mean to run into you like that, so sorry.”

“Calm down, Belle, it’s all right. What’s the hurry?”

“Just in a hurry to see my buddies, that’s all. I mean the rest of my buddies. Did they behave for you?”

“Yes, and how is your little stowaway?”

Taking a deep breath, Belle glanced over her shoulder one more time. Not noticing any shadowy figure, she then placed her suitcases on the ground and gave Starlit a big hug. “Now I’m good, let’s go.” Belle did not want to alarm Starlit, who could sometimes be on the paranoid side. She would often tell Belle to be careful; lock the door, you should not go certain places alone, look inside the car before you get in, and so on. Belle wanted to avoid a lecture from "Mom" in case this was just her imagination.

When they reached the car Belle looked at the back seat lying flat. There was a litter box centered on potty pads there, to Belle's delight, and she said to Starlit, "Good job, thanks!" She placed her suitcases back there and unzipped one of them a little. After getting settled in the front seat she began to relax and become herself again, or so she thought.

Starlit said to Belle, "You look like, well like you're glowing. You're exceptionally happy, you must have needed that vacation more than I realized."

"Oh yes! I did, it was wonderful." Belle thought to herself, *Glowing, oops, better power down before I give things away.* As they drove away from the station, another usual May shower began.

By bragging about her stowaway on the drive home and asking questions about her buddies, Belle avoided giving Starlit a chance to question her. When they pulled into the driveway Belle hopped out, thanked Starlit for picking her up and taking care of everything, and said as she headed toward the house, "Come for dinner Saturday and we'll catch up then. I want to get settled. I'll call the guys and tell them to come too. Luv ya! Thanks again!"

Starlit gave three quick toots of the horn and called out the window, "Forgetting something?"

Belle turned, throwing her hands up in the air, and ran back to the car. She opened the back door, apologizing as she began gathering her things. After stuffing the stowaway in one suitcase and zipping it, she removed the pads out from under the litter box. She gently shook speckles of litter off the pads into the litter box, then placed them in it, right side down. She put on her backpack, then turning one suitcase on its side, she set the litter box on it. Starlit got out of the car to help. She picked up the other suitcase that Belle had placed on the ground then closed the door. They had not even gone through the front door when Belle said, “Thanks again for everything. I hate to rush you but I want to get settled, then spend time with the critters, luv ya!” She gave Starlit a kiss on the cheek and went inside.

Belle got safely into the house to Starlit’s satisfaction. As she drove away, she thought to herself *She loves her buddies so much it’s so precious.*

Saturday evening came quickly. All week long and now during dinner Belle was rehearsing in her mind how she was going to present her news. She was excited and scared at the same time. The conversation up to this point was each of her guests catching her up on what they had been doing over the last few months.

Warren wiped his mouth, cleared his throat and said to Belle, “As usual dinner was delicious.” He hesitated, hearing howling in the distance, then leaned in towards her and in a deep tone asked, “What is going on? You are more smiley than usual.”

Simultaneously Starlit and Silas chimed in, “Yeah, what’s up?”

“Love the stereo,” Belle replied. “Let’s get things cleaned up and we’ll talk, or well, I’ll talk.”

Starlit rushed to clear the dishes from the table while Silas went toward the coffee maker. Warren headed for the living room and began fluffing the pillows on the couches. Silas and Starlit glanced at each other, beaming with thoughts about what Belle could possibly be up to. Again, howling was heard, and it seemed closer this time. Starlit said she did not ever recall hearing dogs howl other times she had been at Belle's. Silas commented that it sounded more like a wolf. Then Starlit whispered to Silas, "Warren was right last week when he said he thought something was up. Do you think she finally met someone? Where is she anyway?"

"I saw her head for the bedroom," Silas replied. "Shush, here she comes."

"Okay everyone let's…"

Before she could finish her sentence, they ran into the living room and sat down. Laughing, Belle said, "Did you guys plan that?"

On his way in Silas noticed a small box on the end table. Inside was a new phone. "What's this? Ooh, fancy, high tech; you're stepping up in the world of communication. Maybe you need to c-o-m-m-u-n-i-c-a-t e with someone s-p-e-c-i-a-l."

Belle grabbed the phone with a grin and said, "I will get to that, Sy."

Ow Ow wow woooo. "Must be a lost dog."

"Do not go there, Belle," Warren warned, "no rescue now. I think the dog will be just fine. Please tell us what is going on."

"Remember last week I went on a mini vacation; well, it was really…"

Silas jumped to his feet. "I knew it! You went to rendezvous with your new love."

Starlit, shooting a look at him, commented, "Rendezvous and you knew it?" Then turning to Belle with a gleam in her eyes asked enthusiastically, "When do we get to meet him?" She walked over to Belle and hugged her. "How long have you been seeing him?"

"Wait, wait!" Belle called out. "No, not a new love."

Horrified, Warren, now on his feet, responded, "No! No! Not that lying cheating you-know-who from two years ago!?"

"Please," Belle pleaded, "Please will you all sit back down. Just listen. Now um yes, past love, uh current love, forever love, well furry love is the best way I can describe it."

All three exclaimed, "Furry love!"

"Still love the stereo," Belle said as she giggled. "You mean you went to find more critters in another state?" Starlit asked. She then looked at Warren and Silas and asked, "Does she mean she went to another state to find more critters?" Warren replied, "I guess five furs are not enough." Silas said, "There are plenty around in this state and it's a good thing she doesn't keep all the ones she rescues." They all sat there having a conversation about Belle as if she were not even in the room. Belle just sat there with her head in her hands.

After about five minutes Belle spoke up: "Okay everyone, my turn." Raising her voice a little she repeated, "My turn." Finally, a hush fell over the room. "Please let me talk. You won't guess what's going on. Let me tell you. It's a good thing and yes it does involve animals, but it's not what you think. My mini vacation was a job interview, well umm, um, two job interviews."

Before anyone could comment she put up her hand and said, "Stop, don't say a word." In what seemed like one very long breath and lightning speed she continued with, "I will be working with animals at a wildlife rehabilitation center. The phone you saw is for work purposes only; to send and receive pictures of critters and the grounds, reporting and communicating with the boss, and coworkers, situations occurring or ones that might occur."

While she paused a second to take a deep breath, her friends also felt the need to take a deep breath, and each hearing the others, chuckled. Her lungs now fueled again and slowing down a little, she proceeded with the explanation. "The Center is linked to a sanctuary center which has lots of outdoor space for animals that can't be released back into the wild. There are many, many acres involved. This is prayer answered, my dream job!" Lowering her hand Belle nervously went on. "I know this is a surprise, a shock since I didn't share my intentions. Not knowing the outcome of the interviews and negotiations, I couldn't; I kept quiet, had to. There is more. Other things were going on. Another kind of negotiation was happening, um happened, before this trip. Something else was going on also. Did I say that already? Yes, um now I want to show you a video of where I will be working and living."

Suddenly all of them burst out with questions at the same time. It sounded as if there were ten people in the room talking all at once. "Whoa, hold on," Belle said, raising her hand again. "Let's break to the kitchen for coffee and dessert." Warren smiled and said, "I did not see the usual display of any tasty treats, therefore I determined there may not be any this time." As they rose and headed for the kitchen, Belle walked toward the bedroom hollering out, "Be right there."

Starlit set the table, Silas poured the coffee and Warren turned on some soothing background music, the same roles they took on many times when they gathered at Belle's, but this time they were very quiet as they did so. They were all thinking the same thing, however none of them could bring themselves to say it out loud. Belle would be leaving. Not just to another part of town, but to another state. They were missing her already and began to think about how they had all become close over the years. The fun times, ups and downs together, even tragedy. It was difficult for them to process a separation. All of them had been friends since elementary school.

In the bedroom Belle was reminiscing also. Tears welled up in her eyes as she collected packages off the bed. Quickly dropping them back down and reaching for a tissue she thought, *I can't let them see me like this. Silly me, it wouldn't be the first time.* After wiping her eyes, she picked up the packages again and went to the kitchen.

As she walked in Silas exclaimed, "Edible gifts, that's a new one!"

"Stop that," Starlit said. Placing them on the table Belle turned and said, "Be right back with the inedible cake." They all laughed a kind of uneasy laugh.

One by one each had memory flashes. They were all always there for each other. Warren recalled how Belle and Starlit stepped in to care for the children when Lucy succumbed to her illness. He thought about how Belle was childlike herself yet able to comfort the kids and fondly remembered she also sometimes was childish, as a little smile began to form across his tightened lips. Starlit thought about how Belle would come and prepare meals for her ailing parents. She recalled reading to her parents and smelling the incredible aroma wafting through the house. Silas was thinking of the time Ashley miscarried and Belle was there for them. He also recalled adventures they all had together.

Belle returned with cake: birthday cake. "Wow, was not expecting that," said Silas.

"Looks tasty," Warren said. Starlit happily proclaimed, "I'll get the matches and candles."

The cake was actually four individual ones, connected with a thin layer of white frosting across the top and down the sides. Each quarter section of the cake had the words "happy birthday" and their names written under it. Each section was made of that person's favorite cake and filling. It was colorfully decorated with vines and flowers.

"This is part two," Belle began. "I want us to enjoy our cake and your gifts, then we'll sit back in the living room for part three, the rest of the reveal. You know I will be leaving but it's sooner than you may think." No one interrupted with questions. "I won't be here for my birthday or yours, Silas, and since I was very late for both of your celebrations, I want to celebrate with you now, and celebrate you. Let's have some cake and then you can open your gifts."

The howling started again; *owOwOwooo* was heard several more times. No one said a word as they enjoyed their cake. Gestures of puzzlement were made at each other over the serenade they had been hearing while they ate.

Everybody was now relaxed. Laughter and tears subsided after an hour of celebrating. Things did not pan out in the order she had planned, but Belle had to press on. No longer feeling nervous, ready to pick up where she left off, Belle stood up, smiled then said, "Leave the dishes, let's..." Deja vu, they were gone.

TWO

AS EVERYONE SAT IN THEIR favorite places, Starlit moved closer to Silas on the couch. "Something's outside the window, moving out there," she said.

"It is windy," Warren said, "something probably soared past on the wind." He walked over to the window. "Relax, it is only a bush being moved by the wind." He closed the curtains, walked over to the other window and did the same.

Flipping the switch for the outside light with no results, he asked Belle if she knew it was out. "Sorry, I forgot to replace the bulb. The back one needs replacing too. I'll get it done tomorrow." Warren then sat down saying, "Go ahead, Belle."

"Questions that come to mind may get answered as I explain." This was her way of saying do not interrupt. "First on the video are pictures of some furs." Smiling, she glanced at Warren. "These were taken to see how I interacted with critters and how they reacted to me. Me and momma opossum hanging around, me and her babies..."

Starlit commented with oohs and aahs at the cute critters but squirmed when snakes and lizards appeared on screen. The guys commented with "interesting" and "cool." Several pictures later Belle concluded, "And the zebra, yes that is zebra, who had enough of me."

"Ha ha ha ha!" They were laughing so hard they had to hold their sides as they stared at Belle in a water trough, splashing about and trying to get out. Silas roared with laughter as the zebra turned, kicked the trough, and walked away as if to say, so there and take that too! Belle was laughing also. When they all regained their composure, she continued to the next show-and-tell section of the video.

"So, this is the Center." The camera showed the outside of a rustic-looking building, panned around its well-manicured grounds briefly, then focused on a four-wheel drive vehicle looking much like a glorified golf cart. Belle approaches the passenger side and gets in. Waving at the camera Belle says, "We're off to show you my living quarters." As the camera is mounted on the dash of the cart the picture shakes a little. The vehicle heads down a wide gravel path. Flashes of color dot the grassy surroundings on both sides of the path. Further off the path were various shrubs and trees. Then the camera appears to go off.

Belle explained, "I didn't think it was necessary to film the entire ride to my place. That trip takes quite a few minutes. One day you will see it for yourselves."

The video began again, opening with the cart pulling up to quite a nice stone house, pausing a moment, then proceeding onto a gravel driveway next to the house. Then a smaller, log cabin-style house behind it comes into view.

Belle, while singing the words, "Say hello to the guest house, people," was suddenly startled by Starlit's reaction and dropped the remote. As the cart came closer to the guest house Belle thought she saw something, someone peering out from behind the large tree near it, but she had not noticed this when she was there. Starlit's reaction confirmed that it was not her imagination. Not wanting to let on, Belle asked, "What's wrong?" Starlit, hesitating, said, "I uh, I saw something by that big tree."

Silas placed his arm around Starlit and said, "It's probably just a wolf."

Starlit yelled, "A wolf! Belle, a wolf! Your house is in the middle of the woods, the middle of nowhere, it's not safe!" Squeezing Starlit a little Silas said, "Don't worry Mom, the bear will get it before it can get close to the house."

Everyone laughed except Starlit. Pushing Silas away she continued her objections. "You can't live out there all alone. There's—there's no protection. You can't be serious!" Silas told Starlit they would look into a guard dog for her, two dogs even. "Would that meet your approval?" Warren asked.

She answered, "And an alarm system and bright lights to turn on all around the house too! And that creepy old building needs to..."

Warren interrupted, "Calm down. That is an old barn, just a harmless old barn. We will discuss and consider options later. I believe Belle is ready to resume."

"The guest house is great. You can all come out to visit at the same time; there is safety in numbers after all, Mom. The kids will love it; the girls can stay with me in my house and the guys in the guest house. I know you all get three weeks of vacation time a year so you should be able to come out to visit and stay a week with me. No hotel bill!"

Not wanting to just speak out, Warren raised his hand, waving it like a schoolboy trying to get the teacher's attention. Belle acknowledged him with a nod, and he asked her how she will be able to afford the rent on all that, since working at a rehabilitation center is usually volunteer work.

Agreeing with him on it being volunteer work, she explained she would be working part time at a nursery. The plants and flowers kind. Then hesitating, not sure if she was ready to say it, whispered, "I won't actually be paying rent, it's called a mortgage." Quickly, before anyone had a chance to ask, up went her hand. "Let me explain. The houses are located on forty-eight acres nestled in between acres of sanctuary grounds. The land was owned by someone who didn't want to sell when the surrounding property was acquired by an animal organization for a rehab center and sanctuary. Four years ago, he built the houses but recently decided to sell. My new boss, Ed, told me the story while we were on the phone discussing my visit.

"Apparently the land had been in that person's family for years, several generations. Well, you can see by the decrepit old barn, quite some time. They were finally going to purchase that property. I mentioned I might be interested in buying it provided the interviews went well and I liked the houses. He said they would consider it under certain conditions, one, if they approved of me and I was given the job; two, signed legal documents to sell only to them if I should ever decide to move. I was able to make the purchase because of a project I had been working on the last few months. That was the other negotiation I was referring to earlier."

Another waving hand went up. This time it was Silas. "You could have shared all this with us, Belle."

Then Warren began counting on his fingers and said, "So you were not working on an in-depth Bible study. You turned down multiple invitations from us. You spent all your time on a secret project. You pretended…"

"Not true," Belle interrupted. "I did so do the Bible study, and finished it, in between my project which was a challenge but paid off, literally! Also I told you I felt I had to wait, I was unsure of results and, oh my gosh, I'm sorry. Please, please will you all forgive me for holding back? I'm so sorry; I didn't think it would upset you as much as it has. I'm sorry, I'm sorry."

Unexpectedly their attention was turned to a noise outside. Starlit, speaking softly as if to keep the unknown from hearing, asked, "What is that—who is that?"

Silas got up and headed for the front door. "I've got this," he said. Then a noise came from the back of the house, causing him to turn abruptly. The lights began to flicker. Howling could be heard again. Now Silas went hastily to the back door. He was distracted by a noise coming from above which caused him to trip and fall. Hearing a noise again in the back of the house, he scrambled to his feet and rushed to the door.

Just then all the lights went out. The girls let out a scream. He opened the door. Debris was barely visible swirling around the yard in the darkness. Silas, squinting, tried to see better but just then the lightning stopped, making it pitch dark. He heard a sound, then something or someone hit him in the face. He swung back but made contact with nothing.

The girls were yelling, "Close the door!" In the dark a figure seemed to be moving about. Silas could not make out what or who it was. A high-pitched voice frantically yelled, "Don't let it in, don't let it get in, close the door!"

Again, Silas was hit. He swung at the air. Again, he heard, "Close the door!" This time he listened. As he tried to close it, he was met with resistance. Then—boom! The door gave way, closing with a loud slam. Lightning began flashing now with such intensity it lit up the room enough to reveal a bloody face. The girls screamed again.

"It's just me, it's me, Silas." Peals of thunder shook the house. Large bolts of lightning seem to be targeting the house. *Rumble Rumble Booom! Booom! Booom!* The reverberating sound and blinding flashes of lightning seemed to go on forever.

Suddenly—silence. Darkness, darkness and silence eerily surrounded them. They held their breath briefly. Then a small faint sound emerged out of the silence: plink, plink, plink. "Did you hear that?"

It was quiet a moment, then the sound began again. "There it is again."

Belle answered, "Yes Star, I hear it. I can't tell where it's coming from."

Warren spoke up, "I need a flashlight." The sounds came faster and louder. The house was pelted with deafening noise now. "Hail," Warren said. "This is a hailstorm, and the storm is directly over us."

Starlit began lighting candles. Belle was tending to Silas's injuries. She nearly jumped out of her shoes when Warren came up behind her and shone the flashlight on Silas's face. "I apologize; I was only trying to help."

"Well, it is a spooky night after all," Silas stated. "Not helping," chirped Starlit as she lit the last candle.

The candles provided very little light throughout the house. The pummeling of the hail began to subside. Sounding more like a soft tapping on the house now, it had a lulling affect.

Silas was all cleaned up. Starlit went to put away the first-aid kit as Belle went into the kitchen to fetch something cool for everyone to drink; Warren was fluffing the pillows on the couch again. His way of saying he was ready to hear about Belle's project.

Warren questioned Silas, "Do you know what hit you? Was it a person?"

Silas answered, "I think it may have been the homeless guy we saw earlier going through garbage pails. Belle did leave the gate unlocked, maybe he wandered in. I can't believe anyone was out in this storm. Although it does seem suspicious that those first few noises and the lights flickering happened before the storm actually got started. It was only a little windy then. I wonder if he was up to something else like maybe looking for a way to get in the house."

"Silas, I think we should keep this quiet for now and make sure the house is secure before we leave tonight. We will replace those light bulbs as well."

"Okay, Warren, Star is coming, just smile. That was stupid of me to open the door with all that stuff flying around. Sorry to scare you, Star, and boy that wind! It was so strong I barely got the door to close!"

Nervously she said, "I thought someone was there, Sy." Silas quickly replied, "Just your imagination, all that stuff flying around, you know."

As they all sat down and got comfortable, Silas commented on how the candlelight cast interesting shadows. Starlit was making faces. She was not a fan of shadows. "What was that? I saw a shadow scurry across the room and..." Before she could finish her sentence, the shadow leapt into the air towards her and she let out a scream.

Warren sprang into action and caught the shadow in midair. "It is the stowaway," he said with a smile.

Returning to the living room at the same time Belle said, "Oh sorry, I must not have closed the door all the way when I went to check on the critters. Warren, would you mind putting him back in his bedroom?"

"I will go and tuck him in, do not start until I return."

"Well that certainly was not my imagination, Sy."

As Belle placed the drinks on the table she asked, "What do you mean, Star?"

Silas answered, "Just the debris flying in the wind and all, seemed like someone was outside, just junk and imagination, that's all. Yep, a black cat, a storm and a blackout are sure convenient for a spooky night." He went on to say he thought they should tell some ghost stories, but Belle could see Starlit was upset so she changed the subject.

When Warren returned, he sat down and called out, "Quiet on the set; Belle, the stage is all yours."

All listened intently. Disbelief struck all of them. Belle actually finished something she started. Not only that but it was successful. They did not interrupt. She went on to explain a lot of time was spent researching. Awestruck by the drawings and plans she showed them, their mouths hung open. Warren had a sense that this meant little Belle had grown up some. She stuck to doing something that led to completing it. He felt proud of her. Silas was blown away. Never had he known Belle to show an interest in doing something like this and certainly would not have thought her capable. Starlit was excited for Belle and of course the mom in her wondered if she was able to get enough rest during all of this. How was she able to work, then come home, do this plus take care of critters and everything else? Then she thought, *Ah yes, the power of prayer, that's how*. They had an understanding now of why Belle did not want to say anything. She probably thought she would not finish something she started, as usual. This would be the worst unfinished thing ever to have to face others with. Who knew she had it in her to design houses! Houses someone would actually buy!

Negotiation was not a strong suit for Belle, and she explained where the advice came from. There was a fee for this and the contracts that had to be drawn up, but she would be reaping a percentage of every house that was built. The money she got from selling the plans enabled her to buy her home. It allowed her to put a large down payment on the houses, leaving her with a very small, very manageable mortgage.

It was nearing midnight now. Warren stated he should call Vee and let her know he and Silas would be late.

Belle said, "No, you told her you would be home by one o'clock when you called to check on her and the kids after the storm. We'll wrap things up quickly so you can be on time. I want to set a date when you all come to help me pack. Say two weeks from tonight and reserve the following weekend after that to help load up the moving truck. I will pay Vee for those days."

They all agreed to that. Starlit offered to come next weekend to help Belle sort through some things. She said she would bring her pajamas and spend the weekend.

Warren apologized to Belle for being harsh. He told her they had all been praying for her as they always prayed for each other, but it would have been nice to know to pray for a specific need. Silas and

Starlit apologized as well. Starlit explained that since they usually shared so much with each other, they felt left out and it kind of hurt. Silas said he was a little hurt and angry. Belle apologized again and gave a long hug to each of them.

Bang! Bang bang! The sudden loud pounding on the door jolted them out of their endearing moment. "Don't open it," pleaded Starlit. Silas said, "I'll try this again," as he approached the front door cautiously.

He opened the door slowly and kept back as he did so. The wind was no longer howling but something else was. Through the screen door he saw glowing eyes. He heard a low growling sound. The flickering candle near the door was snuffed out by a slight breeze. A flash of lightning lit up the porch. There was a dark figure with a hood over its head and it leaned toward Silas. A raspy voice asked, "This dog yours?"

In the background Belle called out, "Across the street to the right, fourth house, the yellow one." Silas turned toward Belle's voice, and as he turned back to the figures to repeat what she had said, they were gone! He closed the door and sat back down.

Warren commented as he sat down, "There has been a lot of howling this night. Belle, in all the times I have been here I never heard howling." "I never noticed either," Silas said.

Starlit stuttered, "Don't start, you guys. I still have to drive home alone." Belle could not help thinking to herself that the figure had looked familiar, confirming the train occurrences were not her imagination. She decided to keep that to herself for now. Warren told Starlit they would follow her home to make sure she was all right.

The lights flickered a few times, then came back on and their cheering filled the room. The guys did a security check and placed new bulbs outside. Then each gave Belle a hug and a kiss. They collected their gifts and cake and headed out the door. To all in their cars waving goodbye, Belle called out, "See ya soon; safe home; have a good sleep; luv ya!"

While making sure the back door was locked, Belle noticed something on the floor in a corner nearby. It did not look familiar. Not knowing what it was or where it came from, and too exhausted to think about it, she placed it on a table and began getting ready for bed. She gathered her critters from their room and took them into her bedroom to go to sleep. They would comfort each other; after all it was a trying night for them as well, with the storm and all. She thought about what she saw in the video. *Could have been an animal by that tree, but the person at the door tonight sure had the same outline as the figure on the train. Still couldn't see their faces though. Trainman had sunglasses and a hat, dark hair but doorman had a hood pulled down, oh, a mustache, a blond one, oh no maybe I'm just being like Mom; they can't be related, it's just a coincidence. Gosh I'm exhausted, time for some sleep.*

Belle turned the nightlight switch on, then climbed into bed. She leaned back, gave thanks, and said her prayers. After turning off the light she turned onto her side and got comfortable. Belle could hear the soft purring of kitties in the room and outside, *Ow ow oWoooowoo…*

THREE

BELLE HAD LONGED TO SEE HER FRIENDS. They kept in touch often but it is not the same as being able to see and touch them. She was looking forward to lots of hugs and kisses. It was Monday, and on Thursday she would be able to give and receive them when they arrived for their visit. On completion of work today Belle would have two days to prepare for their reunion. Her work was distracted by thoughts of what she would do on those two days. Looking at the strange item sitting on her desk, long forgotten, she picked it up and reminisced about the night she found it; that stormy night just a few short weeks before she had to leave. It was a hectic time, and she never asked her friends if it was one of theirs. No one mentioned losing anything either. Learning new jobs and setting up a new home certainly had kept her very busy. The year went by quickly. Belle did not think about this object until now.

"I have to remember to ask everyone about this. Maybe hmmm, better while I'm thinking about it, put this in my bag now." As she was reaching for her bag the phone started to ring. Inside the bag were several pockets to choose from, so she tucked the object in one that had a zipper to ensure it would not slip out.

Ring-Ring, ring-ring, ring-ring… "Hey Hound, ya gonna get that?"

Quickly snapping out of her thoughts, she picked up the receiver. "The Comfort Zone, how may I help you?"

Before Belle said anything, her coworker Cypress could tell by her body language and expression it was time to head out.

"Thank you for your concern, someone will be right there. That was someone from the Yancee farm; Momma Possum got out and is sleeping in a bush there. He said it has our tag on it so it must be ours. Better call maintenance to check her quarters for the breach while I go fetch."

"What's the magic word, Hound?"

"Pleeease *and* thank you." Ooh, bonus, you're welcome.

On her way to pick up Momma Possum, her thoughts turned back to the upcoming visit. Her mind planned out the reception meal and dessert. Suddenly her thoughts were interrupted by something moving quickly across her path. Belle's heart pounded, and her eyes widened as she hit the brakes, crying out, "Jesus help me!" The vehicle stopped within inches of hitting deer as they ran in front of her. They flashed past her and disappeared as quickly as they had appeared. The deer seemed panicked.

After Belle calmed down, she thanked God for helping, then she looked around. "What was that!?" In the distance, the direction the deer came from, she saw something. It disappeared into a wooded section before she could make it out for sure. "Was that a bear? I don't think so. What was that?" It was dark in color, large and unfamiliar. All she got was a glimpse of it. "I don't think that was a bear or anything familiar and I don't want to be here if it decides to come back this way, so move it, girl."

A strange feeling crept up in her. Starting to drive again she became more aware and cautious. The Yancee farm was just a few minutes away, and she was anxious to get there.

When she arrived, she mentioned the incident. Mrs. Yancee offered Belle something to drink, then Mr. Yancee walked Belle over to where Momma was. He made light of the incident but that did not make her feel better. With Momma loaded up, she was soon on her way back to the Center.

She made up her mind to pay attention and drive safely in order not to hit any critters that could cross her path. Being too cautious caused her to drive slowly, which made her anxious again because she wanted to get back to the Center before another possible strange encounter. A loud sound interrupted the silence: "...currrshurr—Hound ya—currshurrr there? Out." Startled and nearly jumping out of the seat she yelled, "Yeah! Yeah, I'm here, I'm here!"

Again, the radio crackled and hissed: "...currshurr-shurr, Come in Hound—Out." Realizing he would not hear anything unless she pushed the button, she reached for it shouting, "Yes Cy, I'm here and could you just call me Belle for a change?!" "...rrshurr-What's up, Snippy? Need help? Out." "Nooo, I'm almost there. Out." "... crrshurr-hiss...Good, we need to tie up loose ends before you leave today. Out."

When she arrived back at the Center, Cypress was waiting outside, arms crossed, leaning against the porch pillar. "Belle, what's up?"

"Had a little shakeup. I saw something that spooked some deer I almost hit, but don't know what it was. Sure gave me the creeps though. All I could tell is that it was quite large and not familiar."

"Yeah, there have been strange sightings around that farm, forget about it."

"In all the time I've been out here, now you mention strange sightings."

"Well, no human remains were ever found so nothing to worry about."

Belle sarcastically replied, "Such a comfort, thanks!"

"You've always been the curious kind, Hound, why so shaken?"

"Just tired, I guess. Is Momma's area secure now?"

"Yes. I wonder how she got to the Yancee farm. Let's get her settled and go over some things before you leave."

With the day finally coming to an end Belle headed out the door excitedly. Cypress called after her, "Can't wait to meet your friends."

On the way home she picked up the groceries. The shopping took much longer than usual since she had to stock two kitchens this time. Knowing the guys enjoyed having their treats as much as the kids, she picked up extra baking ingredients so she could leave some goodies in the guest house for them.

It was late now as Belle put away the last of the groceries. Sitting down, she grabbed a pen and a piece of paper to write out her to-do list for tomorrow and the next day. She also wrote out an itinerary for the kids. They would only be staying until Sunday since Warren and Silas did not want them to miss out on vacation Bible school. The first few days would center on them. After church Sunday morning Vee would arrive and spend the day. The kids would return home with Vee, and she would take them to Warren's mom where they would stay until the dads came back from vacation.

Belle sat there with a grin on her face as she thought about the fun stuff she had planned for the kids. She thought about the conversations she had with her friends during the year. Belle did not tell them everything. She wanted to surprise them when they came for their visit but was now concerned they would be upset for her holding out on them again. "Well, not this time," she convinced herself. "It's not the same. I did mention that I had a surprise for them, I just didn't say it plural and gosh it certainly is more than one surprise. They know about the dogs but not their little house, and I know something like that will please them, it's so me. I'm sure they will enjoy all the little surprises." She stood up, stretching and yawning, and said out loud, "Bedtime," then began the nighttime ritual.

She slept well. As Belle was sipping tea, the phone rang. It was her boss, Ed.

"I see, yes, Saturday afternoon, one o'clock. That's okay, I understand, I can make that work. No, no not the Friday or Sunday class, Saturday is better, thanks—bye."

Once a year it was required that all who worked at the Center attend informational classes. This one was supposed to be later on, but was moved up and changed to this weekend.

Belle prepared breakfast, then sat down to eat and contemplate this news. When she had finished eating, she took a notepad and began making some notes. "Hmmm, well, arriving Thursday morning, arrive here around 11:45 a.m., kids leave Sunday evening, okay, sooo critter activities as planned for Thursday, move treasure hunt from Saturday to Friday, good. Visit the Center Saturday morning instead, then take everyone to town. They can see some sights or catch a movie. After class we can go to the aquarium, then dinner, oooh yummy, that great seafood restaurant, yes, perfect."

Ring ring ring... Hope that's not Ed again.

"Hello, oh hi, Nancy." It was the gal from the Yard and Home Nursery Belle worked at. "Oh gosh I didn't realize I left it there. There's a lot I need to get done today; I'll pick it up this evening just before close. Thank you for calling." Belle had left the bag of clothes she took with her to work. This was in case she needed to change from getting too dirty or wet at work. She also had a bag with her when at the Center.

No sooner than the receiver was back in place: *ring ring ring... What is going on?* "Hello? Star, hi! Is everything okay?"

"Yes, I just wanted to hear your voice. I am so excited about coming to visit. It's going to be wonderful!"

"It certainly will. I'm excited too, can't wait!"

Starlit and Belle talked about half an hour. They went over the flight schedule. Belle reminded her to call just before boarding and of the kind of clothing to bring. Starlit informed her that everyone had been packed since last week and all the clothing recommendations were inspected and met by her personally. Belle checked the clock for the third time.

"As long as I've got you on the phone, I want to let you know something came up."

"Bad news?"

"No, just a little interruption. I have to attend a class Saturday that was supposed to be weeks from now. My itinerary has been altered a little. Here's my thought: we do the Center visit that morning then go to town. You guys do something while me and Cy are in class. Thought he could ride with us since the van you guys are renting is big enough, and after class we could all go to dinner. He's looking forward to meeting all of you. What do you think?"

"That would be great. I know the guys won't mind since they've wanted to meet this interesting sounding coworker you spend so much time with, end quote. Do you realize we might have to call one of the "Sy's" by their full name?"

"You're right. Silas and Cypress both go by the same-sounding nickname. I did give that some thought when I first met him, the similar sound I mean, not about them being in the same space. How funny, Sy and Cy. We'll cross that bridge when we come to it."

"So what else will we be doing, Belle?"

"Still trying to get some info? Not giving it up. That's reserved for when you get here." Glancing at the clock again she added, "But there are surprises, quite a few, you'll be pleasantly surprised. We'll have fun. I hate to go but I have a lot to get done for our visit. Okay, yes, great, luv ya, see you real soon, bye-bye." She smiled as she hung up the phone, feeling satisfied that she made the surprise plural.

Breakfast and caffeine had kicked in now and Belle was on the move. She started in the main house. First, she changed the sheets on her bed then placed sheets on the beds in the guest room. Next, she cleaned the kitchen and bathrooms, vacuumed, and dusted. The downstairs did not take long at all, and when she was done, she went up to do the kitty room.

"I'm making good time. Now to the guest house, ready-set-go! I better fill the dishwasher first and get everything fresh. Good, now I'll get sheets on the beds and clean. Okay, finally done with all of that, now what else? I need to get a fruit bowl out and cleaned so there are healthy snacks; now, which cabinet did I put that in? Aha, there you are, and this sectional will be good for some nuts too. I'll need vases for flowers which I'll cut tomorrow, here we go, done! Next are the barn, doghouse and yard. Better start with the yard. The barn and doghouse can wait till tomorrow morning if I run out of time. Then I can get all the baking done in the afternoon."

Everything was going along smoothly until Belle sat on the mower and tried to start it.

"No, no, no, not now! Don't have time for this! You've got to be kidding me, this is ridiculous! Damn it! Come on, come on! Crap!" All this loud ranting brought Guardian and Stance running. They began circling the mower. When Belle realized this, she quit trying to start it. Now as she muttered under her breath, the dogs sat down, looking at Belle, tilting their heads and growling softly.

"Sorry guys, it's all right." She got off the mower, walked over to them, knelt down and gave them a hug. "Good boys, thank you for looking out for me, good boys." The dogs gave her kisses.

"Well, while I'm down here: Father, forgive me for this outburst. Forgive me for this offence in Jesus' name, I'm sorry. Thank you for loving me, that your mercies are new every day and that you always provide for me. Thank you for the many blessings you've given me. Please help me resolve this mower problem in a manner pleasing to you. I ask in Jesus' name, Amen."

Belle realized how hungry she was. She spent a few minutes of play time with the dogs. With one last throw of the toys, she headed to the garden. After choosing some veggies and lettuce she went into the house to prepare lunch. As she entered, the cuckoo clock was sounding. "Wow, three o'clock! No wonder I'm famished."

FOUR

WHEN BELLE WAS DONE EATING, she placed the dishes on the counter and went into the living room. She sat in her favorite chair and took her journal out of the drawer. "Been a while, little book. I need to take a break so let's get caught up."

Sitting about fifteen minutes writing in her journal, she now concluded with her mower incident. As the last thought was penned Belle heard the dogs barking. She finished and placed the journal on the table instead of back in the drawer, debating if there was anything else she wanted to add.

Just then the phone rang. "Hello."

"Wanna call off the hounds, Hound?"

"Hi Cy, just a minute, I'll open the gate."

Belle opened the door and laughed. "Thank you for bringing my bag. I also forgot my other one at the nursery."

"Thought you might want it since you'll be on vacay a couple of weeks."

"Come in, sit down, I'll get you some iced tea. I just finished eating; do you want something to eat?"

"No, thanks, just the tea. You make the best. Hey what's this? You keep a diary?"

"Hands off, that's called a journal. I put my thoughts down and things that go on in my life. I don't do it every day. It's a good way to see where I'm at in this journey on Planet Earth. To see changes in me and in circumstances, answers to prayer, what God has done, that kind of stuff."

"Oh, the God thing," he replied as he squirmed in the chair.

"While you're here, maybe you can help me get the lawn mower started. Things were going great until I got to that. I just can't figure it out."

"You were tired and hungry and ate real late—right? That's what usually happens. You lose track of time, don't take a break, then the brain locks up. Well?"

"Yeah, I'd been working all morning and into the afternoon trying to get everything in order."

"Keep going, recount what you did."

In her mind Belle went over her actions while sitting on the mower. "Ugh! I never refueled last week and didn't check the gas this time. It probably just needs gas!"

"See, you're refueled, rested and your brain unlocked." Tauntingly he added, "Heck, maybe you should have prayed about it."

"Now that you mention it, I did. God guides in different ways, and I believe you showing up was the answer to that prayer. I'm going to share something with you." She picked up her journal, opened it and pointed to the section she just wrote, then said, "Read this."

His eyes widened a little as he read the section where she gave an account of her behavior, confessed to God and asked His forgiveness, then prayed. After a moment of awkward silence he said, as he handed the journal back to her, "Well yeah, I don't know, yeah."

Belle said, "Let's go out to check the lawn mower. I have to get back to work."

"Cy, Ed said you are going to the class Saturday; me too. My friends and I are coming to visit the Center that morning, then all heading into town. I was going to invite you then but since you're here, ride with us and after class we can all go to dinner and visit."

"Yeah, sounds good. Belle, did you notice anything unusual the day you picked up Momma, I mean other than the mystery beast?"

"Yes, her tag was on her right foot and the color looked a little off."

"Why didn't you say something?"

"Just figured it was a mistake. Like the time one of my feral kitties had the wrong ear tipped. It happens. As for the color, sometimes like with two bolts of fabric the dye lots are a little different. I never noticed it before though."

"Exactly, and she didn't have her annual yet."

"I was just about to say it must have happened when they updated her info on her annual. Hmmm."

"I didn't notice it right away. It was just after you left, I decided to check on her one more time. That's when I saw the tag was on her right foot and went to ask if Momma had her annual and mentioned the tag. I was told she hadn't, and they just blew it off."

"Maybe something happened to the tag, some kind of damage and whoever changed it placed it on the wrong foot."

"Maybe; here you go." Cypress handed the gas can to Belle. Sure enough, all that was needed was some gasoline. The mower started right away. Belle shouted, "Thank you, Jesus! I better get to the lawn, it's after four, then I need to do some weeding too. After that it's off to get my other bag."

"No problem, see you Saturday." She walked him to the gate. "Thanks again for bringing my bag."

Heading back to the mower, she was thinking about their conversation. "He called me Belle, not Hound. He seemed really bothered by the tag, so serious. I'll have to think about this later tonight and recall that day."

Belle hopped on the mower, started it, and began tending to the lawn. When the mowing and weeding had been finished, Belle checked the time. It was seven fifteen. Just then the dogs came bounding over, leaping and barking, letting her know it was feeding time. "Seems like the barn and doghouse will have to wait till tomorrow after all, oops and my bag too. I'll get the critters fed, then me. I can get to bed early so I can get up extra early and get started on the rest of my preparations. Come on, boys, come on."

As Belle was preparing for bed, she started thinking about the last day of work at the Center. She saw Momma Possum that morning when she cleaned her area. Her thoughts of her upcoming vacation had consumed her that day and nothing out of the ordinary was coming to mind. Finally climbing into bed, she began her prayers. After she turned off the light, she was thinking about Momma again, then she drifted off to sleep.

Rising at 4:45 a.m., Belle stretched a few minutes and did some exercises. She went to the kitchen to make some tea and sat down to contemplate the schedule for the day. "I can't believe it's Wednesday already. Okay, so I'll head out to do the barn first then get breakfast for all of us. After breakfast I'll clean the doghouse. I want to pick up my bag. Guardian and Stance can take a ride with me to the nursery when I go get it. When I get back home, I'll clean me up and start baking."

Cuckoo, cuckoo, cuckoo. "Eleven already, time to start preparing and baking all the goodies. This is wonderful! I have plenty of time for baking and decorating the cookies without rushing. The cake will have sufficient time to cool so I can frost it later instead of tomorrow morning. So, tomorrow morning after feeding time I can cut the flowers from the garden instead of today, fresher, good. Then I'll fill the fruit and nut bowls, after that, start preparing the reception meal. Oh my gosh, oh my gosh! Tomorrow my dear friends are arriving! I can't believe it, I'm so excited! They should be here before noon—oh my gosh oh my gosh!" Belle did a happy dance across the kitchen floor.

Belle was excited all day. Everything went well and was done on time. She had dinner earlier than usual so she could get to bed earlier and get extra sleep for the big day. She felt as if she were too excited to sleep and decided to take a sleep aid. When she started to feel the effects of it, she began getting ready for bed. Calmer now, she climbed into bed and as she was saying her prayers, she faded off to sleep.

A while later she woke up, hearing the dogs barking. They quieted down quickly so Belle felt all was good. She realized she fell asleep before finishing prayer, so she did so then. Thoughts about what she was going to do in the morning filled her mind, but the sleep aid was working, and she fell asleep again.

Meeowow-PurrPurr-Meeowow. Belle awoke to the sound of a happy kitty, along with licks on her cheek and forehead. "Good morning stowaway, oh you just aren't going to live down that nickname are you boy, oh yeah," she said as she kissed and snuggled him. "I know, I know, it's time for breakfast. Thanks, Micro, for waking me only ten minutes before the alarm was to go off." *Brruurow!* he replied, as if to say you're welcome.

As she rolled over to switch the alarm button off, there was another kitty sitting by the nightstand staring up at her. "Good morning, little Squirrel." Squirrel began to purr louder as Belle acknowledged her. Belle sat up and stretched. The room came alive with loud meows and purring. Two more cats jumped up on the bed to greet her.

"Hi Bunkie, hi Fluff Girly, yes I'll get you all fed in a minute or two or three. I want to snuggle you all first and I'm not rushing this morning." She giggled as Bunkie continued his greeting with obsessive bunking to her arms and hands. "This is great, I had a wonderful sleep, and my best friends are coming today. There's plenty of time to get everything done before they arrive. Bet you guys will be happy to see them again too. They will be surprised when they meet our new buddies. Well, they may not meet Cautious and Candy if they don't come out of hiding, but they'll be surprised there are more of you anyway. Oh, and my barn buddies as well, oh what a surprise."

Cuddles was left in his room last night with the shy ones and the door was kept closed. Belle did not mind Cuddles sleeping with her sometimes if she were going to nap, but as his name denotes, she did not want him cuddling her all night. He would want to sleep on her chest if she were on her back, her hip when she was on her side, or sometimes near her face. He would stay in whatever place he chose until she moved. It was not comfortable to have him on her for a long time. To make sure she would get a good sleep he was closed in his room. Cautious and Candy, brother and sister, did not venture out of their room. They felt secure there and wanted nothing to do with the rest of the house.

Belle's conversation with her buddies was suddenly interrupted by a ruckus accompanied by loud growling and yowling. Pirate came dashing into the room with Pouncer in pursuit. They jumped up on the bed then off, circled the room and dashed out of it. Micro flew off the bed after them. "Well, so much for a relaxing morning, better intervene." As Belle rounded the corner, she saw Pouncer bounding out of a hiding place and landing on Micro. Pouncer, being twice his size, covered him completely. She could hear a muffled meow coming from under the very still Pouncer. He finally moved just enough so that Micro could peek out from under him. Pouncer began to lick Micro's head.

"That's enough, let's get you guys fed." She said as she lifted up Pouncer, "Good thing you're a gentle kitty or you would have to live outside with the dogs."

As she opened the door to the kitty room and proceeded in, a parade of kitties followed behind her. All of them were meowing with anticipation. Two of them began circling her legs as she measured out their food from a large storage container. After scooping out the litter boxes, she gave them fresh water. Belle paused a moment before leaving the room, listening to the sound of them munching. "My turn," she said with a smile and headed for the kitchen.

"Let me see, what do I want to eat this morning? Hot or cold? Definitely tea, so better get that started."

When Belle finished breakfast, she cleaned up then headed out the door to feed all the other critters. With that done, she went to pick some fruit. She took it to the guest house where she washed and dried it. After placing it in the fruit bowl, she put a variety of nuts in the sectional serving tray. Going outside again she selected and cut some flowers for the guest house. As she was arranging them in the vase, she heard the dogs barking, which did not alarm her but then she heard a car horn blaring.

"Oh NO, that can't be them already, this early, its only eight thirty. Oh my gosh!" Her heart was pounding; panic was taking over. She nearly dropped the vase, spilling water as she fumbled to keep it in her hands.

She quickly put the vase in its planned destination and wiped up the water. *Beep beeeep beep*. "Is this the surprise that Star was talking about in the message she left me early this morning?" Belle quickly went to a mirror to make sure she looked okay, then ran to the door to go out and open the gate.

She leapt through the doorway and ran down the walkway. When she saw what was on the other side of the gate, she stopped dead in her tracks. "What? Uh, who? Ooooh, wait a minute; whew." Taking a deep breath and giving a huge sigh of relief, she raised her arm, waving at the truck on the other side of the gate. "Thank you, Lord, as much as I want to see my friends, I'm not ready. Need to have everything perfecto."

While she was entering the code into the keypad, Mr. Yancee called out the window, "Top of the morning to ya," to which she replied, "And the rest of the afternoon to yourself."

"Good morning, dear," said Mrs.Yancee as Belle gave her a hand out of the truck. "We have all the goodies you requested: fresh milk, fresh cream, homemade yogurt, cheeses and goat milk for the cats. Your friends are going to enjoy the farm fresh of it all. I have a surprise for you; I made three dozen dinner rolls for you and a dozen larger ones for sandwiches. You can freeze some and take from the freezer as you need to."

"Thank you! That's great; this is all great! Help yourself to the garden and orchard. I so enjoy this barter arrangement."

Belle reached into the back of the truck to retrieve the baskets for Mrs. Yancee while Mrs. Yancee asked Mr. Yancee to put all that they brought in the refrigerator, and she and Belle headed to the garden. "I was so caught up in my preparations the last couple of days I forgot you were coming today. When I heard the horn, I thought my friends arrived early and began to panic. There are just a few finishing touches left to do, then I need to prepare the reception lunch. I'm actually going to be done on time."

"That's wonderful, dear. Try to bring them by tomorrow. Anytime you can. We can go on a short hayride. The little ones will enjoy that and seeing the animals. Speaking of animals, I went to peek at the opossum in our bush while waiting that day for it to get picked up. Hard to believe it was an adult, she was so small. I knew she was tame, so I picked her up and cradled her then noticed that little heart-shaped birthmark, it was adorable."

"Birthmark?"

"Well, I don't know what else to call it, dear."

Belle's mind was racing now. She tried to recall that last day at work again. Still nothing was coming to mind. She had been so distracted thinking about the visit with her friends she did not notice anything unusual. Now she wanted to go see Momma. "Will you be all right while I go get some things done?"

"Yes dear, go ahead, I don't want you to get behind. Mr. Yancee is here too."

Belle, adrenaline pumping now, was moving quickly. She darted from room to room in the guest house, making sure everything was in place, then headed to the main house and did the same. Opening the refrigerator, she quickly pulled out the ingredients for the meal. All that needed peeling, cutting, chopping, seasoning, and mixing was done in record time for Belle. With that all done and placed in the refrigerator, it was time for a record-breaking cleanup. "Yippee, done! What time is it? Great, plenty of time to run to the Center!"

She peeked out the window and saw that the Yancees had gone and closed the gate after themselves. Grabbing the keys for the car, she jogged out to the driveway, hopped in the car, and took off racing.

FIVE

THE CENTER WAS TEEMING WITH VISITORS. It was difficult to find a parking space, so Belle parked by the delivery door around back. She hurried inside.

"Did you forget something else?"

"Hi Cy, yes, I think, I'll check my desk. I forgot they were doing visitors today, so I'll hurry and get out of the way."

"No prob, gotta run; see you Saturday."

As soon as he turned the corner she headed for the records room. She was determined to see Momma Possum's records for herself.

She closed the door behind her and glanced around the room. There was a separate section of file cabinets for small animals. Finally locating the correct cabinet, she searched for Momma's file. The records showed she was due for her yearly exam in a couple of months and confirmed it was not done early. After placing Momma's records back in the drawer, Belle opened the door a crack to see if anyone was around. She listened a moment to make sure no one was coming, then headed out to see Momma.

Belle approached the handler's entrance to Momma's living quarters and paused to read the schedule. "Perfect! She isn't due for show until this afternoon." Belle entered the quarters and went to Momma. "Hi Momma, just hanging around as usual I see; oh you're so sweet, let me get a look at you. Goodness, you do have a little mark that looks like a heart! You're not Momma!" Belle hurried to find Cypress.

When she found him, he was doing a show and tell. She nervously paced back and forth, waiting for him to finish. As soon as he was done, his last sentence barely finished, she ran up to him, grabbed his arm and said, "You've got to come see Momma now."

He was startled at first but gave in to the tugging on his arm. Belle told him what she had really been up to and what she discovered. In Momma's quarters now, Cypress was examining her. "Belle, there's nothing there."

"Look near her back left leg. Right th-there—but, but it was there a few minutes ago I swear!"

"Hound, I gotta get back to work and you need a major break." He said this as he was hurrying out the door with Belle in tow. "Like ya said, the tag was probably just a mistake; now let go, see ya."

"The tag!" She quickly turned and went back to Momma. Shocked and confused, Belle said, "Welcome home, Momma," as she held Momma's left foot and flicked the tag, now in its rightful place, with her finger. Just then her phone alarm sounded. "Time to get back home. I've just got to figure this out. What is going on? I know what I saw." She flicked the tag a few more times. "Uh darn, it's going to have to wait a bit." Belle hurried to the car. She was cutting it close, getting home before her friends arrived.

She sped into the driveway and came to a jerking halt. She then checked the time. Dashing into the house and out the back door, she gathered Anomaly and Rarity to get them into the barn. They were one of the many surprises Belle had for her friends and she wanted to present the critters to them.

After they were back in their stalls, she looked over the barn. She quickly rearranged a couple of things. "Yes, that's better. This is so much fun. I can't wait to show it all off." All of Belle's bustling caught the attention of P-2 and P-3, who were peering out the top portion of their cage trying to see what was going on.

She walked out of the barn, glancing over the garden and surrounding area to see if anything needed tending to there. "Almost forgot I need to replace the flowers in my house too. Let's see, hmm, did red, white and blue for the guest house. I'll do purple, yellow and pink with a touch of white flowers for mine."

Making a quick selection she started back to the house. The dogs came over to her, wanting to play. After an acknowledging pat on their heads she said, "Sorry guys, not now, it's a big day. I'm busy but you'll have lots of play time after our guests arrive. Not only that but you'll probably get lots of hugs." Then she shouted out, "Okay critters, it's almost show time!" With that said, she went inside to place the flowers in several vases, then went out front to wait for her friends.

The sound of a moving vehicle caught Belle's attention. She walked toward the road and looked in the only direction one could come from. Seeing it was a large van, the happy dance began. Her arms were up in the air waving wildly as she bounced up and down. Warren was driving and began responding by beeping the horn. He gave many short beeps and a couple of long ones as they approached. The kids were yelling out the window, "Aunt Belle! Aunt Belle!"

Warren stopped the van at the end of the driveway and then they piled out and ran to Belle. Starlit embraced Belle and they began to cry tears of joy. The kids latched on and with excitement exclaimed, "We're here! We're here! Yay, we're here!" Belle gave them a long hug and smothered them with kisses. Silas and Warren squeezed their way into the frenzy saying, "We want some too!" They stood a long time greeting at the end of the driveway, then finally Belle said, "Let's go inside and I'll show you around."

Everyone walked up to the house while Warren drove the van up the driveway and parked. Before entering the house, they all looked around. "Oh, how lovely the house is and how beautiful the flowers are, Belle," Starlit commented. "The yard is very nice and the area is quiet and peaceful," Silas said. As he placed his arm around Belle, Warren said, "This is all wonderful!" Belle opened the door and with a waving motion of her hand said, "Come in, come in. The tour starts now."

"This is the guest bedroom, Jasmine, that you get to stay in with Aunt Star. You boys get to share one of the guest bedrooms in the guest house where you'll stay with your dads. This here is my office. Over here is my bedroom."

As they moved from room to room many compliments were given. "Let's skip the kitty room until after lunch. I know some of you will want to hug and play with them and I'm getting hungry. You must all be hungry too, so let's go downstairs for a quick tour. That's the game room as I like to call it."

Belle started down the stairs quickly. When she got to the second to last step from the bottom she jumped off and with her arm sweeping forward, hand stretched out, said, "Ta-da, pool table included!"

Warren was grinning ear to ear and his eyes were gleaming. Not only did he enjoy playing pool, but this table was the same color as his back home. He never liked green or rust tables, he preferred blue. "Very nice, Belle," he said as he walked over to it. "This will be a nice way to end the day each evening after dinner. Your home is amazing."

"Yes, Belle," said Starlit, "it's wonderful, so warm and cozy!"

Silas added, "What a great retreat!"

The kids did not say much. They were busy looking at the games and toys in a section that was for the kids. It had a child-size table and chairs for them and a storage area for games, toys, drawing and coloring supplies. Belle pointed out the couch with removable back pillows that made it wide enough to sleep on. She showed them a half bathroom and the laundry room, then said, "That's it for now; are you all ready for lunch?" All answered yes in unison and headed upstairs before Belle could take a step. They were not just hungry; they looked forward to her cooking as well as any goodies that were usually part of a visit to Belle's.

While Belle was gathering the food, Starlit set the dining room table. Silas was looking out one of the windows and noticed one of the dogs going into a large playhouse-looking structure through a doggie door located in the front of it. It had a covered porch and a little fence. As he was looking at it, he said, "Oh Belle, you didn't—well apparently you did because I'm seeing it with my own eyes."

Everyone went over to the window. "What?" Starlit said, her eyes widening. "That's adorable! Just like you to make a cozy house for them."

The kids kept saying "cool" and asking if they could sleep in the doghouse. As Starlit's eyes scanned the yard she squealed with delight, "Chickens! They're so cute and what a nice house they have too!"

"Surprise, surprise! That's two of many more to come."

"Fresh eggs every morning sounds delicious," said Warren.

"There's fresh milk right from the cow this morning and cream, also homemade yogurt and cheeses all from the Yancee farm. I get goat's milk for the cats from them too. Just wait till you try the meats I get from the Butchers. That's Mr. and Mrs. Butcher and they own a butcher shop, isn't that funny? Oh and Sy, I got a little extra goat's milk this time 'cause I know you like it once in a while. There is some in the guest house for you."

"Thanks! By the way, did you design the dog and chicken houses?"

"I did. Cy from the Center and a friend of his who knows about building things built them, and I helped. They suggested I design doghouses and they would build them so we could all make a little money, but I said I would have to think long and hard on that."

Another sound came from Starlit but not one of delight. "You still have that decrepit old scary barn! Your vegetable garden is near it! Why? That's not safe!" Silas weighed in too. "I agree with Star. You should have gotten rid of it first thing. Probably would have cost a pretty penny though."

"That's another surprise, it's not as it appears; you'll see and you will be amazed. I sure was."

"My curiosity has been stirred, Belle, and I am eager to explore that rickety building."

"Well, rein in your curiosity, Warren, till after lunch." With a ding-a-linging sound filling the room Belle announced it was time to eat.

"Did you all have enough to eat? Good, then let's clean up and go visit the kitties."

The kids ran to the cat room, waiting anxiously outside the door. One by one they called out, "Hurry, Dad, Aunt Belle, hurry." They knew not to open the door without permission.

"Ready, here we go." As Belle opened the door she sang out, "Surprise again."

Cautious and Candy ran and hid as predicted. The kids and grownups were happy to see the kitties. Starlit picked up her favorite, which was Fluff Girly, and fussed over her. Silas picked up his favorite, Pirate, and said his hellos. When Warren picked up his two favorites, Micro and Squirrel, he said to them, "More furs I see. You two do not mind at all I suppose, there is plenty of room for all of you. I see you have outdoor space to use." With a chuckle he added, "Of course, you can always get into a suitcase, little stowaway, if you want some privacy."

The kids were fussing over Bunkie, their favorite. They just loved bunking heads with him. "May I have your attention please, for the official introduction to the new furs. I'll introduce them in the order in which they arrived. This is Cuddles. He was found near a garbage dumpster at three weeks of age and in very poor condition. Next are the brother and sister, Cautious and Candy, hiding over here. They were found when they were about eight weeks old in a box with other siblings. Finally, this is Pouncer, who was found near the barn with several injuries that have left him with some scars. He was about a year old at that time."

Each one of them welcomed the new kitties, then visited and played with all the kitties for a while. Silas commented how he would like to be spoiled like all the critters as he and Starlit marveled at the outdoor patio space for the cats. It had an entrance through one of the room's windows for the kitties and outside there was a door for Belle. There were places to climb and perch on, toys to bat around and a heat source that stood in the middle of the area.

"You know I love your furs, Belle," Warren began in a loving tone. "This is all very nice but that is a waste of heat."

"Wait, it's not, you'll see how it all works when we go outside. Speaking of outside, we should head there. We've been in here almost half an hour. I have a lot to show you, surprises-surprises."

SIX

AS SOON AS THEY WERE OUTSIDE the kids ran over to the doghouse. They crawled through the doggie door and all the adults laughed. It was a giant of a doghouse.

"This way." Belle led the adults to the back of the doghouse where there was a man-door. Since they would not all fit at the same time, they took turns going in and looking around. It had a ramp leading to an upper part that had two beds and tiny windows. The lower part had two more beds, a storage cabinet and two wagons. They were not your ordinary type of red wagons that kids pulled around. These were custom made for working around a yard. They were wider and the sides were higher than that type of wagon and had a door that opened at the back. The doghouse was well insulated and had heat and cooling sources.

"Hey Dad, we can sleep here, there's plenty of beds," said Warren Jr.

"Can we play with the wagons, Aunt Belle?" Mark asked.

"Yes, you can, and even better, you can ride in them while Guardian and Stance pull you. They help me around the yard. I put special harnesses on them and hook them up to the wagons. You can take a ride later. Okay, official intro: these are the boys, Guardian and Stance. They're brothers."

"They are beautiful, Belle," said Starlit.

"You mean handsome."

"O-kay, Sy, I mean handsome, Belle, and they're so well behaved."

"That's because we all went through obedience training. They have a wonderful disposition naturally, which was a big help." She then said with a giggle, "I was harder to train than they were."

They all played with the dogs for a little while, then Jasmine announced it was time to see the chickens and pick some eggs. "You collect eggs, Jasmine."

They all walked over to the chicken house and took turns going in to check it out. "You kids can help collect eggs in the morning for breakfast." There was a fenced area for the chickens that had a bush-like tree in the center. A ramp led upward to a small doorway and over their little entrance was an awning.

"You know I never did name them. When they were babies, I would call out, 'here chick-chick-chickens, here chicky-chicks' and repeat it while I fed them. Now when they're out and about I call them in the same way. It just kind of stuck and I didn't think about names."

After seeing the chickens, they toured the property looking at the flowers, vegetable garden and orchard, then Belle led them over to the cats' yard.

"Let me show you the 'catio.' Look here. The outside of the frame has slots for Plexiglas panels that get installed over the screens in the cooler weather and rubber strips are placed in between the panels. Then over the bottom half of the panels I place heavy canvas which attaches to these rings. It doesn't take very long. The roof is insulated and the heat source is energy efficient. This really is not a big space, and they don't come out here in the dead of winter, so the heat is not on all winter. No A.C. out here for them, only fans."

"Good job, Belle."

"Thank you, Star. Well, let's move on. I have to show you something that might be a little familiar to some of you, but I have to go into the barn. You'll get a tour of it in a little while and see some other surprises inside but in the meantime, wait over here." She motioned with her hand to direct them where to wait.

Belle entered the barn through the man-door, then returned from around the back of the barn. As she walked towards everyone the kids began jumping up and down and yelling "horsies, horsies!"

Warren corrected them, "That is a zebra and a mule, little ones."

Silas began laughing loudly, which set Starlit and Warren laughing as they realized it might be the zebra from the video with Belle in the water trough. Still laughing, Starlit asked, "Is that the one that was in the video you showed us?"

"Sure is."

Silas could hardly believe it. "Aha ha ha! Where's the trough, Belle? Been swimming lately? Ha ha ha!"

Warren said, "It looks as though it has not grown, Belle."

"She—and she—has not grown. The mule is a girl also and is not growing. They are unusually small and no one knows why. Now I would like to formally introduce the girls. The zebra is Anomaly and this gal is Rarity."

Starlit asked, "How did you get them?"

"They just showed up at the Center one day. Not at the same time. Rarity came later on. It's most likely the people who had them couldn't handle them anymore, so they dumped them at the Center which was a good choice. When Rarity arrived, they became friends. It was soon after that the Center allowed me to adopt Anomaly, since she had become attached to me, and I took her home. Rarity missed her so much she became ill. We brought Rarity here and the two of them became inseparable. Rarity recovered quickly, and the Center allowed me to adopt her also. They're best friends now. We have no idea how someone acquired a zebra. These girls get to be in show and tell at the Center, but I told them the girls were on vacation with me. The center has a lot of critters to use for educating the public. You kids get to ride them, but first let me show you what's in the barn. Come on."

When they reached the barn Starlit did not want to go inside.

"It's all right, really, Star. I go in and out all the time. This thing is in great shape."

Warren and Silas began touching, tapping and pushing on the barn.

"This is amazing, Warren. What is it made out of?"

"I have no idea but it was definitely made to look old and decrepit intentionally."

They disappeared around the side of the barn and eventually got back to where they started. "Star, you have nothing to be concerned about. Silas and I have examined it all the way around. This building is sturdy; it only appears not to be which I believe was done deliberately."

Still a little apprehensive to enter it, Starlit asked, "Warren, why would someone want to do that?"

He ventured, "Perhaps the owner wanted it to be a form of art or wanted the antique look. Perhaps it is meant to be a type of scarecrow..."

"Come on guys, step inside, I have some things to show you." Belle took Starlit by the hand and led her through the door. "This area here is my indoor garden. I'll start this garden at the end of September and have fresh vegetables during the winter. The barn is well insulated and has both heat and air-conditioning."

Warren repeated, "Heat and air-conditioning?"

"This is crazy," Silas said. "Look at this; it has a bathroom with a good size shower!"

"It came that way, I didn't have it put in; however, I did add a bed to this cozy little space." Belle walked over to a curtain hanging next to the bathroom and pulled it to the side to reveal a bed in an alcove. "It had this large, built-in bedlike structure, so I put a full-size mattress on it and made a sleeping space. I don't know if that was its original purpose, but I decided to do it. Look, it even has two drawers in the frame. I sometimes like to sleep out here."

As Starlit shook her head side to side she whined in a high-pitched voice, "Why, why would you want to do that?"

"Oh, and I did change the shower head to the kind I can lift off so I could use it to bathe the dogs. It's great, so convenient!"

The kids started saying that they could hear something inside one of the stalls. They ran over to see what it was. Starlit froze in place while the others went over to see what was going on.

"It's okay, Star, that's just P-2 and P-3, another surprise." There was a small stall in the corner of the barn that had a cage inside it, big enough to stand up in. The cage was set back some, leaving an open area as you entered the stall. Belle opened the stall gate, then the door to the cage. As she opened it, she said, "This is the ferret house."

Two curious little critters cautiously came out. Belle knelt down and picked them up. The kids were excited and asked if they could pet them. "You sure can. These are Pirate 2 and Pirate 3. I call them P-2 and P-3, and just like Pirate kitty they like to steal things."

"Soo cool," said Warren Jr.

They had a deluxe living space with several places to snuggle in, tunnels to crawl through and toys to play with. Mark was rolling one of their spheres back and forth between his hands. "This ball is hard," he said, "don't think it will bounce."

"Here's the other one. They're not for bouncing. P-2 and P-3 go inside them and roll around. It's fun for them and they get exercise. Let's put them in. Now watch."

Jasmine was giggling and skipping as she and Mark followed the ferrets around the barn. "Hey everyone, in a few minutes it will be snack time. After that you kids can ride Anomaly and Rarity, then go for a wagon ride."

"You know, Belle, if I weren't seeing all this for myself, I wouldn't have believed it if someone told me about it," marveled Silas.

"Think about it, Silas," Warren said. "Remember, when we were growing up she would rescue critters, make shelters for them and give them toys, therefore this should not surprise you."

"You're right; it makes sense Belle is spoiling her critters," said Silas, and as he patted Warren on the back he added, "Let's head for some treats!"

Back inside the house, Belle laid out some cookies and cake on the table. She placed a kettle of tea and a pot of coffee on a couple of trivets for the adults and then set a carafe of milk out for the kids next to the fruit bowl.

"Almost forgot the cream; here we go. No sugar after dinner, so enjoy it now. Here's cheese and crackers too if anyone should feel inclined to a little protein. After you kids ride the 'horsies' we can go to the pond; it's quite a hike so Guardian and Stance can pull you in the wagons if you get tired. Maybe you'll see some frogs and other critters there."

"Speaking of critters, Belle, I noticed you're missing birds and fish. You always had them when we were growing up. Thinking of squeezing any in?" asked Silas.

"Well actually, Sy, some fish in the future but I don't want birds. I'm thinking about a freshwater tank for the living room and dining room. The dining room one will be the smaller of the two; maybe, I'll see when the time comes."

During their conversation, sounds of delight could be heard along with "yummy" comments, making it very clear each one of them was enjoying their snacks. They all had a little of the treats as well as some fruit and cheese. Starlit asked, "Belle, are we going to see the guest house before going to the pond? I want to get settled and get our luggage unpacked."

"Yes, Star, we are but I wasn't even thinking about the luggage. That would be a good idea instead of waiting till the end of the day to unpack when we're all tired. We should get that all settled first. Seems like we're ready for a quick cleanup and then we can go."

The guest house was smaller than the main house but could comfortably house four to five people. It had two bedrooms, an eat-in kitchen and a full bathroom which was near a small laundry area. There was a finished basement with a couch that convert-ed to a bed, an upholstered chair, end tables, bookshelves, a half bathroom, a play area for kids and, to Warren's disappointment, no pool table.

"You have unlimited access to the pool table in the main house," said Belle. "Even if we gals retire early or want to do something else, you guys can still use it anytime. There'll be lots of time for pool since you'll be here two weeks. You can come and go as you please, make yourselves at home just like it used to be."

"Of course, Belle, thank you," he replied. "Sounds good to me," Silas added.

Starlit went over to Belle and gave her a long hug and said, "I miss how it used to be, so much." They began to get teary-eyed and the guys interrupted before their emotions took over. Silas headed upstairs saying, "Let's get the stuff put away already!"

Warren placed his arms around the girls and led them toward the stairs. "Come on ladies, we have a schedule to fulfill. The children have asked repeatedly about their 'horsey' ride so we should move on."

Everyone pitched in to get their belongings put away. Belle helped the guys in the guest house, then went to the main house to help Starlit and Jasmine.

"Make sure you take something warm for later, Star. It will be cool this evening."

"Okay Belle, I'll look for something now. The weather is really nice out here, it's not hot, just very comfortable. Is it going to be good for our entire stay?"

"I think it will. You know that's always subject to change though, it's the weather after all. We usually get a shower or two this time of the year."

"We better hurry, the guys are done. They're outside playing with the dogs. You can go and play with them too, Jasmine. Aunt Belle and I will be out soon and then you kids will get to ride the horsies."

As Starlit opened the door for Jasmine she yelled out to the guys, "Make sure you take something warm to wear for later on." Just as she was about to close the door, she heard a sound. *OwOwooo... wooOwooo...*

"Belle, I hear a coyote or something outside. Is it safe for the kids to be out there?"

"It's fine. If something was wrong, if there was some kind of threat, the dogs would let me know. I don't even really notice the howling anymore, it seems normal to me with being in the country now."

"Yeah, I suppose, not like when we were hearing all that howling when we were at your house back home, remember?" said Starlit. "Oh, I'll take this for later, it's warm and it has a hood. Okay, now I'm ready, Belle, let's go."

SEVEN

THE KIDS WERE UP ON THE HORSES in no time. Jasmine was on Anomaly and the boys doubled up on Rarity. Belle led them out a gate behind the barn to a trail. They would pause occasionally so the kids could switch around on who they rode.

After a while they started back to the barn. "Aunt Belle, can we ride them to the pond too?"

"No, Junior, I don't like taking them there, they get spooked. Besides that, they need to rest now." They entered back through the gate and after the kids were down Belle locked the gate. "You can all head to the doghouse while I put these girls inside. Sy, would you and Warren get the dogs set up please. Just tell them it's time to work."

"Sure thing, we'll see you over there. Come on, kids."

Mark and Junior wanted up on their dads' backs; they just could not get enough horsie. Silas and Warren galloped and whinnied all the way to the doghouse while Starlit and Jasmine held hands and skipped there.

"Hi Stance, hi Guardian, it's time to work." As soon as Silas said this the dogs started to bark and turn in circles. After two circles they ran into their house, returning quickly, each carrying a harness in his mouth.

"That is impressive," Warren said, and at the same time Starlit said, "That's so cute! They're so adorable and smart."

Silas came from around the back of the doghouse with the two wagons. He hesitated, barked, then turned around twice, causing them all to laugh. He and Warren placed the harnesses on the dogs and hooked them up to the wagons.

"Aunt Star, where is Aunt Belle?"

"She's still in the barn, Jasmine. I don't know what's taking so long, let's go get her."

Back at the barn Belle was examining Anomaly's neck, then went to examine Rarity's. "Hmmm, does seem like it, now what did I do with, oh crap, damn it! Where did that go, s---! I had it..."

Just then Starlit and Jasmine had entered the barn and Jasmine began shouting, "Potty mouth, potty mouth, Aunt Belle has a potty mouth!"

"Belle!" Starlit said sharply.

"You're right, Jasmine, I'm sorry. I shouldn't talk that way, it isn't right, it's wrong. Sorry, Star."

Jasmine gave Belle a hug, then ran out of the barn. Sounding a little sour, Starlit said, "Belle, it's getting late. How are we going to go on this hike and get back to make dinner? I know we told the kids they could stay up a little later than usual while we're on vacation, but this might get very late."

"It should be fine. We're going to barbecue hamburgers and hot dogs by the pond. I made a green salad, potato salad and coleslaw that are already packed up with the meat. Everything else is at the pond including the condiments. When we get back, the kids can wash up and go right to bed."

"Wow, okay, let's go, everyone is waiting."

Belle walked over to a cabinet and opened it; inside was a small refrigerator and freezer. She took out the food and placed it in a cooler along with some ice packs, then placed the buns on top of the packs. When she finished, she put on her small backpack. "Ready, let's go."

Surprised, Starlit replied, "Well. Wow again!"

"Listen up, gang, we're heading up to the pond now and having dinner there." Belle placed the cooler in the back of one of the wagons. The kids wanted to ride in the wagons now, so she told Mark to get in the one with the cooler and told Jasmine and Junior to get in the other one.

As Warren handed Starlit her backpack he said, "There is a refrigerator in the barn apparently that Belle forgot to mention. I did not see one, therefore it must be hidden."

"Yes, Warren, there is, and it is. With so much to show us she forgot that nook. She probably would have showed us but got distracted at some point when the ferrets stirred up before she was ready to introduce them. Remember, the kids heard something moving in one of the stalls? On the way out of the barn she told me there is a place to make tea or coffee and a toaster oven as well."

He replied, "I think it is unusual to have those types of amenities in a barn."

"It doesn't surprise me that Belle would want a setup like that," Silas said. "After all, she is living her dream, country life, critters..."

Belle, Guardian, Stance and kids in tow were way ahead of them on the path. Warren Jr. called out, "Come on, slowpokes!"

"Yes son, we will catch up in a moment."

"I agree with Sy, Warren. Belle is making good use of the barn and she is enjoying things. Although I don't think she would have thought to put a kitchenette in it."

"Or a bathroom," Silas added. "It was probably there already like the bathroom." Starlit said, in a serious tone, "Before we catch up to them, I need to tell you what happened as Jasmine and I entered the barn."

As they walked along the kids would occasionally want to get out of the wagons to explore a little. They pointed out various insects and played hide and seek among the bushes, some of which had huge leaves perfect for covering a child. With excitement in his voice Junior, pointing to an unusual, tiny fluffy critter said, "Look at the upholstered worm!"

Puzzled, Starlit asked, "The what?"

"Caterpillar," answered Silas. "He's most definitely Warren's son, Star."

"That does confirm it, Belle. I remember now how when we were kids, Warren used to call caterpillars upholstered worms. There are a lot of wildflowers along this section of the path, but I haven't noticed any bees."

"I think they are out here mostly in the morning. Hey kids, let's move on."

As they walked on, they talked and laughed about the things they did as kids. Warren proudly pointed out other similarities Junior portrayed.

The dogs stopped abruptly and began to growl. "What is it, boys?" While everyone began looking around, the dogs lay down and became quiet.

"Anyone see anything?"

"No. Nothing."

"Me either." Belle was standing near Guardian and he began to tug on her pant leg. "I think he wants us to get down; we should get down, and you kids get in the wagons, keep quiet. Sy, get down."

"I have a better running start from this position."

"Quit it and sit it, wise guy."

Guardian stood up, sniffed the air, then lay back down. Warren whispered, "I noticed the birds are no longer chirping."

"I don't hear the frogs either, said Belle, this is weird."

After about ten minutes the dogs stood up and began to walk, and the birds and frogs could be heard again. They all proceeded on but were feeling uneasy.

"Well, that put a dent in the mood," said Starlit. "Should we even keep going?"

"If it weren't all right the dogs wouldn't let us."

After a few minutes they came to a bend in the path. As they passed through the bend and approached the straight part of the path, they could see something had come by at this point. There were marks across the path that looked as if something was dragged by. The dogs started sniffing around the area.

"What do you make of that, Warren?"

"I am not sure, Silas. There are some footprints both human and animal, some are old..."

Starlit interrupted, "Guys, let's go, the kids are getting restless, and we need to keep moving so it doesn't get late. I don't want to be out here when it's dark!"

The kids climbed out of the wagons and stretched. They wanted to walk some more now. On they went, and in about ten minutes they finally reached their destination. The pathway led to a space that opened to a small parklike area, and just beyond it was a pond.

"This is, this is..."

"Come on Star, spit it out, let me help—unbelievable."

"Yes Sy, and I was going to say wonderful and beautiful!"

"You mean you were trying to, right Warren?"

"Yes, Silas. I can see why Star was unable to articulate her thoughts."

"You kids can go and play while I show the grownups everything. I'm going to unhitch the dogs and they'll go with you. Good boys, watch the kids now, guard."

With excitement in her voice Belle said, "So this is it!"

There was an array of colorful plants and wildflowers surrounding the variety of shrubs and bushes that filled the landscape. A fire pit in the distance had large flat stones around it for sitting. There were two picnic tables with lemongrass strategically planted around them. A large structure about thirty feet from the tables housed supplies and all you needed for a picnic. It had a sliding door with a slide bolt on it. Inside were small folding tables and a refrigerator. On one side of the refrigerator was a row of cupboards and closets, and on the other side a countertop and sink.

Behind this structure was a large storage shed. Belle began showing them each section. "There is something to drink in the fridge and ice ready in the freezer. The paper plates, cups, napkins, and plastic utensils are in this cupboard, also plastic tablecloths. These closets have camping chairs and blankets. The long utensils for the grill are hanging on the side of the wheeled table next to the grill parked over here, and hanging on the side of the closet next to it are aprons."

Remembering suddenly and pointing with her index fingers on both hands, she added, "Oooh, very important, the fire extinguisher; isn't this great!"

"What, no bathroom, no shower, Belle?"

"Actually, Sy, there is a bathroom but no shower, down that path. It's hard to see from here and there is a mini dumpster too. The guys from the Center come to collect the bags from it. They bring them up to the dumpster at the Center so they can be taken on garbage day by the town's waste management service. I clean the bathroom as much as possible when I'm out and about, and I'll call the septic cleaning service to empty the tank when it's needed. It had been emptied before I moved in, so it won't need to be done for a long time. Some people who work at the Center like to come out here occasionally for lunch."

"That's nice of the Center to let you use all this."

"Correction, it's nice of me to let others use it; this is on my property—surprise! They take care of the garbage as a thank-you."

"And let me guess, it's also a thank-you because you leave treats once in a while too."

"Silas knows you well," said Warren, and then he asked, "Is there anything else you would like to tell us?"

"Yep, this is all solar powered and if we're here when it gets dark, we can turn on the lights, so you don't have to worry about the dark, Star."

"We still have to walk back in the dark."

"Not if our chefs get going; we should have time to eat, take a stroll around the pond and leave before it gets dark, which will be about nine thirty. We should be home in twenty minutes if we keep a good pace."

"But it took us an hour and a half to get here."

"Well Star, that's because I took us the long way. Part of the trails and paths we took were through the sanctuary grounds." With a big grin and pointing over her shoulder Belle said, "We just have to go back in that direction!"

Silas and Warren began cooking while Belle and Starlit got a tablecloth and set up the table. The kids were playing and laughing. As they ran along the pond you could hear splashing sounds made by frogs escaping possible capture. The dogs were keeping an eye on the kids as they were frolicking about. They would yip and wrestle with each other periodically, but when the kids started to wander too far, Guardian and Stance were on it and herded the kids back to an acceptable place.

Warren Jr. realizing this, made a game of it. He even instructed Jasmine and Mark to quietly sneak away, but the dogs were on them before they could reach their destination. They would jump up and down with excitement when the dogs came running and giggle when they circled them.

Play was interrupted by the sound of a bell ringing, signaling it was time to eat. The kids trotted off toward the picnic tables with the dogs following behind them.

Unexpectedly Guardian charged forward, barking fiercely and startling the kids. Jasmine let out a blood-curdling scream. Hearts pounding, the adults moved quickly towards the children. The dogs were circling a creature, growling and pawing at it relentlessly.

Starlit was horrified. She picked up Mark who had fallen and held him tightly. She told Junior to take Jasmine's hand as she took hold of her other one and led them quickly away.

Belle instructed the dogs to herd the creature away from the water. Silas had grabbed his backpack as they headed towards the commotion. He reached into a small, zippered pouch in one of the outer pockets, made a quick assessment, took aim and yelled out, "Clear!" Belle called the dogs and then–BANG!

Warren stood in front of the creature waving his arms wildly, trying to distract it as it tried to turn toward a large bush nearby. Belle commanded the dogs to herd again.

"Silas, would you care to take another shot?"

"No, brother, I'm good, it's good, give it another minute. See, lights out. Gee Warren, are you losing faith in me?"

"I apologize for the momentary lapse, brother. Belle, I think we should leave it to the dogs, we need to see to Star and the children."

"Okay, Warren; Guardian, Stance—guard! I better call the Center. They're going to love this."

"Is someone there at this time?"

"I'm calling the bat phone. It's an emergency phone that forwards calls to whoever is volunteering to receive emergency calls on any given day."

As they approached the kids, the kids ran to their dads; they embraced. Silas and Warren reassured them. "The situation is under control, children, it cannot harm you."

"Does that mean it's dead, Warren?"

"Asleep, Star," Belle answered as she was ending the phone call to the Center.

"I see, yes, asleep is nicer."

"No, I mean sleeping, for now, but will be awake later." Starlit gasped, and then rolled her eyes.

"Someone from the Center will be here to get it, but it will be a little bit. I think we should eat; everything is ready. You kids hungry? Come on, sit down."

As they sat down to eat, a little breeze came up and the scent of flowers drifted into the picnic area. Silas gave thanks and asked the Lord's blessing over the food. They all said Amen and began feasting. Warren said the meat was delicious as Starlit and Silas nodded their heads in agreement. Everyone was very hungry, and even the kids ate more than usual. It was now a relaxed atmosphere. As they began slowing down on eating, conversation broke out.

Just as they had finished eating, a truck from the Center pulled up.

EIGHT

"Hi guys. Sorry you had to make a trip out here. Goliath is over that way."

One of the guys walked with Belle, Silas, and Warren while the other drove the truck over to the critter.

"It's a big one all right; however, this one might need a name change. The one we caught yesterday is much bigger."

"Bigger! Another one?! How many of these things are out here?"

"Only the two. We have a video of them being dumped by the Center doors the other night. They were wheeled up to the door in a very large crate. The two guys, well we assume guys, had covered their faces and the vehicle they came in was out of camera range, so we don't know who they were; anyway, while rushing to get away they didn't realize the latch wasn't secure on the crate. When they dropped the crate off the door opened a little and eventually the snakes made their getaway. Soon as morning came and Ed viewed the tape, he called a hunt. We'll need you all to help lift it into the truck."

"Thank you for taking care of this. By the way, this is Warren and Silas; this is Steve and John."

They struggled to get the creature loaded up in the truck. "This sure is a workout, Steve."

g in there, Silas, we've almost got it. You didn't realize how solid and heavy this thing would be, did you?"

"No, this certainly isn't your average pet!"

"Well, that's it, thank you, Warren, thank you, Silas for your help, and it was nice to meet you."

"You guys want a bite to eat?"

"No thanks, Belle, we're good. See you later."

"All right, see ya—bye."

When they returned to the table, Warren told Starlit and the kids what had happened and reassured them that there would not be any more creatures. Belle fed Guardian and Stance, then said she wanted to get something out of the shed and would be right back.

When she returned Starlit shouted joyfully, "A guitar!"

"Yep, just like the very one you have back home. I took it up here the other day so we could have a sing-along out here. I'll clean up while you all get started."

"Thanks, Belle, this is great and good timing. I say we start with some worship songs."

"Indeed, that would be wonderful," said Warren.

When they finished singing, they packed up and then went for a stroll around the pond, which was long and kidney shaped. Trees, shrubs, tall grasses, and rocks were spaced intermittently near the edge of it. Honeysuckle bushes filled the air with their sweet aroma. The end of the pond furthest from the picnic area was shallower and had water lilies in it. Off the outer curve of the pond in a small open area stood a stone pedestal with a sundial on top of it. Not far from that was a large rock formation partially covered with flowering vines and surrounded by bushes and trees.

As they were approaching the area of the sundial a beautiful peacock wandered into view. It opened its tail and displayed a wonderful fan of color. Large feathers of blues and greens with iridescent spots in them glistened in the sun. There was a peahen nearby that he was trying to win over. They all stood very still and watched the pair as they wandered off. With excitement Starlit said, "God is awesome! He's created so much beauty and we get to enjoy it!"

"Speaking of beauty," said Warren as he gently swept his hand over the top and down the sides of it, "this old sundial is grand." As Belle approached it, she had a peculiar look on her face. "What is it, Belle?"

"Something's familiar, Warren, but I can't quite put my finger on it."

"You have been here before."

"I never really looked at it—looked at it, you know, studied it. Hmm."

Then he said, "This piece under the stylus looks as though it could move."

"Oh Warren, that's not possi…"

"You were saying, Belle?"

Jumping up and down Jasmine yelled, "Daddy! Daddy, you made lights over there."

"Look, look," Junior said, pointing.

"Belle, isn't that the path we go back on?"

"Yes, it is, Star."

"Another surprise, no wonder you didn't say anything when I said I didn't want to have to walk back in the dark. I like pleasant surprises. There have been some very nice ones but this one is especially nice."

"I didn't know the path lit up!"

Starlit, with a little panic in her voice said, "Oh no, they went out and it's starting to get dark. Warren?"

"I moved it slightly. This time I will move it further. There are notches on the dial; I will try three notches and time it."

Together the kids said, "Yay, Daddy, they're on, they're on!"

"I don't hear anything," Silas said, as he was watching the time also. "No ticking sound, nothing. Time is just about up and... lights off. Well, that settles it, Warren, it is a timer. That was three minutes. Belle said it would take about twenty minutes if we moved quickly sooo, how about you set it for thirty minutes and we start home."

"Yes, I agree, will do."

Everyone checked to see if they had everything. Warren told the kids to get in the wagons which were positioned side by side. He set the timer and off they went. Still full of energy, the kids were talking with each other about their adventures from the day.

"How could you not have known that there are lights out here on this path, Belle?"

"I had no idea Star, really. I never noticed any fixtures during the day. Never saw lights in the distance at night from the house either. That's probably good, 'cause that would mean no one else knows about it. The previous owner probably spent some late hours out and about, so he put them in and obviously could well afford that. Next time I'm out here I want to get a better look at that sundial. I never would have thought that any part of the dial moved..."

Silas interrupted, "You would have eventually once you spent time near it. You would get curious as usual and start poking at it.

But it seems you don't spend a lot of time out here. I can tell by the dust on the Bible that's in the picnic area."

"Well, that's for anyone who might want to read it, you know, or get curious and check it out. I have mine at home and, well, I've been busy and none of you picked it up this evening!"

"Relax, just an observation and a tease."

"Uh okay, sooo Star, are you enjoying our lighted walk?"

"I am. This is nice..." As she was speaking a familiar sound emerged: *Owwooo woo...* "Um, as long as that coyote doesn't come over here."

"Wolf, Star, it's a wolf, different sound and bigger by the way."

"Sy, don't start, please. It's such a nice night and if the dogs aren't reacting then it must be all right."

"Bravo, Star," Warren said.

"You can still talk, brother!" Silas taunted. "I thought the cat might have gotten your tongue, you know, big cat, mountain lion."

"Give it up, Silas," Warren chuckled.

Silas whispered, "You've been very quiet, Warren, what's up?"

He whispered back, "Later."

The path was wide enough so the dogs and wagons could travel side by side with the adults next to them. It was a clean, well-traveled path. The night air was cool and the sound of a breeze could be heard rustling through the trees. As they hurried along the path, the kids became quiet. They had finally lost their energy. Up ahead the lights from Belle's barn came into view. Guardian and Stance let out several soft yelps of excitement.

"Belle, why are the dogs acting up?"

"It's nothing, Star, they're happy to be home."

Suddenly a horrible distressing sound came from up ahead. Starlit yelled, "Oh my gosh, something is hurt!" Silas and Warren moved quickly ahead. Belle called after them, "Guys, wait! Wait!" The scream sounded again. Belle yelled again loudly, "Stop, it's okay!"

Warren and Silas stopped and turned towards Belle. "What do you make of that, Warren?"

As they looked back at Belle, they could see the dogs sitting calmly. Belle was motioning to them to wait there. The guys looked at each other, shrugged their shoulders and waited.

Laughing Belle said, "I'm so sorry, you reacted the same way I did when I first heard it. No one is hurt, just hungry. That's Rarity and that's how she sounds when she does talk. Mules in general have a sound like they're in trouble. I'm sure glad she doesn't talk much. All the critters are overdue for their dinner, so guys, you can help me feed them and Star, you can get the kids ready for bed; that way we can get done quickly."

"That is a good plan," Warren replied.

"Yes," said Starlit, "just give me a minute to get my heart back in my chest, then we can move on."

At last, they were back home. Warren opened the gate, waited until everyone was in, then closed and locked it. Starlit headed into the main house with the kids so she could start a bath for them. Jasmine got to use the bathroom tub in the master bedroom while Junior and Mark used the one in the hallway bathroom.

When Silas unhitched the dogs, they ran around the yard checking everything out, and retreated to their doghouse. When all the critters outside and inside were fed, Warren announced it was time to "rack them up." With a smile on his face, he headed down to the pool table. Belle told Starlit the kids could all sleep in the guest room for now, and the guys could carry the boys out to the guest house when they headed there later. Starlit forgot to get the toothbrushes for the boys when she went to the guest house for their pajamas, so Silas went to get them. When he returned, he gave the brushes to the boys and went downstairs.

All cleaned up and in their pajamas, the kids wanted to go to bed right away. They were exhausted. Starlit took them downstairs to say goodnight to their dads, then right back up. She and Belle tucked them into bed. After they said their prayers, Junior mumbled something about a surprise and "twins" in his backpack.

"We'll take care of the surprise in the morning, Junior," Starlit said, "when we're all rested." Then she whispered, "Belle, grab his backpack while I plug in the nightlight."

"I wonder what kind of twins are in this backpack. Ready, here we go, and I better be very careful."

Belle searched carefully and slowly as she went through each section of the backpack. She was gently moving and lifting items, giggling at some of the things in it. "Well, hello little critters, would you like to come out? This is a surprise, Star."

"Actually, Belle, the surprise he was talking about is a separate one. We thought you would get it tonight, but it got late and the kids were so tired. No, I know that look and I'm not giving any hints, it'll have to wait until morning, say after breakfast."

"All right, all right, I obviously don't have a choice."

"The kids were so excited about the surprise, they wanted me to call you and tell you we had one. That was very early in the morning before we left to come here. I was instructed not to tell you what it was, but that there was one."

"I remember the message. The Yancees came early to drop off my order which I had forgotten about, and when I heard the horn blowing, I thought it was you guys coming early. I thought that was the surprise you meant in the message."

"We're going to have to return these little turtles to their home tomorrow. I'll see what I have to keep them in. The Yancees want us to stop by, so we can take them home on the way there. We'll have lunch before we go. As long as we're at the pond we can hang around a bit for the kids to play and fire up the pit to make s'mores. I'll call Mrs. Yancee in the morning and tell her we'll be there late afternoon."

"Those turtles are so tiny, Belle, are they going to be all right? Poor things must be scared. I think this is the first time Junior collected anything alive and moving. Usually, it's just little stones or sticks we'd find, much like these. A few times he had tiny clumps of moss which he called velvet grass..."

Silas and Warren were downstairs, playing pool. "This is great, Warren! We can do this every night if we want to. So, what's on your mind?"

"Belle seems a little different, Silas. Her language and quick temper indicate it."

"Yes, the way she reacted to what I said about the dusty Bible and how she spoke in the barn seems to hint at that. You know she likes things to be perfect though. It's probably just a little stress but, you're right, she was lacking on the self-control. Are you going to talk to her about it?"

"Not now, perhaps in a day or two. I would like to observe a little longer. In the meantime, rack them up again."

"Great shot, Warren! I can't believe you made that! You always do well under pressure."

"You also, Silas, I can recall many times you performed well while under pressure. A recent 'giant' encounter comes to mind."

"Boy, Warren, that thing was unbelievable. I knew giant snakes existed, but I never expected to meet one face to face. I'm happy we won't be seeing any more and I know the others are too."

"It's really nice out here. I don't know what days Belle has planned for fishing, but I am looking forward to it. She also mentioned a dart board that needs to get put up down here."

"This looks like the spot she has in mind. I'm going to check out the closet. Yep, here it is along with the soft board to protect the wall, we can take care of it later in the week."

"That's a good size storage closet. Hey, sounds like the girls are headed this way."

Belle and Starlit joined the guys in a game of pool. They talked, laughed, and teased each other over some of the things that happened during the day. Belle shared with them the events regarding Momma Possum and what had happened at the Center. She described the marks she found on the necks of Anomaly and Rarity, and pointed out she found a needle cap which confirmed her suspicions that blood was drawn from them. No one from the Center told her they needed to test them, and they would never just show up without calling first, so she was concerned. She apologized to Starlit again for her bad language. The incident with the spooked deer and Cypress mentioning strange sightings in that area brought chills to her as she told the story. She did not know what she had seen, but knew it chilled her to the bone.

"I do believe this all sounds strange, Belle," Warren said as he placed his hand on her shoulder. "There are some other strange things around here, for instance the barn, its amenities, the sundial that turns lights on, unusual indeed."

Silas said, "You know brother, I agree with you. Why not just a switch on the wall at the picnic area? There's one to turn on the other lights. I see your wheels turning, Warren."

"I'm really tired, guys, we can talk some more tomorrow," said Belle.

"I'm ready for some sleep too," Starlit agreed. "The mystery can wait."

They headed upstairs. Everyone said goodnight and one by one gave each other a hug and kiss. The guys scooped up the boys and headed out to the guest house. Everyone got ready for bed and as usual, said thanks to Father God for who He is and for the day.

As Belle began drifting off to sleep her eyes opened suddenly; she sat up quickly and said out loud, "The thing, the thing, that object, oh my gosh I forgot all about it! Darn, no, it'll have to wait till morning, I'll remember now. But, maybe, well it's late, I'm so tired." Yawning, she flopped back down onto the pillow, closed her eyes, then opened them again, closed them, and opened them again, like a little kid trying to resist the temptation of sleep. She let out a sigh, closed her eyes for the final time and fell asleep.

She began having dreams about the object. It grew larger and larger, then smaller and smaller. When she reached for it, it would disappear. As she roamed from room to room searching for it her legs moved normally, but each time she would encounter the object her legs moved in slow motion. It floated away as she slowed down, making it difficult to catch it. She found it again downstairs and, inches from her grasp, it dropped to the ground then vanished. As it vanished it made a loud thundering sound.

Belle jolted awake. "Oh, just a dream…that—that was weird. Okay, I think I'll go put that thing in the kitchen, so I don't forget to take it out in the morning."

NINE

"GOOD MORNING, BELLE. Something smells real good."

"Good morning, Star. That's the blueberry muffins in the oven you smell, part of the menu for this morning. There'll be yogurt, fruit, bacon, eggs, and toast also. Coffee and hot water for tea are ready, help yourself. Did you sleep okay?"

"I did. Jasmine is still sleeping; have you heard from the guys yet?"

"No, not yet. I knew the kids were exhausted so I expected them to sleep in. When they get up, they can help collect the eggs for breakfast. I remembered as I started out to the coop that they were looking forward to that, so I came back in. Habit, you know, to just head out there first thing. I'm hungry, how about you?"

"Famished for sure, smelling the muffins has taken its toll."

"They're done and I made them small so let's have one with our tea."

"No argument here. Since it's just us, a little girl talk, too, Belle... Well, you know David and I have been dating about four months now but I'm not sure I want to see him anymore. I think he is more serious about our relationship than I am and I'm not ready for serious. We talked about it, and he said he understands but thinks we should still date. What do you think?"

"Star, if you don't really want to continue in the relationship, you shouldn't. Why did you start? Were you looking for a potential life partner? Are you ready to get married but he's not the one?"

"Belle, I think that's it. He is just not the one. I would like to marry someday but how long do you date someone before you know it's him you should marry?"

"You said he's not the one after four months, and I've heard of people saying they knew in just three months the person they were with was the one, then got married. I say end it and continue in prayer for guidance in the matter. You want God to lead you in His purpose for your life. He will let you know who and when."

"Thank you, I agree. What about you. How about this Cy guy?"

"No, no, definitely not interested in him that way and definitely unequally yoked. We just work together. Star, I don't think I ever want to get married. I don't want to maybe go through what Sy and Warren have gone through. Like, look at Sy. Ashley refused to accept the Lord. She resented him for going to church without her, and totally lost it when she miscarried with their second baby, and then abandoned him and Mark. He only married her because she got pregnant, as was the case with Warren and Lucy. Granted Lucy was a Christian too, but the guys didn't love them, they just wanted to do the right thing and it was disastrous. Lucy died and left Warren with the twins to raise on his own, and Sy was left to raise Mark on his own."

"Belle, I didn't realize you were so fearful of marriage, but as you said, God will lead you in His purpose for your life and if it is His will, He will let you know who and when. The good news is God is a God of second chances and both the guys are free to marry again, if they want to, and they did have other people around them to help through the difficult times. We even helped, remember? I know you dated a couple of bad apples so I can see you having trust issues too; just don't write off marriage altogether."

"Hmm, I don't know. It's not something I need to really think about now anyway. It can sit on the back burner for now, a year or three or say, ten."

They laughed over Bell's statement as they continued to sip tea and eat their muffins. Starlit reached over to get another napkin and sitting on the table next to the napkin holder was the object.

"What is this?" she asked Belle as she turned it in the palm of her hand.

"That answers the question of, is it yours, since you don't know what it is. I found it the night of the storm back..."

Just then Jasmine entered the kitchen. She was rubbing her eyes and yawning. In the middle of the yawn she asked, "Can we pick some eggs now?"

Belle walked over to Jasmine, picked her up and said, "When you wake up a little more, sweetie, and the boys get here then we'll go get the eggs; in the meantime, how about some juice?"

Starlit placed the object back on the table, then got up to go look out the back door. "Well, speak of the little angels, they're headed this way with the guys. I'll get the dining room table set up and get Jasmine out of her pajamas."

"Thanks, Star, but I'll take Jasmine to change while you do the table, then we'll get eggs."

The kids loved collecting the eggs and were talking about getting them again tomorrow. They wanted to make a contest out of it to see who could find the biggest one. It was quite a surprise when pale green eggs were found among the brown ones. They had seen the usual white and brown in stores but never green. Mark thought Belle colored them, and she had to explain they were made that way by the chickens.

Everyone enjoyed a wonderful breakfast. When they were finished eating, the kids went to play with the kitties and the grownups cleaned up. As Silas was putting something away, he noticed the object on the little table in the kitchen and picked it up. With a puzzled look on his face, he asked, "Belle, what is this?"

Belle and Starlit looked at each other, then in unison they said, "Well, that answers the question of, is it yours," as they giggled.

Warren walked in at that moment and asked what was so funny. Silas held up the object and said, "Apparently this is," then placed it in Warren's hand.

Warren asked, as he examined it, "What is this?"

Silas said with a big grin, "I don't know but that answers the question of, is it yours."

The girls laughed and Belle said, "So since it's not mine either—well, now it is, that concludes that question. Now the questions are: what is it and where did it come from? I found it a long time ago but with moving, starting new jobs, and setting up house I had forgotten about it. Anytime I spoke with any of you it wasn't on my mind. I discovered it the night of that big storm…"

Just then Junior came in and took Starlit by the hand, pulling her to the doorway. He began whispering something. She leaned down to hear what he was saying. The two began whispering back and forth to each other.

"What is going on over there?" Warren asked this as Starlit motioned with her eyes and tilted her head to say, "come here." He placed the object on the table, then went over to Starlit and Junior. "Yes, I see," he whispered. "Go fetch the children, I will have Belle and Silas join us in the living room."

They finished up in the kitchen and went to the living room to wait for Starlit and the kids. "Something is up, what is it?"

"Something nice," answered Silas.

Starlit came in but the kids were not with her. "So, Belle, remember I said there was a surprise for you? Well, here it comes." Nothing happened; she repeated, "So here it comes." Then a little louder this time, "So here it comes!"

The kids came bumbling through the doorway and lined up next to each other, holding something that lay rolled up across their arms, shouting, "Surprise!"

They each had a line to say, starting with Mark: "We give this gift," then Jasmine: "With all our hearts." Then Junior spoke: "And Aunt Star's and Dad's and Uncle Sy's," and then all together they said, "We love you!"

Starlit got up and went over to the kids. She took the item and held it up, letting it unroll. Belle shouted, "Oh my gosh, it's beautiful, oh you guys! What a wonderful surprise! You kids did a great job keeping this a secret."

Then Jasmine said, "Now you can cuddle with us even when we're not here." Tears started flowing from Belle's eyes. "Thank you, thank you everyone, such a treasure! I can't believe it! Oh I just love this, thanks!"

The gift was a throw blanket with a picture of the kids, Starlit, Warren and Silas on it that filled almost the entire blanket. Belle wrapped herself up and twirled around the room in it. Then she gathered the kids in her arms and gave them hugs and kisses. Belle walked towards Starlit, "Okay, it's your turn, you guys," she said as she hugged her first, then Warren and Silas. "Very nice surprise, thanks again."

As she wiped the tears from her cheeks she said, "I have a little surprise too. You're all going to have little treasures of your own; we're going on a treasure hunt this morning. We can start anytime."

The kids all exclaimed as they jumped up and down, "Yay! Oh boy, a treasure hunt! Wow, treasure, let's go!"

"I'll get the clues, then we'll head to the garden first to get some tools for digging." Out they went, and the object was forgotten about.

The hunt took them all around the back and front yards, into the barn, doghouse, and chicken coop. Most items were not buried and when it came to digging, the kids especially enjoyed that. Belle did not have treasure in every location the clues led to. Some had instructions to the next site, which then had more instructions. There was a little something for the grownups along the way also. They each received two treasures of their own.

Guardian and Stance followed along from the time the hunt began until it ended. Everyone enjoyed how eager they were to join in. On two occasions the dogs gave away a hiding place. When the kids got to the last location, which was marked with a large *X*, they began to dig. Up out of the ground they pulled an item that was wrapped in a black plastic bag. They opened the bag and took out a mini treasure chest. Inside it were chocolates wrapped as gold and silver coins and three pirate costumes. The kids were ecstatic and of course wanted to dress up right away, so they gathered all they had gotten from the hunt and headed back to the house to change into their costumes. Once the costumes were on, they ran outside to play.

"That was fun, Belle, and the guys seemed to enjoy it too," said Starlit. "When did you do all that?"

"Last weekend, that's why everything was in sealed containers. I had lots of fun setting it all up. Where are the guys? Never mind, let me guess, they went to play a game of pool, didn't they? I have something for us to do. You can help me pick some fruit and veggies for the food bank. Someone will be here around noon to pick it up. Normally that would get done on a Saturday, but since we're doing the Center visit then and going into town, I asked them to pick it up today instead. Sometimes I bring the food to them.

"Oh yeah, I spoke with Mrs. Yancee this morning. She wants us to stay for supper, said to come around four. We can have lunch, then go to the pond to let the turtles go and have s'mores for dessert while we're there."

"I can't even think about food now, I'm still full from breakfast, Belle!"

"We have a long time before lunch, Star, and we can go work up an appetite in the meantime. Let's go get a box from the barn and start picking."

As Belle and Starlit picked the veggies, "pirates" would run in and out of the garden demanding booty. They held out their little sacks and the girls gave them some grape tomatoes. Another time they gave them blueberries. When they were in the orchard, they gave the pirates some cherries. Belle told Starlit that they would be leaving the box out front at the end of the driveway in the storage container next to the mailbox. It was there for the very purpose of storing the donations for pick-up. Returning to the house, they found the guys sitting in the living room.

"Hello ladies, what have the two of you been doing?"

Starlit answered Warren. "We picked some fruit and veggies for the food bank and fought off pirates while we worked."

Then he said to Belle, "I was pondering the incident regarding Rarity and Anomaly. When would it have been possible for someone to have drawn blood from them?"

"The only time I can think of is when I ran to the Center to see Momma. That seems like the only time in the last few days where someone would have had time and I wasn't here. When I got back from the Center, I hurried to get them into the barn before you guys arrived but didn't notice anything. Maybe I didn't since I was in a hurry."

He said, "I see, however you found the needle cap in the barn. I suppose they went back into their stalls then came out again."

"While we're on the subject I'm going to call the Center and talk to Ed. I'm just going to ask if he sent anyone..." She took out her phone and made the call. "Hello, this is Belle, can I please speak with Ed? Hi, Ed, sorry to bother you, I'll make it quick. I have a question: did you by any chance send anyone to take blood samples from Anomaly and Rarity? I thought so but I had to ask. No, I'm not sure. I'll figure it out, thanks. Oh, oh wow, thanks for letting me know—bye.

"As I thought, he said he didn't have anyone come for samples and if he needed any he would have called first. He was telling me that those giant snakes both died. The strange thing was that they identified their species, and they were four times the size they should have been. I wonder why they died. Maybe they were just old. Anyway, back to my critters. It could be that maybe a needle cap was in my pocket somehow and fell out in the barn, or the marks on their necks were just bug bites? I don't know what to think!"

They discussed different possible scenarios but could not come to a definite conclusion. Starlit believed it was just a mistake on Belle's part. That the cap was probably there from some other time and only noticed now. Silas thought the marks were from insect bites or that a little branch may have poked them when they were out on the trail. Warren said he was still processing and had no comment.

In the meantime, the pirates were still on the run and the clock was ticking on. Before they knew it, it was time to start preparing lunch. Starlit gathered the kids to get them changed and cleaned up before lunch while Belle started getting food ready. Warren and Silas went outside to play with the dogs for a little while until lunch was served.

At last, the lunch bell rang. Everyone gathered to the dining room. Warren gave thanks and they began to eat. Belle told them that they would be going to the pond to take the turtles home and light the fire pit while they were there to have s'mores. She reminded them to make sure they had backpacks with extra clothes for the evening. When they were done, they gathered their belongings and the turtles and headed for the garage.

"We should take Rover, my ATV, up the short path to the pond. When we're done, we'll take sanctuary ground out to a street road to the Yancees'. This is country, so it'll be all right to be on the street with him. I didn't think about showing you the garage; there was so much else to see and after all it's just a garage."

When they entered Silas said, "This is a nice garage—roomy." As Warren walked over to the ATV he said, "And this is a good-looking vehicle."

Knowing Starlit might not be thrilled to travel in the woods at night, Belle pointed to the ATV's roof which had lights on top, in front and back, then reassured Starlit that on the way home those lights would be on so they could see far ahead and behind. "He's small but will seat four. The kids can ride in the back storage area, there's a cushion there or they can sit on laps. Under that storage area is space where we can put our packs. Rover has heat and air-conditioning too. Give me the packs and hop in."

TEN

BELLE PULLED OUT OF THE GARAGE and drove onto the road alongside the house. They passed the driveway gate to the back yard and proceeded on the portion of the road that turned and ran along the fence past the back of the guest house. When they reached the beginning of the path to the pond she stopped.

"So, there are some rules to follow. Kids, no standing at any time even if we stop, and when we stop, don't get out unless you are told to. We generally only go up to twenty-five miles an hour unless we are on a street road, and when we are on the road, seat belts are to be on. There's only one long belt in the storage area so for added safety, I'll have to close that window before we leave for the Yancees'. Now one of you guys can drive to our destinations and the other can drive on the return trip."

As she stepped out of the ATV she said, "Should I flip a coin?"

"Silas can drive first, I will wait."

"Thanks, Warren. All right, I'm ready, let's get going!"

When they arrived at the pond, Belle instructed Silas to park behind the picnic building.

"You guys start a small fire, please, the wood is in the shed; we'll get the turtles back to where they belong and be right back. Junior, can you show us where you got them from, do you remember?"

Starlit was holding the container with the turtles as they followed him to the shallow end of the pond. They put them out under some tall grass near the edge of it. Mark and Jasmine waved goodbye to the turtles and said, "Be safe." "Aunt Belle and I are going back now, don't be too long."

The kids lingered for a while talking about the turtles and other critters. Junior seemed disappointed but he understood it was best for the turtles. He stood there staring at the grass, then Jasmine took him by the hand and tugged him away. She began to skip, and he responded, "Aw come on, no skipping." Mark said, "Yes skipping," and began skipping as he took hold of Junior's other hand. After skipping along for only a minute Junior said, "Race you to that tree!"

He broke free of their grip and ran forward as fast as he could. Mark and Jasmine chased quickly after him. They climbed the little tree and pretended to be pirates looking out of the bird's nest atop the mast of a pirate ship. One of them called out, "Land ho, s'mores ahead!" Starlit and Belle had just arrived at the fire pit.

"Mmm mmm, so good," Silas said as he licked his fingers.

Warren nodded his head in agreement as he wiped his mouth with a napkin.

Starlit stood with her hands on her hips, staring at them, and said, "Really guys? Five more minutes, you only had to wait five more minutes."

"Sorry, Mom," replied Silas. She laughed and said, "You're forgiven, since you left plenty for the rest of us."

When the kids got there, Belle handed them each the ingredients to build their s'mores and a stick. After they all had their fill, the kids went off to play and the adults went for a walk. Belle and Starlit stayed close enough to keep an eye on the kids since the dogs were not with them. Soon they gathered the kids so they could explore a little further away from the pond.

"This sundial is grand indeed," Warren said.

"You seem to be quite drawn to it," said Silas, "and where did the girls go? I thought Belle wanted to get another look at it."

"Star mentioned earlier both of them wanted to see the flowering vines on the rock formation. I believe they went in that direction; however, they have been gone a long time—perhaps we should look for them."

Silas replied, "We better hurry then, they might need rescuing, the pirates could be holding them hostage."

As they approached the area of the rock formation, they could not see the girls or kids, but they could hear something. *BzzzZZzzBzz...* The closer they got the louder the buzzing sound.

"That explains why they're not here. Those bees weren't going to let anyone get close enough to the flowers, so they obviously ventured someplace else. Any ideas, Warren?"

"This is a large formation and if I know the children well, I believe we should investigate the other side of it. We will go this way," he said, as he pointed to the left. "Silas, leave the bumblebee alone, you need not shoo it away; they are harmless and Belle would not approve; you could injure it."

"She's not here so it shouldn't bother her. I think it's following me, why is it following me!"

"I will report the incident to her," Warren said with a smile, as he gave a gentle little punch to Silas's shoulder.

"I hear the kids, Warren." When they turned the corner, they could see the kids climbing a smaller portion of the rock formation about a quarter of the way on.

"As I suspected," Warren said. Upon arrival the guys joined in climbing with the kids. The girls had been reluctant to climb but now that the guys were there they joined in also.

The landscape was as beautiful on this side of the formation as on the side of the pond and picnic area, with various trees, shrubs, plants, and some scattered wildflowers nearby. The wildflowers were tall daisy-like flowers, mostly golden yellow, and situated in small patches throughout the area. Other patches had pale yellow and white flowers peeking out among the darker yellow ones, while a few other patches consisted of only white. There were other wildflowers, short with tiny, light lavender-colored flowers that gave off a strong sweet fragrance. Butterflies were fluttering from flower to flower. Some of the butterflies, the larger ones, were black and yellow.

With the climbing out of their systems now, they walked along the formation opposite the direction they had come to continue exploring. They seemed to be far from the end of the formation. Their intention was to go completely around it, but as they got nearer to the end their attempt was interrupted by a long and wide wall of thorny rose bushes and a familiar sound: *bzzBZZzzbzzBzzzz BZZzzbzzBzBzzz...* The area to the left of the rose bushes was dense with trees and bushes. There was no trail in that area, so with no other choice, they turned and headed back the way they had come.

When they finally got back to the pond area, Belle headed towards the sundial immediately. Barely getting a glance at it Starlit said, "Belle, it's three fifteen already, we have to leave."

"Gosh the time flew; yes, we better get going, I don't want to be late to the Yancees'."

Warren checked the extinguished fire to make sure it was not smoldering, then made sure the doors were closed on the buildings. Silas pulled Rover out while the girls gathered kids and belongings. Once they were all settled in Rover, Warren said, "Onward, brother."

It was a pleasant ride. Along the way they saw some small animals scampering about the bushes, running up and down trees and chasing one another. Colorful birds of different sizes and species could be seen throughout the drive. They could hear chirping sounds in different tones and pitches as the birds called to one another. They came upon several deer heading away from them toward a small clearing. To everyone's wonder, a huge buck appeared. Silas stopped so they could watch them a minute or two, then moved on. Just before they were about to exit onto the street road, they stopped to belt in the kids and close the window.

They could hear a loud knocking sound. Warren pointed toward the sound. It was a large woodpecker. Its head was red with black speckles and a black beak; its body was white with black speckles on the wings and tail. Its head was moving so fast it struck everyone as funny and they all laughed. Jasmine wanted to know if it would get a headache from doing that. Her dad told her God created those birds that way and it was not harmful to them. He explained how they foraged for food by drilling into branches and trunks of trees with their beak to find insects under the bark to eat. She said she was happy God created her not to eat bugs. Mark scrunched his face and said, "Me too."

Silas drove onto the street. Belle told them the path across the street was the path on the Yancee property that led to their farm where she saw the big bear, but they were staying on the street because it was faster to the farm. She said "bear" since children were present, however, the adults knew she was referring to her frightening experience.

Silas was happy to be able to go faster than he had been. At 50 mph he made sounds and motions as if he were in an auto race. He pretended he passed the lead car and was heading for the checkered flag. Warren became the announcer, giving the final moments of the race. Raising his voice a little, he announced Rover to be the winning vehicle of the first annual Woods 500 Auto Race. They all cheered. It was not long before they arrived at the Yancees'. Belle had hoped to be a couple of minutes early but was happy they were not late; it was exactly 4:00 p.m. Mrs. Yancee had just come out the door to greet them.

"Hello everyone, welcome! Mr. Yancee is getting the hayride ready with our grandchildren. They are close to your ages," she said as she looked at the kids. "Let me guess; you are Mark, you are Jasmine and Warren Junior."

"Yes, ma'am but just Junior, please, and we're twins," he said as he pointed to Jasmine.

She continued as she pointed to each person: "This is Starlit, Silas and your dad, Warren and your dad and yours. I've heard so much about all of you—it's so nice to meet you. Let's get you on the hayride and afterward Mr. Yancee will show you the animals while I get supper together. My son and daughter-in-law will be joining us at supper."

"We would love to help in the kitchen."

"Of course you would, Belle, that's why I have an apron for you dear, and I know I have one you can use also, Starlit. It will be so nice to have girls in the kitchen again."

"You guys have fun, we'll see you in a bit."

During the hayride Mr. Yancee did some storytelling. They rode all around the farm and near the orchard. The kids tossed hay on each other while on their journey and spent a good amount of time trying to get it all off when the ride was over. They visited all the animals on the farm. The grandchildren took the kids up in their tree house while the adults were talking. A little while later Mrs. Yancee yelled out from the porch that it was time for supper, and they all hurried to the house. Mr. Yancee gave thanks, and they began to eat. Many compliments were given about the meal and when they were done, they retreated to the living room for a short while.

"This has been a great evening and I hate to say it but it's getting late."

"Thank you. Star, we do need to go, big day tomorrow. Thank you so much, Mrs. Yancee, Mr. Yancee for having all of us over. And it was very nice to meet all of you," Belle said as she walked over to the Yancees' son, daughter-in-law, and their kids.

There was a lot of handshaking and hugging going on. When they were on the porch Mrs. Yancee said, "Belle, I have something for you, dear. That box next to the chair has some red plums, a jar of plum jam, apples, and an egg crate with duck eggs. You know people usually have apple, peach and plum trees too but your place only has pear, nectarine and cherry trees, go figure. Anyway, I thought your guests would enjoy all these."

"We will definitely enjoy these," Warren said as he picked up the box, "thank you kindly, Mrs.Yancee."

"My pleasure, it was very nice having you all. We'll have another get-together before your vacation ends."

"Wonderful," he said, "I can assure you we will all look forward to gathering again."

Silas handed the keys to Warren and said, "I can still drive, I'm up to it."

Warren closed the keys in his hand and answered, "You just sit back and relax." As soon as the vehicle began to roll a voice softly said, "Don't forget to put the top lights on." Belle responded, "Star, that will have to wait until we're off the street. Seat belts, Junior, can you do that back there now?"

"Yep, I got it, okay, done!"

"Good job."

When they were off the street Warren put the top lights on, and to Starlit's delight they could see very well ahead, behind, and well to the sides. As they moved along, they would periodically see glowing eyes staring at them. A few times they heard owls hooting, which the kids would imitate.

"Daddy, does the monster come out at night?"

"There are no monsters out here, Mark," Silas answered. "There are no monsters period, why do you think that?"

"The Yancee kids said there is, near the farm," Jasmine said. Junior added, "And a big one!"

Starlit and Belle looked at each other, Starlit's eyes wide as saucers. "Oh, it's okay, it's just a bear and bears don't come out at night. The kids were teasing you, trying to spook you, that's all."

Just then something large swooped down behind the vehicle and the kids let out a scream. Warren hit the brakes. "I do believe the Yancee children have succeeded," he said, as he turned and looked back out the rear window. He could see something large moving away from them, disappearing into the darkness beyond the lights of Rover. It appeared to be carrying something.

Junior shouted, "Whoa, a pterodactyl!" Mark and Jasmine shouted, "Monster!"

Starlit asked as calmly as she could, "What was that thing?"

"Some kind of large bird," Silas said. "Kids, just a big bird, that's all. Mark, not a monster."

"Your dad is right, Mark," said Belle. "It is a big bird, a great gray owl, actually. It's one of the largest owls. They can grow up to thirty-three inches which is almost three feet and their wingspan can be up to five feet! Did you know owls can't chew their food? They swallow it whole. Their stomach dissolves what it needs, and then expels, um the owl coughs up, what it can't use, like bones and fur. That's called an owl pellet."

Starlit moaned, "Eeew-yucky," and Jasmine replied, "I'm glad God made me chew my food." Mark and Junior thought it was cool and wanted to see some owl puke. "No, kids, it's pellets. They are long shaped, dry, and not liquid."

"Eeew again, can we go now?"

Warren said, "Yes, Star, moving on."

Belle instructed Warren to turn off the path to another one which led to a different way home. This one brought them to the same road at the corner of the guest house from the opposite direction. If they had continued straight, they would have ended up at the beginning of the short path up to the pond again. Instead, Warren turned, went past the driveway gate to the back yard towards the street, turning there into Belle's driveway.

As they turned onto the road by the guest house the dogs were waiting there for them. They sensed their arrival was about to occur and came out to happily greet them. They ran along the length of the yard as far as they could go as the vehicle traveled along the fence. Once inside the garage, everybody slowly got out of Rover. Starlit said, knowing that the guys would want to get at least one pool game in, "I'll meet you all downstairs in a few."

The kids gave goodnight hugs and kisses to their dads and Belle. Silas and Warren helped Belle take care of all the critters while Starlit got the kids ready for bed.

"I'm sitting this one out, you guys, go ahead," said Belle. "The couch is calling me."

"Me too," said Starlit as she yawned. Then she asked, "Do you think the Yancee kids really saw something too? It seems like quite a coincidence. Yes-no-maybe, earth to Belle?"

"I was just wondering about that. I don't know if they actually saw something or just heard of others seeing something, but Cy did mention strange sightings in that area and I'm sure I did see something unusual."

"Well, I'm glad we didn't see it or anything creepy, though we did see a flying dinosaur."

When Starlit said this, Silas spread out his arms flapping them. Making a flying motion, he moved toward her. As he approached and got close, he made a low deep cawing sound followed by a slightly higher-pitched cawing, his interpretation of what a pterodactyl might sound like.

Starlit ducked and giggled, then Silas said, "All in all this was a great day."

As Warren hit the eight ball he added, "And a wonderful way to bring it to a close!"

ELEVEN

THE KIDS SAT AT BREAKFAST DRESSED in their pirate costumes. They wanted to be able to go out playing as soon as possible. Mark was the one who found the biggest egg this morning and made sure to remind everyone.

Belle took the crate of duck eggs out of the refrigerator, walked over to the table and said, "Look at these," as she opened the container.

Junior shouted, "No way!" Jasmine asked, "Did that hurt the chicken?"

Laughing, Belle said, "These are duck eggs. Ducks are much bigger than chickens, so it didn't hurt since the ducks are bigger. You're eating some duck eggs right now, what do you think?" They all agreed the eggs were yummy. When they finished eating, they left to play outside, and the adults stayed at the dining room table.

"I enjoyed driving Rover. I'm sure glad we took the scenic route," Silas said, with a huge smile.

"I know, I know it's all country, but I knew you would like the off-road aspect, that's why we did it that way," said Belle. "It's easier to see the wildlife and it worked out too since we had to take the turtles home. Anyone want something more to eat?"

They decided to have fruit. The fruit bowl was filled with an assortment of color: orange, green, purple, yellow and red. It was in the center of the table and on either side of it were two small vases with light pink flowers adding more color to the table. They munched and talked awhile. When they had their fill, they cleaned up and moved to the living room.

Silas said, "The pirate costumes sure made a big hit with the kids. Mark asked me if he could sleep in his; of course I said no. He and Junior were reading one of their treasures before going to sleep last night, and Warren and I snacked on one of ours with a glass of milk. We might all gain a little weight on this vacation with all the goodies you have, Belle, but it will be worth it."

"Thanks, Sy, we'll just have to do a lot of hiking, that's all. When we go fishing, we can take Rover part of the way then hike. The place I have in mind is an hour drive from here. It's a good-size lake that has some cabins near it. We can rent what we need to fish and purchase bait there. No motorboats are allowed on the lake, only small sailboats, canoes, and paddle boats. We can rent paddle boats and get a little exercise from that too. We'll go fishing sometime after the kids go home."

"I appreciate good conservation, more places should follow suit on preserving our waters," Warren said. "It may not be feasible to be conservative on all waterways, but an effort should be made to prevail on the majority. Belle, remember when you said there was something familiar about the sundial? I believe it is the markings on it that have remained in the back of your mind. These markings are on the sides as well as the top of the sundial. I examined it while you gals were exploring and determined they are similar to, or the same as, the markings on the object."

Belle got up quickly and went to get the object. She came back, sat down and began turning the object, studying it. "You're right!

That's it! I just couldn't register it at the moment. I wonder if it was somehow a part of the sundial. Maybe there were more, like a decoration around the bottom of it, you know, like giant marbles or something, a kind of art-like feature."

"Well, you'd think they would have made them sit permanently in their place if that's the case," Starlit said, "and then no one could have taken them."

"I saw no evidence on the ground that would indicate such a theory," Warren replied.

Then Silas said, "I can picture a bunch of them scattered on the ground around the sundial, and if they were taken a long time ago weather could have erased any imprints on the ground."

Belle said, "We can figure that out another time; what I want to know now is how did this get in my house, the one before I moved out here. Remember I said I found it the night of the storm."

Just then the cuckoo clock in the living room began tweeting. "We better get the kids changed and ready to go the Center, Belle," said Starlit. "I want us to have time to see everything at the Center and leave there with enough time for you to get to your class on time."

"I have a thought," Silas began, "did you visit the picnic area when you came out for your interview?"

"Of course I did, I wanted to see everything but I didn't see this or take it."

"But maybe whoever you were with slipped it into your bag or backpack, whatever you had with you, as a keepsake or something."

Starlit stood up, crossed her arms, and said, "Okay, enough, this is your mother speaking, now get moving!"

Frowning, Belle placed the object down on the end table. Pirate was nearby and as they walked out of the room, he jumped up onto the table and began to paw at the object. He then tried to pick it up in his mouth, but it was too big so he decided he would have to push it. Almost as if she sensed something was about to happen, Belle shouted, "Oh no!" She turned quickly causing the others to turn around.

At that same moment Pirate pushed the object. With a few quick tapping motions, it rolled slowly across the table to the edge and stopped. "Pirate, no!" Belle shouted. Warren moved quickly trying to intercept it, just as Pirate gave one last tap and over the edge it went. The end table on this side of the couch sat at the edge of the area rug. When the object went off the table it hit the wood floor with a loud thud.

Belle shrieked, "Oh my gosh, did it break?"

Silas asked, "Which, the object or the floor?"

Warren answered, "The object is intact but the floor has a minor dent in it."

"Are you sure?"

"I know a dent when I see one."

"I mean the object." Belle took it from Warren's hand and looked at it carefully. Then she knelt down and ran her fingers over the mark in the floor. Warren gently lifted her by the elbow saying, "We need to hurry now, please place the object somewhere safe." Belle walked over to her favorite recliner, opened the end-table drawer next to it, the one with her diary in it, and set the object inside.

The van traveled along toward the Center while the kids talked excitedly about going to the zoo. They talked about big animals they would see, like elephants and giraffes. "Maybe we can ride camels," Jasmine said. "Not me," said Mark, "I want to be on the elephant!"

Belle explained it was not a zoo and those animals would not be there. She told them there would be some large birds, eagles to be exact, hawks, other birds, and animals. She also said they would learn how the animals came to be there and what can be done to help prevent bad things from happening to other animals in the wild.

"You won't be able to feed the critters. I'm glad we don't have elephants, Mark. They're so big it can take over two to four hundred pounds of food a day to feed them and that would cost a lot of money. Since you like elephants, here's another little fact about them: in some places on an elephant its skin can be up to an inch thick! The Center is also one of the places I work so I wanted to show it to all of you. My other job is at a nursery where they grow flowers, trees, plants, and vegetables."

"Can we see that too?"

"If we get done at the Center early, Jasmine, we can stop by there, it's on the way in toward town."

At the Center, Belle briefly introduced her friends to her boss and coworkers since she did not want to keep them from their work. Cypress said he was looking forward to visiting on the way to town and at dinner as he was leaving for his assignment. Belle showed them her little work area and pointed out the pictures she had of them on her desk. She told them she spent most of the time feeding the animals, cleaning their living quarters, and surveying the grounds for anything that looked unusual. The time at the desk was for typing brief reports and updating information. After the quick tour inside the Center, they went outside to the first show and tell.

"That's a real big kitty, Aunt Belle."

"It's a bobcat, Jasmine. The speaker is about to begin; let's listen and learn."

"Hello everyone, I'm Steven and this is Kit. Kit is a bobcat, a cousin to the lynx. They are similar in appearance but the bobcat is a little smaller. They weigh about twenty pounds, measure about twenty-five inches long and stand about fifteen inches tall. Their tail can be four to seven inches long. These cats are nocturnal, resting during the day and coming out at night. Bobcats will rest in dens inside rock crevices or hollow trees and can have several shelter dens within their territory such as brush piles, rock ledges or stumps. They are quite elusive and are seldom seen. Meat is what's on the menu for these kitties. What that means is they are carnivores; they don't eat plants. When a bobcat leaps it can cover ten feet. These cats are quiet but will yowl and hiss at times, especially during mating. A female can have six kittens and the kittens will stay with the mom nine to twelve months…"

When the speaker was done, they moved on to another show and tell, then another. Eventually they came to one about an opossum. Belle said, "This is Momma, the one that you guys saw with me in the video."

"He's sleeping," Mark said.

"It's a she. Momma and all opossums are nocturnal. That means they sleep during the day and are awake at night. They are arboreal, meaning they sleep in trees, and marsupials, which means they have a pouch to carry their babies in. When they're in danger they sometimes pretend to be dead. Let's listen and see what else we can learn."

The kids and adults loved seeing and learning about the animals. They came to the last show and tell that they would have time to see before having to leave for town. It was Cypress who was the speaker for this station.

"Good morning, thank you for joining us. My name is Cy, and I would like to introduce you to Frosty. Frosty is a snowy owl. These owls grow about twenty to twenty-eight inches tall with a wingspan of forty-nine to fifty-nine inches and can weigh three and a half to six and a half pounds. Although it weighs about half as much as the great gray owl, its feet and talons are larger than the great gray's. They see well at night and in the daytime. It can move its head side to side quickly but cannot move its eyes around. They have two sets of eyelids; one set is see-through. That set closes to protect the eyes when swooping down on prey and flying around trees. They have ear flaps on each side of their head hidden by soft feathers. The feathers on their face are disc-shaped and funnel sound into the ears.

"They usually live in the far north. Its white color makes it hard to see in the treeless snow-covered land it comes from. Usually more active during the day, that's called diurnal, unlike other owls that are nocturnal, active at night, these guys hunt insects, birds, and small mammals such as mice and voles. They go where they can find food and some winters may fly south, which is how this one ended up in our neck of the woods. Frosty was found on the ground with a broken wing. We don't know how the injury occurred, but the wing did not heal to its normal functioning capacity, leaving us unable to release it back into the wild. Frosty has been happily living with us for three years now."

The morning passed by quickly. They did see most of the animals and the ones they did not see, Belle and Cypress told them about as they traveled into town. Belle told them she would show them pictures when they got home.

There was time enough to only drive past the Yard and Home Nursery that Belle worked at. A slow cruise through the parking lot revealed shrubs, trees, and lots of color from the variety of flowers behind the fence. They made it into town with minutes to spare. Warren dropped Belle and Cypress off for their class. As they got out of the car Warren said, "We will return at four o'clock."

Class ended a couple of minutes early. Some people stayed around a few minutes to talk. Belle and Cypress left after a few brief comments with others then went outside to find the van waiting for them. Warren had arrived on time at four o'clock as he said.

Belle said, as she got into the van, "That was really good, the time sure flew by. All that note taking and learning has made me hungry."

"That is good news," Warren said. "We are all hungry as well and will have to have an early dinner since we are having a guest tonight. Vee called; she will be arriving at the house tonight about seven thirty. She wanted to have more time here and come to church with us in the morning. I told her we would be dining at a seafood restaurant and asked what we could bring home for her."

Excited, Belle replied, "What a nice surprise, I'm glad she was able to change her flight. We better get going; turn right at the second light."

"This is a lovely place," Starlit said, "I could make this a habit."

"Me too," said Silas. Then he told the waitress to put everything on one check. "Dinner is on us, Cy."

Cypress thanked Silas, then ordered a glass of wine while waiting for dinner. He suddenly became aware that no one else ordered any kind of alcohol and said, "Uh oh, I'm sorry, that's right, you guys don't drink."

"It's all right," Silas said, "go ahead. Some Christians drink; we choose not to but it's fine if you want to."

The salad and appetizers arrived. Silas gave thanks and asked a blessing over the food. Then he said to Cypress, "I heard you went to church a couple of times with Belle. Are you still going?"

"No, it's just not my thing. I'll probably go on holidays, maybe. Pastor Bill is nice and I liked some of the things he said but, well, I don't know."

Warren said, "Pastor Bill does not sound familiar." Then he asked Belle, "Is this pastor new? I do believe this is not the name you have mentioned before."

"Well, no, not new. It's a different church. This one is a little closer. Pastor Bill does give some good messages."

Warren was not happy to hear this news. "Belle, you know better. Going to a church because it is closer to home and convenient is not acceptable."

They went back and forth for a while. Starlit and Silas had their say as well. Cypress finally said, "Well, I didn't know Christians argued."

Silas explained, "We are having a discussion and yes, Christians might argue a little. They can disagree at times. Christians aren't perfect people, just saved sinners."

There was a couple sitting at a table nearby that kept looking over at them. They had been listening to their conversation. When they saw that the group was finished with dinner they came over to the table. The guy asked Warren if he was a pastor. Warren said, "I am not but I will be happy to answer any questions. Bring your chairs over and sit a few minutes with us."

The guy explained that he and his girlfriend had gone to a church a few times. When an altar call was given, they both wanted to go forward but hesitated. They felt that it was too late now. Warren said they could pray now and accept Jesus into their lives, and he would be happy to pray for them. He told them they did not have to be in a church building to accept the Lord. The couple said yes.

Cypress became very uncomfortable and excused himself to the men's room. As he got up Belle said, "We could wait a couple of minutes." To which he replied, "No, no go ahead," then walked away. You could see the look of disappointment on Belle's face as she nodded her head.

When they were done with prayer, Belle reached into her bag for paper and a pen. She wrote out the name and address of the original church she had attended for the couple, along with the service times. "We will all be there tomorrow morning at the early service, hope to see you there." They said their goodbyes and the couple left.

Cypress had been gone for the entire time the couple had been at the table. It was as if he were watching and waiting for them to leave, and he returned as soon as they walked away. Silas said, "Don't sit, we're leaving now." The girls and kids got up to go see the fish tank again before leaving. On the way out, Cypress said, "Dinner was great, thanks again."

TWELVE

AS THEY CROSSED AN OVERPASS the van became full of "what was that and did you see that" questions. "Warren, you have to turn around and go back, we need to get that critter out of there before it gets hit by a car," Belle cried.

"It must be terrified," Starlit said, "it looked like it was clinging to the railing. It seemed to be about the size of a small dog, but I don't know what it was, it's dark over here. I think it moved a little, I hope it doesn't try to run."

"Could have been a raccoon," Cypress said. "They can use their paws like little hands. We might have to stop cars from coming onto the bridge so we can guide it off and we can't get too close; it could be mean."

Warren said, "I am stopping here since there is no room on the overpass. You will have to walk the rest of the way. Take the flashlight from the glove compartment, Belle."

"I have one in my pack," Silas said. He took it out and handed it to Cypress, saying "Good luck." As Cypress took hold of the flashlight Silas held on to it, giving a little resistance as Cypress pulled and tried to take it.

"Thank you, Silas," he said as he gave a yank to take it. Belle and Cypress started toward the overpass. Starlit called out, "Be careful!"

Belle's heart raced as she tried to keep up with Cypress. He was determined to make this a quick rescue and was walking very fast. She had to trot to catch up to him. Several feet before the critter, they stopped then proceeded slowly so they would not startle it. Upon approaching the critter Belle was shocked. "Do you see what I see? I can't believe this, how did he get here?"

"Tossed out a window maybe," Cypress replied, "or maybe it jumped out the window."

"Very funny. I can see why it appeared to move, a breeze from cars passing by would do that."

"I think we should rescue it," he said as he took off his jacket. He bent down and as he wrapped the critter in it, he said, "I'll try not to hurt it. Get that smile off your face, Belle."

She said as she held out her hand, "Well, I can't help it, seeing your tender side, you know. I'll take the flashlight while you carry him."

"Belle, you don't know if it's a he or she."

"I know but I usually say he for some reason."

As they got close to the van the adults were waiting outside of it. Starlit had her hand over her mouth. Cypress and Belle had their heads hanging down. "This appears serious," Warren commented.

Silas said, "I don't see any resistance or hear anything."

Cypress replied, "It's, well, a little stiff." Starlit said, "How sad, we were too late."

Just then Cypress and Belle looked at each other. Then he said, "It could use a bath and a decent burial." He shook his head from side to side, seeing the look on Belle's face, but she could not contain herself. She burst out laughing. "Guys, this is very embarrassing, we just rescued a stuffed animal!"

All of them were stunned and silent for a minute. Cypress uncovered it and showed it to them. It was a little stuffed teddy bear. He told them its arm was through the railing space, making it look like it was holding on.

Silas broke the silence with a chuckle first, saying, "You guys were so serious when you headed out." Starlit said she was very happy it turned out that way and was going to tell the kids everything was okay. As she turned to get in the van she giggled and said, "It was great seeing you in action, Belle, very entertaining."

Warren said, "This has been entertaining indeed," and then let out a hearty laugh. Everyone was laughing now. Silas said, "You know, Belle, we might or might not let you live this one down."

Belle laughed and said, "It's good to stay in practice you know, that was a good drill!"

They dropped Cypress off at the Center by his car and said their goodbyes. Belle waved out the window as they drove off. "Was it just me or did anyone else sense a little tension between the two Sy's?"

"Yes Star, I did. It was as if two siblings were sparring with each other," answered Warren.

"That's a good way to put it," Starlit said. "They did seem to poke and jab at each other throughout the night." Then she teased Silas saying, "Did big brother pick on you?"

"Quit it," he said. "I feel bad that I behaved the way I did, he just got to me, sorry. I can't believe I said, 'I was named after a biblical character, not a tree like you'! Guess I wasn't thinking."

Starlit reminded him, "Well, as you said at the restaurant, Christians aren't perfect people."

"I can't believe his birthday is the same month as mine..."

Starlit interrupted adding, "And he's seven days older, little brother."

"He is not my brother, not until he accepts the Lord anyway, and I didn't like the fact that he knew Belle's nickname either. Belle, that bothered me, did you tell him ours?"

"No Sy, I didn't. Mine came up one day when he noticed I could smell things others couldn't or didn't notice and I just said that's why they call me Hound. It just kind of came out."

"That's enough," he said, "let's change the subject. What are you going to do with the bear?"

"First he will get a good cleaning, then when I get a chance, I'll donate him to the charity center."

"Do you think it might have been put there because of an accident?"

"No, there haven't been any accidents in that area. I don't think we'll ever know how he got there, but what I do know is he sure got our hearts pumping."

It was not long before they were home. Belle wanted to get the food for Vee warming so it would be ready for her when she arrived. As she was turning the oven on Silas called out, "Belle, I'm going out to feed the critters while you're getting things done."

"Thank you," she called back. Starlit suggested she get the kids ready for bed early since they seemed wiped out. Jasmine was a little apprehensive because she wanted to see Vee and show her around. Warren said to her, "You can stay up to say hello to Vee, then you need to go to bed. Tomorrow after church you can give her a guided tour. Jasmine?"

"Oh, o-kay Daddy," she replied as she took hold of Starlit's hand.

"Belle, I will tend to the cats while you take care of the dogs."

"Thank you, Warren. It sure is nice to have a couple of farm hands."

When Vee arrived, it was a little after 7:30. The kids ran over to her and hugged her. They each began telling her what they wanted to show her. Belle told them Vee needed to eat her dinner and reminded them they could show her around tomorrow. Since the kids were very tired, they did not put up much of a fuss. They said their goodnights to everyone, and their dads took them to the guest room.

The girls sat and talked with Vee as she ate her dinner. "Belle, I hear a lot of howling outside. It sounds closer than when I first got here."

"It's okay, it's nothing to worry about. I'm so used to it I don't notice it most of the time."

Vee, sounding a little nervous replied, "Oh sounds like it happens often. I suppose it's normal for out here, which makes sense since it's the country. I'm done and ready for the tour, Belle, thank you for dinner, it was so good!"

"You can see all of outside tomorrow when the kids show you around. They're looking forward to that. Don't mention I showed you the kitty room since that's on their list too. These are the new kitties Snuggles, Cautious and Candy, they're brother and sister, and this is Pouncer, you know the rest. Say hello to Vee, kitties!" Belle then told Vee the story of each new kitty.

"Oh, Belle, this is great. I love their room. Hi, stowaway, I've just got to give you some kisses. I can't believe he got into your suitcase that day when you left to come out here. How'd that go again?"

"I had a sleeper cabin and as soon as I got on the train, I went to it. I wanted to get my things put away then go see the dining and viewing cars. When I placed my suitcase on the seat, I heard something. After opening it carefully I stepped back quickly, not sure of what was in there. As I stepped back a little black head poked out. I couldn't believe it. The first thing I thought about was him going potty. He didn't in the suitcase, so I quickly came up with a kind of litter box, anticipating he'd need to go. Sure enough he did. I'm glad I had a cabin. That made it easier to conceal him, that and the fact he's a quiet kitty.

"It was a good setup, toilet and sink right in the room. It was a tiny room but it worked out. By placing toilet paper in the makeshift litter box lined with a plastic bag I was able to flush the used paper. There was a window covering on the door to the cabin that I kept closed for privacy, and I was able to lock the door whenever I left the room since cabins came with a key for securing your things. At night when it was bedtime, they had someone come to pull down the bunk, so I had to stuff him back in the suitcase for a few minutes and cover the litter box. It was a challenge to get food for him, but I managed. It was kind of fun."

"That's so funny, I wonder if he knew you were going somewhere or if he just wanted a place to sleep."

"I'm not sure, Vee, but they do seem to know something is going on at times. So now I'll show you the game room downstairs. The guys are probably there already playing pool."

The girls played a board game while the guys played pool. They talked for a long time and began yawning a lot. "I'm so tired, Belle, I think I should get ready for bed," Vee said.

Starlit said, "You'll be in the guest room with me and Jasmine; come on, I'll take you up. You'll be sleeping in the top bunk, above Jasmine."

"Good night, Belle, I'm so glad I had this extra time tonight to visit and I'm looking forward to tomorrow. It will go by too fast, I'm sure. We don't have to leave for the airport until three so I want to see as much as I can."

"My gosh, I just remembered we will be getting home late tomorrow night. It's a good thing that VBS starts at nine thirty in the morning, since the kids will get to bed late."

"I'm glad we'll have a few hours more to visit too."

"After the kids show you around, we'll have lunch up at the pond, you'll see everything. Have a good sleep."

"Good night, all."

Starlit and Vee went upstairs while Belle put away the game. The guys had just finished their last game of pool and went to sit with Belle. Warren began to speak, "You do know, Belle that I, we, care a great deal about you? We are concerned about Cypress, his character, which is why I believe Silas reacted the way he did, although not tactfully."

At that moment he looked at Silas, smiled, winked then continued. "We believe he is having a negative effect on you."

"Oh stop, please, I don't think so. I appreciate the concern and love, that you guys care, but don't blow things out of proportion. I'm very tired, let's talk some other time. We have to get up early and I need the sleep."

When she stood up the guys stood up. Silas said, "You do need to sleep for sure, you're cranky." He kissed her on the forehead and said, "Me too, good night." She quickly headed up the stairs.

"Well, Warren, maybe tomorrow we can try again, after Vee and the kids leave. Maybe Star could be there too."

"Yes, we should all be together," Warren said as he put his arm across Silas's shoulders and walked him toward the stairs. "We need to gather the children from the guest room so the ladies can go to sleep, then to sleep ourselves."

In the morning the kids were raring to go. They showed Vee around the yard, going out to the orchard first then to the vegetable garden, pointing out their favorite veggies. The doghouse was next. As Junior was taking Vee to the doghouse he explained how it was big enough to sleep in. She was amazed with it.

When she came out, Jasmine took Vee by the hand saying, "We need to eat," and they skipped to the chicken coop. She showed Vee how to "pick" the eggs for breakfast, then beckoned her to hurry so they could go see the kitties.

Belle prepared breakfast while the kids took Vee to the kitty room. When the food was ready, she rang a bell signaling it was time to eat. The kids ate quickly. They wanted to show Vee more before leaving for church. "We don't have time, kids. You can show Vee the barn when we get back from church while I gather food to bring to the pond, and when we get there you can show her around. Afterwards we'll have lunch. Come on, time to go."

They all got in the van. Belle was about to get in when she heard the phone ring through an open window. "Be right back."

When she returned to the van, she announced she had some news. "Mrs. Yancee's daughter-in-law's mom passed away suddenly, leaving behind some critters. There were takers for all but one, her little dog Willow, and they thought of me. I said I would take her. Willow is familiar with me and has even been here a few times. As a matter of fact, Pouncer and she took a special liking to each other. The Yancees will come to the second service today and bring Willow with them so I can take her when we are on our way out."

Starlit said, "Belle, should you be taking on more work, you've stretched yourself so thin already!"

Silas said, "Yeah, you need to get your priorities in better order."

"It's fine," Belle said sternly. "She won't be a problem. She is tiny, only eleven pounds, don't pick on me, I can handle it."

"We better get going so we won't be late," Starlit said.

After service was over, they went to the gathering room to visit a little and the Yancees were there. There was usually about fifteen minutes to visit between services. When it was about ten minutes into the break, Mrs. Yancee took Belle by the hand and said, "I better get you the little one."

Mr. Yancee stayed behind while the others went to get Willow. Warren drove the van over to Mrs. Yancee's car and they waited for Belle in the van. Belle was handed a travel bag, a suitcase, and a dog crate with Willow in it. As she was walking over to the van, Warren asked, "Is there a child attached to this on-taking?"

Silas answered, "She didn't mention two dogs but it looks as though there are enough supplies for two." As Starlit looked out the window she said, "That is of course her food and water dishes, food, treats, a tiny bed, maybe two, and the rest clothes."

Silas and Warren said in unison, "Clothes! Are you serious, Star?"

"Yes Sy, I am."

He replied, "That is crazy, a dog with a wardrobe, no way. Why do people do that?"

She answered, "It is necessary, you'll see."

When Belle got to the van, she asked everyone to get out so they could meet Willow. She placed everything in the van except the crate. When she took her out of the crate Jasmine yelled, "She's naked!"

Silas slapped the palm of his hand to his forehead. Warren said, "Indeed it is necessary," and Starlit said, "That's weird but she's so cute!"

Silas asked Starlit how she knew, and she told him Belle had mentioned Willow to her during one of their phone conversations a while back. Then he asked, "Why is she not wearing anything now?"

Starlit said, "Because it's warm enough in the car."

Shrugging his shoulders he replied, "Oh, oh of course."

The kids loved Willow. As he pointed to her elbow Junior said, "This is kinda like plucked chicken wings!" Mark gently poked her skin. He couldn't seem to pet her like you would a dog that had fur on their body. Willow had cream-colored fur on her face, tail, feet, and ankles but none on the rest of her body.

"Come on now, we have to get home," said Belle. "I'll leave her out of the crate so you can visit with her in the van."

Immediately upon arriving home from church the kids wanted to take Vee to the barn. The guys went with them while Belle gathered food for lunch. Starlit packed up the kids' belongings so they would be ready to leave to go home with Vee.

It was not long before it was time to head up to the pond. Belle and Starlit placed the kid's suitcases in Vee's car, then put the food in the van since Rover could not accommodate another adult. Starlit said she was going to take one last look around to make sure she got all the kids' things, and Belle went to the barn.

"Hey everybody, we're leaving for the pond. I'll put P-2 and P-3 back in their cage and you can go play with Guardian and Stance a few minutes before we leave since they're not coming with us."

"I'll help you, Aunt Belle," Mark said.

"Thank you."

The ferrets were in their spheres rolling around and P-3 happened to be near his cage. Belle took him out of his sphere while Mark looked for P-2. After P-3 was set inside his cage Belle went to look for Mark. He was in the tack room toward the back with his back towards the door. Belle called out to him as she entered the room. He turned around and was holding the sphere with P-2. He smiled, stood up, walked toward her, and said, "Got 'im!"

"Good job," Belle replied. Her eyes widened with surprise as she caught a quick glimpse of something behind him. She took the sphere from him, tucked it under her arm, then placed her other hand on his back and quickly escorted him out of the room.

Just then Starlit and the twins headed towards them. Belle began to hum a tune, flashing her eyes at Starlit. Junior took hold of Jasmine's hand and said, "Come on, Mark, that means the grownups want to talk. Whenever there's that humming that means we're not supposed to listen."

"When did you get so smart, Junior?"

"Uh, Star, you go with the kids, I'll be right out." Starlit complied immediately.

As soon as they left Belle went back into the tack room, but everything appeared normal. "Must have been my imagination—no, no, I know I just saw something or seemed to, what timing! I've got to go. I'll be back, little room." While she was walking out of the barn, she began to doubt herself again. Frustrated, she repeated as she left, "I'll be back, little room." Then she went to get Willow.

When Belle returned, Starlit flashed her eyes at her, giving short quick nods with her head towards the barn. Belle motioned with her eyes as she shook her head slightly from side to side. Starlit knew that meant "not now" and she would have to wait until later to find out what happened. Belle said, as she snuggled Willow, "This little girl will need some extra love and attention, so we'll take her to the pond with us."

THIRTEEN

VEE'S PREDICTION CAME TRUE and the time passed by much too quickly; next thing she knew she and the kids were in the car waving goodbye. Vee was instructed to call them just as they were boarding the plane and as soon as they landed. The kids were told to be on their best behavior and listen to Vee. Since the flight out to Belle's was an exciting experience for the kids, they were looking forward to going on the plane again. The kids were still waving out the windows after the car pulled out of the driveway and had traveled halfway down the road.

"That was a very good visit with Vee, I'm so glad she was able to be here. Funny how we adults got teary-eyed and the kids didn't. Maybe next year the kids will be here for the entire time, if VBS isn't changed again."

"What happened anyway?"

"They didn't say," Starlit answered. "All I know is they changed the date before they printed the invitations so that was not a problem, but since we had made all our arrangements and reservations to come out here, that became the main issue for us. Praise God for working it all out for us!"

"Yes, thank you, Jesus. How about some iced tea? We can sit out here or inside."

"I would like to be in the house for a little while," Warren said. Silas said he wanted some fruit and headed into the dining room. The girls carried in the pitcher of iced tea and the glasses. Silas began to pour the tea while Warren went to put on some background music. They talked for a short time, then Belle said, "I need to see where Willow is, be right back."

She was only gone a minute and was smiling from ear to ear when she returned. "It's so adorable, Willow is cuddled up with Pouncer and they're sleeping on my bed." She sat back down and continued to talk about Willow. When she concluded, Warren began to speak.

"Now that just the four of us are gathered, we need to speak on a more serious subject. Please listen and understand that this is difficult. I apologize in advance if anything sounds harsh; it is not meant to be. There are some issues we have all noticed."

"Yes," said Starlit. "You don't seem to be completely your old self, or should I say your old, old self has surfaced. We all have slips now and then but you seem to not notice."

"Or not care," added Silas, "which is a great concern. As Star said, you have stretched yourself too much and in doing so, you're neglecting your spiritual health. You have added more working hours at the nursery and hours doing volunteer work for the Center, depleting the volunteer time at church."

"You are no longer in a Bible study group," Warren added. "Please consider all of this and make the necessary adjustments needed to get back on the correct path."

"We love you, Belle," said Starlit. "We want the best for you, we're very concerned."

"I'm sorry, guys. I don't know what to say, I'll figure it out. I know you care. I work more hours because sales are down on the houses. It's been a while since anything has come in from that. I love being at the Center, but I should spend more time here."

Starlit said, "Don't figure it out on your own, that's not good; pray about it, and get with God. Tell Him your concerns. We'll pray too."

"Am I that bad?"

"You're side-tracked, Belle," said Silas, "that's all."

Then Warren said, "There is the concern about your social life as well, the people you go out with and where you go."

"If you're referring to the Center, well, they're my coworkers and I don't drink or go out a lot."

Warren continued, "You are not being a good representative of your faith. You must consider the people you keep company with, what influences you are around and keeping a check on self-control in situations. We know you have to be with coworkers at the Center, but you have a choice to not be with them elsewhere. You said yourself that you and Cypress have gone out alone. That should not be."

Belle became overwhelmed. She tried to justify certain things, then agreed she should change but would revert to justification again. She said she was having a difficult time processing all of this but would pray about it. She stood up and began to pace back and forth. Warren said firmly, "You do not need to pray about Cypress, just stop going out with him."

"It's fine Warren, really. Nothing is going to happen!" Belle went on justifying why it was all right as she continued to pace.

Warren had had enough. He stood up and said, "Belle, I forbid you to see him outside of work."

Starlit gasped, and then looked at Silas as he looked at her. He mouthed out to her, *Ooops*. Belle stopped. She took a deep breath then tried to speak. Still overwhelmed, she said, "I will consider everything you've all said, thanks. I have to go check on something." She turned and rushed out of the dining room, then went out the back door. She had a few seconds of a head start before Warren charged out after her. Starlit and Silas sat there with their mouths hanging open.

As Warren came out the back door, he saw Belle going into the barn. With determination he moved swiftly in that direction calling out, "Do not run away from me."

He entered the barn and found her in the tack room. "Belle, please calm down, I do not want you to be angry."

She replied, "I'm not, I'm not, just—well, I don't know." He continued to talk as she looked around the tack room. She went over to the shelf along the length of the back wall and began to examine it.

"Belle, what are you looking for?"

"I'm not sure," she said as she bent down to examine under the shelf. "I thought the floor moved or seemed to earlier when Mark was in here." That statement sent Warren into silent mode. For two or three minutes he watched Belle go underneath the shelf, searching the underside of it and then the supporting post in the center of the shelf. She came out from under the shelf but was still crouching down. "Hmmm, I wonder..."

Just then Warren placed his hand on her shoulder and gently said, "Belle, a moment, please."

She stood up and said, "Yeesss?"

"Seriously, what are you looking for? What do you mean the floor moved?"

"I think I figured it out. Let's see if I'm right." She bent over, standing back from the post a little, poked her head behind it and said, "I think it's this knothole that might do the trick." She pushed on it and in it went.

A section of the floor to the left of the post slowly dropped down several inches, then moved to the right, revealing an opening that an adult person could fit through. She joyfully announced as she sprang back up, "I was right, it wasn't my imagination!" She had a small flashlight in her pocket that she had grabbed off the table in the barn as she entered. Belle took it out of her pocket, turned it on and started through the opening.

"Stop, Belle! Do not go down there," Warren warned. There was a ladder attached to the back wall down inside the opening and she began her descent. Warren demanded, "Come back, Belle! Stop! You do not know what is down there. Belle, that flashlight is not sufficient. Belle?"

After hesitating briefly, he began his descent down the ladder after her. It was very dark. When he reached the bottom, Belle was standing a couple of feet from the ladder, sweeping the flashlight from side to side. She could not see anything. "You're right, Warren, this flashlight won't do, this light is so dull. I should have changed the batteries. Let's let our eyes adjust a bit, maybe that will help. I can't believe this is here. Why in the world would anyone have a basement in their barn?"

He said, "I do believe we will add this to our list of mysteries. In the meantime, we should leave and return when we are better equipped."

She did not argue with that. He stepped aside to allow Belle to start up the ladder first. Looking up, she started her ascent. When she was on the third rung of the ladder, she let out a shriek. "Warren, the door is closing!" She picked up the pace, going as quickly as she could with Warren close behind. Still several rungs away she yelled at the door, "Wait—wait—no!" as if it were going to listen.

The last bit of light from above disappeared as the little door closed completely. She reached the door and began pounding on it. Belle was breathing heavily. Warren was tapping Belle on the leg. "Belle, stop, calm down, it will be all right. Look around for a latch or another button to open the door."

She searched but to no avail. "I'm not finding anything, Warren. Let's go back down and switch so you can try."

He was not successful either. He tried calling out to see if anyone would answer. There was no reply, so he went back down the ladder. Unable to find a light switch they had to depend on the one little dull flashlight they had. Belle was clutching it tightly. She took a few steps forward, trying to see something, anything, but there seemed to be only dark empty space all around them. "This is not happening. I can't believe I'm stuck down here with you."

Surprised, he replied, "Still miffed I see. Please forgive me, Belle. I think it best for us to be allies right now…"

"Sy, they have been gone a while, should we go intervene? I can't believe Warren forbade Belle to see Cypress," said Starlit.

"Thank you for clarifying that, Star, I wasn't sure I really heard that—you know I did, but I was stunned."

They went outside and looked around. Not seeing them, they went to look in the barn. Starlit called out their names but there was no reply. She called again, loudly, as she stood by the tack room; still no reply.

"Maybe they went for a walk, Sy. I can't even call them; they left their phones in the house since we weren't going anywhere." When they left the barn, they walked to the gate that was near the path which led to the pond. Silas called out their names but there was no answer. "Let's give it some more time, Star; they're probably having a good heart to heart."

"I'm done, Sy, it has been forty-five minutes and I'm worried, we have to do something."

He replied, "Maybe we should go up to the pond. We'll take Rover so it will be faster and take Guardian and Stance too."

At the pond they did not see them either. They drove around that area calling out their names.

"Star, I thought for sure they would be here, now I'm worried." He looked at the dogs and said to them, "Where is Belle, find Belle!" They started to bark.

"Sy, do you think they understand?"

"I don't know." They kept barking. He opened the door and got out of Rover. The dogs jumped out and ran to the path that went back to the house.

"Quick, Sy, follow them. I'm not sure if they understood you or they just want to go home, but go!"

Sy drove fast, faster than he should have been going. When they got back, Starlit jumped out to open the gate. The dogs were barking and turning in circles. As soon as the gate was open just enough for them to fit through, the dogs dashed past Starlit and headed for the barn. Starlit ran after them.

Sy decided to leave Rover there. He got out, closed the gate and ran to the barn. Just before reaching the barn Starlit began calling out, "Belle? Warren?" Silas called out also. They found the dogs in the tack room sniffing around. Starlit, with disappointment on her face said, "Well, that was a bust. What do we do now?"

While Silas patted the dogs he said, "Let me think a minute." He left the tack room and Starlit followed.

Silas sat in a chair at the table while Starlit walked around the barn. The dogs stayed in the tack room, lying down in the middle of it.

"Okay hmm, Belle said she wanted to check something out when she rushed out of the house. Do you think she really meant that or was that just an excuse to leave?" Starlit perked up and answered, "She really did want to check out something! The twins and I went into the barn; she was just bringing Mark out of the tack room in a hurry while humming the signal tune. She said she'd be out in a minute, so I took the kids and left right away. I tried to get some information from her later on but she hinted it had to wait."

"Anything else?"

"Yes, she had one of the ferrets in its sphere under her arm; well, I suppose that isn't anything really. Now what?"

"Food, that's what, I'm hungry."

"Sy, how can you think of food at a time like this?!"

"I will think better, come on."

"Feeling better, Sy?"

"I am and you should have a little something too."

"In a minute; I want to see where the dogs are, I haven't seen them in the yard anywhere."

"While you're doing that I will put Rover away, for now, and when you get back you better eat something."

After Silas put Rover back in the garage he went into the kitchen. Starlit was sitting at the table nibbling on some fruit. Willow was on her lap. "The dogs are still in the tack room," she said.

"The tack room, Star?"

"Yep," she answered.

"You mentioned Mark and Belle were coming out of there in a hurry. When you got there, she was giving you the signal tune which means she was trying to avoid him seeing or hearing something. Maybe by chance he did, I need to call him, hold that thought."

"Great idea, I hope he did," she said excitedly.

"Don't get your hopes up too high, Star. I want to be hopeful too, but I also don't want a big letdown… I'm sorry Star, I can't get through right now, bad signal up there, I guess."

"This is frustrating, Sy, I don't know what to do."

"First, how about you eat something more substantial than fruit, then we get all the critters fed and after that I'll try again."

Starlit was anxious. She could not wait until she finished all her food. With her second bite of food just barely swallowed, she asked Silas to try calling again. He made several attempts but had no success.

"We might have to wait until they land and Vee calls us," he said. Starlit looked at him with a stern expression and said, "Mother says you will try again."

"Yes Mom, finish your food. I will try again and as soon as you're done, we'll get the critters taken care of. It's a little early for them but I don't want the interruption later."

Starlit and Silas helped each other feed all the critters. Guardian and Stance were reluctant to leave the tack room but Silas was able to coax them out. After they finished eating, both dogs roamed around the yard checking out everything, then instead of going into their doghouse as usual they went into the barn.

FOURTEEN

SILAS HAD ANOTHER FAILED ATTEMPT at contacting Vee and now Starlit had tears welling up in her eyes. This unexpected event, along with discovering how Belle had changed, was certainly not the vacation they had looked forward to. It seemed as though much more time had passed than had actually gone by since Belle and Warren went missing. The waiting was agonizing.

"I hope they get back before dark, Sy."

"Come on, Star, we should take Willow outside for a little bit."

"Okay, I'll get her harness and leash. I'm not comfortable letting her run loose since she's so little. It's cooler out now so I better put her jacket on her too."

They walked around the yard alongside the fence line. When they got to the orchard Starlit stopped, turned to Silas and said, "Sy, I need to take my own advice; *we* need to take my advice. I told Belle she should bring her concerns to God."

"You're right," he said, "we should pray and seek His help." They sat down right where they were, and Willow crawled onto Starlit's lap. Starlit and Silas joined hands and Silas prayed out loud.

Back at the barn Belle was still complaining. "Stuck with you of all people, trapped with you, ooh brother." He let her go on for a short time, then said, "You are ranting, Belle," as he softly pressed two fingers over her mouth.

She stopped yapping and nodded her head yes. He took his fingers away and she said, "Warren, I'm sorry, you're right, this is not the time. I need to get a hold of myself, this is too much dark for me, I'm so nervous."

He whispered, "Calm down, take a deep breath and let it out slowly. Do that again. Silas and Star will find us."

"But how? I never told Star what happened. I gave her the signal tune that something was up when she came into the barn with the kids but never told her what I thought I saw, I put her off. This is my fault and I can't fix it. I'm powerless."

"There is One who has power," he said. "Think, Belle, think back to earlier today. What advice did Star give you?"

After a moment she answered, "I should pray but I better repent first." She closed her eyes, bowed her head slightly and said a silent prayer. When she was done, she opened her eyes as she was lifting her head.

Warren smiled, placed his arm around her and began to pray aloud. Belle could feel herself relaxing. When he was finished, she told him she was feeling better. "This is so strange being down here."

She said as she shook the flashlight, "I wonder how long the batteries will last in this thing. That was stupid of me to rush down here knowing they needed to be changed."

Warren replied, "O ye of little faith. You heard me ask for longevity for the batteries during prayer, trust Him. God cares about all of our concerns whether they are large or small. He will take care of this need."

With a slightly forced smile she said, "You may have to remind me again." He gave her a look of compassion. "It's so cold down here, I'm really feeling it now, Warren."

As Silas closed his prayer a breeze kicked up. "I'm cold, Sy, we should go back in the house. Even Willow is cold, I just felt her shiver," said Starlit.

"Sure, come on," he said as he helped her up.

She held Willow close then said, "Let's see if the dogs are in the doghouse before we go inside. Oh, they're not, now I want to see if they're in the barn."

They walked quickly to the barn. Starlit entered first. As they stood looking into the tack room Silas placed his hand on Starlit's shoulder and said, "Well, Star, there they are and they seem to be settled in here for the night. We should say goodnight to them. Hello, boys," he said as he patted them on their heads. Both dogs made a little whimpering sound.

"Sy, they seem sad, they know something is wrong and I think so too. If Belle and Warren knew they were going somewhere for a while they would have come back for their phones first."

They were standing right over Belle and Warren but had no clue to that fact. Belle asked Warren to call out to see if anyone would answer this time. Her reasoning was that Starlit and Silas were most likely looking for them and would surely look in the barn too. He climbed halfway up the ladder and began to shout. He did so several times but there was no reply. He climbed up further and shouted again. He then went to the top and tried pounding on the door; still no reply. Belle was disappointed. When he got back down Belle said, "Okay, I'm still calm but I don't know for how long, and I'm so cold."

"Stand close to me," Warren said. He placed his arm around her saying, "We cannot walk around but perhaps we can sway side to side to warm up some."

Starlit and Silas started leaving the tack room. Just outside its door, Silas's phone rang. "Yes! Vee, that was a missed call from me, everything is fine; yes, I just need to talk to Mark a minute. Oh—oh yeah, that doesn't surprise me, great. Um Mark, please. Hello? Hellloo?"

Starlit was tugging on his arm anxiously. "I'm sorry, Star, we lost the signal. We'll wait in the house; she knows I want to speak with Mark so she'll probably try again. What I did get before we lost contact was that there is some minor turbulence, and the kids are enjoying it as if they're on a carnival ride."

She said, "That doesn't surprise me either."

Just after they sat down in the living room she said, "Sy, please try to call." He did but was unable to get through. Another attempt was made and as he put down the phone he said with a grin, "We need to ask the dogs why they want to stay in the tack room."

"What!" she exclaimed. "Really, not funny."

"Sorry, Star, thought I could lighten the mood. Truth is I don't know what to do. I thought about maybe taking a ride to the Yancees' and asking for help. It's still light out so maybe we could get people to help search around. Leave Willow here," he said as he took her hand and helped her up off the couch. "We'll take Rover again in case we need to go off road."

They were about a quarter of the way to the farm when the phone rang. Silas stopped driving. "Mark! Yes okay, stop and listen to me, I need to ask you something very important. When you were in the tack room with Aunt Belle, what were you doing? The little room in back, Mark. Think, you went to get P-2, what else? Are you sure? I have to go, buddy, I love you; we'll talk again soon. New plan Star, we're going back. There could be a trap door like the one near the bathroom in the barn."

"Why would there be one there, Sy? The one near the bathroom leads to a large crawl space under where all the plumbing is for the bathroom and sink."

"I don't know, Star. Belle's place isn't your norm after all; maybe we didn't notice the one in the tack room."

"Well, if there is a crawl space there, why would Belle go down into it and pull the lid on the opening? Was she trying to hide?"

"Maybe that's what happened! Warren is out looking for her but why, then why didn't he get us to help look for her. Why didn't she answer when we called out?"

"I have no idea, Star."

Starlit yelled, "Oooh—deer!"

He said, "Yes, dear?"

"No! I mean animal—watch out! Slow down!"

He was traveling much too fast; he swerved to miss the deer and ended up in a small ditch. "This is not good, are you all right, Star?"

"Yes, I am, you?"

"I'm good but this will take a few minutes." He got out to assess the situation, then got back in Rover. He began going back and forth between drive and reverse, pressing the accelerator each time. He put it in drive one last time and as he pressed the accelerator, the rear wheels kicked up some dirt and Rover sped forward.

"Great, here we go—woohoo!" His adrenaline was pumping and he was talking fast. "When we get to the house, Star, call Mrs.

Yancee and tell her we might need help. If you can't find Belle's address book, then get the number from her phone. Tell Mrs. Yancee to stand by and we'll let her know if we need the help." He was still speeding even after their ditch experience.

Starlit did as Silas asked while he ran to the barn. He entered the tack room in such a hurry, he alarmed the dogs and they began barking. "Easy guys, it's all right." He hugged and patted them to calm them down as his eyes searched the floor. He was not seeing anything. He stood up and looked around the room carefully. "I don't get it," he said out loud.

Starlit asked as she approached the doorway, "Get what?"

"I don't see anything," he said. "Mark said he saw a cave when he got the ferret. I thought maybe Belle had opened something."

"Look at Stance, Sy, sitting under the shelf. It's kind of cavelike if you use your imagination. You know kids have a great imagination; Mark was probably pretending to be in a cave."

Silas replied, "He did say he got P-2 before the ferret fell in the cave. It doesn't make sense. I want some cookies. What did Mrs. Yancee say?"

"You want some cookies?"

"Yes, Star, I could use a little sugar rush."

"Well, I could use some tea right now anyway and I didn't speak with Mrs. Yancee. There was no answer and I didn't want to leave a message."

As they were leaving the tack room, they both turned and saw Stance pawing at the floor under the shelf. Sy said, "I think they're confused too."

"Are you enjoying the cookies, Star? I'm surprised you are eating any."

"Craved some Sy, that's all, not really enjoying them. Speaking of eating, I'm glad we fed all the animals early, but we forgot about..."

Realizing what she was about to say, Silas joined in and both said, "The ferrets!" He said, "They are easy to forget since they're quiet and in the corner out of sight. We can go feed them when I'm done, I am enjoying my cookies. I'm ready now," he said as he stood up. They started to leave for the barn, but Silas dashed back into the kitchen and grabbed a cookie to go.

"I'm glad you remembered them, Star. Now that they're fed, I want to go back to the tack room." When they entered, Stance was lying under the shelf. "Something is up," Silas said. "With what Mark said and the dogs acting this way, there has to be something to it. There has got to be a connection."

"Look! Sy, Stance was sniffing the post, now he's licking it. What does that mean? Does it mean anything?"

He called Stance out from under the shelf, then crouched down and went under it himself, examining it. He looked up at the underside of the shelf then turned his attention back to the post. "I wonder if... "

Starlit cried out, "What?" "Star, stay back," he said as he came out from under the shelf. He said, "I can't believe it but I think I figured it out. There are some knotholes..."

"Knotholes," she yelled in a panic, interrupting him in midsentence, "now what has that got to do with anything? They've been gone over two hours and you're wasting time looking at knots in wood!"

He took her by the shoulders. "Stop," he said, "calm down." Then he drew her to him and hugged her. Starlit began to cry. "Shush," he said softly and gently patted her on the back. "Give me a minute, Star," he said as he let go of her. He poked his head under the shelf, standing back a little from the post, then said, "Not this one, how about this one." He pushed the knot and in it went. The floor dropped down and as he said, "I can't believe this," Starlit began screaming frantically, "Belle! Belle! Belle!"

When the door opened slightly, Belle and Warren could see light emanating from above and hear the screams of Starlit. At the same time Belle was screaming back, "I'm here." Warren was yelling, "We are down here, we are well!" Fearing the door might close, Belle climbed as fast as she could. "Slow down, Belle," Warren said.

"It might close, Warren!"

"They will open it again if it should."

In her panic she missed a step and slipped. Warren steadied her. "Easy," he said, "we are almost there."

Silas helped Belle out of the opening. She crawled onto the floor and sat there shivering. When Warren climbed out, he sat on the floor next to Belle and held her. Starlit and Silas sat down and held them both in silence for a few minutes. Belle was still shivering. The mom in Starlit kicked in; she stood up and said, "Come on, we need to get you guys warmed up and get you some water."

When they stood up, Belle was still clutching the flashlight. She turned the light toward her face. The little dim light got dimmer and dimmer, then died out completely. She looked at Warren. He nodded his head and smiled.

Belle lay on the couch covered with a blanket and Warren sat in a recliner wrapped in one. Starlit was heating soup for them to eat while Silas brought them a glass of water. Both of them were quiet.

Sensing that neither of them wanted to talk, Silas went back to the kitchen. "This has been a strange evening. I want to know what happened, Star, but I don't want to push anything. I suppose they will talk when they're ready."

"That could be awhile, Sy. I made enough soup for all of us and it's ready. I'm going to put salad and rolls on the table, then come and get…"

Just then Belle walked into the kitchen with the blanket wrapped around her, saying, "I've got to feed the critters." Silas placed his arm around her as he led her to the dining room. He told her, "We have taken care of all the animals, now let's take care of you two."

"Thank you. Thank you both."

When they were done eating, they stayed at the dining room table for a short time. Not wanting to get into certain details, they briefly explained what had happened. Everyone was curious as to what it looked like down in the basement of the barn. Warren expressed that they needed to be well prepared for the exploration. They all agreed to put off making plans until the morning. Tonight, they would need to rest well.

Belle did not want to think about the barn any longer or of the conversations that took place after the kids and Vee left. She stated she wanted to watch a movie, then turn in early. Starlit, noting the expression on Belle's face, said, "I would like that too." The guys as well, pool did not call to them tonight.

FIFTEEN

THE GUYS WERE UP BEFORE THE GIRLS. They were making plans for their exploration while sipping coffee at the little table in Belle's kitchen. Starlit took a deep breath, enjoying the aroma of coffee she inhaled as she walked toward the kitchen. She was surprised, expecting to see Belle, when she saw the guys. Warren informed her the dining room table was set for breakfast already as he poured coffee for her. Silas told her that he and Warren would be the chefs for breakfast as soon as Belle was ready. Starlit thanked them and said she was looking forward to that.

"I thought Belle was going to let the dogs come in the house when they followed us to the door last night," Starlit said. "Instead, she had reassured them she was okay, gave them hugs and kisses and told them it was bedtime. Their reaction was so precious when Belle came up out of the floor. They didn't seem to want to leave her."

Starlit walked over to the window, looking towards the chicken coop, and asked, "Did you get eggs yet?"

As Silas was answering no, she said, "I can't believe it."

"We have time," he replied.

"No, not the eggs, come see this." Silas and Warren walked over to the window. There was Belle coming from the doghouse wrapped in a blanket. "Guys, I think she slept in the doghouse."

"Well, that was appropriate," Silas said. "Did you girls have a talk after we left?"

"No Sy, Belle didn't want to talk. I did go to her room to ask her again before turning in but I heard her sobbing. I thought maybe I shouldn't bother her, so I went to bed. She probably went to stay with the dogs because she knew they wanted to be with her."

"I believe it was best you let her alone," Warren said. "A wrestling match is going on within. It may take her time to process all we had told her."

Silas said, "Proverbs 27:5 to 6a comes to mind: Better is open rebuke than hidden love, Wounds from a friend can be trusted."

"Indeed," said Warren.

Belle went to the chicken coop to get eggs. She took off the blanket, folded it and set it down. After placing the eggs in a basket, she put the blanket over her arm and headed to the house. She arrived in the kitchen, surprised to see everyone. She said, "Well, we're all up early, good morning! Is everyone hungry?"

"We are," Silas answered as he took the basket from her. "Warren and I will make breakfast this morning. You go freshen up while we get it ready. By the way, why did you sleep in the doghouse?"

"I didn't, I was just tucking them in their beds since it was still early. They slept with me in the barn because that bed is big enough for the three of us. I felt bad leaving them last night when I came in, so I decided to go out and let them sleep with me in the barn. They were very happy about that. Thanks, guys, for breakfast, I'll be right back."

Warren noticed the blanket was the gift they had given her. Mentioning it to Starlit and Silas, he said it seemed a good sign that she chose that blanket instead of another. Starlit believed it meant there was still a strong connection between them all. That confronting Belle did not push her away and although Belle did not want to talk, she was considering what they had told her. It appeared the blanket was her way of staying close, cuddling with her loved ones, and contemplating their concerns. They all agreed to continue praying for Belle daily, together and independently. Wanting to support Belle in this new development as well as the mysteries that previously came about, they agreed to hold back voicing their concerns. They would concentrate on finding answers to those mysteries.

When Belle returned, breakfast was ready and they retreated to the dining room. After Warren gave thanks, Belle announced she had figured out what was down in the basement. She said, "It's a root cellar. That would make sense since there had been a vegetable garden located just outside of the barn originally. Could be why there is a kitchenette in the barn. Maybe we'll find some jarred goods or bulbs of some kind that were forgotten about. It's probably a small room, maybe six feet by six feet with lots of shelves."

"That sounds good," said Starlit. "I know canning veggies preserves them for a very long time, oh and fruit too, after all there is the orchard. There is no stove, maybe they took it out or used a pressure cooker; anyway, I can hardly wait to see if you find any canned goodies."

"Don't you mean, we," Silas asked. "You sound as if you aren't going down with us."

"I'm not, Sy."

"You used to be adventurous when we were kids, Star."

"That's the key word, Sy, kids—I grew up."

Warren cleared his throat and said, "We will need someone topside to open the door since we do not know how to open it from below. Perhaps we will find a way eventually, until then someone will have to stay above."

Starlit, raising her hand with a big smile on her face, said, "I gladly volunteer as door keeper!"

"Your service is accepted," he said.

"Thank you, Warren," she replied as she did a little victory chair dance.

"You are welcome. Now with that settled we should talk supplies. We need ample lighting. Each of us should have flashlights, extra batteries, a jacket for warmth and carry our phones. We know it is soundproof, so when the door closes we will call Star to see if the call goes through."

They did not rush through breakfast. You would have thought they would want to get started right away; instead, they sat a long time. Belle was in a great mood and there was no tension in the room. Conversation took place around some of the adventures they shared as kids. They could not believe how long ago that was.

Starlit began to feel the excitement of seeing what was in the basement of the barn. Her curiosity was growing, and she mentioned she would like to go into the basement to see it but after the others had done so first. Then as long as someone stayed upstairs to man the door she would go down. Silas teased Starlit, patting her on the back and congratulating her on yielding to the kid inside. All were looking forward to figuring out the seemingly odd events that had occurred lately.

After cleaning up the dining room and kitchen they began to get ready to explore the basement. Belle said she had two lanterns, a couple of spotlight flashlights, four regular flashlights and extra batteries. She told them the lanterns and flashlights were bright and did not need batteries, so they decided not to carry extra batteries. If for some reason they needed batteries the house was not far away.

Starlit helped Belle feed the cats and dogs while Warren and Silas fed the chickens and the horses. The guys took care of the chickens first, then went into the barn. Belle went out to the dogs while Starlit fed the cats. When Belle came back in the house, she fed Willow then gathered the lanterns and flashlights. Just as they were about to go out the back door, they noticed the guys poking their heads out of the barn door. They were peering out toward the gate that led to the pond. Belle immediately told Starlit to stay still and not to make a sound. To their amazement, Guardian and Stance were by the gate nose to nose with a wolf! They sniffed each other and the dogs rubbed their bodies along the gate; the wolf was doing the same. Tails were wagging, no sounds were made. Suddenly the wolf turned and ran off. It was small, most likely young. When it was just barely out of sight it stopped, turned and looked back at the dogs, then took off again.

Everyone came out and met at the gate. "Belle, the dogs didn't bark, they gave no warning," Starlit said, somewhat distressed.

"Well, it's obvious to me they might be friends," Belle replied, rather surprised. "I really don't know what to make of it!"

Starlit, very concerned asked, "That is very unusual, isn't it? What are you going to do about it?"

Silas replied, "Ground the dogs and tell them that's what they get for fraternizing with the enemy and don't do it again."

"Seriously Sy," Starlit snapped. "Belle?"

"I'll just keep an eye on it somehow, Star. I don't know if this is the first time this happened or happened a few times."

Hand to his chin, Warren said, "I believe we could add this to the list of seemingly odd occurrences to investigate. We should see the basement now."

As they walked toward the barn, they heard a familiar sound in the distance... *OwOw owooo...*

They started down the ladder, Belle leading the way. After they reached the bottom and the door closed, Warren called Starlit. The call went through; Starlit was thrilled. Knowing she had contact with the others was comforting to her. She wanted to know what they had found, but Warren said he or someone would call back in ten or fifteen minutes. Flashlights swept back and forth, up and down. What they saw was nothing any of them would have imagined.

"Definitely not a six-foot by six-foot room with lots of shelves, Belle," Silas said.

"Yeah, no kidding, what is all this? Why is it here?"

"It appears to be a laboratory or what is left of one," Warren answered.

"Yes, I see, I'm familiar with the items in here," said Belle. "If I didn't know any better, I would think I'm at the Center. This is strange, why is it here?!"

There were several workstations composed of short counters, each having a space for a chair to fit under and two drawers on each side of that. Only two stations had chairs. One of those had a microscope on its counter. There was an area on one wall which had some hooks with a lab coat hanging on one. A shelf held boxes of face masks, gloves, and face shields. Another area had a long table with some equipment on it: an incubator, centrifuge, and a sterilization unit for sterilizing instruments. Warren walked over to the station with the microscope on it and set a lantern next to it. He began opening the drawers, searching each one carefully. Silas went to another station and opened drawers there. Most were empty but he did find a few items.

"Did you find anything, Warren?"

"Indeed I have, Silas."

Belle did not say a word but walked slowly towards the station Warren was standing at. There were Petri dishes, vacutainers, syringes, glass slides, plastic pipettes, and needles with caps in the drawers. Silas asked Belle if she was all right as he shone the flashlight in her face, which was pale. The reality of what she thought happened to Anomaly and Rarity hit her. Someone had drawn blood from them! But why, she wondered.

"Guys, this is so unbelievable, it's not making any sense. Why is this here? Why would someone take samples from the horses?"

Just then Warren's phone rang. It was Starlit wanting to know if everything was okay. She was anxious to hear from them. "We are well," Warren answered. Then he said, "We will be up in a few moments. I am not going to tell you anything; you need to see this for yourself."

Silas said, "Come here, guys, you've got to see this. There is an office over here with two desks in it."

Belle and Warren passed through a doorway that had a curtain instead of an actual door. "These file cabinets are empty," Silas said, "but this one is locked so I'm guessing there are files inside with information."

Belle walked around the office briefly. "Don't try to open it, Sy, leave it alone. Whoa! Brain overload, I can't think, let's go back up and let Star take a look at this."

As she headed for the ladder something caught her attention when the light from the lantern shone on it. She turned to investigate. They had not noticed this as they walked away from the ladder toward the middle of the room after their descent.

Belle held the lantern up high with one hand and with her other hand directed the flashlight up, across and down the other side of a metal door. Stunned she called out, "Hey guys, there's a metal door over here, kind of like a garage door. I thought things couldn't get any stranger, what could it possibly be for?"

Silas was behind her at this point. He called out, "Warren, come and see this."

Warren called back, "I am looking at the other door on this side of the barn."

Belle and Silas together shouted, "The other door?"

"Yes, and the vehicle for which they are meant."

They shouted together again, "Vehicle!" They began walking over to the other side of the barn to join Warren. "How did we not notice these things?"

"We were focused on what was directly in front of us at the time," Silas answered. Then he said, "Maybe we shouldn't let Star see all this. She might just start packing up your things and make you move."

"I'm certainly not going anywhere. I will, with help from all of you, get to the bottom of this. I must know why this is here. We better let Star come down now."

Silas noticed a small door barely six feet high. He thought maybe it was a storage closet that held some supplies for the car, which was an electric car. Perhaps it stored a spare battery and spare tire, maybe some cleaning supplies and tools as well. He opened it but it was empty. The space was small inside. One side had three shelves and the other side only two with a larger space between them. The back wall of the closet had two narrow short shelves. He closed the door and caught up with Belle and Warren as Belle pulled out her phone. As they walked toward the ladder, Belle called Starlit to open the door.

When they were back in the tack room they just stood there in silence. Starlit was surprised by that, expecting a surge of information from Belle at least. Warren handed Starlit a flashlight, hooked a lantern to a belt loop on her jeans, took her by the arm and escorted her toward the little door. He began to descend the ladder and motioned for her to follow. She was being cautious as she placed a foot on each step, descending slowly as Warren hurried down. He was at the bottom while she was only halfway there. He walked over to one of the workstations and set a lantern on it. His arms were folded as he waited for Starlit.

When Starlit got to the bottom and turned around, Warren unfolded his arms and opened them wide as if to say welcome. Her mouth hung open as she moved toward Warren. She moved the flashlight slowly back and forth, shining it on each workstation.

He motioned to her to follow him. Holding aside the curtain to the office section, she stepped inside reluctantly. After inspecting it he led her to the side of the barn with the car. He pointed to the garage door and told her there was another one on the other end they would see as they were leaving. The whole time they were looking around she could only shake her head from side to side.

Starlit continued walking around slowly, looking at all she could. Warren let her do so without saying a word. She peeked into a tiny bathroom that had a toilet and small sink. When she had seen enough, she motioned to Warren. They were going toward the ladder and Warren shone the light on the garage door near it. As she started up the ladder she loudly said, "Nope!" Warren called Silas. When Silas answered the phone all he heard was, "Incoming!" He told Belle and they prepared for Starlit's arrival.

Starlit began to speak or tried to. "No-oh-oh-oh-no," was all that came out at first. Then she said, "Ooh, can't be, just one little jar of fruit and maybe a jar of asparagus, that's all, that would have been enough. Even a sack of potatoes but nooo, just weird, strange. I don't know what, this is not acceptable…"

A little smile started to form across Belle's lips. She glanced at Warren and Silas. Silas said, "Wait for it." He began to count out softly, "Three-two-one," then Starlit blurted out, "Belle, you can't stay—"

Silas and Warren together interrupted and said, "Belle's not moving."

"What!" Starlit exclaimed again. "What!"

"I'm not moving, calm down. I know what we've found is a shock, it's okay, really."

"How can you be okay with this, Belle?" Huffing, she then asked, "How did you guys know what I was going to say?"

Silas shrugged his shoulders and said, "What do you mean, Mom?"

Warren and Belle had smiles on their faces. Silas tried to keep a straight face but could not and let out a little chuckle.

Frustrated, Starlit gave up, knowing she was outnumbered; the others were not going to back down. Belle gave Starlit a long hug. She reminded her she had been living here a year and had been safe. Belle explained she wanted and needed to find out all she could about this basement and the other things that had gone on. No longer frustrated and calmer now, Starlit did a rewind in her mind of what just happened, and realizing how well they all knew her, she chuckled. "I get it, guys," she said. "I know why you said what you did now and why you laughed!"

Warren smiled, placed his hand on her shoulder and suggested they go in the house for a while.

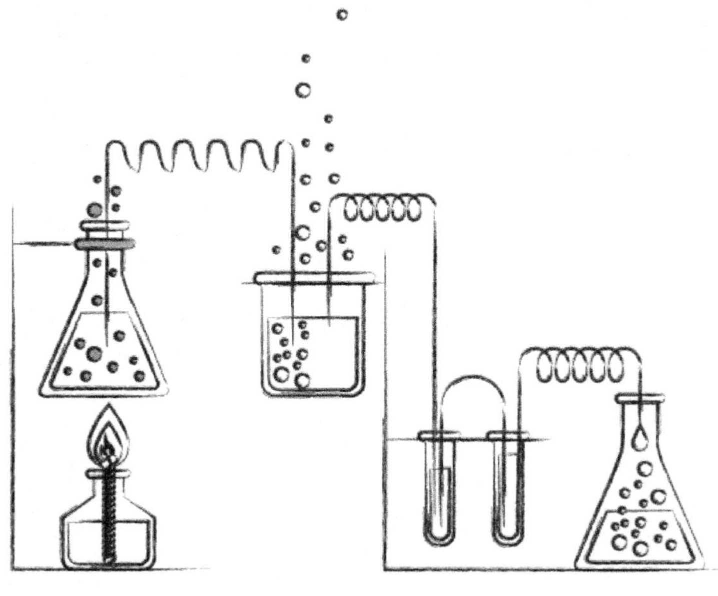

SIXTEEN

"HOW LONG WILL THE CAR need to charge, Warren?"

"I do not know, Silas; I am not familiar with that vehicle. We should check in two hours to see if it is ready to drive. The car will seat only two, therefore we must decide who will go with Belle."

"Warren, you can drive, I can walk, and you'll probably have to go slow anyway. At some point we could switch."

"Possibly Silas, however we do not know how far we will be going, although you and I are good hikers so that may work."

"I have an idea, guys. Maybe we could figure out a way to make something and hook it to the back of the car. You could take turns sitting in tow and driving. You like building things, Sy, what do you think?"

"I'm all for that, Belle. While we're at it maybe I should make it big enough to fit supplies, since the car is small and has no trunk or a roof rack. Do you have anything around here we could use, Belle?"

"A couple of things, but I know the Yancee farm has some stuff we could probably use. Warren, you look as though you disapprove."

"I approve of a towing method; it would be convenient. I disapprove of anyone gaining knowledge of what has come to light. We should plan on the hiking probability and look at the items you have. Perhaps there will be something sufficient for making a trailer that would accommodate supplies."

"He has a good point, Belle. You shouldn't share this with a-n-y-o-n-e."

"I get your drift, Sy about Cy. I agree I don't want anyone to know about this. It is strictly between the four of us only."

It was still morning. They gathered items Belle had, taking them to the basement to assemble. Those items consisted of two old, large skateboards, two small pieces of wood paneling, three short planks of wood, a three-foot piece of wood molding, tools and a bag containing hardware. The plan was to nail the small pieces of wood to the skateboards to connect them together and offer support for the two pieces of paneling which they would nail over them. The molding would attach to it as a tow bar they would somehow hook to the car. Using bungee cords, they would secure supplies onto the base. It would have been ideal if they could have fit one of the dog wagons through the opening; they were built to hold heavy loads.

Warren went down first and waited at the bottom of the ladder for the first drop. Silas lowered the tools and bag of hardware with a very long rope that was laced through the top portion of fishing net. Inside the net was a small blanket that contained the items.

Warren loosened the rope and took out the items. Silas pulled the netting back up and filled it with the skateboards and down they went. Next were the pieces of wood and the paneling. The paneling was difficult to get through the opening. It had to go through it diagonally and without the blanket in the netting. Silas and Warren set down two lanterns and began building their little trailer. It did not take long to get it together.

"Warren, I'm thinking maybe I could stand on this, straddling the supplies or stand over one skateboard as if in skating position with the supplies over the rest of the base. I'll add a post with handles after I attach this tow bar."

"Silas, your weight on the skateboard portion would be supported well. Standing in either position will work. The battery needs to charge longer; now would be a good time to search for wood to make a handle. Upon inspection I have discovered a place to attach the trailer under the vehicle's bumper. It is equipped for towing."

"That's great, Warren. I noticed the seats in the car may not be wide enough for two to sit side by side but there is a little space, we should be able to put some supplies in the car and on the floor with the passenger."

"Wonderful observation, Silas."

When they went to get the wood, they collected enough to make the post with two handles. You could hold onto the lower part if you were sitting or onto the top if you were standing.

The guys finally finished their project. Satisfied and proud with their accomplishment, they were ready to go up to fill the girls in on the plan. Silas called Belle and told her they were ready for the door to be opened. As they were about to ascend, Warren's flashlight shone between two rungs of the ladder, revealing something.

"Look here, Silas. I do believe this could be the..."

Before he could finish his thought, Silas pushed one of the buttons and the doorway above opened. "Well, look at that," he said and proceeded to push the other one, and on came lights. "I can't believe it, Warren! This makes a big difference on how it all looks. Over there, is that a thermostat?"

He walked over to it and turned on the heat. "Well, that'll take the chill off of things," he said. He started up the ladder quickly and with enthusiasm. The girls were dumbfounded when they arrived in the tack room and the guys were there.

"How did you get out?"

"When you and I were trapped and searching for a light switch, Belle, we looked on either side of the ladder, top and bottom, when in fact, the buttons in this case were located between the ladder rungs at the bottom. There were two buttons, one for the door and the other for lights. Silas discovered a thermostat and turned on a little heat."

"Lights!" she exclaimed, "We have lights! Star, we have lights, heat and a way to open the door from in the basement!"

"That's great," Starlit said, "all of that is great! I will however still be the doorkeeper, just in case."

Warren smiled and said, "Come, ladies, we have to prepare for our exploration."

Supplies were gathered: flashlights, water, clothes. They planned on taking some of the tools that were in the basement and decided to include a small shovel. Everyone took snacks consisting of protein bars, jerky, nuts, crackers, and dried fruit, then made sure all phones were fully charged.

"Well, that does it," said Silas. "I think we are as ready as we can be, are you ready, Belle?"

She replied with confidence, "I am, Sy. Lunch is ready, the table is set, let's eat. We'll be having a special dessert. I made a small pineapple upside-down cream cheesecake."

"Mmm, I could eat just that for lunch."

Starlit said, "No, you won't just eat cake; you will eat something healthy first. And by the way, I'm not so sure I am ready for this," she added. "How in the world did the car get down there? What if you run into someone down there?

"Belle and I have been discussing that. There are risks; I'm concerned for all our safety. Yes, I am curious but very concerned as well."

"We will be cautious," Warren answered. "We will not separate from each other. There are many questions which we are looking to answer. This exploration is something Belle desires. She needs answers. We do not know how far the tunnels go or if they each branch off into more. We only know there are two entrances. Belle, have you decided which one you want to explore first?"

"I have given it some thought. The direction of the one on the far end of the barn faces the road in front of the house. There isn't anything in that direction except the ruins of an old boarding school. The one closest to the ladder faces the direction of the path that goes to the pond. Let's start by the ladder. I wish I could be in two places at the same time; I want to know everything now but can only go in one direction at a time."

Belle got up from the table, went to the living room, and returned to the dining room with the object. "I have been thinking about this. It has a slight flat spot on one side which is how it sat on my desk at the Center. I think it is just a paperweight. I think the sundial and it are just something the previous owner probably made and just put a design on them he liked. Maybe I did pick it up to look at when I was here for the interviews and forgot. I was being shown so much and we were talking, so I might have just dropped it into my bag or something, not positive but it is possible."

Silas looked at Warren, then asked Belle, "Didn't you say you found it on the floor by the back door at home after that big storm?

How did it get there? You seemed sure previously that you didn't take it, and after all that's not something you just forget being that it's so odd."

She shrugged her shoulders and did not have an answer, but Silas thought he might. Warren gave an approving nod to Silas.

Silas proceeded to tell Belle what had happened that night; the secret that he and Warren kept about what they thought was a homeless man that tried to get into the house. His theory now was that the man was startled when Silas suddenly opened the back door to see what was going on and dropped the object. He may have been trying to retrieve it by hitting him to distract him. With no success the man rushed off, leaving the object. "That raises more questions, like who was that person and why was he in your yard?"

"I have a confession of my own. Mainly I didn't say anything at the time because I didn't want to alarm—Mom." Belle looked at Starlit with a half-smile and apologized. Starlit covered her mouth with one hand and wagged a finger of the other at all of them. She could not believe what she was hearing from them and could not speak, but the message was loud and clear. She did not want to hear anymore right now.

Belle continued. "When I was on the train coming home from my interviews, I thought someone might be following me, watching me. Since there were people I saw multiple times aboard the train I thought it might be my imagination, but then one time as I was returning to my cabin, I thought I saw that person trying to see into the window of it. The night when the man came to the door asking if the dog belonged there, I thought his outline was familiar, like the guy from the train. Later when I thought about it again, I realized there were some little differences between them though, so I'm not sure if they were one and the same."

"Could have been disguises," Silas said.

"Do you think this could all be related somehow?"

"I'm not sure of much, Belle, only that we need to stay alert and be careful."

Warren added, "We should stay calm, avoid panic, and keep in mind no harmful events have occurred. Star, you have the dogs with you and can contact us by phone. You also have the option of joining us."

"I'm okay, Warren, yeah, I'll stay," she said. "This has been a lot to swallow but you're right, nothing bad has happened. We should clean up, then you guys can get started."

They were all in the tack room holding hands and praying. When they were done Starlit gave each of them a hug and reminded them to call and check in every thirty minutes. Down into the basement the others went.

With the car battery fully charged they could start their journey. Warren secured the trailer to the car; Silas placed some supplies on it, leaving himself space to place his feet, then put bungee cords over the items to hold them on the base.

"Ready for a trial run, Silas?"

"Yes, Sir Warren," he answered.

Belle and Warren got in the car, and he started it. Silas stood on the trailer, his head and chest above the height of the car. He held the handle at the top of the post they added. Warren slowly drove to the door by the ladder and stopped.

"This is really good, Warren, a little noisy but not as much as I thought it would be. How are things with you, Belle?"

"A little tight Sy, with these supplies but doable. I'm ready to go. I hope the remote Warren found works now."

Warren pushed the button with the up arrow on the remote and the garage door opened. The door opening was small; the side view mirrors looked as though there might be six inches on each side of them that would clear the opening. He pulled forward slightly then turned on the headlights.

Smiling, knowing what was on the remote, Belle said, "It sure is dark in there, Warren."

He pushed the button that had a picture of a light bulb and the tunnel lit up. The light was not bright but it was better than none. "Thank you."

"You are most welcome."

"Wow that helps, but I would prefer to be able to see far ahead," Silas said. As they passed through the opening the space on each side of the car increased. Belle let out a sigh of relief. After driving into the tunnel about ten feet the garage door closed behind them. Warren said, "I did not close the door; there must be a sensor or perhaps a timer that triggers the door to close."

When they had driven a short distance Warren called out to Silas, "How are you doing back there?"

"Great! It's just like skitching when we were kids, cold air in the face included."

Warren and Belle laughed. "I can't believe this is happening. It's something you see in the movies; underground tunnels, laboratories, weird things going on, and like a moth to a flame we're drawn in."

They sat in silence the rest of the way down the tunnel. The tunnel was narrow with a low curved ceiling made of various materials. The lights were tube shaped and running along the high point of the ceiling which was about seven and a half feet high. All of them were anticipating that something could happen at any moment. Belle would turn to check on Silas often, then lean forward again trying to see as far ahead as she could.

The tunnel began to curve and change direction. So far, they had not seen any tunnels branching off this one. It was unfamiliar territory, so it seemed to take a long time to get to the end. Factoring in someone in tow added to the slowing of time.

They approached what looked like an end to the tunnel. Warren slowed down and stopped a way back from the end. He and Belle got out of the car, Silas stepped off the trailer and all went and stood in front of the car. There was a half-circle area on each side of the tunnel near the end where there was room to turn the car around. In one of them was another car. They walked to that car, which turned out to be a single-passenger car with a trailer hitched to it that had sides. The trailer was large enough for someone to sit in. Both car and trailer were painted in a camouflage design like the double passenger car they were driving. They continued past the car, then observed an odd-looking floor in a circular room. Around the perimeter of the room on the walls were lights that went up the wall every few feet, lighting up a tunnel that went upward. Beyond the floor opposite where they were standing was a huge metal beam with something protruding from its bottom that continued out to the floor.

"My goodness, what is that!"

"I do believe it is our way up," Warren answered. "Up is where we need to go."

"Whoa! I'm guessing mega elevator," Silas exclaimed. The guys turned to go back to their car, but Belle just stood there staring at what they just discovered. She stepped closer to the floor as she looked up, staring with her mouth open. Silas went back and stood near Belle, then tugged on her sleeve to get her attention. As she acknowledged him, she whispered, "Lights… Camera… Action."

SEVENTEEN

WARREN CAUTIOUSLY DROVE ONTO the elevator floor while Silas walked on. Belle was in the car with her face pressed against the window looking upward, trying to tell how far up was. Silas was leaning against the car, bracing himself in anticipation of what would happen. On the remote were two square buttons with symbols on them. The symbol was a circle with an arrow in the center. An arrow was pointing down in the center of one circle and up in the center of the other. Warren concluded these were the controls for the lift. He pressed the round symbol with the up arrow. Nothing happened.

Silas stepped slightly away from the car, about to ask why they were not moving, when suddenly he heard the soft sound of a mechanism clicking into gear. He could hear humming and ticking sounds that went on for several seconds. He leaned against the car again and waited for movement. The floor began to move, but not upward. It turned slowly first, about a third of the way around, then it stopped. A few more humming and ticking sounds were heard, then the floor began to move upward. Slowly they ascended the dimly lit tunnel. Finally, the floor came to a smooth stop. The car was now in a position to exit a door it was facing. No one moved yet. They wanted to make sure the ride had ended. After a few moments Warren opened the car door and stepped out. Belle followed.

"This is interesting," Warren said. He walked over to a wall that had several large monitor screens built into it. Below them was a ledge or shelf with some controls. As his finger floated over some buttons, Silas said, "I wonder which one is for the garage door?"

"We could just try the remote when we're ready. Wait a minute, be careful, Sy," said Belle.

"I am being careful, Belle, but we have to press something to see what it does." As he was about to push a button he said, "I hope this isn't an alarm." When he pushed it, a doorway opened but it was not for the car. It was an opening that was just wide enough to walk through that led to a chamberlike area. The chamber was rocky and on the far side of it was a rocky wall you had to go around to move on. Silas could see light coming from around it. He passed through the doorway.

"Wait, Sy, I'm not ready to go out anywhere yet. I'm still checking it out in here." He stopped and said, "Let me just peek around that wall and I'll be right back."

"If you wait a couple of minutes, we could all go together." As Belle was speaking, he was inching towards the wall then slipped around it. Just then the door closed. He went around the wall into an alcove that was brighter than the chamber area. As he moved forward he heard a familiar sound: *BzZZBbzbzBzzz…zzbzbzbzBZz…*

He turned around immediately and quickly headed back to the doorway, discovering the door had closed. He called out to Belle and Warren, but they could not hear him. Then he shouted several times.

In the meantime, Warren turned on the monitors. Belle was laughing as she and Warren watched Silas calling out to them. "He just couldn't wait, could he? So much for us not separating. I wonder where we are."

"I do believe we are inside the rock formation," Warren answered. Just then Warren's phone rang. He answered it and placed it on speaker. Belle was giggling as Warren said, "Control room; go ahead."

"You've got to let me in, there's no way to open the door from this side."

"You appear to be in distress Silas, stop pacing."

"Hey! Can you see me? Open the door, hurry! There are bees, lots of bees!"

Belle chose the set of buttons closest to the doorway and pressed the one that had a green hue. Before the door was fully open Silas squeezed through it and said, "Hurry, close the door."

"I don't know which one closes the door. I made a quick guess which one might open it; it will close on its own again."

"Why didn't you let me in when I was shouting to you?"

"We had no audio, only visual," Warren answered as he pressed the button under the one Belle had chosen. The door closed. Silas said, "Thank you, I'm better now."

"Look at the monitors. Anything look familiar to anyone?"

"You were right, Warren, we are inside the rock formation and the bees Sy heard are the ones from the giant hive near the flowering vines."

"I believe you are correct. I think the doorway for the vehicle will lead to a path behind the thicket of rose bushes on the other side of the formation."

"Unbelievable," Silas said as he looked at the monitors. "You can see the entire picnic and pond areas and then some, quite the bird's-eye view."

"Whoever set all this up wanted to make sure they could come and go without anyone seeing them. This setup ensures that. They can see quite well if anyone is around when they want to exit. We have to figure out why. What were they doing?"

"I can't imagine anyone exiting past the bees," said Silas.

"Well, Sy, they probably waited until dusk or dark to do so, when the bees go in the hive for the night, which could explain why there are lights at the picnic area and on the path back to house. Look at this screen. The rose thicket looks like it might not be too close to the car path, so they could exit on that side during the day without disturbing those bees."

"How far does your property line run from here?"

"I'm not sure exactly, Warren, but we are close to Center property. Remember, all the land surrounding my property is owned by them."

"I think maybe someone from the Center is involved," Silas said, "but then again why did they let you buy the property? It could be that they thought you would never find the doorway in the tack room."

"I didn't. Mark discovered it. If he hadn't been where he was at the time, doing what he was doing, we wouldn't be here. Not much is making sense; I doubt anyone from the Center knows about this though."

Starlit was in the house playing with Willow while she was waiting to hear from the others. She had the urge to call them ten minutes after they had gone. She struggled to contain that urge and overcame it. Willow was a good distraction and so were a couple of the kitties who decided they wanted to play also. Play had led throughout the house and now they were back in the living room.

Starlit wanted to sit for a little and chose the recliner. After a few minutes she opened the drawer containing the object and took it out. Her eyes started to focus on the markings on it. Seeing the object in Starlit's hand, Willow let out a little yip. "This is not a ball for you to play with," she told Willow, "it's hard and heavy. Now I'm sure you understood every word I just said; I'll just get you a chew toy."

After returning with the chew for Willow, Starlit continued to examine the object. She could not believe her eyes and said out loud, "My goodness, is that possible! Is this what I think it is? Oh my!" The longer she looked at it the more sure she was. What she was seeing started to make sense. The lines and squiggles on the object were shorthand, and since she knew shorthand, she knew how to read what it spelled out.

Astonished with her discovery, Starlit bolted to the kitchen where she left her phone.

Belle answered her phone and put it on speaker: "Hi Star, we were just about to leave and I was going to call you on the way out. I want you to come and see what we found. Please come…"

Starlit interrupted, "I would love to," she said with excitement, "I can't wait, hurry back!" Then she hung up on Belle.

They were amazed at Starlit's response. Warren said, "I am flabbergasted."

Silas said, "Speechless here," and Belle said, "Ditto!" Belle's phone rang again. "Hello, Star." "Belle, I discovered something amazing, I'll show you all when you get here!" Then Starlit hung up abruptly again.

"Makes a little more sense now, knowing something is up."

"That is intriguing," Warren said.

"Still speechless," added Silas. "We better go," said Belle, "I want to see what she found, she's really excited, must be good."

Belle got into the car while the guys made sure the monitors were off. Warren got in the car and Silas stood against it again. Warren pushed the button that would send them down. The floor turned slowly, changing the direction the car was facing, hesitated then began to descend. It seemed to take longer to go down than it did to go up. Finally, they were at the bottom and hurried to get off the elevator.

"We should take the other car back with us."

"Which one of us will pedal it back," Silas said with a chuckle.

"Warren, I would like to drive and Sy can have a turn driving as well," said Belle.

"Yes, that is feasible," he replied. "Silas, you can drive the single and I will be Belle's passenger."

"Great, let's go, I can't wait to see what Star found. And I also want to know where she found it."

"Is the car charged enough, Sy?"

"It is," he said, "lead the way."

Back at the basement they parked the cars and hurried to the ladder. Belle pushed the button to open the doorway and went up first. When she arrived in the tack room Starlit was not there. She looked around but Starlit was nowhere in the barn.

The guys came and stood next to Belle. "I thought for sure Star would be waiting for us in the tack room, Belle."

"I did too Sy, since she was hyped up about something."

"This is concerning," Warren said, as he started to exit the barn.

"I hope she's all right," said Belle.

Warren was ahead of the others and was opening the door to the house already. Belle began calling to Starlit as she and Silas approached the house. The moment Warren entered the living room, Starlit heard Belle calling her name. She was sitting on the floor in the living room with a note pad and a pencil. She looked up and said, "You're back!"

"We are. We expected to see you waiting in the barn and became concerned when you were not there. What are you doing?"

"Star, thank goodness you're okay, you scared me."

"Yeah," said Silas, "we expected to see you in the tack room since you were worked up over something. What's going on?"

She began to explain: "I was playing with the dog and a couple of kitties. I decided to take a break, so I sat in Belle's recliner. Eventually I took the object out of the drawer and began looking at it. The markings stood out to me all of a sudden. Look at this." She showed them the pad.

"Why did you draw the markings on the pad?" Silas asked, "and what are the letters for?"

Warren smiled and said, "Shorthand, excellent, Star, excellent!"

"That is amazing, what do they spell out?"

"I had to be sure, so I wrote it out to clarify what I thought. There are letters that spell out small words, like 'at,' but the letters are far apart from each other as with some of the others. There is one word which is repeated twice where the letters are close together, meaning it is the main word."

Belle shouted excitedly, "What is it, what is it?!" Starlit turned the page over, covering the word with her finger, allowing only the shorthand markings to show at first. Silas made a drum roll sound on the side of the end table and when he stopped, Starlit removed her finger and the word "key" appeared.

"Wow, a key! It's a key; a key to what and to where?"

Warren said, "In time we will know. Indeed, this is progress."

Belle reached out her hand and Starlit placed the object in it.

"That would have to be a pretty big keyhole," Silas commented.

"Belle look at the flat spot. The word 'key' is there," Starlit said. "It runs vertical with the *K* at the top. When you hold it facing you, the other one is to your left on the side of the object."

"I don't see it. The markings don't look the same."

That's because the word is spelled backward. I don't know what that means but it is definitely y-e-k close together, 'key' backwards."

"Other than the sundial do any of you recall seeing these marks anywhere?"

"No, Warren, I haven't noticed any."

"Me either, but I will keep my eyes peeled," Silas answered.

"I second that," Starlit said, "and like Silas, I thought the keyhole must be big, even if only a quarter of this object were to be inserted into it."

"Perhaps it is not a key but an answer key."

"What do you mean, Warren?"

"Star mentioned other words appear on the object. They may spell out a location for example." Warren then picked up the paper Starlit wrote on, handed it to Belle and said, "Please make copies for all of us. We will see if we can decipher a message."

Immediately they began working on their project. They were confident that in a little while a message would be revealed or a location would be spelled out. There were very few actual words though, only consisting of two or three letters. No one was able to make a sentence or come up with another word of any significance. It seemed as though they were just a couple of random words. Sighs and sounds of disappointment could be heard. Enthusiasm began to fade. "I'm done," said Silas, "I need a cookie."

"Must you," replied Starlit.

"We should take a break," Warren said.

Belle said, "Good idea. I could munch on something myself and I think we all need something to snack on."

Belle put some cheese, crackers, fruit, nuts, milk, and cookies on the dining room table. She placed some pistachios and cashews on her plate along with some cheese. The others chose what they wanted and all of them sat there eating quietly. There were expressions of deep thought on each of their faces as they ate.

"You know," said Starlit, "I admit I did need something to eat and feel much better now. We'll figure this key thing out eventually, like Warren said."

"Maybe it's actually a key that will fit something, somewhere, somehow."

"Maybe, Belle, I can't wait to see what you guys found; this is exciting, when do we leave?"

"You have a sparkle in your eyes, Star, so does this mean you're on board?"

"I am, Sy. I don't want to sit around. We came out here to be together. I want to be with you guys, spending time together is important. This is an adventure I also want to be a part of."

"Whoa!" Silas exclaimed. "The team is back together: the Hawk, the Bat, the Hound and the Elephant! Woohoo!"

"Remember, Sy, call me Elle," Starlit said, as they all high-fived each other.

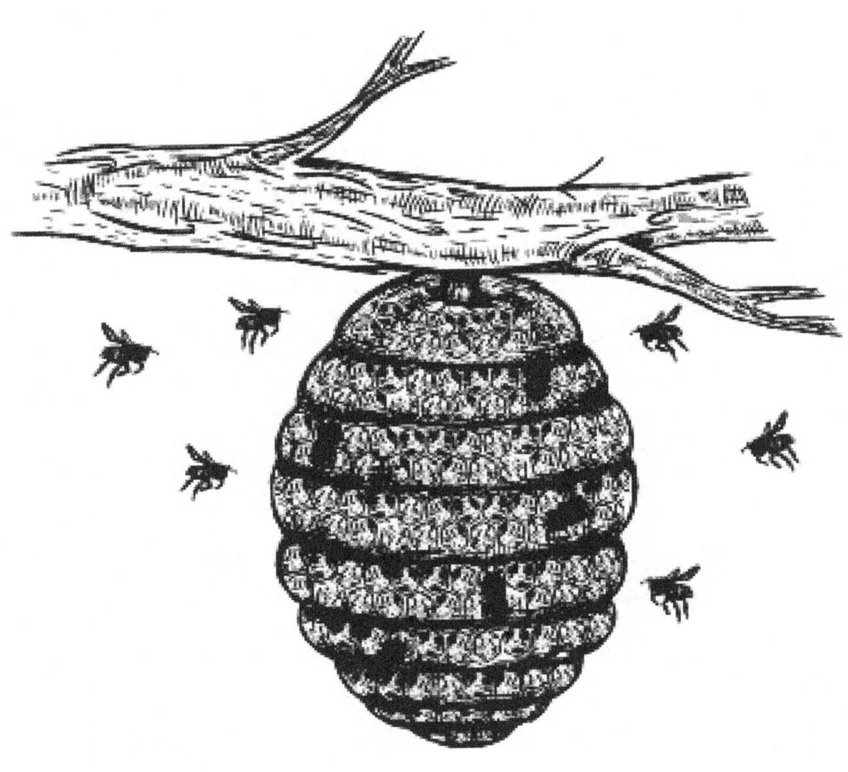

EIGHTEEN

THE TEAM GATHERED THEIR BELONGINGS and went into the barn. Belle made sure to take the object with her. The plan was to show Starlit what they had found and see if they could find a way to open the door that closed on Silas from the outside. They assumed the garage door in the formation room would open with the remote. Belle told Starlit they found another car. When Starlit saw the single car she said, "Who pedaled it back?" Everyone laughed.

"The Bat can drive the single and I will ride in its trailer," Warren said. "You ladies can take the double."

"Would you like to drive, Elle?"

"No Hound, you go ahead, I'm not ready to do that but maybe on the way back." Then she said, "This is weird, calling each other these names after so many years. I feel like since we're adults now we shouldn't, but it is fun."

"There is nothing wrong with a little merrymaking to amuse oneself during times of mystery solving. It can divert stress therefore, let us have fun."

"Fun, well, brother that sounded hard to spit out but I agree, Hawk, we should not get stressed, and so fun it is."

"Do not make me regret using that word, brother Bat," Warren said with a chuckle. The girls laughed while Silas shook his head side to side with a huge grin on his face. Then laughing he said, "Of course not, Hawk; don't stress over it, ha ha haa..."

The cars were lined up in front of the garage door with Belle and Starlit in the lead. Warren opened the door and turned on the lights. As they began going forward Starlit said, "This is a small tunnel, I thought it would be bigger. What happens if you want to turn around?"

"You have to go to the end where there is a space to do that. I suppose you could try backing up, but I wouldn't want to attempt it."

"I'm glad the tunnel has dim lights or it would seem a lot smaller in the dark."

They had just passed through the curve in the tunnel when something changed. Belle stopped. Warren got out of the trailer. He looked behind them, then ahead as he walked over to the other car. Silas got out of the car and followed. "Why are there yellow lights flashing, Hound?" asked Starlit.

"I don't know, Elle, that didn't happen the first time."

"Ladies, stay in the car. We will wait a few moments then move on," Warren instructed.

The flashing yellow lights had long pauses between flashes, which Belle stated made her happy or it would get annoying. The lights were small and located a few inches away from the lights at the top of the tunnel. They were not noticed by anyone previously since they were not on. Nothing was happening; they decided to continue on.

Warren sat facing backward in the trailer instead of sideways as before in order to keep an eye out behind them. They made it to the end of the tunnel without a problem and stopped.

Starlit did the same thing Belle had done; she walked over to the floor, leaned forward and looked up with her mouth open in disbelief. There were yellow lights flashing up the tunnel as well. The mom in her started to rise and began battling with the curious kid in her. She blurted out, "We will go on and be extra cautious, that's all."

"Are you okay, Star, umm I mean Elle?"

"Yes Hound, just fighting a little urge to be overprotective."

"That's why you're the elephant, remember? Female elephants have a strong protective motherly instinct. You have a sixth sense of sorts, too. We're counting on that for this uh, adventure."

"I think I'm a little rusty in that department, but I'll try to get in tune."

"Ladies, time to proceed. Hound, you and Elle drive onto the floor. We will walk on.

"After we get up, Hawk, I'll come back down for the single."

"No, Bat, remember; no separating!"

"Okay, Elle, I suppose it can wait for now anyway," he said.

While traveling up the tunnel purple lights came on next to the yellow flashing ones. Those did not flash, they stayed on steadily. Warren and Silas looked at each other. Belle looked in the rearview mirror at Starlit; no one said a word.

When they reached their destination and had exited the elevator into the room, Starlit said, "Someone is here." She turned slowly, looking over the room, then said, "Oh this is quite a cave!"

"There is no one here," Silas said, "you can plainly see it's just us. Why did you say that?"

"I think her sixth sense might have just kicked in. That was fast, Elle."

"I'm still getting that sense of presence."

"Hawk, turn on the monitors please." Starlit said, "Monitors?"

"Yes," answered Silas, "let me give you a quick tour."

Silas showed her the monitors and controls and walked her over to an area where they could park the single car. He showed her the doorway that he had gone through and explained where it led and about the bees. Back by the monitors now, which were on, she looked at them with wide eyes. One of them had a tiny flashing yellow light on it and another had a steady purple light. On those two screens she could see something moving.

"Your instinct was correct, Elle; there is a presence outside."

"That is amazing, Hawk, she's a keeper," said Silas.

"Indeed, Bat, she is," Warren replied. Then he said, "There are people in the picnic area. The light on that monitor is yellow, however the light on this one where there are deer is purple. The people in the picnic area are closer to this formation than the deer; my conclusion is this: The yellow light is a warning of someone or something in close proximity while the purple light is alerting of someone or something in the distance. This makes it possible to see when it is safe to exit, if indeed that is the intention. In our case, at the moment we cannot exit as we intended."

"Where do you think the cameras are, Hawk?"

"I believe on top of this formation, which would give a three hundred sixty-degree view of the area. See here, I can zoom in. Do you recognize them, Hound?"

"Yes, they are from the Center. It's way after lunchtime though. Something probably came up and they had to postpone lunch. When that happens, we usually get to add time to our lunch. It seems like they're just getting started so maybe we should go back since they could be there up to forty-five minutes. Maybe in the meantime we should go to the other tunnel and come back here later."

On the way back Silas and Warren led the way; Belle insisted. She said since there was no danger it would be okay. Starlit wanted to drive and did not want to feel pressured by someone following her. Belle and Starlit began to fall behind. There came a point where the distance between the cars increased greatly but they could still see the taillights of the other car.

Suddenly Belle told Starlit to stop. Something caught her eye as she looked up when the purple light went out. "Get out, let me out, hurry."

"Bat, the girls have stopped and are out of the car, slow down."

"That's a good thing, Hawk. Hound is probably not happy about crawling and they're going to switch. They should catch up in a couple of minutes once Hound is driving. If not, we'll stop."

"Make sure you have your flashlight, Elle."

"What for? I'm staying next to the car. What are you doing?"

"I saw something on the ceiling by the yellow light back there. I happened to look up after the purple light went out. As we passed under the next light I was still looking up and I think I saw a marking. It's just a few feet back, come on."

"I'll wait here. Tell me if you're sure when you find it and I'll come over."

Belle shone her flashlight up at the ceiling near the yellow light. There was a mark, a symbol. It was the shorthand mark for the letter *E*. Belle moved her light around searching for another mark but could not find one. She walked in the direction they had just come from, as far back as the past two ceiling lights, still nothing. She began to shine her light on the walls, zigzagging back and forth between the two sides of the tunnel as she headed back to the car.

Belle stopped at the darkest point in between two lights. She was very close to one wall. As she turned to look over her shoulder, wondering if she should have gone further back, she tripped and fell through the wall. "Ooh. Whoops! Oww! Oh my gosh what happened? Where am I?" Starlit was looking in the opposite direction at that moment. She turned and did not see Belle. Starlit called out, "Hound, where are you?"

Not quite sure where she was, Belle shone her light around the small dark space. Starlit called out again. Belle answered, "Over here."

Starlit walked over to the sound of Belle's voice. Belle could tell Starlit was standing in front of her as Starlit called her a third time, but they could not see each other. Belle softly said, "Elle, I'm right here." "Where? This is not funny, you're scaring me."

"It's fun, you'll see. Which way are you facing?"

"I'm looking at our car."

"Turn to your left and look at the wall."

"Okay, Hound, I'm looking at it."

"Hold out your hand and walk toward the wall. Now what do you see?"

"Eeek! A hand, now it's gone!" Starlit retracted her hand instantly, placing it against her chest then grasped it with her other one. Then she shrieked in a high-pitched voice, "Belle!"

Belle began to giggle. She put her hand out again, her palm facing up, fingers folded in with the index finger extended. Then she moved her finger in a beckoning motion.

"Hound, is that you?"

Giggling she answered, "It is, Elle, trust me, come closer and put out your hand again."

Slowly Starlit walked toward the wall asking, "What is going on? How is this happening?" As Starlit got closer to the wall Belle reached out, grabbed her hand, and pulled her through the wall. Starlit screamed, "Belle!"

"It's okay, Star, calm down, look. Relax, okay, back in character. This is exciting; it's a hiding place, Elle!"

Meanwhile the guys passed through the curve in the tunnel and stopped when they did not see headlights from the other car. They did not wait long.

"Bat, we are going back now," Warren said, as he got out of the trailer.

"I could back this up, Hawk."

"No, on foot, now, it will be faster." Warren reached for his phone and called Belle.

"Hellooo."

"Hound, are you ladies well? Is the car running?"

"We're good, the car is good. We found something and stopped to check it out. I was about to call you." As the guys approached the car Warren said, "We are near the car, where are you?"

Just then she hung up the phone and poked Starlit. She whispered in her ear, "Now it's your turn to have fun, Elle, they're almost here."

Starlit called out, slowly in a deep tone, "Bat, this is your conscience speaking."

"Did you hear that, Hawk?"

He smiled and answered, "I should not be able to hear your conscience, therefore, no."

They moved closer to where the girls were and Silas called out, "Where are you hiding, conscience?"

"You're getting warmer." There were a few minutes of silence, then he said, "Too long, not funny, where are you?"

Starlit giggled, "Right here and having fun—remember fun, Bat? Follow the sound of my voice."

"Am I getting warmer?"

"That's the spirit, Bat, keep talking." Softly Belle said, as he got closer to them, "Warmer, very warm." Starlit said, "Hot," as he neared their location. Then he called out, "Olly olly, oxen free, come out, come out wherever you are." Belle and Starlit laughed.

"I believe we're standing in front of Hound and Elle," Silas said, pointing to the wall in front of the girls. "I detect the voices are coming from right here, Hawk." Then he said, "There must be a door," as he moved forward almost against the wall.

"Nope, guess again."

"Come on, Hound, open the door."

"I cannot open any door since it's not a door."

"A porthole perhaps."

"Yes, Hawk," said Belle. "Oh, a porthole," Bat repeated.

"Yes," said Warren with a grin, then pushing Silas he said, "Watch your step, Bat." " Whoooaa," he yelled as he stumbled through the wall, "what in the world?"

The girls were laughing as they steadied him. "Okay," said Silas, "I admit I enjoyed that."

"I as well," came from the other side of the wall. "Look," Belle said, to Starlit, pointing to the wall. Floating and waving in the air to capture their attention was a hand. A voice asked, "May I come in?"

"Please, join us, Hawk but it will be a bit tight." He entered saying, "Your porthole, Hound, is a holographic image which makes the wall of the tunnel appear to be there, concealing the actual lack of a wall, the opening."

Standing in the hidden hollow they all wondered why it was there. Warren surmised it was hiding a secret entrance. Silas asked him why he thought that. Warren shone his flashlight on a portion of the wall next to where Silas was standing. One by one they leaned closer to see what the light revealed. "This is incredible," Starlit said. "Is it really possible?"

"I thought it was far-fetched, Hound," Silas said, "but apparently that is a keyhole, well, opening, that would accommodate the key you have."

Belle reached into her pocket and took out the object. She looked at it briefly then said, "Here we go," as she attempted to place the object into the rounded indentation in the wall. It immediately fell out. She quickly caught it before it could fall to the ground. Warren said, "Try placing the object with the flat portion facing in." Belle turned the object and did as he said, and as the object got closer to it, it was sucked out of her hand.

"Uuhh, oh my, Hawk!" It stuck in the wall and with great anticipation they looked around for something to open. Nothing happened.

"I'll try again." Belle pulled on the object and was met with resistance. She pulled a little harder and it released. "That's odd, I don't know why it did that. Maybe this time I should push on it as I place it in."

"Permit me please," Warren said. "I would like to test a theory."

Belle handed him the object. When he held it close to the indentation, he could feel the pull on it. He held on to the object as it went into the space, then he gently pulled back on it. Feeling the resistance, he finally let go of it and said, "I suspected the object or keyhole might be magnetized. I am right."

Belle pushed in on the object and still nothing happened. Starlit asked, "Now what?"

"Try again," Silas said. "This time place the object in and pull it out right away." Belle pulled the object out and tried it the way Silas suggested, with no results.

"I want to take a break," Starlit said. "Just for a few minutes, it's cramped in here and I'm thirsty."

After stepping into the tunnel Belle took a marker out of her backpack and made a small smudge mark on the ground. The car was only a few feet away, but she wanted to make sure they could find the entrance again, especially if they should leave. It was decided that if they left the area, the time and miles would be logged to help locate it again for their return. For now, they were staying. With their fill of snacks and their thirst quenched they were ready for another attempt.

"We should proceed with this endeavor now, Hound."

"I'm ready, Hawk."

"Very well then, I will accompany you to the keyhole. Bat and Elle, stay close to the tunnel portion of the hollow to provide a little more space for us. Please keep watch in the tunnel from time to time. In we go."

"Hound, remember, position the flat portion like earlier."

"Yes Hawk, I will, and I'll put it in the keyhole slowly this time"

"Nothing is happening. What is this mark facing me? Could it mean something? Elle, look at this. What letter is it?"

"It is the letter *I* but the symbol is upside down. Take the object out and turn it. That's better, now the symbol is in the correct position. I don't know if it matters though; an *I* looks the same either way."

"Ladies, it matters. The letter *K* is now at the top. The symbols spelling out 'key' will line up with whatever is on the other side of the wall. It is most likely encoded and when read, activates what is behind the wall. I believe a combination lock is there. We must figure out the correct sequence of turns to open a doorway."

"Hawk, we can't see how many numbers are back there."

"We must work with what we can see and what we know, Bat. When making the first turn on a combination lock which direction do you usually turn it?"

"You turn it to the right."

"Correct, Hound. What follows?"

"You would then turn left, then right, and that is the last turn."

"Correct again. What else do we know?"

"Well, Hawk, the symbols spell out 'key' on the object, which is three letters."

"Yes, Bat, what else?"

"You just turn it three times I guess."

"But like right, left, right."

"Yes, Hound. I suspect it is a simple combination and would like to try it as one-two-three. Place the object in the keyhole. Move it one full turn right, two turns left, three turns right."

Upon completion Belle took her hand off the object, leaving it in place. Above the keyhole a small panel opened up. "Oh no," Belle said. Placing her hands to her face and closing her eyes she dropped her head, shaking it side to side and repeating, "Oh no."

Silas said, "Great! That's great. I thought that sounded too easy; this could take a while." Starlit let out a long loud sigh.

NINETEEN

WHEN THE PANEL OPENED A HIDDEN keypad was revealed. They tried different combinations of the one-two-three numbers but were unsuccessful. Each sensed the frustration the others were feeling. So close but not close enough; they wanted in now, not an hour from now or tomorrow. As they were trying the different combinations, they speculated what might be inside the hidden room. Some comments were made jokingly in an attempt to alleviate their frustration.

"What else can we try? We worked with what we knew, even trying the combinations backward like the backward word key. That was a good suggestion, Elle."

"Thanks, Hound. I really thought that would work. It must be there on the object for a reason."

"Hound, pen and paper please," Warren asked.

"What are you thinking?"

"Perhaps, Bat, the letters of the word key correlate to numbers," Warren answered. "The numbers would then be the code."

"Great thinking, Hawk!"

Warren wrote out numbers up to twenty-six, then under each one of them he wrote a letter of the alphabet. He drew a rectangle around each letter that spelled out the word 'key' along with the number above it. The letter *K* matched up with number eleven, the *E* matched up with number five and the *Y* with number twenty-five. The combination: 11-5-25. They all cheered.

The numbers on the keypad only went up to nine; there was no zero or symbols. Belle's mind immediately assessed what needed to be done and she quickly began entering the combination. She pushed the number one twice to make eleven, then pressed five, then two and five for twenty-five. Expecting to see a doorway open she threw her hands up, waving her arms and shouting, "Wooohooo!"

"I said Woohoo yoo-hoo, yoo-hoo, door, where are you?" Then she shouted, "How about: Open Sez Me. Uhh!" Disappointed, Belle said, "I don't want to give up."

Warren put his hand on her shoulder and said, "You pushed eleven, five, twenty-five, now do it again; then push twenty-five, five, eleven without pause."

"Of course," she said perking up, "the 'yek'!" Silas and Starlit joined in with Belle and they all said, "The backward key!"

The door opened. Slowly, together, as if they were one unit they moved slightly forward and then stopped. Warren's arm extended out in front of Belle as if to stop her from going further. Stunned, frozen a moment, the others could not lift their arms; the light from the flashlights shone on the ground. Their hearts began racing. Adrenaline was pumping in each of them, preparing the body for the flight or fight response.

Belle felt as if the others could hear her heart pounding. The air was moist and cold; dank. Before them in the darkness were eerie, glowing-green ghostly shapes. Some were just mere specks, not so intimidating while others were large and frightening. The odd shapes were suspended at different levels. There were long ones that lay vertical and horizontal, arm-like without fingers. These were suspended higher than some blob-like ones. There was a large orb off to one side that emanated brightly enough to read by. It was not only brighter but a slightly different shade of green. Were they seeing otherworldly beings? Was the large orb their superior? Was it some kind of supernatural phenomenon right in front of them? No one moved as they watched and waited to see if any of the "ghosts" would move or react in some way. Just then the door started to close; even though they were not on the threshold, as one unit again they moved slightly backward.

They stood in silence. Belle was taking long slow breaths in through her nose and letting them out her mouth, trying to calm herself. Actual words eluded Starlit and Silas. Each of them was still processing what their eyes had taken in. No one expected this turn in the investigation. It did not seem to fit along the line of what they had discovered so far.

Eventually Silas managed to say something. "Wow, floating things."

"Glowing green things," Starlit added.

"Astonishing," Warren said.

There was silence again. Whispering, Belle asked, "Other thoughts—anyone?"

Starlit whispered to Belle, "Why are you whispering?"

"Why are *you*?"

"Because you are—do you think they can hear us through a closed door?"

"I doubt it," Silas said. "I couldn't see a lot from behind you guys, how many were there?"

"I didn't count. Did you, Hawk?"

"No, I was attempting to determine what I was seeing. I can tell you, Bat, that there was a very large one off to the side. The green color was a little different than the others."

"I say we go in and I would like to switch places with you, Hound, so I can see better."

"We can swap, Bat, but I might want to wait to go in, you guys can go on."

"I second that," Starlit said.

Starlit and Belle were a little apprehensive but had to know what was in there, so they finally agreed to go along. Warren entered the combination. When the door opened the unit moved forward again, stopping just over the threshold this time. They waited. Nothing moved or made a sound.

Starlit softly said, "Anyone care to set a light on one of those things? I'm not sure I really want to know what they are; maybe we should just leave instead."

Silas teased her and whispered, "If we leave, we should do it quietly and slowly, running could trigger a chase response."

She replied, "You're not scaring me, I-I well, was kind of scared already but that was cute."

Belle said, "I smell dirt, it's a little musty and damp. Something's familiar, I'm thinking it could be something edible."

Warren said, "All lights up, please."

As the lights shone on the ghosts, they grew dim. "Interesting," he said as they focused on the source of the ghosts. Starlit said, "I'm not quite sure this is real." Warren replied, "I assure you it is."

Silas located a light switch. Turning the lights on caused the ghosts to disappear and revealed a small room. Belle was right about smelling dirt. There were two dirt-filled troughs that went vertical into the room and one along the back wall of the room. "Another puzzle piece," Warren said.

"I can't imagine why these are here and why they were glowing," Silas said.

"Still have a great sniffer," Starlit said to Belle.

The something maybe edible Belle could smell, well that would be mushrooms! The armlike mushrooms were in the trough along the back wall growing in tight clusters on branches placed into the dirt. Other mushrooms in that trough were in the dirt directly.

"I would not want to eat these mushrooms," Starlit said, "I might glow too."

"You may be onto something," Warren said. "I read somewhere that scientists use fluorescence-infused dyes that bind to specific areas in a cell to reveal its structure. Perhaps a way was discovered to use bioluminescence to identify or reveal something within a cell or even an organ. We know there is a laboratory under the barn and blood was drawn from the horses, therefore a strong possibility exists. I do not know what was being sought, however this small work area has supplies for collecting specimens and transporting them in these small boxes. I believe the mushrooms are harvested then taken to the laboratory, processed, then again with chemicals, thus creating a formula that could be utilized to identify whatever it is the culprits were looking for."

"Or maybe creating," Silas said, "that could be a possibility too."

"They look like regular mushrooms. It's hard to believe they glow in the dark and harder to believe they're used for experiments. This is more serious than I was realizing or maybe it was just denial, but I'm even more concerned than before about my critters," said Belle.

"I am too," Starlit said as she poked a mushroom. "We've all touched some of these; do you think our fingers will glow?"

"Not likely," answered Warren.

"I'll shut off the lights," Silas said. When he turned off the lights the room was aglow with eerie ghostly green forms again. He asked, "Any glowing fingers?"

All answered no and as he said, "Not mine either," he turned the lights back on.

Warren said, "Not likely confirmed. The bioluminescence in these fungi is more commonly found in marine organisms but there are over eighty species of these fungi found on earth."

In unison the others said, "You read that somewhere," and chuckled.

He smiled and said, "There is also bioluminescence found in an insect, the firefly."

Belle and Starlit said at the same time, "Lightning bugs!"

"I remember we would catch them and keep them in jars with holes punched in the lids so they could breathe." Starlit finished Belle's thought: "We would watch them for a while then fall asleep, and in the morning we would let them go."

Silas commented, "Then you would catch more again that night instead of keeping the ones you had a little longer."

"We didn't want them to get hungry, and since we didn't know what to feed them, we let them go so they could find food."

That conversation lightened the mood a little for a short time. Belle was concerned about her critters. She wanted answers about their unwilling participation in any experiments. Anomaly and

Rarity seemed to be fine. Would they stay that way? She wanted to move on to see what else they might discover. Belle told the others, "I kind of want to go back to our names, for now, anyway. I'm not feeling like this is fun right now, so no team names, but we are a team. We do manage to lessen the stress of things with some of our pleasant memories. We make each other laugh. We support each other with who we are. I love you guys. Thank you for being with me in this." Then she began to weep softly.

Starlit embraced her and held her a long time.

"I wonder if there are more hidden rooms and how many," Silas said as he walked around the little room. "This is some setup, timers, temperature and humidity controls... We should go. If we drive slowly and shine lights on the walls and ceiling of the tunnel, Warren, maybe we will find more symbols that mark other locations."

"We need to start somewhere, Silas, that is a good plan. Belle, are you ready to move on?"

"Yes Warren, let's go." She wiped the tears from her eyes, took a deep breath and said, "Okay, moving; go, legs."

They first drove back in the direction of the elevator. Everyone looked intently at the ceiling and the walls on both sides of the tunnel all the way to the elevator and did the same on the way back to the point where they had found the hidden entrance. A couple at a time searched on foot, pressing on the walls as they moved along and hoping to have a hand disappear inside while the others stayed in the cars, rolling slowly along.

Now they were past the hidden entrance and heading in the direction of the barn. Starlit was walking ahead of the others at this point. Every now and then she would duck and swat at the air.

"What is she doing?"

Starlit swatted the air and called out, "Bat!"

Silas answered, "I haven't found anything, you?"

"I thought we were not using the team names right now."

"I'm not," Starlit said, "just warning you that there are bats, the animal kind, flying around."

"What! Guys, do you see anything?"

"Nothing," Silas answered.

"No, Belle, neither do I. I have not seen anything unusual. I believe Star is tired, perhaps ill; she appears to walk off balance at times."

"Star, stop, wait up. Are you okay?"

"I'm not feeling well," she answered. Her eyes looked glazed over. Warren said, "I do believe we should go home now."

"I don't want you guys to stop on account of me. Just take me back so I can lie down for a while."

"Maybe you have a fever, you shouldn't be alone."

"No, it's okay, really, then you can pick up where you left off."

As they approached the house Starlit commented on the pretty butterflies near the bushes. There were none there really, but she saw them. Belle took Starlit's temperature, but she did not have a fever. She did say she was feeling slightly nauseous, had a headache and that her head felt weird. All she wanted was to lie on the couch.

Belle went to the guest room to get a blanket and pillow for her. Belle told Starlit that her phone was on the end table, and she would call her in an hour to check on her. She emphasized Starlit should not hesitate to call them if she felt worse or needed anything. After getting Starlit settled the rest of them took a little break before heading back to search the tunnel. It was late, almost evening.

Belle's phone rang. She reached for it quickly, answering, "How are you?"

"I'm feeling a little better, Belle. I just woke up. It's five minutes before the hour was up so I thought I'd call you first. How are things with you guys, any luck?"

"No, so we're going up to the formation room now to look for a hidden room there. After that we'll be back and have dinner."

"Sounds good, see you all soon and I'll tell you about my odd dream at dinner. I think the dream lasted the entire time I was asleep. It was about the kitties, very odd; I'll tell you later."

"Okay, bye."

Starlit freshened up and went to see the other kitties. Cuddles had slept with her on the couch while Pouncer and Bunkie slept on the love seat with Willow snuggled next to Pouncer. It was comforting to know that they stayed with her. Starlit said hello to Micro, Squirrel, Fluff Girly, Pirate, Candy and Cautious with a hug. She seemed to be examining the critters as she petted each one. Her odd dream about them was still fresh in her mind as she contemplated it.

Only a few minutes had passed when she heard the dogs barking, then the house phone rang. She left the kitties and headed toward the kitchen. The dogs were still barking so she went and looked out the window.

There was a car at the gate with its window down. When she peeked through the curtains the driver saw her and began waving his phone out his window. At the same time the phone stopped ringing.

She recognized Cypress, walked over to the control on the wall and opened the gate for him. As he drove in, she could see someone was with him. Starlit opened the door and waited to greet them.

"Hello Cy, come in."

"This is my cousin Ben; Ben, this is Star."

"Come sit in the living room. The others are out on a hike; sorry you missed them. I wasn't feeling well so I came back. I just woke up a few minutes ago; let me get these off the couch, I'll be back in a minute." Starlit took the blanket and pillow back to the guest room. Afterwards she went to the kitchen, placed cookies and three glasses of iced tea on a tray, and returned to the living room.

Both the guys said thank you, then Cypress began to speak. "I took a chance that you guys would be here; I figured you wouldn't be though. I wanted to show Ben Belle's place so we just figured we would drive past and look at it. If anyone was home, then we would stop in and visit for a few."

"Yeah, and I had some questions that Cy thought you all could answer," said Ben.

"Okay," said Starlit, "maybe I can help."

Cypress tried to speak but was obviously uncomfortable; Ben took over. "I wanted to hear about this Christian thing. Cy wasn't quite sure how to explain it."

"I see," she said, "I'll do my best to explain."

"Well, a Christian is someone who believes that there is a God. They believe God created the universe and everything in it, including us. He sets the rules. God is holy and pure, we are not. We are sinners and that sin separates us from Him. Jesus, His son, God the Son, came to earth in human form. Jesus left His heavenly throne and willingly came to earth to be an atoning sacrifice for our sin, dying for our sin and dying for us in our place. He saved us from eternal suffering in hell. This is taught in the Bible and the Bible is God's written word. It was written by the hand of men, but the words came down from heaven given by the Holy Spirit of God. When we acknowledge by confessing to Him we are sinners, asking for his forgiveness, thanking Him for dying for us and asking Him into our lives, we are saved and born again spiritually. We are no longer separated from God.

"Jesus bridged the gap between us and the Father. Now we are reconciled to Him and can have a relationship with Him. It's not about religion or traditions, but the relationship, which is what God desires, He loves us. We can't do any kind of work to get to heaven, however, in light of what Jesus did for us on the cross we desire to do good works. Salvation is a gift from God. Christians are not perfect people and will never be, not this side of eternity anyway. It's necessary to get into fellowship with other Christians and be in a church that teaches God's word, all of it. Also, because we're Christians doesn't mean life will be perfect now. There are difficulties in life, but we turn to Him for help. We have to make a choice. No one is saved and a Christian because he goes to church or because they're born into a Christian family or born in the United States. Anyone can pray anywhere and ask for forgiveness; they don't have to be in a church to ask Jesus into their lives..."

TWENTY

THEY CONTINUED TO TALK AWHILE. Ben had some questions; Cypress just sat there listening. The others arrived back home. When they came out of the barn Belle recognized Cypress's car. This was most unexpected, and she was disappointed. Any other time she would not have felt this way but under the circumstances, she did. They did not find another hidden room but did discover something, and now they would have to wait to share it with Starlit.

"Before we go in would you please help me get the outside critters fed and watered? It might be a late night and I don't want to take care of them late."

They approached the house. As Belle opened the door she called out, "Hello everyone, we're back." As they entered the living room she said, "Hey Cy, surprised to see you, what's up?"

"Hi Belle, this is my cousin Ben."

"That's Warren and Silas. Silas goes by Sy, S-y."

"Hi all," Ben said. "So how come the *y* in your name, Sy, not S-i?"

"I liked the way it looked," he answered, "it pronounces and sounds as an *I*, like in the words apply and fly so, S-y."

"I see, anyway, it's my fault for the intrusion. I had some questions about what a Christian was and Tree-man—sorry, I mean Cy—suggested you guys could help."

"Tree-man, I like Ben already!" Silas said.

Starlit pointed her finger at Silas and with a little smile said, "Don't start Sy, behave." Then she said, "Yes, they thought we would be out but Cy wanted to show Ben the house, so they drove over. I happened to be here, and we've had a nice conversation."

"Wonderful," Warren said. "What have you learned, Benjamin?"

"Guys, stay for dinner. It won't take long to prepare. I'll defrost some homemade sauce and boil up some ravioli. We'll have salad, a veggie and garlic bread."

"Thank you, Belle, sounds great," Cypress said.

"It sure does," said Ben, "thanks."

Starlit set the dining room table then helped Belle in the kitchen. The guys engaged in conversation along the lines set up by Starlit. Dinner was done quickly, and a mouth-watering aroma filled the house.

Ben heard a bell ringing and jokingly asked, "Is that the dinner bell?"

Warren answered, "Indeed it is," as he patted him on the back.

Silas said, "Belle enjoys ringing it to let people know it's time to eat, a habit she developed that I like."

"It is different," Ben said, "but I like it too."

The Christian conversation concluded during dinner and then the conversation became more general. They talked about Belle's property and critters. There was mention of the Center and each had a little say about themselves. No one desired dessert since the meal was very filling. The girls began yawning.

"I'm sorry, excuse me," Starlit said. "I know I took a nap but I'm still feeling tired."

"I'm tired from a long hike, sorry, guys."

"We'll help clear the table, Belle," Cypress said. "It's the least we could do since showing up unannounced."

"Yes," said Ben. "Dinner was very good, thank you for your hospitality."

"You're welcome, Ben; it was very nice meeting you."

After cleaning up Cypress said, "We won't keep you any longer, thanks again for having us."

"You're welcome." Belle gave Cypress and Ben goodie bags to take with them. They said they were looking forward to munching the goodies tomorrow. As they drove off everyone waved and Belle called out, "Safe home, take care."

Eager to get back to business they all rushed inside. "I better get Willow and the kitties taken care of."

Warren said, "We will all assist you, Belle."

Starlit had become off balance a couple of times but insisted on helping so they could get done. It only took a few minutes to get the inside critters taken care of, then quickly off to the living room they all went.

Warren began fluffing the pillows. Silas shook his head side to side as he smiled and watched him. No one knew why that was Warren's thing, he just always did it. Silas thanked the fluffer as he took a pillow, placed it on his lap then rested an arm on it.

Starlit tucked one behind her back and placed another under her knees as she lay on the love seat. Belle sat in her recliner without taking a pillow and neither did Warren as he sat on the couch with Silas. "Oh, this feels sooo good."

"I'm cozy comfortable too, Belle."

"You speak for us as well, Star; this outing was tiring."

"Yes, Warren, she does, but I would say exhausting. It took a lot out of me."

"I agree with Sy, exhausting is more like it. Star, you seemed fuzzy during dinner and you lost your balance in the kitty room. You didn't eat much either, are you still sick?"

"I'm feeling ill, a little and still fuzzy as you put it. My headache is gone but I have a slight heaviness feeling in my head. It's not as bad as earlier. Hopefully I'll be myself tomorrow. So, tell me already what happened during my absence."

Belle began: "We went back to the formation room to have a look around. There were no hidden rooms we could find, but Sy was poking around near that doorway that leads out to the giant beehive and got himself locked out again. Warren pushed the button that opened it last time to let him back in and noticed something this time we hadn't before. A little bee symbol appeared on the monitor for that area the cameras were covering. It was in the bottom corner of the screen. When Warren said 'look at this' and pointed to the bee, its wings were up. Well, I thought it was so cute and of course had to touch it. When I did the wings went down. It didn't matter if you pushed the open or close button; each caused the bee to appear. I did it a couple of times, then Sy tried it."

"Yes, but I did it out of curiosity rather than cuteness. Then Warren came up with a theory. He wanted me to go back out by the bees but I said no way, so he volunteered. He went out, then I touched the bee symbol to make its wings go down. Warren called and said the bees disappeared! Belle touched it now, up went the wings and he said they're back. With another touch the wings went down, and they were gone again!"

"Indeed, they were. I told them my theory was correct, that the bees were a holographic image. The hive was there when the bees disappeared, therefore, I concluded it was manmade. The day we were looking for you gals after you had gone to see the flowering vines, we noticed the path faded out and ended. That made sense since no one would chance walking near the huge beehive you could see up ahead. With no sign of you gals, we turned back. The hive was created as a deterrent, it obviously works.

"I walked to the sundial to test another theory. Contemplating a few moments, I pushed down on the piece under the stylus this time instead of just turning it like previously, which had turned on the pathway lights. Estimating the amount of time I would need to get back to the formation entrance, I turned it accordingly, arriving seconds before the door opened. When it opened, Silas was there to welcome me."

"Belle and I could see Warren on the monitor and watched him the whole time! It was great and amazing Warren figured out the stile had a dual function."

"It was exciting to have something figured out."

"Could we get a game of pool in and finish this conversation downstairs?"

"Sure, Sy, but I'll just, we'll just watch, right, Star?"

"Yep, that's good for me."

"Are you sure you don't want in on the game?"

"Yes, we are, Sy, go ahead."

"Okay, Star. Well, getting back to the entrance. Warren was correct about that too. There didn't seem to be anyplace outside of the doorway that the key would go into, so he thought maybe the sundial was involved, genius. Now with no real bees I went out to look at the hive along with Belle while Warren stayed inside. There are some flat rocks that kind of form steps going down to the ground. As we were about to go back up the steps Warren made the bees appear, buzzing and flying they were. It was so incredibly real, for a second I forgot they weren't, panicked and ran up the steps to the doorway. I could hear Belle laughing loudly. That triggered the memory they weren't real, and I started laughing.

"When I turned the corner of the wall in the chamber I bumped it, fell to my knees and crawled laughing all the way to the door. I sat trying to regain my composure. Belle peeked around the wall, laughing still, then came and sat next to me. That's when I noticed a marking that looked as though it might be one of the key symbols. I pointed it out to Belle. She confirmed it was."

"I have to interrupt, I thought you guys had searched for one and didn't find any, Sy."

"We did, Star; I was just about to tell you that when we looked around, we didn't look below our waist. It was down low.

"As we were looking at the marking the door opened. Warren had been watching us. When he saw us examining that portion of the wall, he opened the door wanting to know what we discovered. So, there are two ways to open the formation entrance from the outside!"

"Sy is very happy, as you can see, that he was the one who noticed the mark. Warren has two more theories. I'll turn it over to him to explain."

"Thank you, Belle. The marking has an indentation above it unlike the one for the key we have. It is a tiny rectangle shape approximately an inch long and half-inch thick, a keyhole. Neither is noticeable, they blend into the texture of the rocky wall. With this type of surface, no one would think anything of it. You would have to know as we know that the marks, resembling scratches, mean anything. I believe there is another key specific to that keyhole."

With wide eyes Starlit exclaimed, "Another key! Oh my gosh! How are we going to find that? I wonder if there are more holograms like the tunnel wall and bees too! Goodness, okay, go on I'm ready, wait a minute, okay, now Warren."

"Remember when Belle discovered the symbol on the ceiling of the tunnel. It was the letter *E*. This symbol is the letter *K*. I believe there could be another hidden room which may have the symbol for the letter *Y* marking its area. I do not know if that would mean a third key as well. Perhaps this would be the last hidden room, totaling three. Time will tell."

"Amazing, Warren, it's hard to believe. This is boggling my mind—well, what's left of it anyway."

He said, "That brings me to another subject, Star. When we were in the mushroom chamber you were at a different trough than the rest of us at first. Did any of the mushrooms you touched there look different than the others?"

"Actually, now that you mention it, Warren, yes, there were a couple of different ones. They were whitish and the tops had what looked like speckles of cake crumbs on them. When Sy turned off the lights so we could see if our fingers glowed, those mushrooms didn't glow. I didn't notice any more like them in the other troughs."

Belle was alarmed and distressed in hearing this. "Oh my gosh, Warren, do you think those mushrooms made Star sick? Like food poisoning? Should we take her to the hospital? Star, do you think you should see a doctor?"

Calmly Starlit replied, "No, I don't think I need to, not now anyway. You could stay with me in the guest room tonight though, since I do feel ill."

"Of course, I'll do that; I'd feel better being closer to you. You guys could stay here tonight. One of you could stay in my room and the other on the couch upstairs or down here."

"Silas and I will stay down here," said Warren. "One of us will use the luxurious air mattress you have in the closet over there."

"That sounds good to me, Warren, so what about the mushrooms?"

"There are some that have psychoactive and hallucinogenic properties, Silas. I believe that is the kind Star touched. Some of the chemical that causes that reaction can be absorbed through the skin in the correct conditions. The color of these mushrooms can vary, depending on the geographic location; they can be orange, yellow, red or white. Some can grow very large, up to a foot high and have caps the size of a diner plate." He then smiled and said, "Yes, I read that somewhere."

Puzzled, Silas asked, "Why do you think those kinds of mushrooms would be used in experiments?"

"I am not convinced that is the case," Warren answered. "I am however satisfied it was purely accidental."

"I'm happy to hear that and choose to believe it," said Belle. "It's a terrible thought that my critters would have frightening experiences. I never did notice any strange or unusual behavior or anything weird. I definitely agree they were not grown intentionally."

"I have a thought about the ghostly mushrooms, Belle. Warren thinks that the glowing mushrooms could be used to identify a cell or organ. Maybe someone was trying to find out why the horses can't reproduce. They are very small, so something isn't right."

"Not in the case of Anomaly; mules are born sterile, Sy, but them being small could be a possibility. I want to know who the someone is, or who they are. This is all scary; strangers lurking about underground, secret rooms, and a lab. You know if we had discovered ancient tunnels, ancient ruins and such, that would be really fun, but these things are current."

"I still don't get a feeling of ill-will," added Starlit. "My sixth sense is not wary."

"Thank you, Star, for the reminder."

"You're welcome, Belle."

"Yes, as we have discussed before, no harm has come. I would like to believe that none will however, we do need to stay alert."

"And thank you, Warren, for that reminder. "

"You are welcome, Star."

They changed the conversation to Cypress and his cousin. They talked about how Ben listened intently and contemplated what was being said, while Cypress sat there expressionless as it was explained why bad things go on in the world, things such as crime, murder, broken families, and deceit. They happen because we are sinful by nature, born that way. He was told Jesus taught even if you did not do such things outwardly, only thought them, you were as guilty as if you had done them. The thoughts come from out of the heart and the Bible teaches the heart is wicked above all things. They explained God created us a certain way. He gave us rules to follow; dos and do nots for our own good, knowing how our hearts are, to protect us. People wanted to do their own thing, without God, and what we see around us is the result, the consequences of doing our own thing. God created us for His pleasure and purpose. Ben was also told God has a plan and purpose for each of us and we need to establish a relationship with God. We need to seek His will and His purpose for us in our lives. Although Ben did not receive Jesus that night, they were hopeful he would. They would add him to their prayer list which Cypress was already on.

"You think we should all go to sleep so we can get an early start in the morning?" asked Starlit. "I would love to see the bees disappear and reappear. Hopefully we can find that other key and another hidden room."

"If you're feeling up to all that in the morning, Star, we would love to."

"You ladies go ahead, it is only ten o'clock. Silas and I will gather what we need for tonight, then play another game."

"Okay, good night, guys, we'll see you in the morning."

After the guys had gathered what they needed for the night they prepared for bed. Realizing how tired they were, they sat and talked for a short time instead of playing another game of pool, then went to bed. They both fell asleep right away.

The girls sat up together on one bed and talked a little. Belle told Starlit she and the guys spoke to the kids briefly. They had a great time at VBS and wanted her to tell their Aunt Star they would pray for her to get better fast. Starlit was touched by that. She felt bad; she missed talking to them. Starlit thanked Belle for staying with her and after they hugged, Belle climbed into the bottom of the bunk bed. Just before falling asleep, Starlit moaned, "My weird dream, that dream I wanted to tell you; never mind, too tired, another time, night-night."

"Night, have a good sleep."

Belle was fighting sleep. As she was thinking of places to search for the second key, she faded in and out of sleep. It was a jumble in her mind. She could not concentrate on a plan. While drifting off to sleep again Warren's words echoed through her mind: "Time will tell, time will tell…" Finally, she fell into a deep sleep.

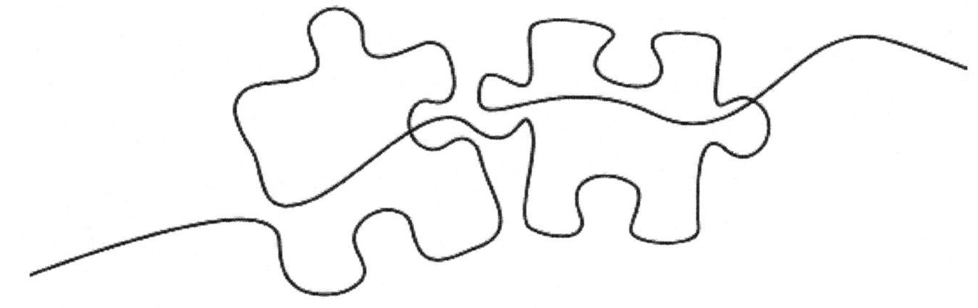

TWENTY-ONE

IT WAS JUST BEFORE DAWN Tuesday morning. Starlit woke up very early and hungry. She went to the kitchen for a little bite to eat. When she looked out the window, she noticed the dogs were out and about. Along the back of the yard beyond the gate that opened to the path to the pond, she thought she saw the faint outline of a vehicle there. Light from the yard did not shine far enough up the path for her to be sure, but since the dogs were not barking it did not concern her. After a quick thought of, *it must be the mushrooms still,* she turned, picked up her plate and sat at the little table in the kitchen. When she finished eating, she cleaned up and took her cup of tea into the living room to read some scripture from her Bible and pray.

Not much time had passed when Belle woke up and went to the kitchen. She saw that there was hot water ready and made herself a cup of tea. Aware that Starlit was in the living room she sat at the kitchen table with her Bible, not wanting to disturb Starlit. Belle was trying to get back on track with morning devotionals which she had come to neglect the past several months. She had managed to say prayers most nights and give thanks to God before going to sleep, but they were quick and not so deep. Belle had been struggling with what her friends had told her. This morning though she confessed to God her distance from Him. After apologizing for her behavior, she apologized for letting so much of what He had blessed her with get in the way of their relationship.

Acknowledging that she had gotten carried away with critters and work, Belle asked for forgiveness and guidance onto the path that was His will for her. When she was done, she got up and made another cup of tea.

The guys woke early as well. They stayed downstairs having their devotionals. After, they dressed and then played a game of pool.

Starlit went to the kitchen for a second cup of tea. By this time, it was light out. She noticed Belle walking out to the chicken coop and decided to set the dining room table for breakfast while Belle was getting eggs. When Belle came back, she put down the basket of eggs and gave Starlit a long hug while asking her how she was feeling. Belle started a small pot of coffee for the guys while Starlit went to the basement door. She opened the door slightly and gave a listen. Surprised to hear they were up, she called down to them that coffee was on, then told Belle the guys were awake. They hurried to get dressed, returned to the kitchen, and started breakfast before the guys came up.

Gathered at the dining room table now, Warren gave thanks and they dug in. Starlit told them about the weird kitty dream she had the day before while she was taking a nap. She described shapes and bright fluorescent colors that were on the kitties. Some had square shapes, some triangles, and some circles. The shapes were different sizes in colors of red, yellow, green, and purple. All the boy kitties had blue mustaches and the girls had pale pink on the tips of their tails. When a kitty rubbed against another the color of its shape changed to the color of the kitty that it touched. The kitties also talked to each other in a human voice.

Starlit then mentioned what she thought she saw on the path but since the dogs were not barking, she figured it was still the effects of the mushrooms. Silas commented that she must have been overly sensitive to them. It was understandable having the dream, since that was soon after contact with the mushrooms, but seeing things now he thought was unusual. Warren added that sometimes it could appear you are seeing something depending on how light reflects on an object or objects, in this case the moonlight on the trees and shrubs near the path. They teased Starlit a little, saying she should let them know immediately if she saw colorful flying saucers or little green and purple men.

When they were done with breakfast and had everything cleaned up it was only seven o'clock. Surprised at how early it was, they talked about going for a hike to get some exercise and fresh air before going underground. It was a beautiful morning and everyone was for hiking. Everything needed for the hike was gathered. As soon as all the critters were taken care of, they headed out. Choosing to go the long way around they started up to the pond area. The plan was to enter the formation room, show Starlit the disappearing bees, then back home the short way.

The morning air was cool, but the sun was warm on their faces. As they traveled along a well-used path, they came upon one that was not so well used and decided to take a detour. This path was one of a couple they had passed when they were on their first hike together but did not pay attention to them. Belle had seen them also prior to her friends' arrival but never made the time to explore them, and now seemed to be a good time.

The narrow, overgrown path went on through the trees before leading to a rocky area. It then began winding back and forth through the rocky terrain. Here and there they would see some tiny wildflowers growing in crevices on some of the rocks. A couple of squirrels dashed over and around some large rocks, pausing on top of one to stare at the intruders. One of them chattered loudly then both disappeared down the other side of the rock. Everybody was amused by that and laughed. The further they went the more rocks they encountered.

The path came to an end. Spreading out around and beyond the faded path they discovered the ground was mostly rocks of all sizes. Bushes, shrubs, and small trees had grown up between many of the rocks in the outer areas off the path; beyond that were tall trees all around.

Each of them had gone in a different direction but stayed within view of each other. No one found anything of interest. There were the usual sounds of different birds calling to one another, little animals foraging and insects crawling and flying about. There were some different size nests up in a few of the tall trees. Silas came across his favorite kind of nest and as soon as he heard buzzing, he turned and went quickly back to the faded path. The others came back when they noticed he was in a hurry to get there. He told them it was a small nest of bees, and he was sure they were real. Warren patted him on the back, then they all turned and walked down the faded path towards the main one.

The second faded-out path was about ten minutes from the first one. It led through a dense wooded area. They could hear a woodpecker seeking breakfast. As they continued the path began to go uphill, and as they moved further on the air seemed to get colder. Clouds drifted into the area and darkened the already low light due to the dense tree canopy. They were hoping it would not shower but stopped to get their rain gear out of their backpacks just in case.

After getting prepared they proceeded on with a quicker pace than before. Farther up the path they came upon small low-hovering patches of fog. Silas could not resist and used the word "spooky." Starlit was not happy about that and decided they should sing uplifting songs to brighten up the atmosphere. As they were singing and walking along, they came to a slight bend in the path which appeared to end. Pushing through some brush that had grown up in the path, they were able to move on. Belle thought she could see something up ahead. The rest of them noticed too. In the distance it looked like a door frame freestanding between two large trees. When they approached the frame, they could see it was made from logs. They passed through the opening into a tiny clearing. Inside the clearing they saw some logs forming a square around the outer part of the flat ground. There was enough room between the ends of each log to walk through. The flat area was covered in debris consisting of leaves, needles, and sticks. There was no fire pit, but they thought there might have been at one time. It seemed a good place to take a break, so they sat down on the logs to rest and talked for a short while.

One subject was the odd area of numerous rocks. Belle had not noticed any other areas on her land or sanctuary land that had a rock accumulation like that. She mentioned she had not been everywhere on sanctuary ground though, just like she had not even explored all of her property yet. Could be there were other spots like it. The other subject was the place they were at now. They wondered who made the little clearing, or perhaps it naturally existed and someone made use of it, a little nook to get away in and have some quiet time.

Speculation arose that it was there from a long time ago when there were few trees. With time the trees grew, causing the area to get dense. It was up high so it must have had a good view at one time, but now with the view obstructed it was not utilized much, which would explain the faded overgrown path.

During the time they traveled on the main path again the clouds cleared away. They stopped to take off their rain gear and were happy that it never rained. The temperature was warmer now, but they kept on light jackets. Finally arriving at the pond area, Starlit gave a shout out to the Lord that they had made it.

Standing by the sundial, they were getting ready to open the formation door. All of them looked around to make sure no one was there. Belle had binoculars and she scanned all around to see if anyone was within viewing distance of them. As Silas was about to set the dial, Warren spoke up saying he figured out why the rocks were there.

He told them the following: "The rocks were most likely from the tunnels, placed there out of the way. I believe the pond was created and rock removed from that area was dumped out of the way in that same location. All the soil from the tunnels and pond excavation were spread around the area we are standing on. This being a large area made it perfect for dumping the soil here. Someone created the picnic area, the pond and all the area around the pond, strategically placing rocks, tall grasses, and other greenery next to the pond and throughout the surrounding area. Other rock was utilized for seating around the fire pit." He concluded with, "All meticulously and attractively done."

That was a jaw-dropping explanation but it made sense to all of them. The rock and soil had to go somewhere. This was a perfect area to create what was there now. Silas stated that manmade ponds and even lakes do exist in various places, so it was not unusual someone would want to make a pond. He added that the pond and its setting were quite a bonus for Belle. Belle accepted the explanation with great satisfaction and thanked Warren for coming to that conclusion. Silas finally set the timer for the formation door. Starlit was thrilled that she would soon get to see the disappearing bees, and they went inside.

When Starlit saw the bee on the monitor she, like Belle, thought it was cute and had to touch it. She giggled when the wings went down. Belle took her outside to look at the hive while the guys stayed inside. It amazed her when the bees and their buzzing disappeared and reappeared. They went back inside. Starlit shook her head and commented someone went to a lot of trouble to do all of this and that they must have spent a long time, probably years, creating it all. Silas added to that, saying it must have been quite an expense as well. Warren only nodded in agreement; he was deep in thought. As Silas would put it, his wheels were turning.

While there they searched again but did not find another key. They headed home for an early lunch, then would go explore the other tunnel. Belle and the others were excited to see what might be on the other side; they all began walking fast.

TWENTY-TWO

BY THE TIME THEY REACHED HOME the clouds had returned. The air was thick and they could feel a mist on their faces. As they approached the house the wind kicked up. The dogs were happy to see everyone, but when the wind started they began to bark and circle the four of them. Belle gave Guardian and Stance some praises and a thank-you, then instructed the others to hurry inside and stay there.

She ran to the chicken coop to get the chickens in their house while Guardian and Stance herded Anomaly and Rarity into the barn. When the chickens were secure Belle ran to the barn to close in the horses. The others watched from a window in amazement at how Belle and the dogs worked quickly and flawlessly. The dogs knew they each had to stand guard once the horses were in their stalls, keeping them from leaving the barn until Belle could get there to close the outside doors to their stalls. Although the others could not see that side of the barn, they knew the dogs got the horses in their stalls and would keep them at bay until Belle arrived. After Belle ran into the barn the dogs emerged and waited by the main door for her to come out. When she came out, she gave the dogs hugs and praises then sent them to their house. It started to rain and appeared to be doing so sideways due to the wind. The dogs stood on their little covered porch and waited for Belle to get in the house before retreating into theirs.

"Wow, Belle, that was great!"

"Thanks, Sy. This storm is a surprise. With the dogs acting that way it tells me it's going to be quite a storm."

"Warren and I watched the news this morning and the weather showed a small chance of a passing shower. We were maybe going to catch the outer edge of a storm passing over half of the bordering states. Apparently, the wind changed."

"I better get out of these wet clothes. In the meantime Sy, would you see if there is any weather broadcast on now about this?"

"Warren went downstairs already, probably to do just that but I'll go down and join him."

I'll get the table set for lunch, Belle, while you change and the guys are watching TV."

"Thanks Star, I'll be right back."

"We'll have soup, salad, and dinner rolls, Star. I'll start the salad while you do the soup, please."

"Of course, love to."

"I'm putting celery, cucumbers, radishes, black olives, and a little onion in with salad greens, romaine lettuce, and a little kale. I'll have green olives with pimentos in a little bowl on the side since you guys don't like them in salad. I'm kind of craving them today."

"That sounds so good, Belle. I'll get the soup started and set the dressings on the table. After that I'll check on the soup and warm the rolls. I sure hope it stops raining by the time we're ready to go out to the barn. Seems silly to have to put on rain gear just to run out to the barn, then take it off right away."

"Yeah, it does but we can leave all that in the barn and not pack it around with us since we won't be outside."

"That's right, good idea."

"I don't mind a little rain either; I won't have to water anything!"

"Belle is not going to be happy to hear this report, Warren. The wind not only changed but it's a slow-moving system that will last till morning."

"It will not interfere with our plans, Silas, since we will be underground. The other plus is Belle will not have to water the lawns and gardens."

"Good point, brother. I wonder what we'll find on the other side, one tunnel, two, more mushrooms?"

"I do not believe there will be mushrooms, Silas. There was a large amount growing in the chamber we found."

"That makes sense, Warren. I wonder how far the tunnel or tunnels go or why there are any more at all. I can't wait to get this all figured out. I sure am glad Star is good with all this."

"I concur, Silas. She is doing well. Shortly we will see what is on the other side. Hopefully we will have answers before our vacation has concluded. I would not want to leave Belle without having solved these mysteries."

"I know what you mean, Warren. Star might decide she's packing Belle up after all if we don't find answers. She may, depending on what the answers are, pack her up anyway and I might just want to help too."

"Indeed, Silas, indeed."

Warren nodded as he spoke those words. He was definitely in agreement with what Silas said. Silas had chuckled after he made that statement, but Warren sat there with a serious look on his face, rubbing his chin with his thumb and forefinger. Silas said, "Come on, brother, let's go upstairs, I can smell lunch."

Having finished her soup and salad, Belle opened a roll and spread cream cheese on it. She cut some green olives in half, pressed them into the cream cheese, then covered them with the top portion of the roll. "Mmmm-yum, dessert," she said.

The others were staring at her. "Uh, I'll just have some fruit," Starlit said. Silas said, "You sure like the strangest things, Belle," as he reached for a banana.

Warren took a piece of fruit and set it down saying, "I shall try Belle's invention first." He repeated the steps Belle did to make the olive cream cheese roll. He slowly lifted it up and examined it before taking a bite. He carefully sank his teeth into the roll. As he chewed, a grin formed on his face followed by, "Mmmm. This is tasty, however, not dessert," he said. Everyone laughed. After he finished the roll, he picked up his nectarine and said, "*Now* dessert."

By the time they finished lunch and cleaned up, the wind had calmed down to more of a breeze. The rain was lighter and no longer going sideways. That was a relief to Belle.

The dogs were sitting on their porch watching everybody as they went toward the barn. Rumbles of thunder could be heard. Just as they were about to enter, a lightning bolt flashed over them. Before going into the tack room, they all removed their rain gear and draped it over the chairs and table in the barn. Noticing the fans in the barn were not on, Belle said, as she walked over to the wall control, "I didn't shut the fans off." When they did not come on, she tried a light switch. The light did not come on either.

"We better check the circuit breaker," Warren said. He opened the door to the circuit panel and examined the breakers. The ones for the fans and lights had tripped off. "As I thought," he said. Flipping them back to the on position, he told Belle to try the fans and lights again. "Oh, good they work, thanks, Warren. What about the appliances?"

"None of those breakers tripped," he answered. "I will go below first and check to see if the lights are working."

As they stood in the tack room Warren crouched down near the hatch door to the basement. He peeked under the shelf, reached for the knot that would open the door, and pressed it in. The door began to open, but he held in the button a few seconds then let go of it. To his surprise he could see the lights on below.

"Stay back," he whispered, "and stay here." He started down cautiously. The others quickly looked into the opening, and they too saw the lights. The door closed and they waited. Finally, after what seemed like a long time, the door opened. Apprehensively, they stepped back away from the opening. "All clear, you may descend," they heard.

Down they went, Silas leading the way. As soon as Belle was off the last rung, she asked Warren, "What is going on? Was someone here?"

Starlit answered, "I don't think so. I'm not getting a sense of that. How the lights are on I have no idea, though."

"I do not know either," Warren said.

"You know, I think I have a theory this time," said Belle. "Warren, you seemed to have been holding the button in. I just pushed it and let go quickly."

"Me too," said Silas, "let's test your theory, Belle. When I get to the top, open the door then shut the lights."

Silas started up the ladder. After the door closed, he pushed in the knot and quickly let go of it. The door began to open. He looked into the opening, and it was dark. He called down and told them what he had done. "Now I will try holding the knot in a little longer after the door closes," he said, "so don't do anything."

Belle called back, "Okay, Sy, we won't."

This time he pushed it in and held it a few seconds. The door opened and when he looked down the lights were on. He said to himself, "Well that's nifty," then started down the ladder. When he got to the bottom he said, "You were right, Belle, when you and I pushed the knot we pushed it in then quickly let go. That caused the door to open, but to turn the lights on you have to hold it in a few seconds."

As Warren gave Belle a side hug he said, "Good job!"

"Thanks. It never did make sense that you could turn lights on after you came down and only when you were going up. It's funny we spent time looking for a way to turn them on from up there and couldn't, only to discover it by accident."

Silas replied, "So far that seems to be par for the course around here. Come on, let's go."

They paired up and got in the cars. Belle wanted to ride in the trailer of the single car which Silas was going to drive. Starlit was Warren's passenger and they would follow the others. Silas pushed the button on the remote to open the garage door. This tunnel was a little wider than the other one. It had lights too and they were not very bright, either.

They entered slowly and, as with the other side, the door closed behind them after they traveled a few feet. Continuing at a slow pace, Belle looked at the sides and top of the tunnel with a floodlight, hoping to find a symbol. They decided they would get out of the vehicles later to search more closely. For now they wanted to see how far the tunnel went. Only traveling a few short minutes, they came to the end. Here there was a mini cul-de-sac for turning around. They made their way around the half-circle, now faced the direction they had just come from, and stopped.

"We could have walked all the way here, Warren," Starlit said as they got out of the vehicle.

"Indeed," he replied. "We will have more time to search now." He took a flashlight and began to examine the walls. The others did the same.

Belle continued to use the floodlight and examined the top of the tunnel where she was standing. Then she began to move in the direction of the barn. Silas, Starlit and Warren carefully pressed the walls as they walked along.

"Would someone like to switch with me? My neck is getting tired."

"I will."

"Thank you, Star."

"You're welcome. I expected the tunnel to go on further. Do you think this side was never finished?"

"Perhaps," Warren answered, "or perhaps it was not necessary and all they intended is in this short stretch of tunnel, we just need to figure out what was intended. I conclude there should be a hidden chamber somewhere in here based on what we have seen so far."

"I don't know, brother," Silas said, "we have been searching for a long time now with no results. We're almost back to the garage door."

"When we get there, Sy, we'll turn around and search again," said Starlit, "all the way back to the cars."

Belle said as they were about to get in the cars, "I was hoping we would see something we might have missed. I can't believe it, nothing."

Starlit sighed, "Yeah, three hours and nothing to show for it."

There were a few groans of disappointment as they got into the cars. Flashlights swept up and down as they slowly drove back towards the barn. Belle was driving this time and Silas was in the trailer. As they neared the garage door Belle did not open it; she stopped the car and just sat there.

Warren called out his window, "Belle, is the remote not working?" She did not answer. He got out of the car at the same time Silas got out of the trailer. Silas asked, "What's up, Belle?"

She got out of the car, waving her hands around her head to express she had an idea, saying, "Guys, guys, where haven't we searched?!"

Puzzled Silas asked, "Seriously, are you serious?" As Starlit was approaching he said, "I think we pretty much covered everywhere."

Belle spun around with her arms spread out while joyfully announcing, "No, we didn't! Not right here, here by the garage door! These last couple of feet around both sides of the door should be scrutinized."

"She has a valid point," Warren said, "We need to inspect this vicinity."

After taking a drink of water Silas said, "Okay, I'm in, makes sense." Then he reached into his backpack saying, "But first, cookie, anyone?"

"I'm for a quick break," Starlit said as she walked over to get her backpack out of the car. She grabbed Warren's backpack also. When she handed it to him, he thanked her then looked at Belle, who was reluctant about taking a break and said, "We will take a few moments." He placed his hand on Belle's shoulder and smiled.

The break was over quickly; the search began. It did not take long before someone called out a discovery. "Over here, I have located a keyhole."

The others immediately came alongside Warren. "It's the *Y* symbol," Starlit said.

"It is also for the key you have, Belle," Warren said as he held out his hand.

Belle reached into her pocket, took out the object and placed it in his palm.

"Thank you," he said. Smiling he added, "Congratulations on another proved theory, Belle, kudos to you. None of us thought the keyhole would be located a foot inside the opening of the garage door." This seemed strange to them but then again, it was all strange.

"Hurry, Warren, I want to see what we found!" Silas said. "This is kind of like a treasure hunt. Maybe we will find gold instead of green glowing things."

When Warren placed the object in the indentation, he felt the magnetic pull. He was about to make the first turn of the object when the object suddenly turned itself. It turned completely around in a full circle and stopped.

"Whoa! Did you see that?"

"We did, Sy," answered Starlit, as she and Belle stepped back a little, not knowing what to expect next. They stared at the object, not sure what to do, and waited.

About two or three minutes passed but nothing had opened up; not in front of them anyway. Belle looked down the tunnel and she could see light emanating from the wall. This was on the same side as the keyhole. Pointing she shouted, "Look, down there." She sprinted in that direction before the others responded.

She ran back and forth between two openings. As the others approached, she was standing near the first opening and said, "It looks like two doorways! Let's look in here first." The first opening in front of them was similar to what they had found in the other tunnel. It was an alcove, only this one had a large door inside. This door's top portion was made of glass, and it had a doorknob.

"An observation space, interesting," Warren said. "There does not appear to be anything to observe, it may be empty; however we will take a closer look."

He led the way in, and all were silent as they looked around.

"These are stalls but they have been cleaned," said Belle. "I wonder what kind of animals were in here. I wonder how long ago."

"We'll probably never know, Belle," said Starlit, "but I'm glad there are none now. The other chamber is probably the same. I'm going over there now."

"Wait a minute," Silas called after her, "no separating, remember, Mom?"

"Sorry, Sy, lost my head for a minute."

The two of them walked into the alcove with confidence. "Wow Sy, this one is different." Their eyes searched around the room through the glass part of the door. "I don't see any mushrooms, Star. Strange how there are ledges with small bushes and shrubs. Look over there, a mini waterfall with a small pool and that side has a smaller one. Let's go in."

"Sure Sy, you go first. Yuck, it smells in here."

"Sure does, I don't see any critters yet, but you can certainly tell they were here. So, we can walk here on these pathways, Star, but there's no way to get up into the enclosure. If you want to get up there you have to go over these support walls. I think these walls are about two feet high."

"Sy, why do you think there's clear edging?"

"Probably so you could see the critters and at the same time keep them from getting out onto the walkways. Wait a minute, that other area has a clear partition all the way up to the ceiling. Oh, I see now, back here, Star. Both sides have narrow steps. That side you can step over to get in or use the steps, this side has a little clear door you open to get in. Look how different the terrain and vegetation is on that side compared to this side. Tall grass, some shorter grass, patches of grass, some small rocky spaces, and some bare soil. I noticed temperature and humidity controls on either side of the main door too. What's that look on your face about, Star?"

"Uh, just wondering what kind of animals, must have been small; hope they're not still here. Oh goodness, I hope they're not snakes, eewww, revolting, or lizard things either!"

He chuckled. Silas walked through the observation area to the tunnel and called down to Belle and Warren, "Come see what's in here, guys."

As he was calling to them Star stammered, "S-s-Sy, th-the rocks are mo-moving!"

"Hurry guys," he added, "I think Star is hallucinating again."

Belle entered first with Warren close behind. "What is this? Sure is strange to see a habitat down here; okay, silly to say since we found a mushroom habitat underground. This place has an odd smell in here, kind of musky, definitely smelly."

Warren responded with, "I do believe that is an understatement, Belle." He then turned to Starlit and asked, "How are you feeling? What did you see?"

Speaking slowly, she answered, "A couple of rocks seemed to move a little, uh just a little."

Suddenly something ran past one of the waterfalls. Starlit pointed and yelled, "Giant—big rat—giant rat!" They all turned to look. The giant rat quickly burrowed into a hole in the soil and disappeared.

Belle was able to see it long enough to identify it.

TWENTY-THREE

"I CAN'T BELIEVE IT, THAT WAS NO RAT, that was an armadillo!" Belle cried. They all repeated together, "Armadillo?"

"Star, show me the moving rocks, where were they?"

She pointed to a small bush. "Give me a leg up, Sy."

"Okay, then Warren, you give me one up," he said.

Belle and Silas made their way over to the bush. Silas said, "That is kind of rocklike," as he moved closer to them. He crouched down, reached out and touched one.

Suddenly *SNAP!* Startled, he jumped up. Starlit screamed, "Sy!" He replied, "I'm all right, didn't get bit, Mom."

Belle gently picked one up, held it briefly then set it down again as she began to speak.

"Unbelievable, guys, what we have here are two different species of armadillo. These two tiny, rocklike critters are three-banded armadillos and the only ones that can roll into a ball. The one you touched, Sy, was not closed tightly, they sometimes do that intentionally, quickly snapping shut to startle you and scare you off. These critters are great diggers but don't dig in defense or to find shelter. They'll roll up inside their armor for protection and prefer to rest under bushes instead of in burrows. The three-banded live in dry climates. I think they're kind of funny-looking-cute. The three-banded are not native to this country. The 'giant rat' is native to the United States and cannot roll into a ball. That's why it burrowed to safety. I think they're cute. It's called a nine-banded armadillo but can have seven to eleven bands, and as you could see is much larger. It does live in burrows and warm wet climates. Another little fact, the nine-banded critters can move along the bottom of rivers holding their breath for up to six minutes! Well, I know all that, but not what in the world they're all doing here."

"Thanks for the lesson, Belle. I'm happy to hear the little rock wasn't trying to bite me. The terrain in this habitat makes sense now too."

"I'm happy it wasn't trying to bite you too," Starlit said, "but I would feel better if the two of you came down from there. I want to leave and get some air."

"In a minute, I want to look around to see if any more are here or if anything else is."

"That's another reason I want to leave," Starlit replied. She looked at Warren and said, "Would you, please." He took her by the arm, and escorted her out to the tunnel.

While the two of them waited there, Belle and Silas had searched the area. Nothing else was found. They came down the narrow steps and went to the stairs to the other area. Silas climbed up, opened the Plexiglas door; then Belle said, "You know, Sy, we could have just gone up the steps on the other side if you had mentioned them."

"True, but it was fun climbing over the barrier, and besides I was so excited I didn't think of it…ha ha."

"I agree, that was fun." Belle could see several holes dug into the soil but did not see any armadillos. There were no signs of any other critters either. She approached the exit and said, "Well, that's it Sy, nothing; sure is muggy in here."

"We didn't find anything, Star, no more armadillos or other critters."

"If there were more of the nine-banded they were probably in burrows. We would have to come back to check later or tomorrow night to give them a chance to emerge again. They are nocturnal so nighttime would be best. The three-banded sometimes will forage during the day but I don't remember if the nine does. I would like to approach quietly and unnoticed to avoid scaring them into hiding. I'm guessing the lights are on a timer to mimic day and nighttime for them. I can't believe I'm talking about this. Such an unusual find, why are they here?"

"Indeed, unusual," said Warren. "Another puzzle piece, however, the puzzle is not forming a picture yet. I believe we need to compile a list of all we have found so far along with any incidents that have occurred."

"I like that, Warren. We could do it like they do in the detective shows."

"Thank you, Silas, perhaps not exactly like the shows though."

"I doubt Belle has a bulletin board."

"No, brother, but she does have an easel and pad. We packed it up with the games, Warren, remember?"

"That's right; I have a Pictionary game with an easel that holds the very large drawing pad that comes with the game! Woohoo—I'm excited now, Warren!"

"Warren? You're deep in thought, what is it?"

"We must consider something," he said as he turned to look at Starlit, standing at a distance. "Star was clearly not hallucinating; perhaps she did see a vehicle on the path."

Suddenly Silas turned and ran toward the basement, saying, "No! No!" The others immediately followed. "Silas, what is it?" Warren called after him.

He explained, "I just realized that if Star wasn't hallucinating about the rocks moving, and she did see a vehicle up on the path, just a hunch, maybe someone was here."

They followed him down the tunnel into the basement, then to the office. As he went through the doorway, he could see that the drawers to the filing cabinet that had been locked were slightly ajar. "I knew it!" He pointed and shouted at the same time, "There, look at the cabinet!"

He walked over to the cabinet, slightly pulling on each drawer and peeking inside. He angrily pushed in each one saying, "Empty, empty…" and when he came to the last one, "Darn it! Well, that settles it, Star, you were not imagining a car up on the path. Whoever it was must have been down here during the night! I wish I had broken into the cabinet now."

"Calm down, Sy," Starlit said as she walked over to him. "It won't do any good to be angry. Hey, look behind the cabinet." She bent down and removed a piece of paper that had fallen behind it. Raising her voice in alarm she shrieked, "Monsters! Oh how awful; they cut off the head of a fox and put it on a large bat! That's sick! What other horrible experiments did they do! No, these people are dangerous after all, I don't get a sense of that but my head says so! Maybe this was a joke of some kind…"

Starlit paced back and forth, ranting a few minutes while waving the paper around. When she realized the others were silent and staring at her she paused, held out the paper and screeched, "Well, would you look at this!!"

When the others looked at the paper, each had a reaction of their own. Warren grinned a little, holding back a full-on smile, Belle had an expression of "no big deal" on her face. Silas laughed and said, "You never did care much for animals other than cats and dogs, so you don't know much about any others. Didn't you ever watch nature programs? Even I know what that really is. It's a bat with the head of a fox, no, I mean, it is actually a very large bat that's called a flying fox because its head looks like a fox, but it is one animal, not two stitched together, ha ha… Oh, and it eats fruit."

"He is right, Star, it was not an experiment made to look that way, but it might have been something experimented on. I wonder what other animals were involved. I'm sorry you got so upset. We should go; I want to get that list started and let's make sure we add that critter to it."

"Before we do, Belle, I would like to look at that circuit breaker."

"Sure thing, Warren, I hadn't noticed it before; then again none of us were looking for one down here earlier. I'm glad I know where it is now."

"That's pretty big, Warren. I guess it would have to be to house all the breakers for down here."

"Yes to that, Silas and perhaps something else, my hunch this time. Look at the location of it in relationship to the desk. Notice also it has double doors. Ladies, I believe we are about to discover something else for our list."

The girls moved in closer. Warren held the handle of one door and Silas held the handle of the other. Together they counted down: "Three-two-one—open!" Warren's hunch was correct. There was something besides the breakers inside.

Silas was fascinated. "Would you look at that? I'm shocked that I'm not shocked. Nothing is going to surprise me anymore. It just figures there would be monitors down here too, and I can guess what they'll show. Warren, would you do the honors?"

"Umm, Belle, be prepared for what you might see and hold Mom down."

Starlit and Belle looked at each other. Moving closer together, standing side by side, they placed their arms around each other's waists.

When Warren turned on the two monitors, each had a split screen on which could be seen four sections showing a 360-degree view of Belle's property! The girls' knees buckled slightly. Starlit's mouth hung open and Belle softly, almost whimpering said, "Someone has been watching me. Has someone been watching me?"

Warren walked over to the girls. He stood in front of them, placing a hand on each of their shoulders. In as soothing a tone as he could, he said, "No, I believe watching the horses, and likely to see who may be around but not to ogle anyone. It is four o'clock; we should go home to start that list with yet another entry for it." He looked directly at Starlit. Softly he said, "Belle is not moving." He smiled, placed his index finger under Starlit's chin and pushed up, closing her mouth, then led them to the office doorway and said, "You two go on, we will fetch the cars and return immediately."

Holding hands, the girls walked toward the ladder. Warren went quickly back to the monitors. "Silas, look here," he said. Warren slid open a panel located on a narrow shelf below the monitors. "I thought this might open but did not want to try it with the ladies here after seeing their reaction to the view on the monitors."

"Oh, okay, Warren, I lied, I am surprised. How did you know it was there and what was in it?"

"I did not know either. Silas, this is between us for now, we will show these to the gals later when their shock fades. Hurry, place these in your backpack; we must leave."

After retrieving the cars, they joined the girls in the tack room, then the four of them walked home in silence. The girls went to sit in the living room as soon as they entered the house. They appeared to still be in shock and stared at each other in silence.

The guys went into the kitchen to prepare snacks. They set everything on the dining room table. Silas poured hot tea for Belle and Starlit, coffee for himself and Warren. Warren entered the living room to find the girls sitting quietly. He waited a moment then said, "Ladies, please join us in the dining room."

After sitting down and taking a few sips of tea, Starlit said, "Thank you." Belle then said, "Thank you, guys, this is nice." Both girls went silent again, obviously still processing what they had just seen. The guys did not push for a conversation, they just ate their snacks and sipped coffee. Starlit broke the silence.

"I get it," she said, "we have to press on. I'm not in panic mode but am very concerned. That was a shock, realizing there are cameras here, not just at the picnic area."

Belle, nodding her head in agreement, said, "Certainly was and is."

"Oh, and that bat thing sure was a shock also. I am a bit embarrassed though, that I didn't know it was an actual, real, well you know." The others giggled a little.

"So, Belle, would you please tell me about that animal?"

Belle hesitated a minute, then shrugged her shoulders and answered, "Sure. Let's see..." She took a sip of tea and started to talk.

"The one in that picture was a giant golden-crowned flying fox. Another kind is the gray-headed. Their wingspan can be six feet. They hang from leafless trees. Bats have good vision, but those bats have the best eyesight of them all. Their big eyes help them to see better at night. They don't use echolocation but depend on their eyesight and sharp sense of smell to find fruit and flowers to eat. Oh, and bats are mammals, the only mammals that can fly.

"When the fruit bats go out to eat, they take their young with them. Other bats don't take their young because the weight of the babies makes it difficult to hunt insects and other animals. Yes, there are bats that will eat small animals. Bats are a mysterious species. Scientists don't know which animals are their closest relatives. Um, well, that's it."

"Thank you, Belle, that was enough information, it was good. It's hard to believe it exists. The face was a little cute but that body, creepy. Two animals stuck together, just weird."

Seeing that the subject got Belle talking and broke the ice, Silas said, "It is one animal. It's not the only one though, that looks like it has different animal body parts. Belle, tell her about the duck-billed platypus."

"Wonderful idea," Warren said, "please do."

Belle went ahead and told her about that critter. The conversation took their minds off the camera discovery and alleviated the shock. The girls were feeling better and ready to move on to creating the list before dinner. They talked about actually giving it a name. The final choice was to title it the "Discovery and Incident Fact Sheet." The sheet would be divided into two parts, with the words Discovery on one half of it, and Incident on the other half. They all went downstairs. Silas told Belle he would help her set up.

Silas should have opened the file cabinet drawers all the way; one in particular held something they could have added to their Discovery and Incident Fact Sheet…

TWENTY-FOUR

SILAS HELPED BELLE GET THE EASEL and pad out of the closet downstairs while Starlit and Warren sat talking on the couch. They decided to stay downstairs for now to work on the list. Once the easel and pad were set up, Belle began to write. On the left side of the sheet, she wrote Discoveries, on the other side she wrote Incidents, underlining each title. She jotted down a couple of things that came to mind first. The others would call out a discovery or incident and Belle would add them to the list. Nothing on the list was appearing in the order it happened. They wanted to list everything they could think of and then would number each one, eventually rewriting the list in chronological order.

"This is good; we have a visual in front of us that we can refer to. Hopefully these puzzle pieces will start fitting together."

"I have one, Belle," Starlit called out. "The dogs and that wolf, you should add that too. That was unusual. I think it should go under Incidents."

"Yes, good, thanks."

"The hologram bees," Silas said. "That should go under Discoveries, and the hologram wall in the tunnel too."

"This is getting to be quite a list. Warren, I think you mentioned the most."

"Belle, what about what we talked about a while ago? The guy in the storm back home and the one on the train should go on the side of Incidents. I'm not sure if there is a connection but we should keep it in mind."

"What about the howling that night? Could that have been a wolf? I think it sounded like one and maybe it's the same one that was at the gate with the dogs."

"I agree with you, Sy," Starlit said. "It's creepy to think that it started way back then but with all we have found and seen, I think it could be related."

"Good point, guys, I'll note it."

After Belle wrote a note on the list she went to sit on the couch with the others. They all read the list over and over. Silas got up and went to stand in front of the list at the easel. He said, "Now let's number these in the order they occurred." A few times he had to place a line through a number and renumber it.

It was not very long before the numbering was complete. "Sy, please rewrite the list without the cross-outs, it will look better," said Starlit.

"Thanks for that, Star; I would like it to be neat. Thank you, Sy, for doing it."

"You're welcome, Belle, I'm enjoying it."

"I was just thinking about the Momma incident," said Belle. "It wasn't her in her quarters, then she was in her quarters. That switch didn't take long. Maybe someone at the Center is involved or someone was pretending to be a visitor, slipping in to put Momma back after maybe taking a blood sample from her. I keep juggling that back and forth in my mind, I just don't know for sure; anyway, since she is unusually small for her kind of opossum and the horses are small, I think there is a connection there."

"Indeed, Belle," Warren said as he nodded his head.

"The giant snakes," Silas chimed in. "They were four times the size they should have been according to what you said your boss told you, Belle. I think that is related, so one thing we know for sure, animals are being experimented on, but we don't know what was trying to be achieved. We know they wanted it kept a secret."

Sounding annoyed, Belle snapped, "Obviously, Sy, give me something more!"

"Oh no," Starlit said with a horrified look on her face. "What about that thing you saw, Belle, the encounter near the Yancee farm? That thing was a giant too! Do you think it was an experiment that escaped, and could that creature wander this way?"

"It hasn't so far, well, not that I know of anyway. I'm not even sure what it was, still, it was strange and gave me chills. Sy, I'm sorry I snapped at you."

"I forgive you; I understand the frustration."

"The Center, Belle, maybe someone is involved."

"Go on, Sy, what are you thinking?"

"That rocky area is on Center property. Why would the person excavating on this property dump stuff on somebody else's property? After all, there is enough land here to have done that. What do you think, Warren?"

"Perhaps that area was a part of this property at one time, Silas. Remember, the property surrounding Belle's was acquired by a rescue organization. The previous owner of this land did not want to sell his property to them but maybe he did sell them a portion, that being the rocky area now belonging to the Center and Sanctuary. We know eventually the owner decided to sell the rest of his property a few years later. Belle was informed about that decision and now it belongs to her."

"You're tapping your forefinger on your chin, Warren, what are the wheels churning up?"

"I do believe I said informed, Silas, informed, perhaps we should keep that in mind, you might be on to something."

"Yes, that's right Warren, Belle was informed. Belle, you were just making plans to go for a job interview; why would your potential boss tell you about that? It must mean your boss Ed is definitely involved."

"Not necessarily, Sy. Maybe he just innocently mentioned it, you know, it just came out."

"Either way, I believe it is suspicious."

"But why, Warren, are you saying someone at the Center knew I might want to buy the land? So it could tie into all of this? This is crazy, I can't imagine how or why."

"As Silas mentioned before, the incidents on the train and at home, perhaps someone wanted to investigate the person who was buying his property, perhaps investigating her friends as well."

"I think Warren is right. That owner could have stopped the sale if he didn't like something. There were obviously no objections though, since the deal went through in what, about three weeks. That is unusual and seems to indicate someone wanted you to have it."

"Okay, Sy, could be, I don't know. I'll note it on the Incident side. Oh Sy, you go ahead and write it since you're standing right there.

Just write 'Note: Possible Center involvement' for now. I can't think of anything else.

"Well, you know that actually sums it up just fine. Getting back to the animals, some are exotic animals, others weren't, not sure what that means but it is both. Whatever they were trying to do, something went wrong. Some of the animals had stunted growth and some overgrowth. I wonder if they were trying to breed exotics with domestics. Ugh! Puzzle pieces, no picture yet. Well, I guess that's it."

Warren cleared his throat. "There is one more discovery that can and should be added to the list. Silas, would you please get your backpack."

"Sure, be back in a minute."

"While he is fetching his backpack, I will explain what occurred. There was something I noticed in the breaker box besides the monitors. With you both reacting the way you did regarding the images on the screens, I decided to wait before sharing this discovery with you, and Silas agreed. Now that you have recovered, we will show you. Under the monitors was a narrow ledge. It appeared to have a panel that might open. It did indeed open and the contents are now in Silas's backpack."

Starlit responded with, "I'm glad we're sitting down."

Hearing Silas on the stairs, Belle loudly said, "Come on, hurry Sy, I'm anxious to see what you have."

He removed several items from his backpack and placed them on the coffee table in front of them. "Wow! I can't believe it. This is great! We would have been okay with this, right, Star?"

"Yeah, we w-w-ould have; hmm-um, Belle, there are two of one kind and three of the other. I'm thinking there were probably four of each originally."

"That is correct," Warren said. "Unless there are others we have not yet found, but based on this find and what we already have, I am inclined to agree with your thinking, Star."

"And that would be?"

"Could be there are four people involved, Belle," Silas answered. He said, as he pointed, "There are three of this one, meaning one is out with someone and that same someone has the other kind, which you have one of also, leaving these two."

"Or maybe these are just spare keys! Look, this rectangle one must be the one for the formation room! Even if there were four people involved, these are here which I'm thinking means they're not."

"Good point," Silas said.

Warren, with concern in his voice stated, "There is a possibility then of their return."

On hearing that and feeling weak, Starlit leaned back on the couch. Knowing the answer already, she put her hand to her forehead and said, with the sound of defeat in her voice, "Suitcases anyone?"

Excited, Belle jumped up, went to the pad, and added, Circuit breaker = hidden panel w/spare keys. "That makes twenty-nine discoveries! So far, that is. We should go to the formation room door and try the key to see if it is for that door."

"It is getting late; we should have supper and get a good sleep," said Warren.

"You are a killjoy, Warren, but you're right, we should. The formation room isn't going anywhere. I'm actually tired anyway. Will you guys please take care of the critters while we get dinner started?"

"Yes, of course, our pleasure."

"Thank you, Warren, thanks Sy, thank you."

"Before we go up, Star, I want to look over the list one more time. It'll only take a minute and the guys will be busy awhile with the critters."

When dinner was finished and cleanup complete, Warren announced he and Silas would gather their belongings and go back to the guest house. He stated they all needed a good sleep. The girls were tired and ready to turn in for the night even though it was early. Silas was hoping to play a game of pool but he sensed something was up, so he followed Warren's lead. Everyone was looking forward to the formation room key check in the morning. They set a time to gather for breakfast and said their goodnights.

The girls waved as the guys walked across the yard to the guest house. As they headed toward the guest house Silas whispered, "Okay, Warren, I want to get settled fast, then I want to know what's on your mind."

Belle, obsessed with the list, whispered to Star, "I want to look at the list again before turning in, just to make sure I don't have to add anything else or change anything around."

"The list looks good to me, Belle; we should go to bed now."

"I'm tired, I agree. I'll look at it again with fresh eyes in the morning."

"The guys seemed to be in a hurry, and it was strange that Warren set a time for us to have breakfast, don't you think?"

"Warren knows I want to check out the new key and start as soon as possible, that's all, Star."

<u>DISCOVERIES</u>

2) Before country: strange object on floor
5) Belle finds ndl cap, ndl marks on horses
7) Sundial = timer, lights up path
8) Realize markings on Sundial & Object similar
9) Barn, Tack Rm = hatch door to basement
11) Lab. Office = one locked cabinet, others empty
12) Electric car, two garage doors, tunnels
13) Car elevator, second car w/trailer
14) Formation Rm = monitors/cameras
15) Object = key
16) Warning lights = tunnel & monitors
17) Symbol for E on tunnel ceiling
18) Hologram wall
19) Hidden Rm = bioluminescent mushrooms
20) Bees are hologram
21) Sundial opens outside door = Formation rm
22) Symbol for K, different keyhole = Form. Rm
24) Symbol for Y, keyhole = second tunnel
25) Tunnel 2 = hidden Rms: 1 Empty/Armadillos
27) Picture of Flying Fox bat
28) Circuit breaker in office = monitors
29) Circuit breaker = hidden panel w/Spare keys

INCIDENTS

1) Before country: Man stormy night. Man/train

3) Strange sighting near Yancee farm

4) Momma stolen

6) Giant snakes

10) Dogs and Wolf

23) Vehicle on path

26) Locked cabinet opened

Notes: Before country, Howling = Wolf?
Here, wolf at gate. Related to above?
Possible Center involvement

TWENTY-FIVE

SILAS ASKED WARREN TO MEET HIM in the living room when they were done. They took their belongings and put them away, washed up for bed, and retreated to the living room. There they settled down on the couch facing each other. Silas anxiously said, "So spill it already! You didn't want to skip a game of pool and hurry back here for nothing; what is it?"

"We will look at the facts, Silas, starting with the lab being mostly empty. File cabinets in the office were empty except one and then it was recently emptied. The one room in the short tunnel had been cleaned out. The armadillo habitat is there, but for how much longer? Star did see a vehicle on the path early in the morning, before sunrise. I believe this indicates activity during many nights, spending those nights closing up shop..."

Interrupting with a slightly raised voice and a gleam in his eye, Silas blurted out, "And you want us to try to catch him! Warren, I knew you were hatching something but not this. You're right about all of it, I can see that clearly now, definitely moving out. Whoever it is comes after they know we went to bed—uh, gee, I don't like the sound of that now that I said it out loud."

"Indeed Silas, a tad disturbing. My plan is we get some sleep then wake at two a.m. We will take our backpacks but keep them light. The dogs will not bark and give us away since they know us. The main concern is encountering anyone. I do not know if we will, that is yet to be seen but I do know we need to be cautious; there could be more than one perpetrator. We should only confront one perpetrator and be certain only one is present before we make a move."

"I agree, Warren. Before we hit the hay, what do you make of the object turning itself? It didn't do that in the other keyhole, how could that be possible? We had to enter a combination."

"I am not sure, Silas. Perhaps the sensor behind the wall was programmed to read one or two of the letters, thus causing the mechanism on the other side to be set in motion. When it engaged, the gears began turning, the object moved. When the turn was completed, the task was done and the door opened. No combination needed to be entered."

"I can live with that explanation, thanks, Warren. One more; the guy on the train and the wolf, you know I think it is related to here. I believe he was checking all of us out too, but why take your pet wolf with you? How could he get it on the train? Why would anyone even have a pet wolf?"

"That is three questions, Silas, however, think: Center and Sanctuary for wildlife."

"Of course, Warren, an injured wolf that couldn't be returned to the wild! He raised it as a pet and companion."

"Perhaps injured as a pup, Silas, and raised by this person, hence a possible Center connection. I believe that person had a sleeper cabin and likely listed the wolf as a service animal. We should retire to bed now."

"I hope I can sleep, Warren. I know, instead of counting sheep, I'll count cookies, ha ha, or glasses of milk with pictures of goats on them."

Chuckling, they headed off to their bedrooms.

For a short time, the girls sat at the little table in the kitchen. They were in their pajamas and sipping on warm milk. Belle often had warm or hot milk to help relax her before bedtime. It seemed difficult for Belle to let go of the day; she wanted some resolve. Even though she knew morning would come quickly and the key would be checked then, the answer was desired now.

"Belle, let's set our alarms very early, that way I can help with the animals. I'll take care of the cats and dogs while you take care of the rest, then we can make breakfast. When the guys come, we can just eat and be on our way."

"That sounds great, thanks, Star. You know, I appreciate all the support you and the guys have given me through all of this. I have thought and prayed about all that you guys talked to me about. Uh, you know, how I had changed, umm, all that. I've been praying for guidance on a plan to reorganize and prioritize my life and get back on track. The Lord put it on my heart to apologize to all of you first."

Belle reached out across the table and took hold of Starlit's hands. She gave them a gentle squeeze and said, "This is difficult to face and to do but God is helping me. Star, I'm truly sorry I hurt you and offended you. Please forgive me."

"I forgive you, Belle, and I love you. Thank you for the acknowledgement."

"I love you too."

"What else did He say?"

"Nothing yet on the plan but I will keep inquiring. In the morning I will apologize to the guys. I want to speak to them individually though, this is very personal."

"Speaking of morning, Belle, we better get to bed." They embraced a long time, then kissed and went to their bedrooms.

Parting, they called to each other, "Good night, Belle."

"Night, Star, have a good sleep. Love ya."

"Love ya too."

The guys fell asleep with no problem but waking up for Silas was a different story. Warren held a glass of cold water in his right hand. He stared at sleeping Silas a moment with a smirk on his face, then dipped his fingers in the water. As he flicked it on Silas's face he chuckled. Silas stirred a little and groaned. Warren flicked a little more water on him, put down the glass, picked up a peanut butter cookie and waved it under Silas's nose a few times. Silas opened his eyes slightly.

"Good morning, sleepyhead, time to get up."

"What time is it, Warren?"

"Fifteen minutes past the time you should have been up."

"Yeah, sorry, that's right; we were going to get up at two a.m. I wish you had waited another minute before waking me; I was dreaming about a cookie and was just about to eat it."

"Your dream is about to come true, Silas, here is your cookie but have a protein shake first."

"You must have waved that cookie under my nose, causing it to incorporate into my dream and my face is wet, you must have splashed me with water."

"Indeed I did, enjoying every second of doing so; it was fun."

"Yes, I can tell by that ear-to-ear grin. Now please step aside, Warren, and I'll get ready in a hurry so we can go."

"Since peanut butter is your favorite, I will take your cookie to the kitchen while you are getting ready, alleviating the temptation to eat it now. In the meantime I will set up our backpacks."

Warren left the bedroom. He turned, went back to the bedroom and poked his head through the doorway saying, "There will be a shake ready for you."

"Thanks Mom, ha ha, I mean Dad. Warren, be there in a few minutes."

They peeked out a window, examining the yard before opening the door. Satisfied it was all right to proceed, they quietly left the house. As they were slowly walking toward the barn the motion sensor lights turned on. That triggered the dogs to come out of their house. Heads high, the dogs sniffed the air. They let out soft sounds as if to say hello and began wagging their tails. They approached Silas and Warren, who greeted them with pats on their heads. Silas, whispering, said, "Hi Guardian, hi Stance; good boys, stay now, stay."

The guys continued toward the barn. When they had gone through the barn door Warren turned, closed the door partially and watched through the opening to see if anybody was there or if the girls might be up, possibly seeing that the lights in the yard were on.

Not seeing the girls looking out, he was certain they were in the clear and closed the door.

"Silas, when I open the hatch I will push in the button, quickly releasing it. We need to see if lights are already on, which would indicate the presence of someone. If it is dark, we can descend. Once we are down, we will go to the armadillo habitat. Please turn off the light in here; I have my flashlight ready and will push the button."

"Oh, good sign, Warren, no lights. I'll push the button to turn them on. Hey, it's not working, the door is closing now. Guess I'll try again after it closes all the way; sorry, Warren. Here goes, I'll hold it in a few seconds and there we have it, open door and lights. After you sir, I'll be right behind you."

"Someone has been here, Silas; the double is gone but the trailer was left. We will open the garage door and look down the tunnel. If we see light coming from the side of it or the car itself, that would indicate someone is down there. That being the case we will leave since we do not know if there is more than one perpetrator."

"Unless, Warren, we see them, then we should run because if we see them, they see us."

"Indeed, we will move out quickly. Stand to that side, Silas, I will stand on the other and open the door."

As the door began to open Silas and Warren crouched down, at the same time poking their heads around the edge of the door frame. They peered under the door before it was a quarter of the way up. As the door went up, they both eased themselves upward, eyes wide and fixed down the tunnel. It appeared to be all clear, no light, no car.

"It is not far, Silas; we will jog down, make a quick inspection then return to the barn. Insert the key the instant we get down there."

"I see the lights, let's go. You were right, Warren, the bushes are gone, no little rocks, both ponds and waterfalls are gone as well. I'm guessing the burrowing 'dillos are gone too since some of the soil is missing over there. Do you think they'll be back to clean the rest of the chamber out tonight?"

"Perhaps, I am not sure, however we need to move on. We will take the single and drive to the mushroom chamber to see if that has been cleaned out. First, we will exchange our trailer for the bigger one. I will sit in that, you can drive."

"Sure thing, Warren, I'll drive now, we'll switch later. Come on, race you to the car!"

"Wow! This chamber was definitely cleaned out. Not a speck of soil has been left, Warren. It looks like they must have vacuumed it out of the troughs, vacuumed and washed the floors too."

"Spores, Silas, spores, most likely to ensure all the spores were removed. It was a thorough job; time consuming. They had several hours to complete this. Since there are less than two hours until sunrise, perhaps they will be back to do more in the habitat, however I doubt they will finish there tonight; at the very least they will bring the car back. We will go to the formation room now."

"What if someone is coming back in the tunnel? We need a plan; do you have a plan?"

"Yes Silas, I do. If anyone is heading back in the tunnel, we will be able to see headlights, however not if two or one are in the car, unless we wait until the car is close which might not be wise. You will turn the car sideways as much as you can to block the tunnel, then we will run back to the barn. They would have to pursue us on foot. A lone perpetrator may not do so; either way we would have a head start. You will go up the ladder while I wait near the bottom. I will be able to tell how many there are when they near the garage door. If more than one, I will open the hatch and head up. I believe whether one or two, they would not follow us out of the barn. If there is one perpetrator, I will call to you and pursue him."

"Perfect, Warren! I would quickly join you and we will interrogate him. I am hoping it plays out that way; it sure would be great to finally get some answers."

Silas drove faster than normal in an attempt to save time. Warren was in the trailer watching ahead and behind as they traveled. When they reached the elevator, Silas paused a moment before driving onto it. He was a little disappointed they had not encountered anyone. The elevator was set in motion and began to rise slowly. It reached its destination in the formation room. The floor turned slowly. Suddenly, just before the car was fully positioned in front of the garage door, the door began to open.

"You are truly in a hurry, Silas, do not drive forward yet."

"That wasn't me, Warren, I did not press open on the remote, I didn't. Look, look! Headlights! Hey, the car is turning sideways and blocking us! Didn't see that coming, that was our plan!"

"Silas, he is alone, on foot—quickly, he has a major head start. Take your backpack."

Silas grabbed his backpack and put it on as he ran. They approached the car, then split up. Silas ran around the right side of it while Warren ran around the left side. Warren suddenly tripped and tumbled from the waist up into a trailer. He quickly righted himself, shook off his hands, wiped dirt off his face, spit then started moving again, this time with his flashlight in hand.

Warren was able to see part of the first trailer but not the other trailers hitched to that one. He did not anticipate a line of trailers to slow him down. He navigated past all of them as quickly as he could. All the trailers had higher sides than the one they had seen attached to the car originally and were longer.

Silas had no idea what had happened. He was focused on the person he was chasing. Warren could see light from Silas's flashlight bouncing around. As he got closer to Silas, he noticed the light stopped moving. When he caught up to him, the two of them stood still, huffing and puffing slightly.

"Darn it! I lost him, Warren, I can't believe it. Without a full moon it's hard to see, well, at least we do have a little light from it, better than none. He must have gone off the path or into hyper speed and is way in front of us."

"Silas, I have a spotlight in my backpack; I will scan the area with it. Here, take my flashlight, use it with yours to scan. Do you see anyone, Silas?"

"No, not so far, hold on, I think—never mind."

"Silas, I have him located now but I will keep scanning and not give that away. We will have to split up. This is what we will do…"

They jumped into action, the chase was on again. Running around bushes and hopping over smaller ones was taking its toll. The ground was uneven. Twigs were snapping and breaking underfoot. Branches from larger bushes and from small trees resisted as they pushed passed them. Several times both of them were hit in the face with branches: *Whack! Whoosh! Snap! Snap! Smack!*

Silas was gaining on his target in spite of the obstacles he encountered. He stretched out his arm, his fingers as far as they could go.

A few more inches and he grabbed hold of the jacket the man was wearing. They fell to the ground and wrestled. The man's face was covered with a ski mask and Silas tried to pull it off. They rolled and struggled, then the man broke free, sprang up and began running.

Silas scrambled to his feet quickly, hesitating as he located the direction the man ran in. He called out to Warren, who had lagged behind. In motion now, Silas again called out, "Warren, over here, hurry, this way. Warren?"

"I am coming, Silas, continue on, go, I will be right behind you!"

TWENTY-SIX

BELLE WAS STARTLED AWAKE BY barking dogs. She waited a few minutes, but they did not quiet down. As she started out of bed a knock came at the door. She grabbed her robe as she headed for it. The knocking got louder and faster.

"I'm coming, Star, hold on. Come on, let's look out the windows to see what's happening, I won't just run outside."

"The dogs sure sound angry, Belle. I hope it's not the mad scientist creeping around. I don't see anyone, do you? The guys must be hearing this too, do you think they are? With the security lights on I can't tell if they are looking out of their windows. How come the security lights aren't on around the side of the house?"

"Something has to go past that area for the sensors to pick up and then the lights will go on. Whatever or whoever is out there didn't go over there."

Snap! Whack! "Ouch, this is getting old!"

"I agree, Silas; we have taken a beating, however we must endure. Movement, over there to the right, pick up the pace. We should split up again."

"Whoa! Warren, what is that? Watch out! It's coming right at us..." Before Silas could finish his sentence, Warren shoved him out of the way. As Silas steadied himself, he finished that sentence with a yell: "Get down!"

"The dogs are by the gate to the path. Oh, look, just outside the gate, a raccoon, thank goodness, just a raccoon! It's almost out of sight and the dogs are not barking as much. Yep, there we go, they're quiet now."

"They're amazing, Belle; they're standing there watching to make sure it doesn't come back. Such good guard dogs and so cute! My, that was a huge raccoon, Belle. You know, I think the guys slept through all the commotion. We'll just have to fill them in later. What time is it anyway?"

"It's three twenty; we should go back to bed. I really don't want to stay up till four thirty. Getting up at four thirty is early enough."

"We'll have plenty of time to get everything done by our breakfast appointment. Come on. Good night again, Belle."

"Ditto, Star."

"Bird of prey, Silas, owl I believe. It was honing in on an early breakfast. This has set us back; we have lost the perpetrator. Onward, we will continue in the direction we were going before the interruption."

"Look, Warren, broken branches, we're on the right track. This way, it looks like he changed direction. Over there, that looks like the silhouette of a human." *Crunch! Crack! Snap!*

"It appears he has heard us, Silas, hurry, I do not want to lose him again."

"I'll head this way, Warren, you go that way."

Silas caught up to the man again. He jumped on him; they fell to the ground rolling back and forth, muttering and groaning. The man overpowered Silas as they got to their feet again, then he pushed Silas against a tree. The man turned to run but Silas grabbed him and pushed him back. He tried to pull off the man's mask but was blocked by two forearms forcefully pushing him backward as the man moved forward. Struggling with all their might, the two of them swung around and around…

<><><>

"Good morning, Belle, again, teehee. I was actually able to get back to sleep, how about you?"

"Me too, I slept well. Let's get the critters started and meet in the kitchen when we're done."

"I'll see you in a few minutes, Belle."

Warren was catching up and closing in on the fighting duo. He was just a few feet away when suddenly he tripped over a large branch, stumbled forward then fell to the ground, grunting and groaning. Warren did not get up right away; he was feeling dizzy, so he stayed down. Silas and the man were both tiring. During their struggle Silas noticed they had neared a path. He tried to steer the man away from it, fearing he would outrun him if he made it to that path. They struggled with each other as Warren approached them, staggering.

Silas, noticing something was wrong with Warren, hesitated, giving the man the upper hand. The man pushed Silas away from himself, breaking free. Silas lost his balance, down he went, and the man took off. Warren came and stood next to Silas. Silas got up and they leaned on each other, watching as the man sped away from them at an amazingly super speed.

"What in the world just happened? Did you see that, Warren? He flew out of here, poof, gone!"

"Indeed, he did. He appeared to be sitting on something, obviously camouflaged, a getaway vehicle waiting out here in case of an encounter, like with us."

"You know, Warren, I noticed he was edging near to that path and that explains why he was going in the direction of it. The way he took off was like he was on a motorcycle, but I couldn't hear anything. That's not possible, no sound, totally quiet, wow! I wonder what that vehicle really is, even with a little light from the sunrise I couldn't tell what it was. You're leaning on me hard, brother, are you all right? Warren?"

"Aw-grrr-uh."

"I see, okay, sit down a minute. Here, have some water. You sure are sweating more than you should be."

"Thank you for the drink, Silas. The sun is up now, we need to leave; take the compass from my backpack, and find the direction home, please."

"I will, but you need to rest a few minutes."

"I can't believe the guys are late, I'm hungry."

"We should go get them, after all they set a time for breakfast—come on."

"They probably snuck back here after we were asleep to play pool, it got late, and they overslept."

Belle knocked on the guest house door several times with no results. Starlit tried knocking next with the same results, then Belle turned the doorknob. "No answer, no way. The door isn't locked, Star, we're going in… Hello, hello! You have company, are you dressed? Hello?"

"That's odd; maybe they're hiding, you know, joking around. You check the closets, I'll go downstairs."

Starlit bounded down the stairs, confident that is where the guys would be. She looked around then shouted up to Belle, "They're not down here." Belle shouted back, "Not in any closets either. Their backpacks are gone; they must have gone for an early morning hike."

As Starlit got to the top of the stairs Belle said, "Still, they should have been back in time for breakfast; like you said they set the time, after all. I'm hungry too, let's go back home. If they're not back in a few minutes, Star, we should eat. I'm going to."

"I will gladly join you."

“I’m surprised the girls haven’t called us yet, Warren, we are late. I am not looking forward to telling them what we did and what happened. How are you feeling?”

“Under the weather, Silas, not myself.”

“Hold on, Warren, we’re almost home; the garage door is just up ahead. I remembered to grab the remote when I got out of the car so we would be able to open the garage door when we got back. I’ll move the cars around so we can take the double, that way you can sit in the car while I drive. It’ll only take a couple of minutes to unhitch the trailers and make the switch, then we’ll be on our way.

“I say we eat now, Belle. I think I’ll have coffee this morning.”

“I was just thinking the same thing. I’m looking forward to my sticky pear-oatmeal muffins. As a matter of fact, since the coffee and muffins are ready, we should have them first and something afterward.”

“I like that idea and then we can have, say a veggie omelet with cheese.”

“You got it, Star, thanks for helping with the critters and setting the dining room table.”

“You’re welcome. I’ll bring the muffins to the table while you get the coffee.”

“Here we are, coffee and cream.”

“This muffin is wonderful; it’s so delicious and moist, Belle… Belle, I just got the strangest feeling. Something is wrong; I think it’s the guys. My senses are jittery.”

"That's probably just the coffee, Star, it is a little strong. I'll go make the omelet now, be back in a few minutes."

"I'll come with you; I want to look out the window for the guys."

"You are worried, Star."

"Yes, I am. I cannot shake this feeling. If they're not back shortly I am going to call them."

"Come on, let's have our omelet, then you can call."

"We're halfway home, Warren, hang in there. I'm sorry that you're sick. When we get back to the barn I want you to go up the ladder first, that way I can steady you if you have a problem."

"Belle, there was no answer on either of their phones; it went right to voice mail. Do you think they remembered to take their phones with them? Let's go back to the guest house and take a look. I still have a bad feeling."

"I have to admit, I am concerned now. Here is what we'll do, we will check for the phones then take Rover up the short path and look by the picnic area first. I have no idea if they went that way, but we have to start somewhere. We can take the dogs too. Let's make sure we take our phones and backpacks…

"Actually, Star, you go to the guest house to look for the phones while I get the keys to the secret places, then I'll pull Rover around to pick you and the dogs up."

"Got it, let's hurry. I can't believe I'm going to say this but when we get in Rover, please drive fast."

"Warren, the yellow lights are flashing, someone is out there. I wonder if Speedy is back. Maybe he came back for the car and trailers."

"I do not believe he would come back during the day, Silas."

"Warren, maybe he would if he had company. This situation could be getting serious."

"Please stop the car, Silas; I need a moment of no movement."

"We're going to lose our voices if we keep yelling out their names!"

"Yeah, Star, my throat is getting dry, I need to take a drink of water. As long as we're here by the formation I want to see if the other key will open the outside door. I'll make it quick so we can continue our search; come on."

"That's amazing, Belle, the dogs are not bothered by the bees. They must know they're not real! Hurry, try the key. Great, it does open the door, the dogs, oh no! I can't believe they just ran inside like that, Belle."

"Guardian, Stance come! Come on boys, come, good boys. Yes, good boys, I just have to give you hugs and kisses. Sorry, Star, they enjoy exploring new places. Sorry boys, we don't have time to explore here or to play. We'll make time to play later; right now we have to find Warren and Sy."

"Belle, the dogs are going back to the door!"

"Go back, follow the dogs, and open the door again!" The dogs nearly knocked Starlit over as they pushed past the girls and ran into the formation room.

"Belle, I sense the guys were here, I'm sure of it and the lights are on."

"The lights came on when we came in, Star. The dogs are by the garage door and Stance just picked up something in his mouth. Good boy Stance, come here, what do you have? This is Sy's phone, Star, your senses and the dogs were right, the guys were here. I think we should leave and look around outside again."

"Silas, please, stop."

"I did, Warren, we are not moving. You're starting to worry me."

"I see, maybe I will close my eyes a moment. In the meantime, Silas, you should call Belle to let her know we are on our way. The ladies know by now, not only are we late for breakfast, we are not home. Do not mention I am ill."

"Okay, I won't. Uh-um-uh, Warren, my phone is missing. I will have to use yours, please."

"Certainly Silas, here you are."

"Thank you. No wonder we haven't heard from the girls, Warren, my phone is missing and yours is off! Here goes: Hi Belle, yes, fine. I'm sorry, we should have contacted you sooner, just lost track of time and well, I lost my phone and Warren's phone was off, just realized that. Great! Great! I'm very happy Stance found my phone, tell him I said thanks. ETA on when we'll get home? Um, we are on our way, almost there, say ten-ish. See you soon, bye."

"Silas, did Belle say where Stance found your phone?"

"No, Warren, and I didn't think to ask."

"Star, they're fine. They lost track of time. I didn't tell Sy where his phone was found because I didn't want him to know we were here, yet. Let's hurry home. He said they should be back in about ten minutes; they should get there before us. Guardian, Stance, come."

The girls arrived back home and called out to the guys but received no reply. They went into the house, but the guys were not there. The next stop was the guest house, thinking the guys wanted to freshen up, but they were not there either. No sign of the guys anywhere. The girls stood out in the yard in silence as they turned about every minute or two, watching and waiting.

Belle was about to phone Silas when Starlit pointed to the barn. "Look, the dogs are going into the barn."

"Of course, the guys were in the formation room and took the tunnel back. The dogs probably hear them; hurry, let's get in the house."

"I'm still getting an uneasy feeling, Belle, even though they're back. *Are* they back? They should have been out of the barn by now. What is going on?"

"Probably greeting their greeters and delaying facing us, heehee. There they are! We'll greet them at the door."

"Belle, do you see what I see? That doesn't look good; come on."

"What happened to you guys, you're both filthy and oh my gosh—and hurt!"

"Bushes and tree branches, that's all, Belle, nothing major. We'll wash up, change and be over in a few minutes."

"Are you sure you are all right, Sy?"

"Yes Star, sorry we messed up on the time, we got carried away."

"Indeed, we did, I apologize, ladies."

"Warren, you don't look right, what is it?"

"I am a little weary from overdoing it, Star. I fell; the wind was knocked out of me briefly but Silas took good care of me."

"You guys need to eat. Coffee and muffins are ready and when you get back, I will make the rest of breakfast for you. See you in a few minutes."

"We'll wait until you get in the guest house before we go inside and please don't be long."

"Yes Mom, bye, see you in a few."

"You know, Belle, my senses tell me something is going on, something isn't right, they're holding something back."

"Yeah, and look at Warren, he is a bit unsteady. I wonder if he hurt himself more than he is willing to admit or more than he wants us to know. Hopefully he will feel better soon. Maybe he'll have a quick recovery after eating something. Star, do you think he might have broken something, like a rib or two? Can your sixth sense pick up on something like that?"

"Not really, Belle, only that they are holding something from us. Hopefully they will come clean on what really happened out there. Even though it was dark they would have had their flashlights with them and been on a path or trail, so why all the scratches and cuts? Why would they go off any path or trail? Do you think they were chased by an animal? Gosh, Belle maybe that large thing by the Yancee farm did come over in this direction! It is out there, out there somewhere."

TWENTY-SEVEN

"SOMETHING CHASED THEM, Belle, that could explain why they weren't on a trail and why they were delayed in getting back. If I were running for my life, I would not be looking at my watch to check the time."

"Maybe, could be a possibility. What about the formation room, Star? How did they wind up there? If they went for a hike, how did they get in there from the outside? When I went downstairs to get the key none were missing."

"Yes, Belle, I see your point and they obviously came back in the tunnel, which would mean they went into the barn, took a car or hiked through the tunnel. Maybe before they went for a hike they wanted to see if they could find another secret room, Belle, but that doesn't explain their condition."

"No, Star, it certainly does not, and we have a lot of maybes. One thing is for sure, they have a lot of questions to answer. You know, I don't think there are any more secret rooms. Remember, each one we found had a letter from the word 'key' marking its location and we found a room for each letter, making three secret places, just a thought. I see them; they just got out the door and are on their way. Star, no questions until after they finish breakfast; please try to contain yourself."

"I will, Belle, come on, I'll help you with their breakfast. I know they need to eat and recuperate, and then we'll grill them."

"Would either of you like more eggs or bacon?"

"No thank you, I will have a little more coffee though."

"Since Warren is nodding his head and staring at the coffee pot, I think I'll pour him more coffee to help him wash down that muffin."

"Breakfast was great, thanks."

"You're welcome, Sy, it was our pleasure."

"Yes, thank you, ladies, most satisfying."

"You are welcome too, Warren. You sure were quiet while you were eating. You don't look well, I'm glad you were able to eat. You sure uh, ate more than usual too."

"Delicious food, Belle, so good."

"We can tell you are enjoying it very much, Warren, right, Star?"

"Yes, I can definitely see that. You both worked up an appetite, especially you, Warren, you know with all that hiking you did and all. Maybe even a little running too. What else did you guys do; I mean you must have gone off your trail to get all scratched up like that. Warren fell and got hurt; we could see he was off balance when he walked…"

"Mom, we can sit and talk in the living room after we clean up, it will be more comfortable and restful."

"Good idea, Sy, I'll take that; you don't have to help but thanks, you guys go ahead to the living room, we won't be long." "Thanks Belle."

"Let's hurry, Belle; I definitely don't want to be long."

"Star, you weren't kidding when you said we would grill them after they ate. I mean really, three seconds from the last bite, really! Heehee."

"Why are you whispering, Belle, they can't hear us from the living room. Besides, they know we're going to ask questions. I want to know what is wrong with Warren, he's still off balance, and how they got hurt. I'm not sure he should do anything but rest today."

"Have to say I agree with you about Warren, Mom, heehee."

"Thank you, Belle, that is a compliment, I do sometimes enjoy being Mom. Let's get this done, I want my answers."

"Don't get the wrong impression, Star, I want answers too. There are enough unanswered ones already; they don't need to add to the list. Whatever they were doing I'm sure it was to help get answers for me, as a nice surprise but it seems doubtful that was accomplished. If there was any good news, they would have told us as soon as they got back. Ready, let's go."

When the girls entered the living room Warren was fluffing the pillows. According to Silas, Warren was on his third round of fluffing and Silas had no idea why. Everyone sat down. Warren explained he had come up with the idea and plan they would carry out. This was, as Belle predicted, their attempt to gather information and give her answers. Having trouble staying focused on the subject, Silas would finish some of Warren's sentences. Finally, Silas just took over and told the girls what had occurred from the time they went into the barn until their arrival home. From the cars, the different trailers, to the chases and fighting with the perpetrator, the empty mushroom chamber and partially empty armadillo habitat, every detail he could think of.

Warren sat there nodding his head, occasionally softly saying, "Indeed." Silas ended their story with the man taking off with what looked like superhuman speed, explaining the man was in fact on some kind of camouflaged vehicle that was fast and amazingly quiet. When he was done, he looked over at Warren who appeared to be in his own little world. Silas stood up, went over to Warren and began looking at his head. He separated and parted portions of his hair, examining and feeling his head. As Silas pressed here and there, he would ask Warren if it hurt. Warren would reply with no each time, occasionally giggling and slightly swatting at the air.

"You read my mind, Sy, I was wondering if he might have hit his head when he fell," said Starlit. "Belle had wondered earlier if he may have broken a rib or two also. Would you please poke around his ribs when you're done with his head, Doc? I suppose it's not that serious though since he did have an appetite and quite one at that. If he did hit his head, we need to keep a close watch on him—anything?"

"No, Star, no bumps or cuts up here. Come on, Warren, let me help you up; I want to feel your ribs. I will be gentle, tell me if anything hurts."

"No, no, no, no…I am intact, Silas, thank you."

"Warren, there is something wrong, you are not yourself."

"I agree, Silas; my thought process is intermittently hindered."

"You just had a moment of clarity, brother, there's hope yet."

Belle said, "Warren, sit down; rest a while here in the recliner so you can put your feet up. Whatever it is, we're here for you. I don't have to go anywhere right now.

"We went to look for you guys earlier at the picnic and surrounding areas and while we were there, I tried the key for the formation room. It did open the door, so I know that answer. As a matter of fact, that's where we found your phone, Sy, in the formation room by the garage door. I'm happy you are both here and safe and I don't want to go anywhere right now."

"Sy, I'm also happy the both of you are here and safe, but you could have gotten seriously hurt. What were you two thinking? What if that man had had a knife?"

"He didn't, Star..."

"I'm not done, Sy, what if he had a gun even? You had no idea what you were going to face, it was a dangerous thing to do, trying to confront someone like that. What about us? So far nothing has happened to Belle, but you may have jeopardized that now. If this person or people were packing up and leaving, good, just let them go, but now we don't know if they'll leave in peace! What is Warren doing?"

"Looks like he's swatting at flies or something, Mom, I don't think everything you're saying is registering with him right now."

"So, okay, Sy, I'll repeat it all to him when he is better. Another thing, Sy, all that fighting, I can't stand the thought of you hitting anyone; you're not a hitter and you are a grownup, I can't believe you don't have a black eye."

"Wait, wait, Mom, okay, I get it but now that you mention it, I never hit him. We struggled, wrestled, and pushed each other. I never hit him and come to think of it, he never hit me either! I don't think I was in any danger. He never hit me, he was just trying to get away once he was discovered."

"That's great, Sy, a polite criminal—just great!"

"I know you're upset, Star, all with good reason. I am very sorry to have worried you both. And you are right, we didn't think about any possible harm that could've come from this decision. We were confident we'd be able to handle everything, I'm very sorry. I must insist though, that the fact he didn't hit me means something. He had great opportunity to throw some punches and he didn't."

"That makes me feel a little better, Sy. Star, I think he has a valid point. I agree that he was not in danger, and I don't think I am either. That man wasn't carrying any weapons and didn't use his hands as a weapon; he could have but chose not to. That tells me he really means no harm."

"Bravo, bravo, bravo."

"I don't know if that was meant for me, Warren, or if you're watching your own show over there but thank you anyway. Hey! Wait a minute, um-hmm, this is starting to look familiar, I mean the way Warren is acting. Spacing out, loss of balance, flies or whatever that aren't really there; it reminds me of when Star was seeing butterflies that didn't exist. She was off balance too. Big difference on the appetite though."

"Sy, you said you went to the mushroom chamber, did he touch anything?"

"Neither of us did. Remember I mentioned that it was cleaned out very well, it's not possible he touched any mushrooms. We'll have to wait until he's more with it to ask him some questions. He won't be any help right now. By the way Belle, here's the key Warren took from the end table drawer on the way out last night. I'm going to get a book; I'll stay in here and read while he is, well, doing whatever it is, until he has recovered. You two can go do something if you want."

"Thank you, Star and I will be just outside. I have some things we could do out there, if that's really all right with you, Sy."

"Sure, go ahead, I'll call to you if I need you. Don't look so skeptical, Star; it will be okay. We can even have a changing of the guard later and you can stay with him awhile."

"Yes, Sy, I can handle that. Come on, Willow, let's go outside with Belle, come on girl. Awwww, she doesn't want to leave Warren. That's so sweet; she must know he doesn't feel well and wants to stay on his lap to comfort him."

"I'm not so sure he is actually feeling bad, Mom, ha ha—ahem, uh sorry, go on, we'll be fine, really."

Belle and Starlit did some weeding in the gardens, played with the dogs, and even went to visit the kitties in their catio. They reminisced about days gone by, enjoying the break from the mysteries surrounding them. The next stop was visiting the horses and ferrets.

Eventually they had their changing of the guard. Silas went outside, played with the dogs, and visited the kitties as well. After that he went to walk through the orchard.

Standing under one of the fruit trees he contemplated which piece of fruit to eat. Silas plucked his choice, rubbed it gently with his t-shirt to clean it, then took a bite. He thought about the arrangement Belle had with certain people who came to pick from her trees, like they just had Monday morning before all of them took Starlit into the basement. People would leave her the kind of fruit that she didn't grow, duck eggs and food items in jars they prepared. It was a nice setup and like Belle, they all donated food to the food bank. Belle sometimes took her donations to the food bank herself, helping out while there. Then there were times she and others would meet with their donations and carpool to the food bank together. It pleased him to know it was a caring community. He was very happy for her and thought about how he could get into all that and the country life himself.

For a moment it became a strong temptation to want to move. Suddenly, something occurred to him. He told himself out loud to hold that thought and remember it for later. Silas finished his fruit and decided to visit the critters in the barn before going inside. When he entered the barn, he glanced over in the direction of the tack room. He avoided the impulse to enter the little room. When he concluded his visits with all the critters, he decided it was time to check in.

"Hi, Star, how is our patient and where is Belle?"

"Warren has been sleeping since you left and Belle went downstairs to throw some laundry in. She's probably looking over the list again too. This is a nice break from all that searching, don't you think, Sy?"

"Yes, I agree, I'm certainly enjoying the quietness that is other than Warren's snoring."

"When he wakes up, Sy, I think I'll take him for a walk if he's not off balance still. Willow can come with us too. I think she'll be happy to come along and keep her eye on him. I wonder if he was bitten by an insect that caused this weird reaction."

"I don't know, Star, I never heard of this kind of reaction from a bug bite. Anyway, when I was outside, I went for a walk through the orchard and a thought popped into my mind as I was eating some fruit. I want to mention it to Belle…"

"Mention what?" said Belle, walking in.

"You're back, good, come on, let's sit down."

"As I started saying to Star, when I was in the orchard a thought popped into my mind. I remembered Mrs. Yancee made a comment on the kind of trees you don't have that are more common out here. That's when it hit me. All your trees are of your favorite fruit. I think someone knew that. I think there is a connection for sure that someone wanted you to buy this place."

"I'm not sure about that, Sy; it takes several years for these trees to produce fruit. You don't just plant them one year and the next get the fruit. It's just a coincidence."

"Just a minute, um maybe he is right, Belle, hmm."

"How so, Star?"

"Well, the owner only decided to sell the property last year but he did build the houses four years prior. We were just talking about the orchard while we were in the garden, and you told me how long it can take for fruit to grow and that Mr. Yancee told you your trees were about six or seven years old. I'm guessing the previous owner was living in an old house or cabin, at some point decided to plant the trees, then later on build a new home. Most likely the trees were planted before the new houses were built. If Sy is right, that would mean something is going on that started a long time ago. I have no idea what or why, uh, thaaat's all I have."

"Please reiterate that information."

"Warren, you're awake! How are you feeling? Are you up for a little walk? Belle and Sy can mull over the conversation while we are outside. Belle, you might want to talk to Sy about something else too, wink-wink."

"That's right, Star, thanks, you two go on out—oh looks like you three, with Willow. See you soon."

Warren, Willow and Starlit went for a leisurely walk around the yard. Starlit filled him in on the conversation they were having about the orchard. He was a little more with it now and steady on his feet.

Belle had a heart to heart with Silas. As she said she would, she apologized to him. He accepted the apology and thanked her for it. Silas then apologized for saying anything in a way that may have hurt her. They talked for a while about some sensitive issues. They embraced briefly, then thanked their heavenly Father for the grace He has given them to forgive others as He forgave them and thanked Him for his mercy.

TWENTY-EIGHT

BELLE GATHERED TWO BLANKETS and she and Silas joined the others outside. They placed the blankets on the grass in an area near the catio, overlapping them. Everyone sat down and Willow settled on Warren's lap again. No one wanted to rush Warren into talking about what may have happened to him. He had to this point not mentioned anything but earlier told Starlit he felt a little…dormant. After some small talk the conversation steered back in the direction of the orchard. They went over all of that, each giving their opinion of the possibilities. Belle still thought it happened by chance; just what the person who planted it preferred. Finally she asked Warren about his experience.

"Warren, what happened out there, do you remember anything unusual? We think most of your symptoms were like Star's when she was hallucinating from the mushrooms. A big difference was you had an appetite and she didn't. A few times it looked as if you were swatting at flies."

"Fish, Belle, fish. I saw colorful glowing saltwater fish swimming around my head, which was drifting through dark outer space. The fish were various sizes. Occasionally tiny ones would touch my face."

"Warren, that does sound like mushroom effects, but when we were in the mushroom chamber it had been cleaned out really well; how can that be?"

"Silas, I believe my encounter with a mushroom occurred at the time we began our chase. We left our car, each one of us going around a different end of the one blocking the path. You were a little ahead and did not notice I had tripped over a trailer. I went face forward into it. The trailer was not clean. After I righted myself, I shook soil off my hands and spit out something tiny that had flicked into my mouth. The perpetrator had not cleaned the trailers yet. I believe he intended to make one more trip to the habitat after all."

"I see, Warren; he wanted to remove a little more soil before quitting for the night. You took a more direct hit than Star, she only touched a mushroom, but you ingested some."

"Yes Sy, he did, that's true, so how come you seem to be getting better faster than I did, Warren?" asked Starlit.

"Difference in our body type, metabolism, and the actual amount I ingested, Star."

"Of course, that all figures, and what about the car and trailers, do you think he will come back tonight to get them?"

"Doubtful, he knows we are on to his night vigils. He may wait for a future time or not come back at all. Silas, you appear puzzled, your thoughts?"

"What about the items in the office? What about the laboratory equipment, Warren? I didn't really notice if any of it was still there, did you?"

"No, we were the car by, you know car, we were…"

"You are having a glitch, Warren, I think you're trying to say we were distracted right away when we noticed the missing car and focused on that."

"Indeed, Silas, thank you."

"You're welcome, brother, I'm happy to be your translator. I'm curious now about the lab equipment. Belle and I can go check to see if it's still there while you stay here with Star and Willow. Any objections, Star?"

"No, Sy, I think it is better for Warren to wait a while longer before attempting that ladder; okay, Warren?"

"Indeed, I agree. Belle?"

"I would definitely like to see if the equipment is still there or not. I feel a little hesitant though; I said I wasn't going to go anywhere. If you really don't mind then I will go. If you want me to stay, then Sy, you can't go alone, it'll have to wait."

"You have my blessing, Belle."

"Thank you, Warren, we'll keep in touch. Come on Sy, let's get our things and let's not get side-tracked down there so we can come right back."

Belle and Silas eagerly gathered their backpacks. Seemed silly with the short distance they would be going to be bothered bringing them, however they were all raised with this rule: Never leave home without supplies in the event of an occurrence that could delay your return. All of them kept a complete change of clothes in their vehicles, all the way down to undergarments, shoes, and jackets. They carried snacks and water too. Backpacks were no exception. Belle had learned her lesson regarding exploring without taking supplies and making sure they were adequate. Belle gave Starlit and Warren a hug, then reassured them they would not be long.

"Belle, please let me go down first, just in case."

"Go ahead, Sy, but I think it's fine. No one is going to be there, it's daytime."

"See that, there are no lights on."

"I appreciate your protective instincts; thanks, Sy."

"You're welcome; I'll always look out for you."

"The equipment is all gone! They left the stations. Whatever it is they, or he is doing will be done someplace else. I can't stand the thought of more animals being hurt. We have to figure out where their new lab is! Obviously this couldn't have continued here with us knowing it exists but I need, we need more time. If someone comes back, maybe we can follow whoever…wait, Sy they will come back, I doubt the cars and the trailers would be left, they need them! At the very least the cars, those cars were probably expensive. I know Warren didn't think anyone would come back but remember he's not thinking clearly; he's not fully himself yet."

"Yes, of course, they most likely won't be back right away but they will be back."

"Can you figure a way to track the cars and trailers, some kind of tracking device?"

"I'm not sure, Belle, I can contact a friend of mine and inquire. All these drawers in this station are empty too."

"Let's check the office to see if the furniture is still there."

"Well, it's still here, Belle, I suppose the desks and file cabinets could get left behind since they're nothing special and can be replaced, or maybe they'll be taken later on."

"Sy, I'm going to look in all the file cabinets, especially that last one that had been recently unlocked. Please check the desks, look in and under them. See if there is a hidden drawer or panel somewhere."

"Okay, Belle, but you won't find anything in that cabinet; I looked already, remember?"

"Unlike the thorough search you did on the station drawers, you only peeked in these. You didn't open these drawers all the way, you opened them about two inches, peeked in then slammed each one closed, hothead, ha ha."

"I'm embarrassed to say but you're right, I lost control for a minute."

"It's okay, Sy, I can, without a doubt, relate; let's get started… I found something, a piece of paper in the back of the first drawer!"

"That was quick, what is it? Let me see it."

"No Sy, I'm excited I found it but I want to wait to see if we find anything else, keep looking!" Belle folded the paper and tucked it into her back pocket. When she finished searching in and behind the cabinets, she joined Silas who was examining the desks for a second time. Both of them were convinced nothing else would be found. Belle pulled out the paper and unfolded it. As she laid it on one of the desks she said, "What do you think of that?"

"I think Star will say that's adorable," he answered. Then he said, "You better answer your phone, that's probably Mom now. We really haven't been gone that long but you know her."

Nodding her head in agreement she replied, "I do, really I do, and I agree she would say that's adorable too."

Just as she about to answer her phone it stopped ringing and his phone began ringing. Silas smiled at Belle and said, "Too slow."

When he answered his phone, his smile dimmed. In a serious tone and speaking fast he said, "We're on our way now, be right there. Belle, something is wrong with Pirate."

She quickly folded the paper, placing it back into her pocket as she hurried to the ladder.

Belle rushed into the house. Pirate was lying on the floor next to the couch. He did not appear to be well. Nothing tempted him to move, not his favorite toy or any treats. Knowing Belle would want to take him to the vet, Starlit had already brought a crate into the living room.

They all wanted to go to the vet with Belle. Silas drove, Warren was in the front passenger seat, Starlit was in the back with Belle, and Belle had her hand inside the crate on her lap, gently stroking Pirate. When they arrived at the vet the waiting room was full. It was going to be a long wait since Belle did not have an appointment. When finally in the exam room, it was noted Pirate had an abscess on the back of a front leg and a fever. He was given an antibiotic injection and subcutaneous fluids. The cause of his abscess was unknown at this time, and since he was lethargic it was decided he would be staying at the vet for observation.

"I'm sorry," Starlit said, "I should have stayed a few minutes with the kitties this morning. When I put out the food Pirate went over to it but I didn't actually see him eat. He was moving slowly; if I had waited maybe I would have noticed if he ate or not and could have told you."

"It's not your fault," Belle replied, "it is mine. I should have been spending a little more time with them myself. I didn't think anything of it when he wasn't out in their catio earlier. I should have checked on him then. Also, for him to be that sick it probably started a couple of days ago."

"Pirate is in good hands," Silas said, "he will be fine. From now on we will all take a little more time with the critters when we are feeding or visiting and pay attention to what they're doing. We have all been distracted, Belle, not just you. Keep in mind though since we don't know them as well as you do, we may report unnecessary things."

Warren added, "It is better to err on the side of caution, then Belle can make a determination. I should take us to lunch while we are out. It is not far to downtown."

Silas said, "I'm for that, I am hungry; thank you, Warren and I'll split the bill with you. Belle, do you have a preference?"

"I do, seafood, please."

When they arrived at the restaurant a lot of people were dining outside. There were a couple of tables available there, but Silas asked to be seated inside at a booth, preferably in a corner away from the mainstream. They only had to wait ten minutes and they were seated in a cozy corner out of the way of the main dining area. After placing their orders, Belle reached into her back pocket and took out the folded paper she placed there earlier.

"I think this is why you wanted us to have a more private seating arrangement," Belle said as she waved the paper in the air just above the table surface, "thank you, Sy." She unfolded the paper, smoothed it out on the table and said, "I found this inside a cabinet at the back of the drawer."

"Oh, that's adorable," Starlit said. Silas and Belle said at the same time, "We knew you'd say that!" Starlit asked, "What does it mean?"

"Well, it says Noah's Ark, Phase II," answered Silas. "The ark has lots of animals on it. Look at them; all exotic, that's their main interest. It clarifies the kind of animals being experimented on. I think Belle agrees."

"I do," she replied, "exotic for sure. We can add that to our list."

Warren said, "I believe based on the ark animals, we can rule out breeding exotic and domestics. Perhaps cross-breeding within the exotic species is the intention, possibility to create an odd variety."

"Why would anyone want to do that," Starlit asked, "it doesn't make sense to me."

Silas said, "That's because you're not greedy, they want to make money, of course. If they could come up with some weird, strange and unusual animal, it will sell to the highest bidder, probably not your average-income person either."

Then she asked, "What about Rarity, she's not exotic? Seems there was an interest in her."

Belle answered, "Remember I've mentioned mules are a cross between horses and donkeys, but the mules are sterile. Maybe they were trying to figure a way to avoid sterility in whatever animals they're trying to breed." Pointing to the partial letters under Phase II, Belle continued, "I don't know what words were here. We have *t* and *h* together, torn space then *e* and *s* together, the rest torn, gone. Each line is centered; I don't think a long word or sentence would be here; oh, it figures the paper got torn right at those spots. I can't figure out what was here. Also, what was Phase I? How many phases are there? I was feeling good but now there are more questions, again."

"Here comes the food," Silas said, "we can c-h-e-w on all that while we eat. You can add the Ark and exotic animals to the list later."

Before they left the restaurant Belle called the vet to check on Pirate. He was resting comfortably but there were no improvements in appetite or activity. It had only been two hours since he was admitted. She did not think there would be any change yet but was hoping and was relieved his condition did not get worse. The others reminded her Pirate was in God's loving hands.

Warren said with conviction, "The Lord loves the animals, as well as us, He created. He heard our prayers and will comfort Pirate whatever the outcome, do not fret." Then he closed his eyes, bowed his head slightly and said, "Father in heaven, we lift up our sister Belle to you, you know her troubled heart. We ask in Jesus' name you pour your peace that transcends all understanding over her, that she may rest in you and will trust you in this unsettling time, amen." The others all said, "Amen."

Moved to tears, Belle smiled and said, "Thank you, Warren, I needed that prayer. As you would say, indeed I did."

Silas asked, "Dessert anyone?"

Starlit said, "Not now, later some of that delicious ice cream Belle has at home though; we can digest somewhat before we indulge."

"Wonderful," said Warren, "I would be delighted to have some delicious ice cream."

"Mom, I'm surprised you're not concerned it might spoil dinner since it'll be about three thirty or so by then," Silas said.

"I'll just make a late dinner," Belle replied, "and a light one. We can vote on that when the time gets closer."

The group drove home in good spirits after their lunch. After ice cream they went downstairs to add the Ark to the list and decided to play darts while they were down there. Two darts were missing. Belle figured they were left in the closet and went to get them. She found a box she had not opened in years. She took something out of it, got the darts out of their box then joined the others.

"Look what I found," she said giggling, "I haven't seen this in years. I forgot I even kept it."

The others were studying it as she held it out. "Unbelievable," Silas shouted, "crazy even!" He took it from her.

Starlit gasped, wide eyed, she said, "I want a closer look too."

"What is it, what's wrong?" Belle asked. "Was it silly to keep it?"

Silas passed it to Starlit when he was done. She looked intently at it and turned to Warren asking, "Do you see what we see?"

Warren took it from her, examined it, then asked Belle, "Do you know what this is?"

She laughed, answering, "Of course I do, something from when I was a kid."

"She does not see it," Warren said.

"Definitely not," said Starlit. "For sure, not," said Silas. Then together the three of them, shaking their heads in amazement, all said: "Denial! Denial! Denial for sure."

TWENTY-NINE

BELLE, LOOKING QUITE BAFFLED ASKED, "What do you guys mean? What am I in denial about?"

All the others, perplexed themselves regarding her response, looked at one another for a moment, then Warren said, "Belle, tell me what this is, in detail." He held the item out in front of her, waiting for an explanation.

Finally, she took a slow deep breath and said, "It's a drawing I did for a class project when I was very young, in sixth grade. The teacher liked it, said I did a good job, I got an A, and that's it."

Silas took the drawing from Warren, smiled and said, "This is very good, Belle, and proof Star and I came to the correct conclusion about the orchard."

Belle just stared at him shaking her head side to side as said, "What does this have to do with the orchard, it's a drawing of a house?"

Starlit asked, "Why did you draw it?"

"Well," Belle began, "we were given a choice of several subjects. I chose the one to design a house. I thought it would be fun and I imagined a house I might like to have when I grew up. I guess I had it in me young to be able to design houses, which sure helped with what I did not that long ago. Okay, Warren, why the huge grin on your face?"

"You said, and I quote, 'I imagined a house I might like to have when I grew up,'" he answered, "welcome to adulthood, Belle."

Silas then swung his arm out, sweeping his hand around the room and toward the ceiling, indicating upstairs. It hit Belle like a wave crashing at the seashore and she fell back onto the couch. All she could say was, "No way, can't be, how can it be, no, can't be."

Silas handed her the drawing and sat down next to her. Starlit sat down on her other side, placing her arm around Belle; Warren sat on the floor in front of Belle. They sat in silence for a few minutes while Belle processed all of this.

"I understand what you've all been trying to tell me now, the orchard, this. I don't understand how this could be possible and certainly not why it came to be. I can't believe it; I'm sitting in and own the house I designed as a kid! Look, even the flat brown stones I drew on this page that I wanted for the outside of the house, they are on the outside of the house, amazing! I have no idea who could be responsible for this and the orchard."

"Besides the teacher, Belle, who else saw this drawing?"

"Just Nanny, Sy, I showed no one else that I can remember. I remember her saying my mom and dad would be proud of me, then she put it on the refrigerator. It was there for one week. That was our time-honored tradition; after that I put it away with other school projects. From time to time, I would take out the boxes I kept those things in and look at them but never showed them to anyone. Eventually I got rid of some items. I kept this and a couple of other things along with a ceramic clay pot I made, that one in the living room—remember Star, I told you I made it?"

"Yeah, I do, that was a long time ago, Belle. So, what do you make of this scenario, Warren?"

"A few people know Belle's favorite fruits, Star, it would be a waste of time to pursue that avenue; however as of now we know of only two people who viewed the drawing—good place to start, Nanny first. I believe the key is finding out if anyone else viewed the drawing. It is plausible to conclude the one who had access to the drawing would be the one to have planted the orchard as well as building the houses."

"It's still early; I'm going to call Nanny."

"Sorry that took so long, guys. She was happy to hear from me. I didn't realize so much time had gone by since we spoke last. I apologized and told her I'd call her again next week. We usually talk every other week even if it's brief; I feel badly I didn't call her sooner. We're planning for her to come for a visit. Anyway, she said she never showed the drawing to anyone. That leaves the teacher, I guess. Sy, when you talk to your friend about a tracking device could you ask him how we can find information on someone?"

"I left him a message while you were on the phone with Nanny, just in case, and about tracking again. Belle, I was thinking about the exotic animals being transported. They would have to be in quarantine a very long time and there would have to be licenses or permits for them. Maybe my friend can tell us how to track those, then we could get a name or two of the culprits."

"No, Sy, you don't need permits or licenses to own exotic animals. Quarantine for most is only thirty days but if it is for horses traveling back and forth for publicly recognized shows, then ninety days both ways."

"Thank you for clarifying that, Belle. I can see Warren is in deep thought. He was studying the Ark while I was on the phone. I think he's ready to share his thoughts now."

"Indeed, I am, Silas. I have come to two conclusions; the first, that exotic, wild and domestic animals were experimented on in order to achieve an ultimate goal. Taking into consideration what you both have just said and observing the animals on the Ark, perhaps we were not on the right track with breeding. Notice the animals in the background and on either side of the middle group up front. You have giraffes, chimpanzees, anteaters, gazelles and hippopotamus. The ones front and center are drawn much larger, not just to depict their size but to emphasize their prominence. You have the African lion, black rhinoceros, African elephant, African leopard, and the Cape buffalo, known as The Big Five. These are game animals. No one can possess, sell, import, or export live game animals. Smuggling is the only option."

"Gee, Warren, that would be difficult, to smuggle such large animals."

"Indeed, Silas, hence the experiments. What do you remember about the animals on the biblical ark?"

"There were two of every kind."

"Yes, Sy, but more importantly, and I think what Warren is getting at, is their size!" said Belle.

"That's right, Belle, they were all babies!"

"Correct, Star, babies, small animals."

"Ladies, more than that, I believe the goal is to delay the growth of the baby animals, then accelerate it at the desired time, the ultimate goal."

"So, Warren, you're saying that is the reason for the small sizes of Anomaly, Rarity and Momma Possum; it's what happened to them."

"Yes, Silas, yes, I believe it is what happened to them. These experiments have been going on for many years."

"And guys, don't forget the giant snakes! Remember, Belle said her boss told her they were much larger than they should have been."

"Yeah, Star, and they died. I hope my critters will be okay. Maybe those snakes died somehow because of their overgrowth, in which case the horses and Momma will be fine. I wonder if that creature by the Yancee farm is an experiment that escaped like you thought, Star. Sorry to interrupt, Warren, go on please."

"Thank you, Belle, my second conclusion: someone from the Center is definitely involved. Perhaps two to four people, a group right from the Center. We should not exclude the possibility of women being involved. Not necessarily only older folks either, younger ones could have been recruited, following instructions of a veteran."

"Warren, I'm glad you're back to your old self again," said Belle. "I'm going to accept your conclusions. It all fits in my mind, I feel satisfied that is an answer to some of what is going on. Now I want to know who they are. I want to know who had anything to do with my drawing. We still don't know if the animals and my coming to buy this house are related. I think they must be two separate cases, which makes more sense in my mind. It's obvious to me now, someone did want me here… Star, you have a strange look on your face, what is it?"

"I just got a feeling of peace while I was thinking about the baby animals. I'm confused; my senses are detecting, good things? Seems peaceful, no panic, no suspicions. No way that can be right; after all, the intentions of the experiments are awful. I don't get it. You should add The Big Five and your house drawing to the list, Belle."

"Yep, Star, I will and you're right, your senses are not making sense!"

"I think you need to make a separate list of the older people at the Center, the ones who get paid and the volunteers," said Silas. "Start with that, then we can try to figure out who the recruits are, if that's even possible."

"Good idea, Sy, I'll put Ed at the top of the list. Not only is he an older person, he owns the Center—oh, ooh, his wife! She sometimes volunteers, that's two. Oh my gosh, his brother, I forgot about him! He's a co-owner. He doesn't come around a lot but does volunteer occasionally. Let's see, who else...okay…done. We have four men and two women on the veteran list. The rest are younger people, all under thirty-five years old and out of them, three get a salary."

"What does Ed's brother do for a living? I'm guessing he does work since he is not at the Center often."

"You're right, Star, he does work. He owns a small trucking company."

"Bingo!!"

"Care to elaborate on your excitement, Sy?"

"I will, Belle. It's very convenient having trucks at your disposal so you can transport whatever you may need to sneak back and forth to the Center."

"Oh yeah, that would be; wow, Sy, you said you thought Ed was involved. This makes that, well, I find it so hard to believe. Ed seems to care so much about the animals. He couldn't be cruel to them, experimenting on any; no, I've been looking up to the man, he's taught me a lot, and I can't accept it!"

"Belle, calm down, it is not written in stone, stop pacing please. Perhaps his brother is acting without his knowledge; perhaps it is neither of them. We are not done with the investigation. I understand where you are coming from but please keep an open mind."

"Warren, I cannot do that right now. Okay, I'll calm down, but I can only offer half my mind to be open. I know there are people in this world who are great deceivers, but this is just too hard to accept. My open half is open to the fact we're not done yet, and more likely the possibility he knows nothing about these things."

"I didn't mean to strike a nerve or be insensitive, Belle, I'm sorry. Warren is right about not coming to any conclusions yet. I hope it turns out you're right."

"Thanks, Sy, thanks for that. I really hope I'm right too and that's not a pride thing, I just don't want to be hurt. It really hurts to be deceived by someone you know and trust. I'm so tired suddenly, but I was thinking about that creature, and I want to go to the area where I saw it. It's getting close to the time that happened…uh well, maybe not now, tomorrow; you both look really tired, and you should rest since you didn't have much sleep. Warren did get a catnap but it obviously wasn't enough. I should start dinner; we can explore tomorrow. Star, Sy, would you please both go upstairs and pick our dinner choices, I'm going to call the vet since they're closing shortly and we'll be up in a few minutes."

Belle did not hear the news about Pirate she was hoping for but again his condition had not worsened. Now she finally had her time with Warren to apologize to him. She had a more difficult time doing so with him than the others. He, like the others, thanked her, apologized if he came across harsh and told her he appreciated her confession. They talked awhile, longer than Belle anticipated. Warren stood up when he had finished speaking. He held out his hand, offering to help Belle up. She smiled, took hold of his hand and together they headed for the stairs. When they got to the kitchen, they discovered dinner was ready to be served. Belle thanked Starlit and Silas for preparing dinner.

During dinner Belle told the others some of Pirate's antics, giving everyone a good laugh; then she told stories about the rest of the kitties, ending by reminiscing about the stowaway, Micro. They talked about the recent discoveries and discussed some of the previous ones. The wolf was brought up again. It was mentioned how unusual it was to see and hear it during the day since they are nocturnal critters. Silas said it was probably due to it being raised as a pet. He was not sure why the dogs were okay with it but maybe they sensed it was not wild. Belle said she wanted to spend time with the kitties and the other critters as well after they all were fed.

All that behind them now, they finally made it to playing darts, the girls against the guys. They played until 8:15, then decided to call it quits to get ready for bed. The guys were very tired and lost the last game. Silas had not heard back from his friend yet. Belle was anxious and asked him to call his friend in the morning instead of waiting for him to call back. She wanted to get started searching for info on her old teacher and see if they could obtain a tracking device.

It was lights out for all but Belle; her mind was racing. She sat on the edge of her bed thinking over the most recent events as she rocked slightly back and forth. Thoughts of her old teacher rolled around in her mind. Nothing unusual popped up. He was a young teacher; one of two she had that year. He was kind and helpful to all the students in the class. Belle doubted he could be involved in any way, then, suddenly she remembered, he did mention one time he had a cousin who was in the construction business. She hopped off the bed, wondering if that could mean something, and was just about to open her bedroom door but stopped, turned, and went back to the bed. Deciding to wait until the morning to tell the others, Belle climbed in under the covers, shut off the light, leaned back and heavily sighed as she closed her eyes.

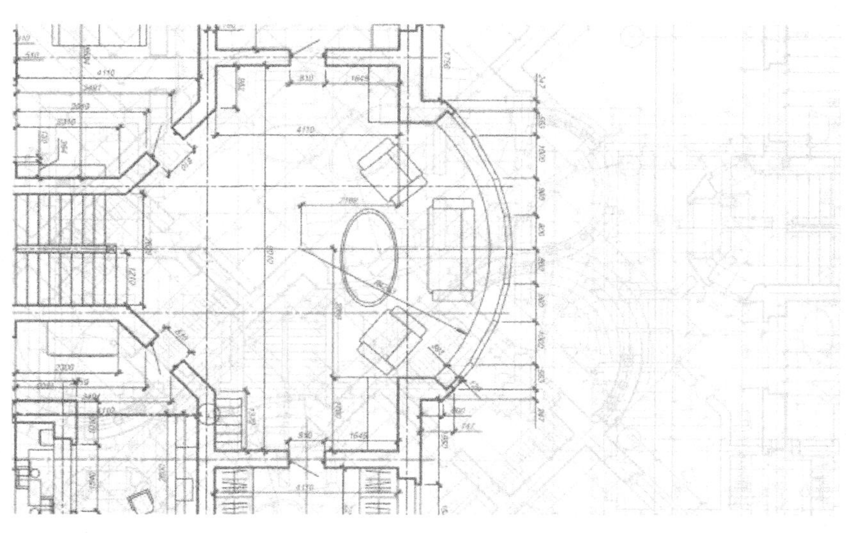

THIRTY

AFTER BREAKFAST THEY COMPLETED chores, then Belle called the vet. She received good news about Pirate. He was eating a little and drinking water now and able to go home at the end of the day if he continued to improve, which the vet was confident he would. All the critters received some attention and play time before Belle, Starlit, Warren and Silas headed out on their search. They gathered their belongings and climbed into Rover, Belle in the driver's seat.

It was a warm sunny morning with glistening dew over some of the landscape. As they traveled along a couple of squirrels bounded across the road in front of them; each one was carrying something in its mouth. They did not see any other animals but did hear some birds calling to one another. Eventually Belle turned off the road onto the path of the Yancee property. She proceeded in the direction she took to their farmhouse the day she had gone to pick up Momma. They traveled through a wooded area and came to a large open area that had some trees intermittently growing among various sizes of shrubs and bushes.

Belle said, "I can't believe your friend hasn't called you back yet, Sy. We kind of have our hands tied for the moment. Maybe in the meantime I'll remember my teacher's cousin's name."

Silas replied with, "He's probably very busy. I'll try him again later, emphasizing it's important."

In a high-pitched voice Starlit spoke up, saying, "I can't believe we are searching for that creature! Worse, I came along!"

"No," Belle said, "not the creature, just evidence, footprints or something. We're looking this morning instead of the time of day I had seen it to avoid an actual encounter. I'm not sure if that was a regular time it foraged but thought we better not take a chance. I really don't want to come up against it. I realized that last night in bed, so here we are now."

She slowed down, then stopped Rover. "This is the spot the deer ran in front of me." Belle pointed and said, "Over there is where I saw it, the creature, the thing, disappear into the woods, then I continued on to the Yancee farm. We can drive a little further in that direction but then we'll have to leave Rover. Hmm, I want to name it, call it something other than the thing or it."

Silas trotted ahead of the others saying, "I'll lead the way and Warren can take the rear for a while." He asked Belle, "How much area will we search?"

Warren chuckled, answering with, "Knowing Belle, all three hundred acres of the Yancee property," and then he asked Belle, "How far to the farm from here?"

"A few minutes by car, not long at all, Warren, about five minutes."

"That's not very far," said Silas, "I wonder if the Yancees ever saw it. You said Mr. Yancee made light of the incident, saying anything could have spooked the deer, kind of sounds like he never saw the thing. You're right, Belle; you should give it a name. I don't like, it or the thing either; 'creature" is out, how about Beastie?"

Starlit rolled her eyes. With a huff she said, "Really, Sy. I think *It* probably avoids being seen; Belle barely got a glimpse of the *Thing* herself. There's a lot of wooded area out here; maybe the Yancees stay close to the farm and never did see the *Creature*."

He replied, "Someone got a glimpse of Beastie, Cy mentioned strange sightings to Belle."

Warren, grinning said, "Perhaps Mr. Yancee said what he did to discourage people from wandering around his property."

Starlit laughed and said, "You mean like what we're doing right now?"

"Indeed," he answered.

They walked to the point where Belle saw the creature disappear into the thick of the woods, then came upon a path. Nothing unusual was found so they continued on. The path curved, turning in the direction of the Yancee farm. Silas was farther up the path than the others; he stopped, then raised his hand to silence them. The others stood still, listening and looking around, quietly waiting for instruction. Silas turned toward them, placed his index finger to his lips, indicating they should remain quiet, and waved his hand at them in a pushing back motion. They backed up. Silas remained where he was, shifting his head around. Stooping down slightly he moved forward a little, stopped, and then moved forward again. He obviously had his sights on something. Eventually he straightened up. Slowly he walked backward toward the others, glancing back and forth all the way until he reached them. He could see that Belle and Starlit had eyes wide as saucers and Warren's brow was furrowed with concern. Silas could tell what they were all thinking.

Whispering, Silas described what he had seen. "There's a short, narrow tiny clearing with what looks like a large mound covered in weeds and vines at its far end; it could be a small cave. The mound sticks out the end of a hill. There was something very large near the inside of the opening. It might have been Beastie. I watched but he didn't move, maybe he could smell me or see me. I was back from the edge of the clearing so I doubt he saw me, but if he did and wanted to chase, I think Beastie would have been in view by now. I'm thinking, like other wild animals, he wants to avoid us. Also a huge log is lying on the ground a few feet from the cave opening. Could be he likes to sit there sometimes or sharpen his claws, scratching on it like a cat. I got a faint whiff of something that smelled awful too. Wait here, I want to take another look. Belle, please let me have your binoculars."

As she handed him the binoculars she smiled, nodded, and said, "Beastie it is."

Teasingly he replied, "Oh, oh sure, I get affirmation on the name now, not…" Then in a slightly higher tone, imitating Belle as he walked away from them, he said, "Sy-Sy, be careful, oh pleeease be careful and come back to meee."

Warren chuckled and the girls giggled, then Starlit said, in her motherly voice, "Yes, Sy, do be careful, very careful please."

Silas being gone too long caused concern; nervously Starlit said, "This is why we shouldn't split up, what happened to that rule? He should have had one of us with him! We need to look for him."

Silas suddenly appeared, running toward them. The girls' eyes widened and their hearts pounded fiercely.

Warren said, "Ladies…" Before he could say any more the girls turned and began running back toward Rover with Warren close behind, urging them to move faster. Starlit could feel her heart pounding fast in her chest. It seemed so loud she was sure it could be heard by the others.

When they arrived at Rover they got in and Belle, hand shaking, started the engine. They watched and could see Silas was almost to them. Starlit screamed, "Hurry, Sy!" He began waving his arms, then he stopped. He motioned to them to come but they stayed where they were. In a normal tone he said, "It's okay, come on." They did not move. Not wanting to raise his voice, he began walking quickly to them.

Warren could see the demeanor of Silas was not one of fear but excitement; he let out a sigh of relief and said, "Ladies, I believe it is safe to exit now."

They did so reluctantly but Belle kept the engine running. As Silas approached he asked, "Why did you guys run?"

"Because *you* were running Sy, why were you running? You scared us."

"I'm sorry, Belle, that makes sense given the reason why we came out here, sorry. I was running because I couldn't wait to tell you what I found. I couldn't shout to you because there was someone out there heading in the direction of the farm, it didn't look like Mr. Yancee either. He was a good distance away, but I didn't want to take a chance and give us away. Come on, you have to see this."

Starlit asked, "Does this mean Beastie is gone, Sy?"

Warren answered, "I believe it does, I trust our brother."

Then Belle said, "I wonder who that was you saw, Sy." As she turned off Rover and removed the key she added, "Must have been someone from the Yancee farm, a relative or friend. Come on, guys, let's hurry."

They walked quickly down the path, slowing their pace as they approached the narrow clearing and pausing at its edge. They scanned the area, looking and listening for anyone or anything.

Silas used the binoculars to view the distant surroundings. He handed them to Belle and said, "Look at the cave." Belle placed them to her eyes, made some adjustments, then asked, "What cave? I see a mound covered in weeds and vines, no opening. Are you sure you saw one? Have you had any mushrooms lately?"

The others laughed, clearly seeing what Belle did and they did not need binoculars. Silas wanted her to clarify with a close-up view of what was ahead of them.

"Definitely no mushrooms, Belle," Silas said, "there really is an opening."

Starlit said, "Just a guess, must be another hologram."

"No," Silas replied, "come take a look." They cautiously walked toward the cave. Silas gently took hold of the vines. As he moved them to the side he said, "This is the door to the uh, cave."

"A well-camouflaged door," Warren said, "unusual for a cave to have a door, unusual indeed."

Laughing, Starlit commented, "No mushrooms after all, the door blends in perfectly with the vines, which are like a curtain. Even when we got close you couldn't tell there was something behind them. So Sy, these were pushed aside, and the door was open when you first saw this cave."

"Yes, and it's not exactly a cave; come in." He opened the door and as they walked in Starlit exclaimed, "Oh my goodness!" Belle said, "Double Ditto!" Warren nodded thoughtfully, thumb and forefinger to his chin.

There they stood in a tiny room obviously built for one, two at most. With four of them there it was cramped. The room was about nine and a half feet wide by ten feet long. The ceiling was about eight feet high. The perimeter was laid out as follows: To the left of the door along the front wall was a wide shelf supported by legs, like a table, which continued to the corner, then along the left wall three quarters of the way down, forming an L-shaped work surface. In that corner under the table was a fan. The left side of the back wall had three short shelves with storage cabinets under them. To the right of them was a back door with a large hook at the top of it. Right of that door was an upholstered chair in the corner and a sconce for light. In front of the chair along the right wall on the floor was a hatch door. Above the hatch on the wall was a tiny door that housed the electrical box. There was a small space after the hatch door, and then you were back where you entered in. The ceiling held lights which were more than adequate for this space.

"It smells slightly like rotten eggs in here."

"Yeah Star, that was the little whiff I got earlier. I'll just sit over in the chair to give you guys a little room to take it all in."

"Thanks Sy, you can narrate the tour while you're sitting there, ha ha."

"Gladly, Belle, you have something in the making over there. You have all the supplies to make the product you desire with enough storage for everything, books to read if you want to sit or take a nap even. When your work is done you open the hatch and store it downstairs. There's a very nice, mostly quiet, generator out back. What do you think, Warren?"

"I believe the slight odor of hydrogen sulfide, the sulfur or spoiled egg odor, is normal for the process taking place. The odor built up while the door was closed. You detected it, Silas, when the door opened, and it drifted with the breeze in your direction. It is unusual to have this located in the middle of nowhere."

"I agree it's strange to have this way out here, Warren," said Belle, "why not just in your own basement after all. I recognize those empty bottles. They had one at the Yancees' when we went for dinner, only it had wine in it. So this is wine being made and there is a wine cellar."

"Yes, Belle, you are correct. I believe this batch was recently stirred. Someone left this fishing book out and opened. My calculation is that person will be back soon; we should leave now. We will exit the back door, take a quick look around, then head back to Rover."

Alarmed, Silas jumped up out of the chair, "Wait! Don't do it, Warren, take your hand off that handle!"

Starlit and Belle, both startled, questioned him, "Why? What's going on?"

"Let me explain!" He shouted, "Warren, wait!"

All were talking over each other. At the same time Warren stepped through the doorway, pushing aside a curtain of vines. Starlit said, "Warren, maybe you should wait," as she and Belle followed him.

Too late! Starlit suddenly weakened. Trembling, she dropped to her knees. Shaking, Belle hid behind Warren, leaning against him to keep from falling. Stunned, no one moved. The frightening sight caused a deep chill in them.

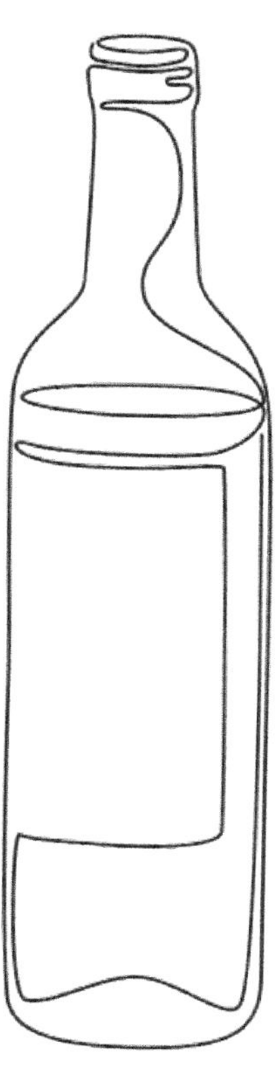

THIRTY-ONE

THE BEAST! THERE IT WAS, behind some vines that were hanging over a hollow in the side of the hill. At any moment it would step out from behind the vines. Beastie waited though, staying still in the hollow, almost frozen with fear itself. Was it being cautious? Did it think it was their prey? Could be it realized it was outnumbered and hoped they would go away or that they did not see it.

Warren slowly lifted his arms up to shoulder height; spreading them out wide, he pushed back slightly on Belle and together they inched backward. Suddenly, when they were just about to reach the place where Starlit huddled on the ground, the vines began moving. Terrified, both Belle and Starlit gasped.

Silas came up behind Starlit and knelt down. She let out a scream. "It's okay," he said as he put his arms around her, "it's just me. It's okay, everyone, look, he's not moving, just the vines are moving with the breeze. He can't move, really it is okay."

Her voice shaking, Starlit asked, "Is it dead?"

"Well, no, he was never alive."

Warren said in a stern tone, "Silas, please expound!"

"I'm sorry, really, I tried to stop you. I was going to explain what was in the back out here, but I didn't get a chance."

Belle sat down and let out a sigh of relief. "This is crazy. Oh my gosh, I'm still shaking." Warren sat down next to her and placed his arm around her. He could feel her trembling.

Stuttering, Starlit quietly said, "I uh-uh, I-I think it just moved."

"No, no Star, the breeze picked up, that's all. Beastie is hanging on a hook and the breeze probably moved him. I think he hangs around on the back door too sometimes, heehee."

"Oh no, you *didn't*! How can you make a joke out of this after scaring us half to death?"

"I wasn't trying to, Belle; really the chuckle just came out. I'm sorry; I am upset it turned out this way, a little nervous you know."

While Silas and Belle were conversing, Starlit was squirming in Silas's arms and then she shrugged herself free. Annoyed, she said, "Yeah, how could you, Sy?" "I'm sorry, Star," he said as he took hold of her shoulders. "Please take a deep breath and try to calm down. Belle, you too please, deep breath."

Warren cleared his throat and said, "This is partly my fault. I was in a hurry and did not heed your warning to wait. I apologize, please forgive me. We should collect ourselves and leave. I do not want to be found here by Beastie's animator. We will talk later. Silas, make sure the room is left the way you found it."

"Sure thing, Warren, you guys head back to the car; I'll check the room and turn the lights off."

"I will drive," Warren said. Belle sat in the front seat and Starlit in the back. Both were relieved to be away from Beastie, even though it was not alive. The experience left an ill impression on their spirits. Silas arrived and he and Warren acknowledged each other by nodding their heads, then they got into Rover.

"Warren, head to the pond please, I want to walk around there. I need to be in a serene place for a little bit. Silas, what was the wine cellar like?"

"It was about the size of what you thought was a root cellar in the barn, Belle, small. There was a narrow small table along a short wall. The longer wall was all wine rack with several bottles of wine, about thirty. That room has very good lighting too. I think you made a good call, Warren; something was in the works, and someone will probably be returning soon. Do you think this is a little business someone has going?"

"No, Silas, it appears the wine is made in small batches. The equipment and lack of barrels to hold large quantities supports my thought on that subject. I believe it is for self-use, a bottle or two to family and friends, done for enjoyment, a hobby."

"Do you think Beastie was created to keep people away?"

"Indeed, I do, Silas, especially little ones. Perhaps the beast makes an appearance on occasion along the outskirts of the woods to scare the children from the Yancee farm, keeping them from venturing in the direction of the still."

"Yes, I believe that, guys," said Belle. "I wonder who the man was that Sy saw, though. Maybe it's someone Mr. Yancee lets use his property or they both make wine. I suppose it doesn't matter, that's a mystery solved, and remember we can't tell anyone about Beastie or the wine-making room."

"I'm sorry again, guys," Silas said, "I should have told you about Beastie first, that would have avoided what happened. I wanted you to be able to touch the costume. It was two pieces, a top and bottom, lightweight. It looks heavy but the material is thin and light. The fur was long but in patches, not solid over the whole costume, you can't tell that from a distance. He doesn't have a face either, just fur. Part of the chest is made to sit on a person's shoulders to give Beastie his height. The person inside can look through an opening to see where they're going that is covered in a brown plastic piece, like looking through sunglasses. There are no feet; the pants part ends at the ankle, and no hands. On both sides of the bottom are two loops that attach to large buttons on the top portion to keep the suit together. It seems easy to get in and out of it quickly."

"Oh my gosh," exclaimed Starlit, "seeing it behind the vines was scary enough! If I could have seen it had no eyes, nose and mouth, wow, that no-face thing might have just pushed me over the edge! I might have just freaked and died right there!"

"I'm not sure how I would have reacted to no face, all I know is what I did see made me want to turn and run but I couldn't."

"I relate, Belle, I froze at the unexpected sight," said Warren. "I experienced a chill up my spine that I had never before experienced."

"I confess, Warren, I experienced the same thing when I went through the back door the first time," Silas said. "We were at a standoff for a few minutes before I realized Beastie was just hanging there. I waited. I glanced down at some point, and I didn't see feet. Then I looked through the binoculars. It gave me a much better view of what was behind the vines. Convinced it was harmless, I went to check him out. I was so excited about all I discovered I ran back to get you guys. I wanted to save the best discovery for last but wasn't expecting it to turn out the way it did. I'm happy to say he was not alive, real but not a live beast. You know, I think we did experience chills when we were younger…"

"Perhaps," Warren interrupted, "however, not so intense. I think the ladies would appreciate it if we avoided a walk down that memory lane."

It was a pleasant stroll around the pond. A breeze was moving the vegetation to and fro. There was life teaming around the area today. Frogs sat on the floating leaf of a water lily. They stood out well against the dark yellow of the lily flower. Two dragonflies hovered over pale orange lily flowers. Their tiny dark blue bodies shimmered in the sunlight. Birds were flying about and singing. To the delight of the girls, a family of quail scurried past them and hid under the cover of some bushes. A couple of wild rabbits were munching on something near the edge of the far side of the pond. Some ducks flew down, quacking, and landed on the pond.

"What a wonderful sight this is today! This is a sight for sore eyes, so refreshing after what we just experienced, a blessing for sure."

"Yes, Star, it certainly is. There's some cracked corn in the picnic shed we can feed to the ducks."

"I'll run and get it, Belle; I assume the corn is in one of the cabinets," offered Silas.

"Yes, Sy, thanks. It's in a large jar on the bottom; just put a little in the paper bags next to it for each of us."

"You got it, I'll be right back."

"I think now that the ducks have had something to eat, I could go for something."

"We can have some snacks for now, Sy, it's a little early for lunch and well, snacks are all we have with us."

"Yes, snacks will be sufficient for now, Belle," said Warren. "Afterward I would like to go through the formation room to where the car and trailers are; perhaps we can plan the placement of the tracking device."

"That's a good idea, Warren, then we'll be ready to set it up. Maybe we'll get two, one for each car."

"Belle, look, there's the quail again! Those little ones are so cute!"

"Yeah, Star, definitely." Then sounding somewhat disappointed Belle said, "I would love to pick them up and pet their little feathered bodies, but we can't."

Starlit replied, "I know. Come on, Belle, let's go over and eat at the table instead of sitting on the ground here."

Everyone was quiet while they ate. They each had carried different snacks and shared them with each other.

Warren broke the silence, "Delightful." He took a long, slow breath and said, "Belle, I believe with the knowledge we have of the surroundings, perhaps you should not allow others on your property any longer."

"You know, Warren, that might be a good idea," agreed Silas. "I might be afraid of the bees, but someone else might not care and could make their way to the alcove."

"No way, Sy, that hive is huge; I don't think anyone would risk getting near it."

"That's right, Star, that's why it was made so big," said Belle, "that and if they did get inside the little space, you can't tell there's a door. The path ends quite a distance from the hive too so I'm confident no one will venture there anyway.

"Besides, I did limit the time anyone can be here; it was legal advice. They can have lunch, clean up and leave. No hiking on the property. If anyone stays for long, it's because I'm here with them like the time we had a birthday party here. No one paid much attention to the sundial either. They acknowledged it was there briefly but didn't step over the wildflowers to get close, uh like we did, they observed from a distance."

Star mused, "If Belle suddenly told people not to come here anymore that would make them suspicious, I think, and then they might sneak coming here."

"Good point, Star, I don't want to make changes. Come on, let's go to the formation room, but first we'll check the area to make sure no one is around."

Warren turned on the monitors first thing and scanned the area. Seeing the portion of the path where the car and trailers were left, he began to nod his head. "Clever," he said, as he rubbed his chin, "clever indeed."

Silas walked over to him and asked, "What is it, you look intense?" Silas looked at the monitor, answering his own question. "Oh yeah, I see, so much for not coming back right away."

Belle shouted, "Not fair! No no, not fair!" The others turned and looked at her, each with a certain expression on their faces, to which she replied, "Well, all right, there weren't exactly any rules, but you've got to admit this is frustrating." She began looking for the switch that would open the garage door since they did not have the remote with them.

Starlit said, "It might make it easier for her to accept that the cars are really gone if she's there outside."

As Belle walked around outside Starlit called to her, "Maybe the double the guys took back to the barn is still there." Belle rushed back in, excitedly saying, "Great thought, we should go look right now, we could still have a chance to get a tracking device set up after all!"

"Do not get your hopes up," Warren said, "I do not believe it will be there." *Ting-ting, ting-ting*… "Silas, your phone."

"Yes Warren, I'll see if that's my friend." He reached in his pocket, opened his phone, and read the message. He rolled his eyes, forced a little smile and in a sarcastic tone mumbled, "Great."

THIRTY-TWO

"THAT DOESN'T SOUND LIKE something I'm going to be happy to hear. Go ahead, Sy, tell us what that is," said Belle.

"Belle, this is a two-part message. When I left the second message my friend started a search for your teacher right away. Your teacher passed away the year after he moved to another school district nine years ago. Then he mentions he detected a sense of urgency in my voice when I left my first message and had already sent out two tracking devices with instructions; they should arrive tomorrow before noon. He got the message early enough apparently and was able to send them out immediately."

"Well, that part is good news! Why the long face, Sy?"

"We won't have anything to attach them to. I'm inclined to agree with Warren; there won't be a car in the basement of the barn."

"We need to go see and I guess it doesn't matter; now that I couldn't remember the cousin's name, I'm convinced there's no connection. In the meantime, we should think about a plan B in case you guys are right about the car. I can't believe I'm about to say this, but could Nanny be involved somehow? What do you guys think?"

"I don't think so," Starlit answered, "I don't think that could be possible at all."

"Neither do I," said Warren.

"I doubt it too," said Silas, "but we'll find the answer eventually, hopefully. Star, you should take a turn to drive Rover."

"You know, Sy, I think I will."

"Well, has anyone come up with a plan B?"

"I'm sorry, Belle, that the car is gone, I know you're disappointed."

"Thanks, Sy, I really thought it would be here. Star, what are you looking at?"

Belle and the others walked to Starlit who was holding aside the curtain to the office space. She stood staring into the office and held the curtain while the others stepped inside.

To everyone's surprise there were extra-large bows on each of the two desks, one purple and one yellow. Around the large bows were small ones of purple, teal, yellow, peach, red and blue. A large bow on the electrical panel/monitor door was red and a small, dark blue bow topped a box which was sitting on one of the desks.

"Major disappointment; these gifts mean these will be left behind and no one will be back, the cars won't be back, and we don't have a chance to put tracking on them; darn it! I have no use for these things. Why would anyone leave them with bows? Is it some kind of 'ha ha you didn't get me, keep this for your troubles' thing?"

Warren stated, "The colors of the bows are each our favorite colors." He then picked up the box, opened it and let out a laugh. "I believe our perpetrator has a sense of humor," he said. Still laughing, he held out the box towards Silas.

"That—is—not—funny," Silas said as he backed up.

"That can't hurt you," said Starlit, "I think it's dead and what are those next to it?"

As Silas's eyes focused on the items in the box he yelled out, "Oh my gosh! Oh no, no..." Starlit asked, "What is it, Sy? You sound like me!" "Really, Sy, you do sound like her."

"Um yes, Belle, I do. Give me a minute here." He took the box from Warren and examined the contents. "Amazing," he said as he poked at one of the items, "it looks so real and sure is a big one. Yeah, Warren, it is kind of amusing now that I think about it, a little anyway."

"Will one of you please let us in on the joke?"

"Go ahead, Silas, tell them," said Warren.

"When we were looking for the two of you out by the formation, uh, when the kids were here, I was being chased by a large bumblebee. I kept swatting at it and Warren threatened to tell you, Belle. He said it was harmless and you wouldn't like the idea of it possibly getting injured. It finally went away. Judging by Warren's laughter, this is that bumblebee along with its remote control!"

"Yes, Silas, I believe the bee is a tiny camera, we were under surveillance," said Warren. "Our perpetrator must have been amused with Silas's antics and decided to leave this as a gift for him, perhaps."

"Warren was right, Sy, I know you don't like bees but there is no need to be afraid of bumbles and besides, you know better, swatting only agitates bees. That's a threat to them and provoking them will make them sting. Teehee, it is funny though, ha ha, you being chased by a bee that wasn't real. I can picture it: you trying to get away from it; bee honing in on you, you ducking and moving about...ha ha ha!"

"I had no idea it was fake!"

Then Starlit asked, "What about that other thing next to the remote, what is that?"

"It looks like a mini television screen," Silas said. "This is amazing technology, high-tech. Everything about this place is high-tech, like what you only see in sci-fi movies, Belle. It sure is strange that your home is surrounded by all this high-tech, over the top stuff; not your normal."

"Indeed Silas, indeed, it is all out of the ordinary, futuristic."

"We still don't know how all the utilities are paid for since they're obviously not on Belle's bill, Warren."

"Perhaps in due time, Silas, we will know. I believe we should figure out how to connect the bee to the monitors and do a test run, rather a test flight, of your little fuzzy friend."

"You guys go ahead. I want to go and add this information to the discovery list," said Belle. "There certainly is a lot of that high-tech stuff around here and I still don't know why I'm in the middle of it. I'm sure glad I don't foot the bill for it all. Come on, Star, we'll let the guys figure out how to get the tiny camera working, or should I say Sy's new pet."

As the girls turned to leave Starlit called out, "Hey Sy, you should heehee, give it a name, heehee."While Warren and Silas were on their bee camera mission, the girls went to the house to work on the discovery list. From time to time, Belle would allow Guardian and Stance to come into the house. This was one of those times and they were happy downstairs with Belle and Starlit.

After Belle finished what she wanted to add to the list, she sat on the floor with the dogs and talked with Starlit for a long time. The girls thought the guys would have been back by now but figured they were still playing with their new toy. They were right.

"Easy, Silas, we do not want to damage the camera. Steady now, good, slow; meticulous landing, brother!"

"Thank you, Warren, we need to practice more. I want to get this flying, maneuvering, and landing down pat, then work on speed before the camera is rolling. Here, Warren, your turn again."

"Thank you, I agree, technique is important. We must perform skillfully every time, until the task comes naturally."

"Warren, the girls are probably wondering what's taking so long."

"Silas, by now they would have concluded we are enamored with our project. They will return here when ready."

"Guardian, Stance, here boys, come on, where are you?"

"Maybe they went upstairs, Belle, I'll go see."

While Starlit was upstairs Belle found the dogs in the utility room. They were sniffing around, mostly near one particular wall. This room had paneling on the walls just like the rest of the downstairs. Belle tried to get them to leave with her, but they would not. She went to the stairs and shouted up to Starlit, "Star, they're down here, come on down, hurry!"

Starlit hurried down. Belle was waiting at the bottom of the stairs. "You've got to see this, follow me. Look at them, they're acting weird. Stance keeps pawing at that wall. I sure hope I don't have mice!"

Just then a peculiar look appeared on Starlit's face. "Uh oh, Belle, my sixth sense is thinking something bigger, as in look for a keyhole."

"What! You think there is an exit here?"

"Well, an entrance too."

"Could be, oh boy…with all that's been found it's possible but why down here? If there is, that would mean, oh, goodness—someone could get in my house anytime! You start on that end, I'll start over here and we'll meet in the middle."

Starlit asked, "You sure you don't want to move now? This is your personal space we're talking about."

With optimism and determination in her voice Belle replied, "That's right, it is my space and I'm going to find out what's behind this wall, if anything, and then figure out how to defend my space! There must be something here, according to the dogs."

"I'm not finding any keyholes, it's all smooth across the paneling, Belle."

"Yep, smooth all the way. Now let's try pushing on each panel from here back to the ends."

They pushed and pushed every panel, one by one, each time saying as they went along, nothing…nothing…nothing. When Belle pushed the last panel on her side a small portion of the wall popped opened towards her. The dogs yelped and turned in circles. For a moment the girls stood staring at each other. Guardian placed a paw in the opening and pulled on the door. Belle commanded him to stop, then told him to wait.

"Good boys, wait. Star, we need to get our packs and lights. We'll take the dogs with us too. I'll close the panel, then we get our packs. Come on."

"Maybe we should get the guys, Belle."

"We'll be fine, I'll contact them in a bit; let's just see some of it first. No one is coming back, Star, no need for me to panic. I shouldn't have reacted that way, I was just surprised."

"Go ahead, Belle, open it; I'm ready." *Woof-woof bark-bark!* "Looks like the dogs are too, ha ha." Belle pushed the panel and slowly pulled the door open. There was a wall behind the door. Annoyed, she yelled, "Oh brother!" Belle pushed the wall jokingly saying, "Open sez me." The wall swung inward. Starlit said, "Good job," and in they went, shining their flashlights into the dark space in front of them.

Starlit was startled as her light flashed onto something, which caused her to jerk slightly and gasp out loud.

"What's that, Belle?"

"They look like old-fashioned torch lights, Star. I doubt they're really that old based on things we've seen."

"Wow, seems narrow in here."

"Give me a minute to look for a light switch. Here it is! Well, they're not that old after all and not bright either, just like the other tunnels. This is maybe five feet wide, definitely a passageway for a person or two only. Stance, stay with Star, Guardian stay with me; boys, guard."

Moving forward cautiously and slowly, they shone their flashlights up and down the walls and along the ceiling as they went. It was a low ceiling, curved, about six and a half feet high. The ceiling and walls were smooth. The torch lights ran along both sides on the walls of the tunnel with alternating spacing across from each other. The bulbs were shaped like flames and the handle part, looking like old wood, was held by a hand-shaped form attached to the walls at its wrist. As they moved forward, the hands on one wall all faced the same way showing the fingers of the hand, while the opposite side showed the back of the hand. The light emanating from the torches flickered like a real flame.

"I wonder if we'll find any tunnels branching off of this one."

"Or if we'll find any keyholes either, Star."

"I'd say that's a dead end in front of us, Belle. That looks like dirt, this tunnel was never finished."

"Wow, yep, dirt from bottom to top."

"Let's go back, hurry, I don't like it here. I like the torches, they're nice, interesting but those hands are creepy."

As they turned to leave Guardian began sniffing around. He moved forward, then suddenly the front half of his body disappeared! Belle said, "Guardian, wait," and he stopped. His back end was in full view, sticking out of the wall with his tail wagging.

The girls broke out in laughter while Stance stood there growling. Belle tried to get Stance to move but he stayed where he was, still growling; that made the girls laugh all the more. The poor dog just did not know what was going on.

"I can't believe I fell for the hologram trick! I should've known better and tried putting my hand on the wall! Good boy, Guardian, come." As he turned around, his back end disappeared and his head and shoulders reappeared, causing Stance to bark. When Guardian moved toward them, Stance backed up growling.

The girls were laughing again. Belle went to comfort Stance and Guardian joined in. After a few minutes they tried to get Stance to go through the wall. He wanted no part of it.

"Belle, he's just not going to give in, I wish there was a way to turn off the wall. Maybe it means we should go back, not forward, a sign or something."

"That's it! We might be able to do just that." "Okay, going back it is."

"No, I mean turn off the wall. I remember seeing an old black-and-white movie where there was a torch light on a wall that opened up a secret passageway. I need to examine this torch closest to the wall, hold on a minute. So, it does not pull down like a lever, nothing twists—oh what's this? Hmmm."

"Where are you going, Belle?"

"To look at the thumbs on the two previous torches; I think I might have figured it out. I'm so excited, Star! There is a slight space under this thumb but not on the others. I want to look at the ones on the opposite wall, too. Yeeha, no spaces, and get ready, I'm going to press on the thumb on that torch by the dirt wall. One, two, three... Woohoo, voilà—no more dirt wall!"

"That was great, Belle! Um, however Stance doesn't think so; he's sitting back there by the entrance to the house."

"Stance, come, it's all right boy, come on." Whimpering, he proceeded toward Belle, let out a little yip, then got quiet as he came alongside her. She crouched down and gave him a big hug. Suddenly she stood up and joyfully shouted, "I know where this tunnel goes, Star!" That startled poor spooked Stance and he ran back to the house door again.

"Oops, I'm sorry Stance, it's okay, really boy. This could take a while, he's just unusually spooked. We'll sit down for a few minutes, and I'll give him some love before we go on. He just needs to settle down first."

"Maybe he doesn't like the hands either, Belle. Could we sit in the house instead?"

"No, I think that would be worse, I could let him go in to stay and we go on without him, but I think it would be better for him to get over it and get confidence back; after all he's a guard dog…

"I think we're ready to try again. Come on, boys, time to go. Good boys, oh yeah happy boys, tails are wagging. Star, don't say a word, just keep going past where, um, you-know-what was. Yes, yes, we made it!"

"So, tell me already, where does this go?"

"I'll tell you when we're almost there."

THIRTY-THREE

"WE'RE ALMOST THERE; can you guess where we're going?"

"You mean this tunnel is ending already? That was about two minutes ago when you said you knew where it went."

"Yes, and we would have been here already if we weren't examining the walls and ceiling."

"What! Give me a hint, Belle."

"Okay, Star, we're walking under my yard instead of across it. There will be a door to a downstairs."

"Huh, I know where we're going!"

Together, with excitement they said, "Into the barn!"

When they reached the door, it had a handle on it. Belle pulled on it and the door opened. This door was a thick wall like the one behind the panel in her house. The other side of the wall at the house had a handle and a release to open the panel to enter her basement. Where they stood now was a second door which had a notch cut into it, with a button inside the notch to open that door. The girls were whispering now.

"Guardian, Stance quiet, wait. Here we go, sez me, ha ha heehee. We need to be quiet, remember the guys are down here—well, they could have left but I want to surprise them if they are here."

"Yes, maybe we can have a little fun with them too."

"Star, you have pleasantly surprised me! Let's make it really good. Okay, shush, I'm going to open this just a crack to take a peek. Umm oh, I'm opening all the way now, come on in."

"This isn't the barn, Belle."

"No, I'm guessing it's the little closet near where the cars get parked. I hear the guys coming this way, we need to be quiet and listen."

"Warren, I like that the camera has the ability to zoom in on anything, amazing. This is a great space to practice. I hate to say it, but we've been here a long time, too long, I'm ready for a break."

"Indeed Silas, a much needed one. I am actually hungry. We will fetch the box from the office then go back to the house."

Belle opened the door to the barn a crack to see if the guys moved to the office. "Are they there, Belle?" "They went to the office, now's our chance."

Starlit made what she thought was a soft ghostly sound, quavering and moaning. Belle placed her hand over her own mouth to keep from laughing. The dogs were reacting, so Belle had to calm them.

"Silas, did you hear something?"

"No, brother, what did it sound like?"

"Mysteriously like a ghost. I did not touch any mushrooms, either."

Just then Belle made some sounds. The dogs let out soft howls, which caused the girls to giggle. "I hope they didn't hear us laugh, Belle."

"Warren, I-I did hear something, ghost dogs?"

"The ladies must have come down, Silas."

As Silas pulled the curtain aside, he said, "Very funny, girls, good imitation of dogs too."

He and Warren walked out of the office. Looking over the basement with puzzlement, Warren said, "There is no one here." "We're definitely in need of a break," said Silas. "Wait a minute—no sounds—let's go."

They started up the ladder. Belle, Starlit and the dogs quietly snuck along the wall of the office. Belle could see Silas going up the ladder first with Warren behind him. She waved at Starlit to follow her but signaled the dogs to wait.

Quickly the girls walked to the ladder, then Belle said, "Hey guys, where're you going, *wooo, ahahaha...*" They heard Silas yell, "Whoa, no way, coming down." Warren backed down the ladder and stood near it, staring at the girls in silence as he waited for Silas to get down. Silas and Warren looked at each other; then Silas asked the girls, "How did you get here?" Warren said, "You must have snuck down while we were in the office and then hid in the closet."

"We could have come down the ladder but how do you explain this?" Belle pointed in the direction of the office wall and called the dogs. "Guardian, Stance, come. Good boys." Warren frowned, Silas stood in disbelief, the girls laughed, and the dogs turned in circles.

"A secret passageway," said Warren. "I do not approve of the location. Silas, the closet has a passageway to the house."

Silas, dumbfounded said, "Mom, you don't seem to be bothered by that! Shocking, this is a whole other ball game, access to the house! Warren, I will help you with the suitcases."

"Guys, my senses aren't giving me any red flags," said Starlit. "Belle likes it and besides, no one is coming back, remember?"

"That's right; I don't feel threatened, especially since no one will be back. If I want to at some point, I can block the panel in the utility room."

"So that's where the entrance is," shouted Silas. Starlit smiled and said, "Deep breaths, Sy, take a couple of deep breaths."

"Silas, it is futile to disagree with the ladies," said Warren. "Please show us the passageway, Belle."

"Sure Warren, right this way. We have to figure out how this one opens. At the house I pushed on a section of paneling, and it popped open toward me. Then there was a thick wall I pushed that opened into the passageway. This could work the same way; I'll try it."

"That didn't work," said Starlit, "now what?"

"This closet is all wood," said Warren, "examine the knots."

"Good call," said Silas. "You were right, Belle, it does pop open towards us."

"Yippee, we're on our way. Wait till you see the lights and the dirt wall! Hopefully Stance will be good this time around."

Belle showed them the handle on the thick door, the notch on the other door with its button, and excitedly pointed to the torches, saying how much she liked them. When she disengaged the hologram, the dogs ran ahead of them and waited by the door to the utility room. After they exited the passageway and closed it, Warren opened it again. He and Silas went in, looking over the doors.

They went back into the utility room with Belle and Starlit, closed the entrance, and all of them went into the main room. Each took a seat while Belle added this new discovery to her list. When she was finished Silas said he and Warren were hungry; Starlit and Belle said they were too.

"Wow, it's really late, way past lunch. I'm thinking we all need some caffeine too," said Belle. "You know, they have a name for when you have a late breakfast and early lunch combined, they call it brunch. What's it called when you combine lunch with dinner?"

"I don't know," said Silas, "but we can have it faster if we all pitch in!"

"Amen brother, indeed we can," responded Warren. As he headed for the kitchen he added, "Much sustenance is needed now." They prepared a smorgasbord meal and settled in the dining room.

"You guys really know your way around a kitchen. I suppose that's because you both have younger brothers and sisters you've cooked for."

"True, Star," said Warren, "eventually they were all taught to prepare meals. We focused on nutritious foods, rarely having sweets."

"Our family did nutritious foods too, but we had our sweets," said Silas. "I think it kind of stands out that I like my sweets. Hey, you know peanut butter cookies have protein, pumpkin pie and carrot cake are vegetables, so I don't feel too bad having them."

Everybody laughed except Belle. She was in her own little world as she poked and pushed her food around on the plate before each forkful.

"Belle, your thoughts consume you, please share?" asked Warren.

"I-uh-I'm upset about not knowing where the animals all went and what others might get experimented on. I hate feeling hopeless. We were so close but now I can't help them." Tears welled up in Belle's eyes. She sniffled then said, "I have no idea still how my house came to be, or the orchard. I thought these were two separate cases but there is still the possibility they're connected. The teacher is a dead end. Who else could've seen my drawing?"

Starlit's eyes welled up with tears as she felt empathy and sympathy toward Belle. The guys had the same feelings. They had all experienced hopelessness at some point in their lives. All of them expressed their thoughts to Belle and did their best to comfort her.

With a sad tone and defeat in her voice Belle said, "What do we do next?"

"We will delay contemplating the events surrounding us for a short period," Warren answered.

"Sounds good to me," agreed Silas.

"I like that," Starlit said, "it would be nice."

"I was going to show you what I can do with Thunder," said Silas, "but it can wait."

"Sy, who's that?" asked Starlit.

He answered shyly, "My bee, I did name him, and he can fly with or without buzzing." She laughed and said, "Such a big name for something so small."

"All right, guys, I'll try to get my mind off things for a bit," said Belle. "What should we do? Keep in mind I have to pick up Pirate soon."

"I know," Silas said with enthusiasm, "we can help you pick out two fish tanks with fish and all the trimmings!"

"Yes, that's good, it's only four o'clock. Belle, you've mentioned the pet store is open until eight and since we have to pick up Pirate at the vet, we can shop right after that."

"You're right, Star. If we hurry and clean up, we can get there, shop and be back to get it all set up and be done at a decent time.

Okay, I'm for that. First thing when we get home though, we'll take care of the critters, then set up the tanks."

"Wonderful," Warren said as he stood up and began clearing the table. With a smile he added, "Tomorrow we rise early to go fishing." Silas stood up, did a little dance while saying, "Oh yeah, I'm ready," and went to the kitchen.

Starlit looked at Belle and said, "Allrightee then, we should get moving; you okay?"

"Yes, it'll all be good for me. We have to take Willow with us tomorrow. I'll get her things packed up in the morning. Come on, let's help the guys and I'll tell you the rest when we're all together."

"So, everyone, here's what I'm thinking: I do want to get away from the mysteries so I will call Cy to see if tomorrow, Saturday and Sunday morning he will stop by to take care of the outside critters. If he will, then I say we stay over near the lake. The kitties will be good for that much time after I set them up and Willow will be with us. The pet store carries decorative dissolving seashells that have food in them. They slowly dissolve, releasing tiny bits of food for the fish, so I don't have to worry about them either!"

"I am elated with your decision, Belle," said Warren.

"I'm so happy, Belle, you're willing to take a break," Starlit said, as she gave her a hug. Silas said, "This is great, we'll have fun. I'm looking forward to it and willing to pay Tree-man for his trouble."

Starlit said, "Hurry, Belle, call him while we finish up here so we know if we can do it."

"I will; be right back."

"What a relief," Starlit said.

"I thought we might have to twist her arm," said Silas, "but she was quite cooperative."

"Yes," said Warren, "she is weary, in need of distraction. When Belle is rested, we can reassemble."

Belle returned smiling and said, "All set! He's coming very early so I can show him everything and Ben will help him. We better get going."

Silas began waving the dish towel and did another happy dance.

At the pet shop, Belle chose small colorful fish, algae eaters, plants, and other items for the tanks. She chose solid dark brown stones for the tank bottoms so the fish would stand out. They went home, took care of all the critters, then packed for their trip. The tank setups were completed next. Belle made sure the tops were secure in case the kitties tried some fishing of their own. Possible kitty invasion attempts were not likely by all but by some, so it was necessary to protect the fish. She was delighted with the way the tanks looked.

The lake and surrounding areas were beautiful. It was a huge lake. You could not see the end of it because it wound around a tree-lined landscape at one point. The lake was marked with different-colored buoys to section off areas of activity. Canoes were allowed in one portion, small sailboats in another, paddle boats in another, and rowboats in yet another. You could fish from a rowboat, the pier or from the shore. There was an area for swimming and wading in also. It had it all, a dream come true for the guys.

Belle liked to fish some, Starlit not at all, but they went out with the guys on the pier. During their time at the lake, they all swam, went out in paddle boats, and did some hiking. When the guys wanted to go fishing again, this time in a rowboat, Belle and Starlit opted to visit the village associated with the lake area. To their pleasant surprise there was a theater offering dinner and a show featuring a Christian comedian. They picked up tickets for the six-thirty show for the four of them. After shopping, the girls went back to locate Silas and Warren to announce their plans for dinner and a show, allowing them plenty of time to get back, wash up and change for dinner. They were happy the girls found out about this and were looking forward to it.

The two days they spent away worked wonders for all of them. They had a great time. Sunday morning, they packed up their belongings, had breakfast, then left the lake to head for the later church service before going home.

THIRTY-FOUR

"I SURE AM GLAD BELLE LEFT GOODIES in the fridge here, Cy," said Ben. "It's really weird that there's one in this barn along with a bathroom."

"The old man that used to live here, Ben, was eccentric; he lived in here while the houses were being built, that's what I heard anyway."

"Yeah, he supposedly lived in here with his animals and if you're going to do that, might as well be comfortable."

"That wraps things up for us; thanks for helping, Ben."

"My pleasure, Cy. I'm going to head to church, want to come?"

"No thanks, not my thing."

"Cy, you really need to make a decision for the best, *your* best. Here it is in a nutshell cousin: God loves us. We're all sinners separated from God because of that sin, bad news. Jesus came to pay our penalty for sin by dying on the cross in our place, good news. We confess to God our sin against Him, ask His forgiveness, thank Jesus for what He's done for us then ask Him to come into our lives. *God loves you.*"

"I like your nutshell, Ben, like a walnut; Star was talking out of a coconut shell, ha ha; she went on and on and on."

"Cy, this is serious, I love you, and I'd like to see you in Heaven one day. We'll be spending eternity either in Hell paying our own penalty for our sin forever or living in Heaven forever. If you die in your sin, it's too late, the decision to reconcile to God is now. Speaking of now I need to leave Belle a note, I don't know why but I have to."

"Hurry up, Ben, so we can leave, I have to wait on you, then make sure the gate is locked after us. I'll think about what you said when I have some quiet time."

"Don't take too long to think, Tree-man. Talk to God, even if you're not sure of anything, tell Him that, and tell Him everything that's on your mind."

Ben turned over the note Belle had left them, took the pen next to it and began to write.

Cypress and Ben parted ways, going in different directions: Ben to church, Cypress to the Center. Belle and the others arrived at church as the first service let out. They met up with Ben in the gathering place and talked for a few minutes while having coffee. He told Belle her animals were a pleasure to care for and that he enjoyed playing with the dogs and ferrets. He watched the kitties when they were in their catio and said Pirate was doing great.

Belle mentioned what they had done while they were away. Before they knew it, it was time to go; they said goodbye to Ben, thanking him as they hurried to the sanctuary.

When Belle arrived home, she left her belongings in the car and ran inside to see her critters, especially wanting to see Pirate. Afterwards she went out back and was greeted by Guardian and

Stance, who knocked her down because they were excited to see her; Belle shrieked and laughed with delight. Next she went to visit Rarity, Anomaly, P-2, P-3 and then the chickens. The others knew Belle would want to see her critters immediately, so while she was visiting them they brought her suitcase and backpack into the house, along with the package from Silas's friend that was sitting by the front door. Belle never noticed the note on the table in the barn.

The guys went to the guest house to put away their belongings. Starlit placed Belle's suitcase and backpack in her bedroom, then went to her own room to put her belongings away. Seeing it was time for lunch, Belle went back inside to start preparing food. Starlit set the dining room table and went to help Belle.

Warren and Silas were outside playing with the dogs. Silas wanted to see the ferrets. He went into the barn and played with them until he heard that wonderful sound of a bell ringing. He put P-2 and P-3 back in their home. On the way out he glanced at the note on the table; realizing it was for Belle, he took it.

As soon as they were finished with lunch, they cleaned up and sat in the living room. "I'm glad we went away for a couple of days," said Starlit. "I had a relaxing and fun time."

"Indeed Star, marvelously relaxing and refreshing," said Warren.

"I think we all agree with that," said Silas. "Good food, good time and best of all good company!"

Belle smiled and said, "Absolutely, I feel great. I think I'm ready to see the trackers in the package now and focus on what to do next."

Silas opened the box with the tracking devices. They all had a turn looking at them. "Maybe in the future I'll have a chance to use them for something. We should look at the list and reassess the incidents and discoveries. Come on, let's go down now."

They talked over what was on the list for a while. When they were done reviewing Silas said, "Let me show you how Thunder flies now, he's upstairs." Back upstairs to the living room they went.

Belle opened the box with Thunder in it. Silas carefully took him and the control out of the box. "You're really good at that, Sy, and I'm so pleased it can't sting you," said Starlit. "Thanks Mom, but please humor me and call him Thunder."

Laughing, Warren said, "Please do, Star, Silas has bonded with his pet."

Belle noticed there was a small cushion in the bottom of the box the objects rested on. For some reason she lifted it up. To her surprise there was a little piece of paper there.

"Look what I found." She unfolded it and read what was on it out loud. "It says 'Genesis 1:26. Then God said, Let us make mankind in our image, in our likeness so that they may rule over the fish in the sea and the birds in the sky, over the livestock and all wild animals and over all the creatures that move along the ground.'"

"Whoa, wait, that reminds me, Belle, I found a note to you from Ben on the table in the barn.," said Silas. "I was going to give it to you after showing you Thunder; I realize now how important it is; sorry, sorry that was really selfish of me.

"He states that this was heavy on his mind and thinks it's a message for you. Couldn't understand it or shake the feeling he was supposed to write this down for you, then writes: 'so here goes'..."

Silas handed the note to Belle. She read the rest, cleared her throat and proceeded to read it out loud: "'Proverbs 12:10: A righteous man cares for the needs of his animals but the kindest acts of the wicked are cruel.'"

"What do you think it means," asked Starlit, "I know what they say but what do you get out of it, Belle?"

"Not sure, does anyone have any ideas?"

"We will decipher some key words first," Warren said, "from the Genesis scripture, those being, our image and our likeness."

"I see," said Starlit, "that would be the attributes of God, His characteristics."

"Correct," said Warren, "the inherent part of someone."

"His kindness and loving nature and patience are some."

"Yes, Silas and merciful, faithful, nurturing, caring and good," added Starlit.

"He is good, always good and so much more! I get it, I get, it is a message," cried Belle. "God works in strange ways sometimes, gives help in ways you wouldn't think of or imagine! Wait a minute, I'll be right back."

"I'm clueless, Warren; do you know what Belle is talking about?"

"Perhaps, Silas; I believe she has gone to retrieve a torn piece of paper."

"She was ecstatic, I hope she's right about what it is she thinks she figured out. I wouldn't want things to revert to the way they were before we went away."

"I am confident Belle is correct about her revelation, Star."

"I hope your certainty proves correct, Warren."

"Well, Warren, you and Belle seem to know the answer to something that Star and I don't. We're left in the dark, brother, unless you want to give us a hint."

"I have already, Silas," Warren replied with a grin.

"Ouch," said Starlit, "he actually did, Sy: the torn paper! We'll have to wait until she comes back because I can't figure it out either. I hear her coming now."

Warren was right; Belle came back to the living room waving the torn paper she went to retrieve. "Got it, these scriptures refer to how man should take good care of the animals and creatures God created. God expects man to care for them like He would. That's the first scripture verse. Proverbs confirms, 'A righteous man cares for his animals.'"

"Warren, tell me what you were thinking," asked Silas.

"We concluded the animals on the Ark were game animals. Babies were to be smuggled and grown to maturity at a delayed rate of growth. The biblical Ark had baby animals on it for two reasons; we failed to realize one during the time we were evaluating the situations."

"I know, I know," shouted Starlit, "it was to save them!"

"Yes Star, that's why you got that feeling of peace when you thought about the baby animals that day. The missing letters on this paper are *e* for the end of the first word; *r*, *c*, *u*, and *e* for the second word. Here, wait, I'll write it out all just like on the picture, three lines each centered under the one above it. I'll underline the letters that were missing from the last line. Now this as a whole reads: Noah's Ark, Phase II, The Rescue!"

"Meaning this whole time everything that was going on was to help animals," Silas said with puzzlement. "Why not come forward and tell us once they knew we knew something was going on?"

Warren answered with a smile, "Perhaps to protect us, Silas."

"Great news! I'm happy my senses make sense now and there is no threat to us."

"Yes, Star, I'm happy about your senses too, more so someone was actually trying to help animals. We've solved another mystery; it feels really good! Now we need to figure out why and how my drawing came to life and my favorite fruits are growing in my yard. Hmm, but there must be a connection between the animal project that was going on and the person who owned this property before me."

"Not necessarily, Belle, could be the underground structures were there and the owner didn't know about it," said Silas. "Remember, the property was in that person's family for generations and only occupied in the last eight years. The underground was probably there for many years. He may not have known about the hatch in the barn tack room or the entrance to your utility room. The secret entrances may have been added after the houses were built and without the knowledge of the homeowner. Warren and I were talking about all of this while we were at the lake."

"I see, Sy, it does sound like it is possible. What do you think now, Belle?"

"Maybe Warren and Sy are right, Star. Let's just move forward on the house and orchard and leave the underground, for now."

"Silas and I also contemplated and conversed on that subject," said Warren. "We remembered some facts concerning Nanny. First, she was left a wealthy woman. Secondly, she had gone away for over a week, leaving you with Star's family."

"That's right, Warren, I remember now; Belle and I camped out in my back yard in a tent a few nights. I don't like tents anymore."

"Okay, I need to think a little about this. When I mentioned Nanny possibly being involved, you all said couldn't be and well, I was just grasping for something, I don't think I was serious? That day I called her though, to ask if she had shown the drawing to anyone; she said no but she didn't ask why I was asking, that is a little concerning. She did see my drawing; she knows my favorite fruits but why have houses built for me and create an orchard, then arrange for me to move away?"

"Perhaps she was going with you, hence the guest house."

"Warren, why do you think she would do that?"

"To give you a new start in life perhaps; an opportunity to fulfill your animal-caregiving dreams, a chance to discover other opportunities, for example. However, she is not living out here."

"Valid point, Warren, why is she not here," mused Silas.

"Nanny is active in the community, Sy," said Belle. "I can't imagine she'd want to leave her home and start over. She hasn't been for a visit yet because she's busy; well, I was too. I think the guest house was just for anyone coming to visit. Ugh! We're back to where we were before, more questions.

"Before we get involved in mystery solving, I want to let you know, while at the lake I did some contemplating also. Regarding the things you guys talked to me about, you were right; I need to get back to church serving, devotions and prayer time. I'm going to cut my volunteer time at the Center, work decent hours at the nursery and hire someone to help me with the outside critters three times a week. I'll see how that goes, I can always add one more day. There's a young girl volunteering at the Center and I'd like to give her a chance to earn some money."

Warren said, "I speak for us all in saying we are pleased with your decision, you will not regret it! This is wonderful news, Belle, wonderful indeed!"

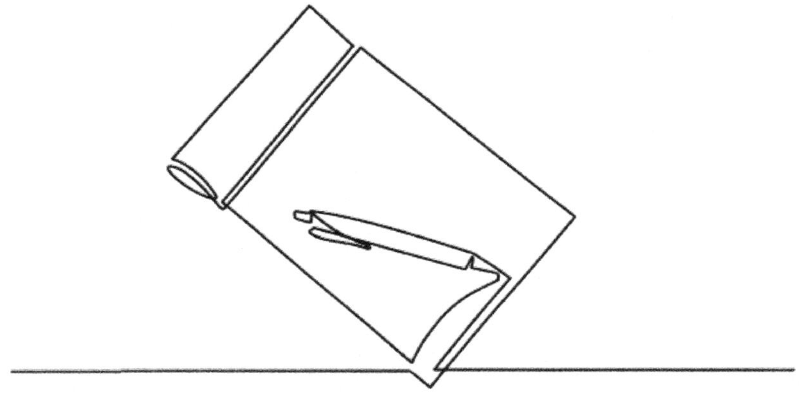

THIRTY-FIVE

"ANYWAY, I DO HAVE ONE MORE thought about Nanny: blueberries. Yeah, I like them a lot but Nanny loved them and so did my dad. She was always making pies, muffins, pancakes and parfaits. Even dark chocolate truffles with blueberries which I loved, and I still like my dark chocolate. If she had anything to do with the houses and orchard, she might have planted the blueberries in honor of her son. Here's a question: why would she keep it a secret and not tell me she arranged all of this? Let's say she did want me to have a new start and explore options, why didn't she just tell me?"

"Perhaps to produce the impression it was your decision; to create the appearance you discovered this on your own."

"Warren, that makes sense, I did gain a little confidence after I sold the house designs and that grew a little more after landing the jobs. It was topped off when I looked at the property and houses. I was feeling like my dreams were coming true. We don't know for sure this is all true unless I straight out ask Nanny, but I don't want to spoil it for her if that was her intention. I can't imagine who her connections were to help carry out her plan; Ed might be involved and I'm not sure if I should pursue that either now."

"With that I'd say there's no connection to the animals and Ed, they're separate circumstances. If he was involved, it was all for the good of the animals anyway. There was never a connection with the animals and Nanny, only the orchard and her."

"That sounds about right to me, Sy so we should call it quits on it all."

"I'm not sure about that just yet, Star, calling it quits; I'll think about it a little more. In the meantime, why don't we play with the tracking devices? We could divide up into teams and take turns tracking each other?"

"Definitely for that, Belle, you can team up with me!"

"All right, Sy, I will, that leaves you, Star with Warren, and Warren, you can have my jeep, we'll take Rover. Just remember if you're off road, it's four-wheel drive and twenty-five miles an hour. We should avoid going to usual places like the pond."

"Warren, your call, hide or seek?"

"Hide is my choice, give us twenty minutes, then start tracking."

"This is perfect, I'm going to enjoy it; let's get prepared. Can I drive Rover?"

"Yes, Sy, you can and for the record, I'm going to enjoy it too. I know you will, Warren; what about you, Star?"

"I like the idea, so far."

"We're heading towards town, Warren; this is good, Belle did say to avoid usual places."

"Indeed, however we are stopping for fuel, not going to town. They will fill up Rover when they arrive, then continue to pursue us."

Belle, Silas, Starlit and Warren spent several hours tracking each other over the countryside. The equipment worked well and had a long-range signal capacity. When it was Warren and Starlit's turn to hide again, Warren suggested their last stop be at the Center. Much to their surprise when they arrived, Belle and Silas were already there in the parking lot.

Belle waved and said, "I was just about to call you guys. We weren't far from the Center when I got a call from Cy. Some unusual animals arrived late Saturday and will be guests of the Center for a while, and he thought we would like to see them. Let's go."

Cypress greeted them when they entered the Center. He led them to an area that had recently been built to accommodate the temporary tenants. The area had a divider made of Plexiglas between two habitats, each habitat having its own door. Two people entered each side of the room with a crate. At the same time, they opened their crates, reached in, and took out the new inhabitants.

Astonished and delighted, Belle did a happy dance. Silas, Starlit and Warren were amazed and bewildered. This unforeseen event left them with a sense of joy knowing Belle was happy. Where did these critters come from? Cypress explained they did not know where they came from, of course. As he spoke, Belle, Starlit, Silas and Warren looked at each other, smiling from ear to ear. What were these critters? They were the armadillos! The four of them finally left the Center to go home and prepare dinner.

"I couldn't be happier about the 'dillos," said Belle. "If they don't stay with us, I know they'll go to a good home which probably won't be soon, so I'll get to see more of them. I know what you're thinking, Mom; no, I won't be adopting them."

"Star wasn't the only one thinking that, Belle," said Silas, "I was too and think it's safe to say it crossed Warren's mind at the same time as ours."

"I understand you guys are reluctant to believe I meant what I said earlier. I will be more responsible, with the Lord's help. It was exciting to see the nine-banded had a buddy and wouldn't be alone. After cleanup I want to add this 'dillo event to the list."

"While you're doing that, we'll catch up on some pool playing."

"You guys don't have to help clean up tonight, Sy, thanks; go on down and start a game."

"Thank you, Belle, we will do that."

"You're welcome, Warren, I'll play tonight too after I get the list updated."

After a couple of games of pool and a game of darts, they all sat down. Belle and Starlit played a board game while the guys watched. As it got late, Silas and Warren fell asleep. The girls became sleepy and decided to leave the game out and clean up in the morning. They did not want to disturb Silas and Warren. Belle figured since the guys did not look comfortable, they would wake soon and go to the guest house.

On the way upstairs Belle told Starlit it was time for P-2 and P-3 to have a bath. Starlit said she would be happy to help, and they planned to bathe them after breakfast, making that the start of the day. By the time the girls were in bed it was after 11:30.

"Warren, Warren, wake up, sorry to shake you. We fell asleep and they didn't wake us."

"What time is it, Silas?"

"Three thirty, I can't believe we slept that long and look—the girls left the game out, must have been too tired to put it away."

"I will take a moment to gather it up and place it on the shelf, Silas, then we will leave."

"That didn't take long, I guess we could go now. You seem to be hesitating, Warren."

"As are you, Silas, what are you thinking?"

"That I want to uh, take a peek in the tunnel down here as long as it's so close, that's what. "

"We should endeavor to make it quick, however I have an unexplainable sense of suspicion that if we should come across something, 'quick' is not going to happen."

"Warren, I think we need to investigate."

"We will need our backpacks, Silas. Only one of us should go to retrieve them."

"This is nice not having to use a key or combination to enter, and I'm with Belle on liking the torches, Warren. The way they flicker like real flames is amazing."

"I fancy them myself, Silas. Stop touching that torch."

"Look, Warren, I can hold my hand over the top and not get burn—ahaaha-ooops!"

After Silas held his hand on top of the torch, all the lights began to flicker rapidly. At the same time, they heard what sounded like wind and the lights went out.

"Sorry, Warren, good thing we have our flashlights." Before they were able to get the flashlights from their backpacks, they heard a sound like rushing water and both sides of the passageway walls lit up in a greenish-blue color. What looked like water flowed up the sides, forming a wall of water on either side of them. They watched in silence with mouths hung open. The color brightened, illuminating the passageway. All of a sudden fish could be seen swimming past them. Along the bottom edges of the water walls were small kelp plants, seaweed, and scattered stones. Warren gave Silas, who was standing in front of him, a gentle poke to get him moving. They walked slowly down the passageway to the end, marveling all the way at the show taking place on both sides of them. About five feet from the doorway to the barn the fish began to go away, then the water receded down the walls and the torches came back on. The sides of the passageway returned to normal.

"That was a major mushroom moment, Warren! How in the world did they do that? Why did they do that?"

"I do not know, Silas, it may remain a puzzle."

"Wow this is great, definitely a splash of Bible."

"Indubitably, Silas. This mimicking the parting of the Red Sea is positively amazing."

"Belle is going to love this, Warren!"

"Indeed, I believe she will, Silas, and not mind this mystery remaining unsolved; we should move on."

"You know, Warren, I think Mom will like this one too, can't wait to see the looks on their faces. Wonder when we'll find maintenance access to everything, there must be something somewhere."

"That may remain unsolved," replied Warren.

"Please, allow me," said Silas as he placed his hand on the door handle to open it. As he opened the door to the closet he motioned to Warren with his other hand and said, "After you." They quietly entered the closet, closed the doors behind them, and waited a minute listening before exiting into the barn.

Whispering, Silas asked, "Do you hear something?"

Warren whispered, "I sure do."

Warren opened the door to the barn just barely enough to see through. Silas heard him gasp. He tapped on Warren's shoulder. Warren turned to look at him; Silas could see the shock on his face. Silas motioned for him to move so he could see.

Silas then peered through the door and gasped. Warren reached around him quietly and gently closed the door, reopened the door to the passageway, then tugged on Silas's arm, urging him to come. Silas stood stunned. Warren pulled on his arm again. Once inside the passageway they continued in whispers. "Now that is something we need an answer for, Warren. I can't believe what I saw, can't accept it," Silas said as he shook his head side to side.

Warren rubbed his chin with his thumb and forefinger in his usual contemplative mode. "Indeed," Warren replied, "we need to contrive a swift resolution to this quandary…"

"Good morning, Belle, are the guys still downstairs?"

"No, I have no clue what time they went back to the guest house, but I think they may need a little extra rest to make up for their not so comfy sleep on the couch. Whenever I fell asleep in an unusual position, I didn't feel rested and something usually hurt. I just put cherry muffins in the oven. The kitties and Willow are fed and watered already. By the time we get the outside critters fed and watered the muffins should be done, then we can wake the guys if they're not up by then."

"I'll take care of Guardian and Stance, then come in and make coffee."

"Good plan, Star, thank you. After you make the coffee you can feed the fish, please. I saved that for you, thought you might like it."

"I would like that, thanks, Belle."

Starlit and Belle finished the chores, set the dining room table, then sat at the little table in the kitchen waiting for the guys. Ten minutes passed, no Warren and Silas.

"We can't make the rest of breakfast until they get here. I say we go calling."

Belle and Starlit trotted over to the guest house. Starlit gave the doorbell a push. When no one came she knocked hard on the door. "I can't believe they're not answering, let's go in."

They called out, but no one answered. "Belle, they haven't slept in their beds!" Raising her voice Starlit said, "This seems all too familiar."

"Deja vu; I don't think it's the same as before though, calm down, their backpacks are gone. They've simply gone hiking." "Then why are the beds not slept in?" "Probably slept at the house till early this morning, that's all, Star."

Warren and Silas were heard calling out to them, "We're back, sorry it got late, where are you?" The girls rushed out, eager to see them. Belle said, "See, they look good, no ruffled feathers!"

"We went right to the house as soon as we got back, it sure smells good in the kitchen," said Silas. "You weren't there. Obviously, you were looking for us, how about I make breakfast to make up for you waiting on us?"

"Coffee is ready, you guys can just go ahead and start on that. We'll get breakfast—oh and we're both happy you're not all beat up again." Belle and Starlit giggled. Starlit said, "You both look kind of tired and hey, aren't those the same clothes you had on yesterday? Well, I suppose you stayed downstairs all night then decided you would change after your hike."

"Yeah, yeah that's it, partly anyway," replied Silas. Warren interrupted quickly.

During breakfast there was some small talk. At one time Warren gave Silas a little kick under the table to stop him from giving away one of the discoveries made during the night. He and Silas had already decided before arriving home that they would hold out on the discoveries until after breakfast, then reveal them.

"Ladies," Warren began, "we have something to show you."

"Can it wait till later? Star was going to help me bathe P-2 and P-3 this morning."

"No, Belle," Silas jumped in, "you have to see this, you're going to love it; you will too, Mom! When we woke up, we decided to go into the tunnel and an amazing thing happened."

Starlit said, "Since you have a gleam in your eyes and are excited, I'm willing to see whatever it is, Sy."

"I'm intrigued; let's go, the critters can wait a little longer," Belle agreed.

When the girls went to gather their packs Warren placed muffins, napkins, fruit, and a thermos of coffee into his backpack while Silas watched. Warren looked at Silas and winked. Silas winked back.

Inside the passageway, Silas explained to Belle and Starlit what he had done with the torch closest to the door they entered. He told Belle to do the same, and so it began. Walking in single file they moved on. The show on the walls amazed and delighted the girls. All the way to the end everyone made comments: Beautiful! Cool! Spectacular! Cute! Wow! Amazing! Look at that one! Wonderful! Whoa! Love it! Marvelous! This is great! Ooh a big one…

With the show over, Warren placed his hand on Belle's shoulder saying, "Please prepare yourself for another discovery; this will be a shock. We agreed to wait until after breakfast since this will take some time. You will have answers." Warren opened the doors.

Silas took hold of Belle's hand and said, "Yes, you will have answers."

THIRTY-SIX

SILAS AND WARREN HAD discovered something that was going to answer some, possibly all, of the mysteries in their midst, but neither Belle nor Starlit had a clue as to what. Starlit looked at Belle and said, "Yay, answers!" Then puzzled asked, "Another piece of paper?"

Belle said, "Diary would have a lot more info."

They had exited the closet and entered the barn. Halfway to the office door, Warren stopped. He said, "Ladies, we have a confession to make. We woke at three thirty, did not go hiking, only exploring underground, and in the process we did encounter someone. This time there was no scuffle." The girls stared wide-eyed into each other's faces.

"Mom, no lecture please," said Silas, as he smiled and gave a gentle squeeze on Belle's hand which he was still holding. "No, no of course," Starlit replied. "I wasn't going to. Who is this person?"

Then Belle asked, "*Where* is this person?"

"Prepare yourselves ladies, for the meeting in the office."

"Wow, okay, the office…let's go."

Starlit asked, "So this person is just waiting for us?" Snickering, Silas answered, "He didn't have much of a choice since we tied him to a chair, Mom. We wanted to make sure he would be here when we returned." "I see," she said.

Silas pulled the curtain aside and led Belle into the office; Warren and Starlit followed. A man was sitting there, tied to the chair of the small desk.

Whispering, Starlit said, "Belle, he looks like…" Interrupting, Belle whispered, "He does, a little but…" "It can't be, though." "No, it's not, this is weird."

Warren said, "While you ladies are processing this, Silas will untie our guest." Warren opened his backpack, took out the thermos of coffee, the muffins, and a banana, and set them before the man. "Thank you," the man said.

Silas took the chair from behind the big desk and arranged it with the chairs by the small desk. He and Warren led Belle and Starlit to a seat, then took a seat themselves. The girls were next to each other and continued their conversation in whispers. Earlier, Silas had jokingly commented to Warren the girls might need cots instead of chairs but they were holding up well. Warren looked at Silas and gave him a thumbs up. The man said, "This is very good, thank you again." He then reached for his thermos of coffee and took a drink from it. Silas and Warren sat in silence. When the man had finished everything, he wiped his mouth and said, "Shall we get on with it?"

Warren was about to introduce the man when Belle spoke up. "Uncle I.Q.?"

Silas said to the man, "That I.Q. part was a tidbit you left out when you introduced yourself."

The man answered Belle, "Yes, Bellerina, it is I."

"So, Belle, he is your uncle; he looks like your dad," stated Starlit.

"Yes, I haven't seen him in years. He's what the family called a bad apple, Dad's older brother, was a very smart kid and had a high IQ but always in trouble. He disappeared one day and now here he is." Then Belle in a demanding tone said, "And why are you is, I-I mean uh, why are you here? What have you got me involved in?"

"It is all true," said I.Q. "The past, that is, I am a changed man. I am a Christian now. Just before your parents' accident, Belle, I reconciled with them. That was a great blessing. I spent time with them on their last mission then I returned home. We had planned to tell you all together after they completed their mission but, so sorry to say, that didn't happen. I had called your grandmother twice during the first few months, but she didn't really believe me. One day I stopped at the house, but you were not there. Nanny and I spoke for some time, but she was still apprehensive, did soften some though. She wanted me to leave before you came home. I left, hopeful that Mother and I would reconcile eventually; she had given me a big hug. I asked for a drink of water before leaving, she said help yourself…"

Belle leapt up out of her chair. With excitement she said, "It was you—it was you! That's when you saw my drawing! How did you remember it? Nanny knew nothing about this house of mine, did she? Did she know about the orchard? What about…"

"Hold on, Belle, take it easy, I will get to all of it," he replied.

"Of course," she said, and sat back down smiling.

Starlit sympathetically said, "That must have been so hard to have your own mother not accept you, I.Q. Is it okay to call you that?"

"Yes, you can call me I.Q., and it was difficult," he answered. "We did reconcile though, Mother accepted me back. I was away a lot, call it mission work, and Mother didn't want Belle to have a relationship with me just yet since I was gone often. She didn't want Belle to fear the same fate for her uncle as her parents so we both agreed to wait until Belle was older. Time went by quickly, I was always busy, things snowballed, now here we are years later. It wasn't until recently I decided to tell Mother about your house and orchard, Belle, just have not had a chance yet. I will not tell her about the subterranean part, she is never to know, I want to be very clear on that.

"During the time spent with your parents, your dad explained about the property here, that it has been in the family for generations, and he wanted you to have a home here. He planned on building a home for his family in the future and wanted to start an orchard first. Again, sorry to say, he was unable to. His plans for the orchard were drawn, so I started it as soon as possible and added the blueberry bushes in honor of him. Next, I renovated the old barn into my unique barn, then eventually would build a house for you to carry out his dream; I thought there should be a guest house also. When I saw your drawing, I decided it would be the perfect house to build for you since you wrote on it, 'my grown-up home one day,' so I took a picture of it with a mini camera."

Belle responded, "A spy camera I'm thinking, mister; call it mission work, what exactly do you do?" Belle caught herself, realizing how she was sounding. "Oh my gosh, I'm sorry. I'm overwhelmed." Slightly nervous she added, "Uh, you know I made the muffins small and, well, you should have something more to eat, Uncle. We should go back to the house, and I'll make you eggs, bacon, toast, or oatmeal or both, after all, we had ours."

"Thank you, I would like that very much, Belle."

Silas stood up, offered his hand to Belle and said, "Bellerina, I like that." She took his hand and said, "Thanks." Warren offered his hand to Starlit and off they all went to the passageway.

In the passageway Belle said, "What happens on these walls is amazing; we enjoyed it, Uncle."

He replied, "It is amazing, done with laser lights, great technology, and if I may say so myself, genius, get my drift?"

"Indeed, we do," replied Warren.

"Yes sir, Mr. High-Tech," said Silas, "I get it."

Starlit laughed, "Certainly do."

"Yep! Sure do, Uncle."

Belle stared at I.Q. as he ate the duck-egg omelet he'd requested. Finally, she said, "I have questions; I'll try to keep them short but I need to back up a little."

"Okay," he said, "what is it?"

"If the land was in my family all this time, why did I pay for it?"

"You didn't," he answered, "you paid for the houses. If you had paid for the land also it would have cost you much, much more."

"I see, well I never did any research on that, I just thought I was getting it cheap cause it was the country!" Everyone laughed. "One more, it's related. How come I paid for the houses?"

Warren said, "Allow me while you finish your meal, I.Q."

"Certainly, thanks," he replied to Warren.

Warren turned to Belle. "You paid for the building materials and some of the labor, Belle."

"But why?"

"Character development; teaching you responsibility, discipline and accountability, quality life living. Not all things should be given to anyone; one must work. Some of the labor was a labor of love, a gift."

Silas added, "Get in good habits, stay in good habits."

"You guys had obviously talked about this already, didn't you? Well, I suppose it makes sense, it reminds me of the warning against idleness in second Thessalonians, chapter three, particularly verses ten through thirteen. Wow, praise God for bringing that to mind! I needed that. I'm happy I have my house."

"I'm happy for you, Belle, that you have your house," said Silas, "thank you, Jesus."

"Amen," said Starlit. "I'm happy you have your house too, even though we went through some strange things. I, myself can't wait to hear the rest of the explanation."

"We will retire to the living room shortly," replied Warren, "and will hear more."

As he took a seat on the upholstered chair in the living room, I.Q. began with, "This property is assured to our family. I would not have sold to anyone. At the Zone I do handyman work. I orchestrated you getting out here by planting a seed regarding sale of this house, and you finding out help was needed there."

"By the Zone you do mean the Center?"

"Yes," he answered.

Silas commented, "The Zone, I really like that, High-Tech."

"There was a rumor going around that an old man owned the property. What about that?" asked Belle.

With a grin her uncle answered, "I wear many hats, disguises if you will. With that said, I would like to tell you about the events that took place before you moved out here…

"You did see someone on the train and that same someone on your doorstep. I wanted to analyze where and how you were living, and your friends as well. There were multiple visits to your town previous to my influencing the circumstances which finally brought you out here. The night of the unexpected storm I was outside near your house. I was holding the key in my hand, tossing it up occasionally. Suddenly someone ran past me and grabbed it. He ran into your yard with me right behind him. The storm was raging at this time. We struggled and the key flew from our grasp. I left and waited by the gate. When the man tried to run out of the gate I grabbed him, searching for the key. It was not in his possession. He said it landed on the porch, the door opened, and he accidentally kicked it into the house. He leaned to my ear and said, 'If you want it, you go get it,' then he ran off."

Silas said, "That man was the one who hit me, Belle, not High-Tech. I'm glad it wasn't you, High-Tech."

"Thank you for that, Silas. Since I had a spare key, I counted it for loss. Figured no one would know what it was so it didn't matter after all, and I moved on. I found a dog shivering near the side of your house, Belle, and brought it to your door to inquire of its home. He was returned home safely."

Gratefully Belle said, "I love that you care about animals, Uncle. By any chance do you own a wolf, and did you have him with you?"

"As Warren would say, indeed I do. I imagine you heard some howling then. He is a she and she was quite young, four months old and finding her voice when we visited your town. Her name is Dainty. As little as she is, she howls big. Being the obvious runt of the litter, having some injuries and no desire to be a wolf, I decided she was unfit and unable to be returned to the wild. After you moved out here and acquired your dogs, I took the liberty of introducing Dainty to Guardian and Stance. They took an immediate liking to each other. Whenever I'm nearby she likes to say hello to your boys."

Belle said with passion, "I would love to meet her, and she is welcome over anytime! If you ever go away on, uh, business that wouldn't allow you to take her with you, she can stay with me."

Star laughed and said, "Strange for me but I would like to meet Dainty also."

"Yeah, Mom, that is strange," said Silas, and Warren added, "Definitely unusual for you." Then he said to I.Q., "Now explain the circumstances surrounding Momma, please and thank you."

"Certainly," I.Q. replied.

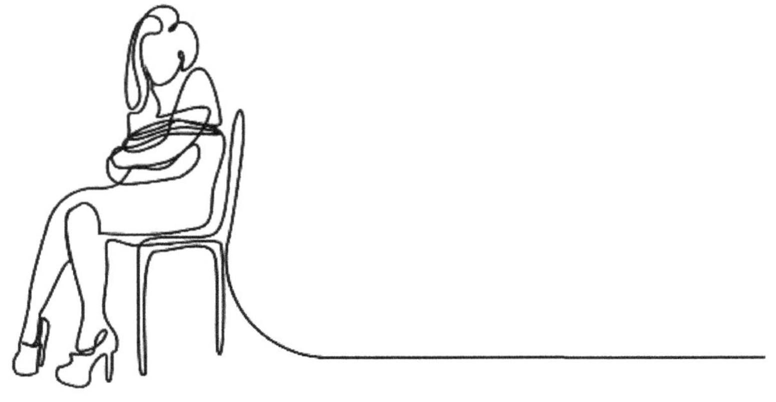

THIRTY-SEVEN

"I DO WANT TO ADD ONE MORE thing about Dainty, though. Belle, she was not a victim of the evil scheme started years ago as was Momma Possum. Now regarding Momma, I needed to follow up on her well-being. Tests proved she was past the critical stage and no longer in danger; her health is good. Afterward I returned Momma to her habitat, took the imposter and proceeded to work at the Zone. Sometime later I heard Belle was on her way to pick up Momma at the Yancee farm. Apparently the Yancee boy found her in a bush near the house and called. Well, that was a surprise to me; I had made the switch from the imposter to the real opossum. I had to act quickly. When I went back to the habitat to take Momma out, I also had to create a breach that she supposedly escaped through since they were going to be looking for one. The imposter snuck out of the sack I had her in. She was active when she should not have been. I didn't notice she managed to get out while I was in the bed of Mr. Yancee's truck helping unload the donations he brought to the Zone. You returned the impostor to Momma's habitat, and I had to wait for another time to switch them out again. Turned out that would be a couple of days later."

"Well, actually Uncle, about three and a half days later…

"I remember it was early Thursday morning, the day my friends would be arriving. Mr. and Mrs. Yancee came over to drop off food for me. Mrs. Yancee mentioned that while she was waiting for someone to pick up Momma, she went to look at her and noticed a cute heart-shaped birthmark. I knew she didn't have a birthmark so I hurried to the Center to look at Momma. Sure enough, there was a little heart on her. Knowing something was up I needed to get Cy to come and look at it. We both had noticed something wasn't quite right with Momma's tag earlier on but figured it was an honest mistake. Now I had to wait for him to finish his show and tell before he could come to look."

"That, Belle, was the moment I had the opportunity to switch Momma for the imposter and Momma was home at last."

"Cy was so annoyed at me, Uncle, after looking and not seeing any birthmark. I was hanging onto him as he was leaving, trying to get him to listen to me. He thought I was having one of my 'worked too long, need a break and some food' episodes. Then it was time for me to leave, I had to rush home and finish getting ready for company. I figured the mystery would have to get solved some other time, but was sure happy Momma was back. Once other things started to happen, you know, turn up, we decided not to tell anyone what was going on, so Cy has no idea. Now I'm really glad it turned out he had to rush off to another show and tell that day."

"Thank you, Belle, Warren and Silas assured me of that already. It is very important it stays that way and I appreciate all of you for your silence."

"We are definitely committed to keeping the secret, Uncle I.Q."

"It's very obvious you're a genius, Uncle, but you couldn't have done all the building and taking care of the animals yourself—who helped you?" Belle asked.

"Belle, that will remain a secret, I am not at liberty to say. Do not be concerned, you are all safe. Let me assure you they are the good guys, and I am as well."

"What about the basement of the barn and the tunnels, Uncle, were they all there before the barn?"

"As I mentioned, I renovated the barn but that old thing was on the property for many years already, Belle. Now the lab was constructed under the old barn intentionally with the hope one day I could acquire the property. When I found out the property was in the family, I renovated the barn and connected it to the lab, then added the shorter tunnel. As far as the other tunnel and formation room, I had that all done long before. After completing the barn and houses I made the picnic building and picnic area."

"Silas told me that Warren concluded the pond and surrounding area were manmade and rocks from the tunnels were dumped where you discovered the rocky terrain area."

"That land is part of your property, Belle, but an agreement for an easement was established for the Zone to use that portion if necessary."

"Now that you mention it, I do recall something about an easement in the contract. Because the property was so large, I didn't actually walk over to look at it, it was just pointed to from a distance; I never explored the area or gave it another thought." "Silas also mentioned Warren figured how the mushrooms were used and he concluded the animal experiments had to do with sizing down large game animals.

"It was quite the illegal scheme which with great effort our team was able to shut down. Warren explained to me, Belle, how you figured out the missing letters from the Noah's Ark torn paper you found and summarized the project's intention of saving the animals. He said Star discovered the shorthand markings on the key and deciphered them. Silas and Warren told me how you all came to the conclusions you did in all you encountered. You work well together; are resourceful and supportive of each other; that is important, you make a good team. Later I would like to show you something."

Silas jumped in and asked eagerly, "About the silent, super speedy vehicle, Hi-Tech?"

Grinning I.Q. said, "That too, but for now I would like to hear about the years I missed with Belle and about the rest of you."

There was a lot for Belle to fill her uncle in on. The others had their chance to talk about themselves and each had brought up a memory about another. Everyone was comfortable with I.Q.; even though they did not know him well, they trusted him. A certain rapport developed among all of them.

Talk went on all day until dinner time. Silas asked Hi-Tech to help him and Warren with the critters while dinner was prepared. During the time I.Q. was feeding the dogs he fed their guest also: Dainty was in the doghouse, unknown to Belle for the time being. After a moment he made a phone call. The person on the other end asked how it was going and he told them he was asked who helped him, but did not reveal their identity. Then I.Q. told this person to be proud of him for not revealing certain other information which he was asked to suppress. His comment was that Belle would understand and forgive him for holding out, they all would. When asked if he determined when he might reveal it, he answered a year might be sufficient time, the whole truth was on hold for now. The other person replied by saying good job, and hung up.

After patting the dogs one by one and saying it was time for him to eat, he told Guardian and Stance to take care of Dainty. On his way back to the house he could see that Silas and Warren were just entering it. He trotted the rest of the way to catch up to them.

"Right behind you, guys," I.Q. called out, "I'll clean the litter boxes while you two feed and water the kits and dog." Warren said, "The ladies will be in the living room shortly, we will meet them there when we are finished. Belle said dinner will be ready in forty-five minutes."

While in the living room waiting on dinner, I.Q. said, "Belle, I would like to introduce Dainty to you now, if this is a good time."

"Yes, Uncle, we have time before eating; bring her in, where is she?"

"With Guardian and Stance, be right back."

Belle was in heaven. Dainty made a good impression on them all, including Willow. She and Dainty settled down together on the floor by the couch.

"The day is passing much too fast," said Starlit. "I have a question, I.Q., about the passageway from the house. Why the house and why so elaborate a scene?"

"Eventually I was going to reveal it to Belle," he answered, "but was not planning on that so soon. Once she knew about the barn and tunnels, I wanted Bellerina to have access with this passageway in style. I wanted to create something enjoyable with significance, the latter being the main objective. The theme I chose was to be a reminder of how anything is possible for God and of His mighty power. His divine intervention in our lives is amazing. He is an awesome God and Father to us all."

Silas said, "You've placed an image in my mind, Hi-Tech, that I'm sure will come to mind when I'm not here at Belle's."

Warren added, "Indeed, you depicted well your intention."

"Yes, thank you, Uncle," said Belle. "When were you going to tell me about all of this?"

He answered hesitantly, "I'm not exactly sure, a few months from now. I did not expect you to discover the entrance to the lab which led to other discoveries."

"Funny you should say that; it wasn't me. It was actually by accident. Mark, Silas's son, was in the tack room getting P-2 and as I approached, I thought I saw part of the floor under the shelf move. It was so slight and brief I thought it was my imagination, but it kept nagging at me and eventually I investigated."

They talked until dinner was ready, then continued their conversation in the dining room. It was getting late, and they were still sitting there at the table. Warren noticed the time and said, "We should clean up, I would like to get a game of pool in before we retire."

"Good idea," Silas replied.

As they were cleaning up, the phone rang. Startled by the information coming from the caller, Belle covered herself by trying to sound matter of fact in responding. The others detected this by the expression on her face. Belle hung up and said loudly, "Oh brother, that was Cy reminding me to be at the Center tomorrow afternoon to help set up for the TCZ annual fundraiser on Wednesday. We have booths to set up for games and tables for food and other things, I completely forgot!"

Starlit replied, "Yes, right, I remember now. That stands for The Comfort Zone, the Center as you refer to it. We made our plans to fly home late Wednesday evening so we could come with you, Belle. With all that has been going on we all forgot."

"Yes, no doubt, we have," said Warren.

"That's not the worst of it, guys, I committed to baking several dozen cookies to donate for sales! You guys go ahead and play a game; I have to see if I have enough ingredients, otherwise I'll need to run to the store in the morning." Disappointed, Belle took hold of her uncle's hand and said, "I was so looking forward to what you wanted to show us, Uncle. I must keep this commitment."

He understandingly and sympathetically responded, "They start at nine Wednesday morning. We'll stay three hours to help out, have lunch, then I'll show you afterwards. There will be enough volunteers there so it's not necessary to stay all day."

"Good plan, happy to hear that," said Silas. "We can help you with the cookies, Belle."

Starlit laughed then said, "You mean help eat them. That's okay, Sy, I'll help Belle and you guys can find something else to do tomorrow. You know, Belle, I'm going to bring my guitar Wednesday for some added entertainment."

"Great! It'll be fun. We can do sing-alongs too, the kids will love it. It will be a good time for all. You guys run along now, we have to see what I have on hand—sorry, Uncle."

Gently he said, "Stop it, Belle, no need to apologize. I will be in good hands with Warren and Silas."

Belle had plenty of ingredients. She had forgotten she planned what she was going to make for the fundraiser, purchasing all that would be needed before her friends arrived for their visit, even animal-shaped cookie cutters to add to the collection of cutters she already owned. During the time Belle and Starlit did inventory, laid out ingredients and supplies for the morning, Silas, I.Q., and Warren played a game of pool. When it came time to say goodnight to everyone, I.Q. told them he would see them tomorrow afternoon at the Zone for the setting up. He winked while reminding everybody that "they do not know him," then he and Dainty left.

THIRTY-EIGHT

IMMEDIATELY AFTER BREAKFAST Tuesday morning, Belle and Starlit began mixing the different doughs. In between batches Starlit did her laundry and packed everything but her essentials in preparation for their departure Wednesday. Warren and Silas took care of all the critters and gave P-2 and P-3 their much-needed bath. They too prepared for going home and did their laundry in the guest house.

Late Tuesday afternoon Belle, Starlit, Silas and Warren carried packaged and boxed cookies out to the car. They arrived at the Center on time to help with the setup for Wednesday's fundraiser. Other than a brief hello upon introduction to all the volunteers, they successfully ignored I.Q. and concentrated on the instructions for the setup, then proceeded to work. It took several hours before everything was done. Knowing it would get late, Belle planned on an easy dinner of stew, salad, and rolls. The stew was ready when they arrived home at 8:30. The next morning they were at the Center nine sharp.

It was a wonderful morning. Starlit played her guitar and sang to the delight of the children and adults. After being relieved from their positions, they wanted to contribute to the cause, so each of them participated in games. On the way out they stopped at a booth which sold t-shirts and purchased shirts for themselves and their kids. This was the booth I.Q. was working. When he handed Belle her shirt, he discreetly gave her a note containing information on where and what time to meet him. Belle waited to read the note until they were in the car.

Lunch was served by Chef Hi-Tech, as Silas called him, at the picnic area. He barbecued chicken and hamburgers. Broccoli salad, potato salad and coleslaw accompanied the meat. It was a pleasant surprise to all of them.

Belle was thrilled. "Uncle, this is wonderful! Thank you for doing this. I'm guessing you had prepared everything and took it up here yesterday morning."

"Yes, Belle, I did." Starlit, Warren and Silas said thank you in unison. They talked about the fundraiser, gardening, and critters, then it was back to business.

Silas said, "I think we're all ready to see what you wanted to show us, Hi-Tech. Where are we going?"

As he answered Silas, I.Q. pointed to the sundial saying, "The formation room."

"We call it the formation room, I.Q., but what do you actually call it?" asked Warren.

"I call it the Den or at times, my Den."

"We're ready, Uncle, let's go."

When they were in the formation room I.Q. took a remote from a drawer, walked onto the elevator and said, "Come on now, down we go." He took them to the location of the maintenance tunnel they had never discovered. They only walked a short distance inside of it since there was a time limit hanging over them. He explained some things including solar panels, batteries, and their location.

Upon returning to the elevator, expecting to go back up, they saw a long narrow car parked on it. Silas walked over to it and began counting, "Two, two and two, it seats six; this is the limousine of the fleet. Where are we going now, Hi-Tech?"

"To the barn," he answered. "I'll drive and Belle will sit with me."

As they were driving, he told them about the garage that stored the many vehicles owned by his team, also explaining about the speedy vehicle Silas inquired of. He mentioned again how he thought they made a good team, adding they each had qualities needing growth and fine tuning.

Starlit asked, "What's that supposed to mean? I get a good impression in my senses when you say it, but I don't know what for."

"Your senses, good example," I.Q. answered. "I must say you need to recognize that is the Holy Spirit speaking to you. It is not a worldly sixth sense."

Warren asked, "Now that the huge undertaking of the animal project has concluded, what will become of all this?"

Smiling, I.Q. looked in the rearview mirror and answered, "There will always be a use for the subterranean complex, it will serve many purposes. Some permanently, others, as they arise. There is coming a time when sound doctrine will not be tolerated. Read second Timothy four, verses three through five. Times are changing already and will get worse. The mission continues."

Silas, in a serious tone said, "Hi-Tech, stop beating around the bush, tell us what's really going on. You sound as if you have some definite plans."

Warren added, "Indeed you do, implying our inclusion in them." At that moment they came to the garage door.

The garage door began to open, and they could see two silhouettes in the headlights scurrying towards the ladder. Belle cried out, "Uncle, look! Who is that? What are they doing in my barn? What's going on?"

He calmly answered, "No one, it's all right, everybody." He turned on the lights in the barn with the remote. As he was pulling forward to the parking area he shouted, "Surprise!"

There sitting by the other garage door were two double cars with large purple bows on them and two trailers. Warren replied with, "A very generous surprise." Silas bellowed, "Indeed!" His statement caused the rest of them to laugh.

"Wow! Thank you, Uncle."

"You are very welcome, Belle. They have been in for maintenance along with the lab equipment. I wasn't sure when they would be ready, but it appears they just arrived."

"So that was why we saw shadows running away," said Silas, "not anyone looking to do harm."

Just then Starlit said, "It's time to go. We have to get our suitcases in the car and leave for the airport."

"Hurry then," said I.Q., "the sooner you get home and settled the sooner we can begin training."

With raised voices they all spoke at the same time, talking over each other: "What!" "What do you mean by that!" "Training for what?" "Are you serious!" "We need details!" "Why?" "Waaait...!"

I.Q. said as he got into the limo, "You will each be contacted by me and visited." He opened the garage door by the cars and drove into the short tunnel. As the door closed, he called to them, "You are all recruited, bowing out is not an option."

Stunned, they stood there looking at each other. Warren opened the garage door. Before it was fully opened, they all crouched down and went under the door. They stood up, speechless at the sight: The car and I.Q. were gone!

DISCOVERIES

30) 'Dillo habitat partly gone

31) Mushroom chamber empty

33) Lab = Equipment gone, stations remain

34) Found torn paper = Noah's Ark, Phase II

35) House picture drawn as kid = living in now

36) Cave = wine making

37) Beastie not real

38) Bumblebee = a camera

39) Passageway from house to barn basement

40) Scripture verse in box

41) Figured out letters missing on torn paper

42) Passageway scene; parting of the Red Sea

32) Captured man

44) Man my uncle

45) Got answers

INCIDENTS

32) Wrestling w/unidentified man

43) Captured a man

46) More Questions

47) **Uncle and limo disappear** = another question

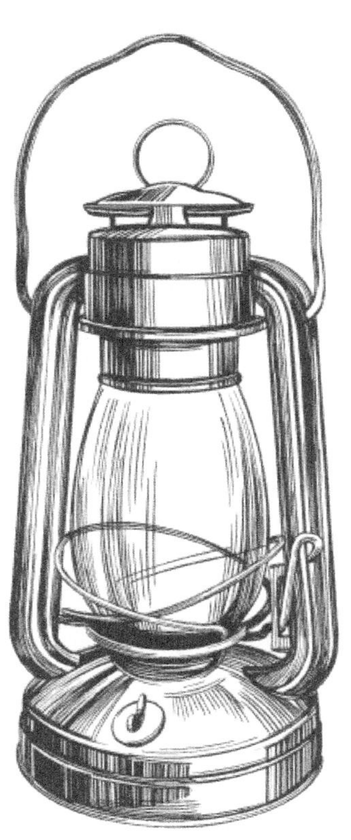

ABOUT THE AUTHOR

Jo has rescued and cared for animals over the years, including some wildlife. She has owned several rescues herself. Completing a veterinary assistance course was helpful in aiding with the care of her critters.

She also enjoys gardening, cooking and baking; sometimes experimenting with creating recipes in both. Jo has dabbled in film photography and was a member of a photography club for about three years, one of which she was the secretary.

While recuperating from the loss of her furry family, she finished this, her first book. Jo, one day when ready, will have another furry family. She plans to continue writing as inspired and is looking forward to what God will lead her in next.

Made in the USA
Monee, IL
17 March 2023

29672313R00236